U0685134

美国文学阅读与欣赏

American Literature：
Understanding and Appreciation

主　编　黄家修
副主编　刘　岩　周静琼
编　写　杜寅寅　张　欣　焦　敏

武 汉 大 学 出 版 社

图书在版编目(CIP)数据

美国文学阅读与欣赏/黄家修主编 . —武汉：武汉大学出版社，
2007.4(2025.8 重印)
普通高等教育"十一五"国家级规划教材
新视角英语文学与文化系列教材/刘岩主编
ISBN 978-7-307-05466-0

Ⅰ.美… Ⅱ.黄… Ⅲ.文学欣赏—美国—教材—英文
Ⅳ.I712.06

中国版本图书馆 CIP 数据核字(2007)第 029750 号

责任编辑:谢群英　　　责任校对:王　建　　　版式设计:支　笛

出版发行:**武汉大学出版社**　（430072　武昌　珞珈山）
　　　　　（电子邮箱:cbs22@ whu.edu.cn 网址:www.wdp.com.cn）
印刷:武汉邮科印务有限公司
开本:880×1230　1/32　印张:18.375　字数:504 千字
版次:2007 年 4 月第 1 版　　2025 年 8 月第 9 次印刷
ISBN 978-7-307-05466-0/I·306　　定价:58.00 元

版权所有,不得翻印;凡购买我社的图书,如有缺页、倒页、脱页等质量问题,请
与当地图书销售部门联系调换。

新视角英语文学与文化系列教材
编委会名单

顾　问　何其莘　陈建平

总主编　刘　岩

编委会　（按姓氏笔画排序）

马建军　王　虹　卢红梅　平　洪　仲伟合

余卫华　李　明　沈三山　郑　超　金李俪

黄家修　傅文燕　彭保良　管建明

作 者 简 介

　　黄家修　1969 年毕业于广州外国语学院英语系，1973 年赴英国，在埃克塞特大学和考文垂教育学院攻读英语语言文学，1981年在北京大学研修美国文学，1991 年在加拿大麦吉尔大学研修加拿大文学并进行学术交流。曾任广州外国语学院英语系副主任、涉外秘书系主任、广东外语外贸大学国际文化交流学院院长、广州翻译协会副理事长等。现为广东外语外贸大学英语语言文化学院教授、硕士生导师。长期从事英语语言文学专业的教学与研究，目前主要担任美国文学、英语诗歌、当代西方文学批评等本科生课程和英国诗歌、美国诗歌等硕士生课程。主要研究方向是英美诗歌、美国小说和文学翻译等。

总　序

我们所处的时代是一个多元共生的时代。国际政治的多极化走向、经济的全球化趋势、社会的信息化局面以及文化的多元化态势正快速改变着我们的生活。科学技术的高速发展以及新兴学科的不断涌现加剧了世界各国文化的交流、碰撞和合作。如何培养适应新时代发展和需要的人才，这是我们这一代教育工作者面临的新的课题和挑战。

高等学校外语专业教学指导委员会英语组于 2000 年 3 月修订的《高等学校英语专业英语教学大纲》明确规定了高等学校英语专业的培养目标："高等学校英语专业培养具有扎实的英语语言基础和广博的文化知识并能熟练地运用英语在外事、教育、经贸、文化、科技、军事等部门从事翻译、教学、管理、研究等工作的复合型英语人才。"这样的描述为我们编写英语专业教材和组织英语专业教学提供了重要依据。我校在长期的外语教学和研究实践中践行"明德尚行，学贯中西"的校训，着力推进外语与专业的融合，致力于培养一专多能、"双高"（思想素质高、专业水平高）、"两强"（外语实践能力强、信息技术运用能力强）、具有国际视野和创新意识的国际通用型人才。这要求全面提高学生的综合素质，包括拓宽人文学科知识，加强人文素质，培养创新精神，提高独立分析问题和解决问题的能力。

正是在这样的环境和背景下，我院精心策划并组织骨干教师编写了这套《新视角英语文学与文化系列教材》。这套教材可以用于英语专业高年级文学、文化、翻译等专业课和选修课的教学，也可以为其他专业的学生提供必要的相关专业知识。我们期待这套教材能够以培养学生人文素质为根本原则，以加强学生人文修养、增强学生创新能力为目标，帮助学生批判地吸收世界文化精髓并弘扬中国优秀文化传统。

　　这套教材的策划和出版得到武汉大学出版社的积极推动和热情支持，没有他们的努力就不会有这套教材的问世。我院教师把多年教学经验积淀成书，每一本教材都凝结着他们的智慧和心血。还有我院一批渴求知识的学生，是他们的勤学好问让我们看到了工作的价值，也正是在教学相长的过程中我们的教材得到了不断的完善。在这套教材即将面世之际，让我们对所有参与教材编写和出版的人士表示衷心的感谢和敬意！也请同行专家对教材的缺憾不吝赐教。

广东外语外贸大学英语语言文化学院　刘岩博士
2006 年 4 月于白云山校区

编 者 的 话

美国从其诞生至今仅有两百多年的历史，但它的文学从殖民时期开始，经过了浪漫主义、超验主义、现实主义、自然主义和现代主义的发展，一直到第一次世界大战以后，异军突起，欣欣向荣。美国文学在其短暂的历史进程中迅速冲出了欧洲文学的樊篱而成长，涌现出了一大批诸如惠特曼、马克·吐温、海明威、福克纳、尤金·奥尼尔等享誉世界的伟大作家，也产生了许许多多题材广泛、风格迥异的文学精品，为世界文学的繁荣与发展起到了十分重要的作用。

美国文学是英语专业本科生的重要课程之一。2000 年全国英语专业本科教学大纲中明确规定："文学课的目的在于培养学生阅读、欣赏、理解英语文学原著的能力，掌握文学批评的基本知识和方法。通过阅读和分析英美文学作品，促进学生语言基本功和人文素质的提高，增强学生对西方文学及文化的了解。"《美国文学阅读与欣赏》是根据英语本科教学大纲的要求，结合当代的文学理论进行编写的本科生教材。这一教材已经在几年的课堂教学中试用。在具体试用中，我们运用了新的教学方法（如交际教学法），在美国文学课堂中进行实践，并取得了一定的成果。有些成果已经在有关学术刊物上发表。

《美国文学阅读与欣赏》这一教材在相关章节中对美国文学发展的各个历史时期的时代背景、哲学和文艺思潮、文学运动和主要作家做了较为详尽的介绍。对所选作家及其作品也做了具体的介绍。结合我们在美国文学课堂教学实践中得到的经验，我们对练习项目做了精心的设计，包括检查学生对文本阅读理解程度的题目，培养学生对文本进行鉴赏的适合课堂上进行小组讨论的题目，以及锻炼学生用书面表达对文学作品的意见的写作练习。

本书由黄家修策划和设计，并担任主审。正式参加编写的人员有黄家修、刘岩、周静琼、杜寅寅、张欣和焦敏。其中第一章、第二章的时代背景部分和第一章中 Edwards 及其作品的介绍和练习题由黄家修编写，这两章的其他作家和所选作品的介绍及练习题由杜寅寅编写；第三章、第四章的时代背景部分由刘岩编家，这两章的其他作家和所选作品的介绍及练习题由焦敏编写；第五章的时代背景及其中四位作家（Carver, Jen, O'Connor, Walker）的介绍由周静琼编写，这一章的其余四位作家、全章作品的介绍以及练习题由张欣编写。黄家修审阅了第一、二章，刘岩审阅了第三、四章，周静琼审阅了第五章，黄家修对全书终审定稿。

本书已列入普通高等教育"十一五"国家级规划教材。在编写过程中，编者参阅了有关的资料，在此向相关的书著作者及出版社表示感谢。在本书的编写过程中，广东外语外贸大学英语语言文化学院一直给予大力的支持，在此我们表示衷心的感谢。本书难免还有许多有待改进之处，敬请使用本书的各界人士不吝赐教，提出宝贵意见，以利今后修改。

编者

2007 年 3 月 2 日

Contents

Chapter One **Early American Literature** ·············· (1)

Jonathan Edwards ································· (12)

Sinners in the Hands of an Angry God ·············· (12)

Benjamin Franklin ······························ (23)

The Autobiography ··························· (24)

Chapter Two **American Romanticism and Transcendentalism** ················ (45)

Ralph Waldo Emerson ·························· (53)

Nature ································ (54)

Self-Reliance ······························ (62)

Henry David Thoreau ·························· (81)

Walden ······························· (82)

Edgar Allan Poe ····························· (103)

The Raven ····························· (105)

Nathaniel Hawthorne ························· (112)

The Minister's Black Veil ···················· (114)

Henry Wadsworth Longfellow ···················· (135)

A Psalm of Life ··························· (136)

Herman Melville ···························· (139)

Moby Dick ····························· (140)

Walt Whitman ····························· (158)

When I Heard the Learn'd Astronomer ············· (159)

1

Cavalry Crossing a Ford .... (161)
Come Up from the Fields, Father .... (162)
Out of the Cradle Endlessly Rocking .... (165)
Emily Dickinson .... (174)
Wild Nights—Wild Nights! .... (175)
A Bird Came down the Walk— .... (177)
I Died for Beauty—But Was Scarce .... (178)
Because I Could Not Stop for Death— .... (180)

Chapter Three　**American Realism and American Naturalism** .... (183)
Samuel Langhorne Clemens .... (194)
The Celebrated Jumping Frog of Calaveras County .... (197)
Henry James .... (208)
Daisy Miller .... (210)
Edith Wharton .... (224)
Ethan Frome .... (225)
Stephen Crane .... (230)
The Red Badge of Courage .... (232)
Theodore Dreiser .... (246)
Old Rogaum and His Theresa .... (248)
Jack London .... (274)
The Law of Life .... (276)

Chapter Four　**American Modernism** .... (287)
Ezra Pound .... (300)
In a Station of the Metro .... (302)
Robert Frost .... (304)
The Road Not Taken .... (306)
Fire and Ice .... (308)
Mending Wall .... (309)

Stopping by Woods on a Snowy Evening ·················· (312)

Thomas Stearns (T. S.) Eliot ···························· (315)

  The Love Song of J. Alfred Prufrock ···················· (317)

Sherwood Anderson ···································· (330)

  Sophistication, Concerning Helen White ·················· (332)

Ernest Hemingway ······································ (344)

  A Clean, Well-lighted Place ·························· (348)

William Faulkner ······································ (356)

  A Rose for Emily ·································· (359)

Eugene O'Neill ·· (372)

  Desire under the Elms ······························ (374)

Chapter Five **Post-war American Literature** ········ (380)

Saul Bellow ·· (389)

  Looking for Mr. Green ································ (391)

Arthur Miller ··· (420)

  Death of a Salesman ································ (421)

Jerome David Salinger ································· (465)

  The Catcher in the Rye ······························ (466)

Flannery O'Connor ···································· (480)

  The Life You Save May Be Your Own ·················· (482)

Allen Ginsberg ·· (500)

  A Supermarket in California ·························· (502)

Raymond Carver ······································ (507)

  What We Talk About When We Talk About Love ········ (509)

Alice Walker ·· (528)

  Everyday Use ···································· (530)

Gish Jen ··· (544)

  In the American Society ······························ (546)

References ·· (569)

3

Chapter One Early American Literature

(1620-1820)

Early Colonial American Literature

Christopher Columbus discovered the American Continent in 1492, but the United States became an independent country in 1776, nearly three centuries later.

The development of colonial America into the United States was recorded by explorers and colonizers from Europe in a literature that began as accounts of exploration and colonization. They wrote of what they saw and what they felt in the New World, and thereby they created a literature that was amazingly rich.

However, the early settlers thought of themselves as Europeans instead of Americans. They observed European customs and habits, and remained European in their ways of thinking and writing. So much of their literature is not uniquely American. It is not really literature either because much of it told people how to do things and was written in the forms of letter, diary and report. Among the early colonial American writers, there were some descriptive writers who contributed significantly to the development of the nation's literature, including **Captain John Smith** (1580-1631) and **William Bradford** (1500-1657).

Captain John Smith was among the members of a small band of settlers who founded the first permanent English settlement in North America—Jamestown, Virginia in 1607. He was born in England of poor farmers, and ran away as a youth to become a merchant soldier. When the Jamestown settlers faced immense difficulties, Smith became their leader, and saved their colony from ruin. He forced the settlers to build defense, plant crops, and trade with the Indians. He started Jamestown on its way to survival. In 1609, he returned to England, and five years later, he was sent back to America by merchant investors to search for gold, collect furs and kill whales for oil. After the voyage, he returned to the Old World, where he spent most of his remaining years writing and rewriting his histories and reports.

His first published work was a letter he had sent from Virginia to a friend in England, where it was printed in 1608 as *A True Relation of Occurrences and Accidents in Virginia*. This account of exploration has been described as the first distinctive American literature to be written in English. In 1616 he published *A Description of New England*. In 1624 he published his most important work *The General History of Virginia*.

"Strongly shaped by a New World consciousness, Smith's descriptions of America were filled with themes, myths, images, scenes, characters, and events that were a foundation for the nation's literature. He portrayed English North America as a land of endless bounty, a land of nourishment and redemption."[①] This confirmed the European dream of America as an earthly paradise. "His delectable vision helped lured many English settlers to America, among them the Pilgrims and Puritans who saw themselves as new saints with a spiritual mission to flee the Old

---

① George McMichael, et. , ed. *Anthology of American Literature*. New York: McMillan Publishing Co. , Inc. , and London: Collier Macmillan Publishers. 1980, p. 2.

World and create a New Israel, a New Promised Land, in the America that John Smith had described. "①

William Bradford was one of the Pilgrims on the ship "Mayflower", which sailed to America in 1620. They landed at Cape Cod and founded the Plymouth Colony. Bradford was chosen as the governor many times, serving almost continuously from 1621 to 1656. But all through his life, he remained a humble man who sought neither personal glory nor riches. Instead, he held fast to his faith in the divine mission of the Pilgrims. His life is an epitome of determination and self- sacrifice that are characteristic of his people.

He began writing his history of the Pilgrims in 1630, which was published posthumously as *Of Plymouth Plantation*, a book that has been regarded as one of the great works of colonial America.

Literature of Puritan New England

3

The Plymouth Colony was the oldest, but remained one of the poorest of the New England colonies. In 1691 it was absorbed by the large and prosperous Massachusetts Bay Colony centered at Boston.

The Massachusetts Bay Puritans were a group of serious religious people who advocated strict religious and moral principles. They believed that the priests and bishops of the Church of England had too much power and too little respect for the teachings of *the Bible* which, they regarded as the revealed word of God. They believed that people should take *the Bible* as their guide to all aspects of life, the Church of England should be purified of its errors, and church worship should be

---

① George McMichael, et. , ed. *Anthology of American Literature*. New York: McMillan Publishing Co. , Inc. , and London: Collier Macmillan Publishers. 1980, p. 2.

restored to the pure and unspotted condition of its earlier days. "For their ceaseless efforts to 'purify' the English Church, to purge it of corruption, they earned the name 'Puritans'. "①

The Puritans adhered to their basic religious beliefs, which had been strongly shaped by the teachings of **Martin Luther** (1483-1546) and **John Calvin** (1509-1564). They agreed with Martin Luther who asserted that priests and bishops should not be regarded as a privileged class that had the right to impose their law upon the Christians, and all true believers were equally divine. "From Calvin's great work, The Institutes of the Christian Religion (1536-1559), the New England colonists derived their basic theological doctrines: of total depravity, that because of the original sin of Adam and Eve, all mankind was born 'corrupt and prone to evil'; of limited atonement, that Jesus' sacrifice had earned God's forgiveness, or grace, only for the elect, a limited few; of irresistible grace, that salvation was ordained by God, and one could neither win nor lose salvation by his own acts; of predestination, that God had predestined all events and selected all those who would be saved in heaven, and all those who would be lost in hell. " ② These doctrines, which may appear harsh, were received with joy and comfort by the Puritans.

The Puritans set an example to the Christian world with their absolute dedication to religious principles. They developed a tradition of preaching and sermon. Sermons were by far the most popular literature of the time and the dominant literary form for the major writers of New England although sermons were more like lengthy exercises in logic than

————————————

① George McMichael, et., ed. *Anthology of American Literature*. New York: McMillan Publishing Co., Inc., and London: Collier Macmillan Publishers. 1980, p. 5.

② Ibid., p. 5.

works of literary arts.

The Massachusetts Bay colonists were devoted to sermons and Bible study, and therefore they placed great emphasis on education. As a result, their colony soon became the educational and cultural center of the English colonies in North America. They founded the first American college, Harvard, at Cambridge in 1636, established the first colonial press also at Cambridge in 1638, and published the first colonial newspaper in Boston in 1690.

In the Puritan period, many of the people who were writing were politically and religiously powerful. This group that ruled was called theocracy. Among them was a minister, **John Cotton** (1584-1652), who joined the Massachusetts Bay Colony and became a religious leader. He wrote many works on the church, and some of them were very influential. *The Keyes of the Kingdom of Heaven* (1644) became the standard congregational guide in New England. Cotton and his group preached for the Puritan church authority.

Toward the middle of the 17th century, there emerged another group of writers who were more sectarian and pragmatic. Then came the Puritan controversy between the two writers, John Cotton and **Roger Williams** (1603-1683). Cotton's autocratic views on civil and religious government provoked Williams to write his famous tract The Bloudy Tenent of Persecution (1644), which was an attack on the "soul killing" requirement of religious conformity.

Roger Williams was born in London to a merchant family and graduated from Cambridge. He became a Separatist and migrated to Massachusetts. In the New World, he argued for a more democratic church government. When the vexed Puritan authorities charged him with brewing discord and subversion, he moved to the Plymouth Colony. In 1633, he returned to the Massachusetts Bay Colony, and became minister of the Salem Church. There he continued to speak against the religious estab-

5

lishment, which he saw as tainted with popery. As a result, he was banished from the Colony. He later migrated to Rhode Island, and established the settlement that eventually became Providence plantation. Under his leadership, church and state were separated; and religious tolerance was maintained. To later ages, Williams stands an apostle of civil and religious freedom.

Another important writer in this period was **Cotton Mather** (1663-1728), who came from a distinguished family in Puritan New England. He was a man of immense intelligence and industry. By the time he was twelve, he had learned Latin and Greek and begun to learn Hebrew. When he graduated from Harvard at 15, his elders counted him among the school's most brilliant students. In 1685, he was ordained as one of the two ministers at one of the largest churches in New England. And he held the post until his death. He wrote over 400 works, which were congested with scriptural and classical allusions. His representative work was *Wonders of the Invisible World*, and his most famous book *Magnalia Christi Americana* was a religious historical miscellany of New England. The bulk of his writing was aimed at reinvigorating the waning Puritanism of his day, but with the coming of the age of Reason and Enlightenment, he became instead a symbol of the Puritan decline.

Another brilliant Puritan essayist is **Jonathan Edwards** (1703-1758), who was the chief minister of the church of Northampton. He sought to teach men their utter dependence on God and to arouse their yearning for an inner sense of God's spirit. His famous sermon Sinners in the Hands of an Angry God terrorized his listeners with visions of unregenerate men helplessly dangled over the pit of hell by a wrathful God. He wrote a few complex philosophical works including *Freedom of Will* (1754), *The Doctrine of Original Sin Defended* (1758) and *The Nature of True Virtue* (1765). Edwards was a prolific writer who published nine major works and numerous sermons in his lifetime. At his death, many of his works still remained unpublished.

In Puritan New England, except for the hymn and the ballad, poetry was of small account. Only three poets have much claim to notice.

Anne Bradstreet (1612-1672) was the first notable poet in America. She was born in England. In 1630 she sailed with her husband and her parents to Massachusetts Bay Colony. Her family settled on a farm near a frontier village on the Merrimac River. She became a dutiful housewife who stole time to read and write poetry. In 1647 her brother-in-low sailed to England taking copies of her poems with him. There, in 1650, they were published under the title *The Tenth Muse Lately Sprung Up in America*. In the remaining years of her life, she revised her early work and composed new poems in the midst of her household tasks. Bradstreet was an authentic Puritan voice in New England. Her best poems, including *Contemplations*, *To My Dear and Loving Husband*, *Upon the Burning of Our House*, showed in great depth the spiritual struggles of a Christian confronting doubt and skepticism.

Michael Wigglesworth (1631-1705) was a typical Puritan poet. He was born in Yorkshire, England. When he was not quite seven, he went with his parents to New England, where they settled on a Connecticut farm. He entered Harvard, intending to become a physician. In 1653 when he was twenty-two, he had a mighty dream in which he saw God seated on His throne on the "dreadful day of judgment," separating the saved from the damned, the "sheep" from the "goats." The saved were glorying in their blessedness and the damned were cowering and whining before their Judge. The dream moved him to swear that he would forever "follow God with tears and cries." It remained deeply impressed on his mind. After he received his BA and MA, he became both a minister and a physician at Malder, Massachusetts. During a long period of bad health, he turned to writing. The most significant result was the long poem *The Day of Doom*, a poetical description of the Great and Last

7

judgment that he had dreamed of years before. When it was published in 1662, it was an instantaneous success. Savored by wise men and simpletons alike, it was perhaps the most popular literary work written by an American Puritan.

A less popular but more significant Puritan poet was **Edward Taylor** (1642-1729), who was born in England, and who emigrated to Massachusetts in his 20s. After his graduation from Harvard College in 1671, he served as pastor of the church at a frontier farm village 100 miles from Boston. And there he wrote many poems, which were largely unknown to his contemporaries. The appearance of his poems in the 1930s, two centuries after his death, revealed a mind radically different from his contemporaries. Taylor wrote in the tradition of the English metaphysical poets, expressing divine and elevated ideas in unrelated and homely terms. He created elaborate conceits and denotating metaphors, and used concrete images to express his intense emotions. His poems stand with the finest literature of early America.

The Literature of the Age of Reason and Enlightenment (1721-1826)

The eighteenth century in America is known as the age of Reason and Enlightenment. It was a time when people gradually turned cool toward organized religion and became critical of governments. They placed their faith in the achievement of a new science.

The Age of Reason and Enlightenment developed first in 17th century England, spread to France and Europe and finally came to America in the 18th century. Its precepts can be found in the philosophy of Descartes (1596-1650) and the writing of Voltaire (1694-1778). Both of them rejected medieval authoritarianism and attacked dogma.

In the Age of Reason and Enlightenment, Isaac Newton (1642-

1727) published his *Mathematical Principles of Natural Philosophy* (1687), which marked the beginning of modern science, and it weakened man's faith in miracles, holy books and the divinity of kings and priests. Gradually, theology became rational; religion became deistic. The idea of progress became one of the dominant concepts of the age.

The British philosopher John Locke (1632-1704) wrote his *Treatise of Civil Government* (1690), in which he argued that governments were not based on divinely ordained hierarchies extending from God through king to men. Governments were the result of agreement between men. So men of the Age of Reason and Enlightenment shaped their beliefs into a celebration of political change.

In the Age of Reason and Enlightenment, the Calvinist view of man as innately evil came under unceasing attack. In his Essay *Concerning Human Understanding* (1690), John Locke suggested that the human mind at birth was a blank sheet of paper, therefore man was born neither good nor bad; all was the result of experience. Some philosophers expressed their optimistic faith in the perfectibility of man. The Swiss philosopher Jean-Jacques Rousseau (1712-1778) even declared that man was not merely free of evil, he was naturally good. With the rise of humanitarianism and faith in human goodness, people demanded more human liberties.

In the Age of Reason and Enlightenment writers took their literary models and critical maxims from Greek and Roman Literature. They thought that literature was to avoid the ornate and the extravagant, and that writing was to exhibit "clear sense".

In the Age of Reason and Enlightenment, America produced two fine poets. One was **Phillis Wheatley** (c. 1753-1859), who was born in Africa and later brought to America. She became a slave of a Boston tailor who treated her well and encouraged her talent. In her master's household she learnt to read and write. Her *Poems on Various Subjects*,

Religious and Moral (1773) was published in London when she was only nineteen. Her poems express the popular sentiments of the age. And she is the first significant black poet in America.

Philip Freneau (1752-1832), a more significant poet than Wheatley, was born in New York and educated at the College of New Jersey (now Princeton University). In their senior year, Freneau and his classmate Hugh Henry Brackenridge wrote the poem *The Rising Glory of America*, which expressed his vision of the glorious future of America. He also founded the National Gazette, a newspaper that became the voice of liberal democracy in American politics. He derived his power and style from English models and his poetry was a fusion of neoclassicism and romanticism. His other famous poems include *The House of Night*, *The Wild Honey Suckle* and *The Indian Burying Ground*.

One of the great writers of the Age of Reason and Enlightenment was **Benjamin Franklin** (1706-1790). As a youth, he was apprenticed to his brother, a printer. At twelve, he published his first works, two ballads. By the time he was sixteen, he was writing for his brother's newspaper, using the pen name "Silence Dogood". When he was seventeen, he ran off to Philadelphia, where he became a thriving printer himself. At the age of forty-two, when he was wealthy and famous, he retired from business to devote himself to science and public service. Between 1757 and 1775, he represented the colonies in England. On the eve of the revolution, he returned to Philadelphia. He was named a delegate to the second Continental Congress. In 1776, the Congress sent him as Minister to France. In Paris, he negotiated the treaty of alliance of 1778 that joined France with America in the war against England. He was the only American to sign the four documents that created the republic: The Declaration of Independence, the treaty of alliance with France, the treaty of peace with England, and the Constitution of the United States. He was a brilliant, industrious and versatile man. His writings range from informal sermons to periodical essays. He writes gracefully and clearly, with a wit which often gives an edge to his words. He is a master of satire and political journalism. His most important works include *Poor Richard's Almanac*, *The way to Wealth* and *The Autobiography*.

Jonathan Edwards (1703-1758)

Jonathan Edwards was born in Connecticut and was educated at home by his parents. A brilliant and precocious child, he entered Yale College when he was only thirteen. After his graduation in 1720, he served as a minister in New York and worked as a tutor at Yale. After the death of his grandfather, he became the chief minister of the church of Northampton, and filled this position for more than twenty years. At Northampton, Edwards delivered a series of sermons that both fascinated and disturbed his congregation. He wanted to restore to his listeners the original sense of religious commitment which he thought had been lost. His preaching brought him fame throughout New England. His sermon Sinners in the Hands of an Angry God, which was powerful in the use of logic and creative in the use of metaphor, became the most famous sermon in colonial America. But he went too far in his attempt to restore the church to its original position of authority, and his indictments of backsliders and arguments over church membership created a furor that led to his dismissal. Retired from the controversies of Northampton, he wrote his complex philosophical works including *Freedom of Will* (1754), *The Doctrine of Original Sin Defended* (1758) and *The Nature of True Virtue* (1765). Edwards was a good preacher and a prolific writer. His close-textured, lucid and precise prose qualifies him as the most sensitive stylist in American Puritanism.

Sinners in the Hands of an Angry God

Introduction

Sinners in the Hands of an Angry God is a fervid and imprecatory sermon which Jonathan Edwards delivered in Enfield, Connecticut on Sunday, July 18, 1741. It was published the same year. In this sermon, Edwards took a line from *The Bible*, and as he explained it, he terrorized his listeners with visions of unregenerate men dangled over the pit of hell by an angry God. It was an exposition of God's vindictive justice and man's natural corruption. However, his intention was to teach men their utter dependence on God, to awaken in them a new sense of sin, and to prepare them to receive God's grace.

From **Sinners in the Hands of an Angry God**[①]

Deuteronomy 32: 35

Their foot shall slide in due time. [②]

In this verse[③] is threatened the vengeance of God on the wicked unbelieving Israelites, who were God's visible people, and who lived under the means of grace;[④] but who, notwithstanding all God's wonderful works towards them, remained (as in verse 28) void of counsel, having no understanding in them. Under all the cultivations of heaven, they brought forth bitter and poisonous fruit; as in the two verses next preceding the text. The expression I have chosen for my text, "Their foot shall slide in due time," seems to imply the following things, relating to the punishment and destruction to which these wicked Israelites were exposed.

1. That they were always exposed to destruction; as one that stands or walks in slippery places is always exposed to fall. This is implied in the manner of their destruction coming upon them, being represented by their foot sliding. The same is expressed, Psalm 72: 18: "Surely thou didst set them in slippery places; thou castedst them down into destruction."

2. It implies that they were always exposed to sudden unexpected destruction. As he that walks in slippery places is every moment liable to fall, he cannot foresee one moment whether he shall stand or fall the

next; and when he does fall, he falls at once without warning: Which is also expressed in Psalm 73: 18-19: "Surely thou didst set them in slippery places; thou castedst them down into destruction: How are they brought into desolation as in a moment!"

3. Another thing implied is, that they are liable to fall of themselves, without being thrown down by the hand of another; as he that stands or walks on slippery ground needs nothing but his own weight to throw him down.

4. That the reason why they are not fallen already and do not fall now is only that God's appointed time is not come. For it is said, that when that due time, or appointed time comes, their foot shall slide. Then they shall be left to fall, as they are inclined by their own weight. God will not hold them up in these slippery places any longer, but will let them go; and then, at that very instant, they shall fall into destruction; as he that stands on such slippery declining ground, on the edge of a pit, he cannot stand alone, when he is let go he immediately falls and is lost.

The observation from the words that I would now insist upon is this. "There is nothing that keeps wicked men at any one moment out of hell, but the mere pleasure of God. " By the mere pleasure of God, I mean his sovereign pleasure, his arbitrary will, restrained by no obligation, hindered by no manner of difficulty, any more than if nothing else but God's mere will had in the least degree, or in any respect whatsoever, any hand in the preservation of wicked men one moment. The truth of this observation may appear by the following considerations.

1. There is no want of power in God to cast wicked men into hell at any moment. Men's hands cannot be strong when God rises up. The strongest have no power to resist him, nor can any deliver[5] out of his hands. He is not only able to cast wicked men into hell, but he can most easily do it. Sometimes an earthly prince meets with a great deal of diffi-

culty to subdue a rebel, who has found means to fortify himself, and has made himself strong by the numbers of his followers. But it is not so with God. There is no fortress that is any defense from the power of God. Though hand join in hand, and vast multitudes of God's enemies combine and associate themselves, they are easily broken in pieces. They are as great heaps of light chaff before the whirlwind; or large quantities of dry stubble before devouring flames. We find it easy to tread on and crush a worm that we see crawling on the earth; so it is easy for us to cut or singe a slender thread that any thing hangs by: thus easy is it for God, when he pleases, to cast his enemies down to hell. What are we, that we should think to stand before him, at whose rebuke the earth trembles, and before whom the rocks are thrown down?

2. They deserve to be cast into hell; so that divine justice never stands in the way, it makes no objection against God's using his power at any moment to destroy them. Yea, on the contrary, justice calls aloud for an infinite punishment of their sins. Divine justice says of the tree that brings forth such grapes of Sodom[6], "Cut it down, why cumbereth it the ground?" Luke 13:7. The sword of divine justice is every moment brandished over their heads, and it is nothing but the hand of arbitrary mercy, and God's mere will, that holds it back.

3. They are already under a sentence of condemnation to hell. They do not only justly deserve to be cast down thither, but the sentence of the law of God, that eternal and immutable rule of righteousness that God has fixed between him and mankind, is gone out against them, and stands against them; so that they are bound over already to hell. John 3:18. "He that believeth not is condemned already." So that every unconverted man properly belongs to hell; that is his place; from thence he is, John 8:23: "Ye are from beneath." And thither he is bound; it is the place that justice, and God's word, and the sentence of his unchangeable law assign to him.

4. They are now the objects of that very same anger and wrath of God that is expressed in the torments of hell. And the reason why they do not go down to hell at each moment, is not because God, in whose power they are, is not then very angry with them; as he is with many miserable creatures now tormented in hell, who there feel and bear the fierceness of his wrath. Yea, God is a great deal more angry with great numbers that are now on earth: yea, doubtless, with many that are now in this congregation, who it may be are at ease, than he is with many of those who are now in the flames of hell.

So that it is not because God is unmindful of their wickedness, and does not resent it, that he does not let loose his hand and cut them off. God is not altogether such an one as themselves, though they may imagine him to be so. The wrath of God burns against them, their damnation does not slumber; the pit is prepared, the fire is made ready, the furnace is now hot, ready to receive them; the flames do now rage and glow. The glittering sword is whet⑦, and held over them, and the pit hath opened its mouth under them.

5. The devil stands ready to fall upon them, and seize them as his own, at what moment God shall permit him. They belong to him; he has their souls in his possession, and under his dominion. The scripture represents them as his goods, Luke 11: 12. The devils watch them; they are ever by them at their right hand; they stand waiting for them, like greedy hungry lions that see their prey, and expect to have it, but are for the present kept back. If God should withdraw his hand, by which they are restrained, they would in one moment fly upon their poor souls. The old serpent is gaping for them; hell opens its mouth wide to receive them; and if God should permit it, they would be hastily swallowed up and lost.

6. There are in the souls of wicked men those hellish principles reigning, that would presently kindle and flame out into hell fire, if it

were not for God's restraints. There is laid in the very nature of carnal men, a foundation for the torments of hell. There are those corrupt principles, in reigning power in them, and in full possession of them, that are seeds of hell fire. These principles are active and powerful, exceeding violent in their nature, and if it were not for the restraining hand of God upon them, they would soon break out, they would flame out after the same manner as the same corruptions, the same enmity does in the hearts of damned souls, and would beget the same torments as they do in them. The souls of the wicked are in scripture compared to the troubled sea, Isaiah 57: 20. [8] For the present, God restrains their wickedness by his mighty power, as he does the raging waves of the troubled sea, saying, "Hitherto shalt thou come, but no further;" [9] but if God should withdraw that restraining power, it would soon carry all before it. Sin is the ruin and misery of the soul; it is destructive in its nature; and if God should leave it without restraint, there would need nothing else to make the soul perfectly miserable. The corruption of the heart of man is immoderate and boundless in its fury; and while wicked men live here, it is like fire pent up by God's restraints, whereas if it were let loose, it would set on fire the course of nature; and as the heart is now a sink of sin, so if sin was not restrained, it would immediately turn the soul into fiery oven, or a furnace of fire and brimstone.

7. It is no security to wicked men for one moment, that there are no visible means of death at hand. It is no security to a natural[10] man, that he is now in health, and that he does not see which way he should now immediately go out of the world by any accident, and that there is no visible danger in any respect in his circumstances. The manifold and continual experience of the world in all ages, shows this is no evidence, that a man is not on the very brink of eternity, and that the next step will not be into another world. The unseen, unthought-of ways and means of persons going suddenly out of the world are innumerable and inconceivable.

17

Unconverted men walk over the pit of hell on a rotten covering, and there are innumerable places in this covering so weak that they will not bear their weight, and these places are not seen. The arrows of death fly unseen at noon-day; the sharpest sight cannot discern them. God has so many different unsearchable ways of taking wicked men out of the world and sending them to hell, that there is nothing to make it appear, that God had need to be at the expense of a miracle, or go out of the ordinary course of his providence, to destroy any wicked man, at any moment. All the means that there are of sinners going out of the world, are so in God's hands, and so universally and absolutely subject to his power and determination, that it does not depend at all the less on the mere will of God, whether sinners shall at any moment go to hell, than if means were never made use of, or at all concerned in the case.

8. Natural men's prudence and care to preserve their own lives, or the care of others to preserve them, do not secure them a moment. To this, divine providence and universal experience do also bear testimony. There is this clear evidence that men's own wisdom is no security to them from death; that if it were otherwise we should see some difference between the wise and politic men of the world, and others, with regard to their liableness to early and unexpected death; but how is it in fact? Ecclesiastes 2: 16. "How dieth the wise man? even as the fool."

9. All wicked men's pains and contrivance which they use to escape hell, while they continue to reject Christ, and so remain wicked men, do not secure them from hell one moment. Almost every natural man that hears of hell, flatters himself that he shall escape it; he depends upon himself for his own security; he flatters himself in what he has done, in what he is now doing, or what he intends to do. Every one lays out matters in his own mind how he shall avoid damnation, and flatters himself that he contrives well for himself, and that his schemes will not fail. They hear indeed that there are but few saved, and that the greater part

of men that have died heretofore are gone to hell; but each one imagines that he lays out matters better for his own escape than others have done. He does not intend to come to that place of torment; he says within himself, that he intends to take effectual care, and to order matters so for himself as not to fail.

But the foolish children of men miserably delude themselves in their own schemes, and in confidence in their own strength and wisdom; they trust to nothing but a shadow. The greater part of those who heretofore have lived under the same means of grace, and are now dead, are undoubtedly gone to hell; and it was not because they were not as wise as those who are now alive: it was not because they did not lay out matters as well for themselves to secure their own escape. If we could speak with them, and inquire of them, one by one, whether they expected, when alive, and when they used to hear about hell, ever to be the subjects of misery: we doubtless, should hear one and another reply, "No, I never intended to come here: I had laid out matters otherwise in my mind; I thought I should contrive well for myself: I thought my scheme good. I intended to take effectual care; but it came upon me unexpected; I did not look for it at that time, and in that manner; it came as a thief: Death outwitted me: God's wrath was too quick for me. Oh, my cursed foolishness! I was flattering myself, and pleasing myself with vain dreams of what I would do hereafter; and when I was saying, Peace and safety, then sudden destruction came upon me."

10. God has laid Himself under no obligation, by any promise to keep any natural man out of hell one moment. God certainly has made no promises either of eternal life, or of any deliverance or preservation from eternal death, but what are contained in the covenant of grace,⑪ the promises that are given in Christ, in whom all the promises are yea and amen. But surely they have no interest in the promises of the covenant of grace who are not the children of the covenant, who do not be-

lieve in any of the promises, and have no interest in the Mediator of the covenant. ⑫

So that, whatever some have imagined and pretended⑬ about promises made to natural men's earnest seeking and knocking, it is plain and manifest, that whatever pains a natural man takes in religion, whatever prayers he makes, till he believes in Christ, God is under no manner of obligation to keep him a moment from eternal destruction.

So that, thus it is that natural men are held in the hand of God, over the pit of hell; they have deserved the fiery pit, and are already sentenced to it; and God is dreadfully provoked, his anger is as great towards them as to those that are actually suffering the executions of the fierceness of his wrath in hell, and they have done nothing in the least to appease or abate that anger, neither is God in the least bound by any promise to hold them up one moment; the devil is waiting for them, hell is gaping for them, the flames gather and flash about them, and would fain lay hold on them, and swallow them up; the fire pent up in their own hearts is struggling to break out: and they have no interest in any Mediator, there are no means within reach that can be any security to them. In short, they have no refuge, nothing to take hold of; all that preserves them every moment is the mere arbitrary will, and uncovenanted, unobliged forbearance of an incensed God.

Notes

① **Sinners in the Hands of an Angry God**: Edwards delivered this sermon in Enfield, Connecticut, a town about thirty miles south of Northampton, on Sunday, July 8, 1741. Benjamin Trumbull's *A Complete History of Connecticut* (1797, 1818) says that Edwards read his sermon in a level voice with his sermon book in his left hand, and in spite of his calm, "there was such a breathing of distress, and weeping, that the preacher was obliged to speak to the people and desire silence, that he might be heard. " The text is from *The Works of Jonathan Edwards*, vol. 7, edited by Sereno E. Dwight (1829-1830).

② **Their foot shall slide in due time**: "To me belongeth vengeance, and recompense; their foot shall slide in due time; for the day of their calamity is at hand, and the things that shall come upon them make haste. "

③ **verse**: a numbered section of a chapter in *The Bible*.

④ **the means of grace**: the Ten Commandments. For Protestants following the Westminster Confession (1646), the "means of grace" consist of "preaching of the word and the administration of the sacraments of baptism and the Lord's Supper".

⑤ **deliver**: rescue others.

⑥ **Sodom**: a wicked city destroyed by a rain of fire and sulfur from heaven (Genesis 19:24).

⑦ **whet**: sharpened.

21

⑧ **The souls of the wicked are in scripture compared to the troubled sea, Isaiah 57:20**: "But the wicked are like the troubled sea, when it cannot rest, whose waters cast up mire and dirt. "

⑨ **"Hitherto shalt thou come, but no further"**: Job 38:11.

⑩ **natural**: unregenerate, unsaved.

⑪ **the covenant of grace**: The original covenant God made with Adam is called the Covenant of Works; the second covenant Christ made with fallen humanity—declaring that if they believed in Him they would be saved—is called the Covenant of Grace.

⑫ **the Mediator of the covenant**: Christ, who took upon Himself the sins of the world and suffered for them.

⑬ **pretended**: claimed.

Questions for Reading Comprehension

1. Who are the sinners in the hands of an angry God?

2. What does the expression that the speaker has chosen imply?

3. Why can't the wicked Israelites foresee the destruction to which they are exposed?

4. Why do wicked men deserve to be cast into hell?

5. Why are the wicked Israelites not fallen already?

6. Is there anything a natural man can do to secure himself from hell?

7. What can keep wicked men out of hell?

8. Why is God so angry with the wicked men who are now on earth?

9. What would happen if God should withdraw his restraining power?

10. Under what circumstances is God under an obligation to keep a natural man from eternal destruction?

Discussion Questions for Appreciation

1. What imagery does the speaker use to describe the invincibility of God?

2. Give one example of the speaker's metaphorical mode of perception.

3. Find two epigrams in the texts.

4. What is the speaker's purpose of depicting such a horrifying image of the wicked men dangled over the pit of hell?

5. What effect do you think this sermon will have on the listeners?

A Question for Writing

What religious doctrines of the Puritans are portrayed in Jonathan Edwards' sermon "Sinners in the Hands of an Angry God"?

Benjamin Franklin（1706-1790）

Benjamin Franklin was born in Boston, Massachusetts on January 6, 1706. His father was a poor craftsman who could not afford to keep his son long in school. But Franklin educated himself by reading widely. At the age of twelve, he was apprenticed to his brother, who was a newspaper printer in Boston. He learned the printing trade and published his first essay in his brother's newspaper. Franklin went to Philadelphia almost penniless when he was seventeen. He soon established himself as a printer, owned his own printing shop, and published the newspaper *Pennsylvania Gazette.* From 1732 to 1758, published his famous *Poor Richard's Almanac* under the name of Richard Saunders. Richard was the kind of man that the Americans called a cracker barrel philosopher, a person who sits around, doing nothing, talking idly, and giving pearls of wisdom. Franklin was ready to give other people advice in common-sense witticisms and maxims. It soon became the most popular book of its kind, largely because of Franklin's shrewd humor.

At the age of forty-two, Franklin retired from business and began his active life in civic and scientific activities. He helped found the Pennsylvania Hospital and the University of Pennsylvania. He encouraged scientific activity in Philadelphia and eventually formed the American Philosophical Society of which he was the first president. He also converted many of his theoretical investigations to practical uses such as bifocal glasses, the Franklin stove, and lighting rods.

Franklin spent many years in England and France, where he was a popular figure among intellectuals and aristocrats. Before the American Revolution he represented the colonies in London. In 1776, at

23

the age of seventy, he joined the committee that drafted the Declaration of Independence. Later he served as the American representative in Paris and helped negotiate the peace treaty with England. In his final years he was a delegate to the Constitutional Convention, and worked for the ratification of the Constitution. He died on April 17, 1790, at the age of eighty-four, as one of the most beloved Americans.

Brilliant, industrious, and versatile, Franklin was a sparkling man. He is often seen as a representative American: practical, witty, ambitious, and most of all successful. With his humble origins, dedication to self-improvement and genius for business and science, he sets an example for "the self-made man".

The Autobiography

Introduction

Franklin has a definite gift for writing. As an author he has the power of expression, and a subtle humor. He began to write his autobiography when he was already sixty-five. His fullest exposition of economic individualism and social mobility is found in *The Autobiography*, which was completed in four stages between 1771 and 1790. *The Autobiography of Benjamin Franklin* is an inspiring account of a poor boy's rise to wealth and fame, and of his fulfillment of the American dream. It is a book on the art of self-improvement. It is a classic of its kind. Using his life story as an example, Franklin eloquently demonstrates all the major principles of the enlightenment in America.

From ***The Autobiography***

Continuation of the Account of My Life

Begun at Passy, 1784

It is some time since I receiv'd the above Letters, but I have been too busy till now to think of complying with the Request they contain. It might, too, be much better done if I were at home among my Papers, which would aid my Memory, and help to ascertain Dates. But my Return being uncertain, and having just now a little Leisure, I will endeavor to recollect and write what I can; if I live to get home, it may there be corrected and improv'd.

Not having any Copy here of what is already written, I know not whether an Account is given of the means I used to establish the Philadelphia public Library, which from a small Beginning is now become so considerable, though I remember to have come down to near the Time of that Transaction (1730). I will therefore begin here, with an Account of it, which may be struck out if found to have been already given.

At the time I establish'd myself in Pennsylvania, there was not a good Bookseller's Shop in any of the Colonies to the Southward of Boston. In New York and Philadelphia the Printers were indeed Stationers, they sold only Paper, etc., Almanacs, Ballads, and a few common School Books. Those who lov'd Reading were oblig'd to send for their Books from England. The Members of the Junto had each a few. We had left the Alehouse where we first met, and hired a Room to hold our Club in. I propos'd that we should all of us bring our Books to that Room, where they would not only be ready to consult in our Conferences, but become a common Benefit, each of us being at Liberty to borrow such as he wish'd to read at home. This was accordingly done, and for some time contented us. Finding the Advantage of this little Collection, I propos'd to render the Benefit from Books more common by commencing a Public Subscription Library. I drew a Sketch of the Plan and Rules that would be necessary, and got a skilful Conveyancer[①], Mr. Charles Brockden to put the whole in Form of Articles of Agreement to be subscribed, by which each Subscriber engag'd to pay a certain Sum down for the first Purchase of Books, and an annual Contribution for increasing them. So

25

few were the Readers at that time in Philadelphia, and the Majority of us so poor, that I was not able with great Industry, to find more than Fifty Persons, mostly young Tradesmen, willing to pay down for this purpose Forty shillings each, and Ten Shillings per Annum. On this little Fund we began. The Books were imported. The Library was opened one Day in the Week for lending to the Subscribers, on their Promissory Notes to pay Double the Value if not duly returned. The Institution soon manifested its Utility, was imitated by other Towns and in other Provinces, the Libraries were augmented by Donations, Reading became fashionable, and our People, having no public Amusements to divert their Attention from Study, became better acquainted with Books, and in a few Years were observ'd by Strangers to be better instructed and more intelligent than People of the same Rank generally are in other Countries.

When we were about to sign the above-mentioned Articles, which were to be binding upon us, our Heirs, etc., for fifty Years, Mr. Brockden, the Scrivener, said to us, "You are young Men, but it is scarcely probable that any of you will live to see the Expiration of the Term fix'd in this Instrument." A number of us, however, are yet living: But the Instrument was after a few Years rendered null by a Charter that incorporated and gave Perpetuity to the Company.

The Objections and Reluctances I met with in Soliciting the Subscriptions, made me soon feel the Impropriety of presenting one's self as the Proposer of any useful Project that might be suppos'd to raise one's Reputation in the smallest degree above that of one's Neighbors, when one has need of their Assistance to accomplish that Project. I therefore put myself as much as I could out of sight, and stated it as a Scheme of *A Number of Friends*, who had requested me to go about and propose it to such as they thought Lovers of Reading. In this way my Affair went on more smoothly, and I ever after practic'd it on such Occasions; and from my frequent Successes, can heartily recommend it. The present little

Sacrifice of your Vanity will afterwards be amply repaid. If it remains a while uncertain to whom the Merit belongs, some one more vain than yourself will be encouraged to claim it, and then even envy will be disposed to do you Justice, by plucking those assum'd Feathers, and restoring them to their right Owner.

This Library afforded me the Means of Improvement by constant Study, for which I set apart an Hour or two each Day; and thus repair'd in some Degree the Loss of the Learned Education my Father once intended for me. Reading was the only Amusement I allow'd myself. I spent no time in Taverns, Games, or Frolics of any kind. And my Industry in my Business continu'd as indefatigable as it was necessary. I was indebted for my Printing-House, I had a young family[2] coming on to be educated, and I had to contend with for Business two Printers who were established in the Place before me. My Circumstances however grew daily easier: my original Habits of Frugality continuing. And my father having among his Instructions to me when a Boy, frequently repeated a Proverb of Solomon, "*Seest thou a man diligent in his calling, he shall stand before kings, he shall not stand before mean Men.*"[3] I from thence considered Industry as a Means of obtaining Wealth and Distinction, which encourag'd me: tho' I did not think that I should ever literally stand before kings, which however has since happened; for I have stood before five,[4] and even had the honor of sitting down with one, the King of Denmark, to Dinner.

27

We have an English proverb that says,

He that would thrive

Must ask his Wife,

it was lucky for me that I had one as much dispos'd to Industry and Frugality as myself. She assisted me cheerfully in my Business, folding and stitching Pamphlets, tending Shop, purchasing old Linen Rags for the Paper-Makers, etc., etc. We kept no idle Servants, our Table was plain and simple, our Furniture of the cheapest. For instance, my Breakfast was a long time Bread and Milk, (no Tea,) and I ate it out of a two penny earthen Porringer[5] with a Pewter Spoon. But mark how Luxury will enter Families, and make a Progress, in Spite of Principle. Being Call'd one Morning to Breakfast, I found it in a China[6] bowl with a Spoon of Silver. They had been bought for me without my Knowledge by my Wife, and had cost her the enormous Sum of three and twenty Shillings, for which she had no other Excuse or Apology to make, but that she thought *her* Husband deserv'd a Silver Spoon and China Bowl as well as any of his Neighbors. This was the first Appearance of Plate[7] and China in our House, which afterward in a Course of Years as our wealth increas'd, augmented gradually to several Hundred Pounds in Value.

I had been religiously educated as a Presbyterian[8]; and tho' some of the Dogmas of that Persuasion, such as the Eternal Decrees of God, Election,[9] Reprobation,[10] etc., appear'd to me unintelligible, others doubtful, and I early absented myself from the Public Assemblies of the Sect, Sunday being my Studying-Day, I never was without some religious Principles; I never doubted, for instance, the Existence of the Deity, that he made the World, and govern'd it by his Providence; that the most acceptable Service of God was the doing Good to Man; that our Souls are immortal; and that all Crime will be punished and Virtue rewarded, either here or hereafter; these I esteem'd the Essentials of every Religion; and being to be found in all the Religions we had in our Country, I respected them all, tho' with different degrees of Respect as I found them more or less mix'd with other Articles which without any Tendency to inspire, promote, or confirm Morality, serv'd principally to divide us, and make us unfriendly to one another. This Respect to all, with an Opinion that the worst had some good Effects, induc'd me to avoid all discourse that might tend to lessen the good Opinion another might have of his own Religion; and as our Province increas'd in People, and new Places of worship were continually wanted, and generally erected by voluntary Contributions, my Mite⑪ for such purpose, whatever might be the Sect, was never refused.

Tho' I seldom attended any Public Worship, I had still an Opinion of its Propriety, and of its Utility when rightly conducted, and I regularly paid my annual Subscription for the Support of the only Presbyterian Minister or Meeting we had in Philadelphia. He us'd to visit me sometimes as a Friend, and admonish me to attend his Administrations, and I was now and then prevail'd on to do so, once for five Sundays successively. Had he been, *in my Opinion*, a good Preacher, perhaps I might have continued, notwithstanding the occasion I had for the Sunday's Leisure in my Course of Study: But his Discourses were chiefly either polemic Arguments, or Explications of the peculiar Doctrines of our Sect, and were all to me very dry, uninteresting, and unedifying, since not a single moral Principle was inculcated or enforc'd, their Aim seeming to be rather to make us Presbyterians than good citizens. At length he took for his Text that Verse of the fourth Chapter of Philippians, *Finally, brethren, whatsoever things are true, honest, just, pure, lovely, or of good report, if there be any virtue, or any praise, think on these things*; and I imagin'd, in a Sermon on such a Text, we could not miss of having some Morality: But he confin'd himself to five Points only, as meant by the Apostle, viz. , 1. Keeping holy the Sabbath Day. 2. Being diligent in Reading the Holy Scriptures. 3. Attending duly the Public Worship. 4. Partaking of the Sacrament. 5. Paying a due Respect to God's Ministers. These might be all good Things, but, as they were not the kind of good Things that I expected from that Text, I despaired of ever meeting with them from any other, was disgusted, and attended his Preaching no more. I had some Years before compos'd a little Liturgy, or Form of Prayer for my own private Use viz. , in 1728, entitled, *Articles of Belief and Acts of Religion.* ⑫ I return'd to the Use of this, and went no more to the public Assemblies. My Conduct might be blameable, but I leave it without attempting further to excuse it, my present purpose being to relate Facts, and not to make Apologies for them.

It was about this time I conceiv'd the bold and arduous Project of arriving at moral Perfection. I wish'd to live without committing any Fault at anytime; I would conquer all that either Natural Inclination, Custom, or Company might lead me into. As I knew, or thought I knew, what was right and wrong, I did not see why I might not *always* do the one and avoid the other. But I soon found I had undertaken a Task of more Difficulty than I bad imagined: While my Care was employ'd in guarding against one Fault, I was often surprised by another. Habit took the Advantage of Inattention. Inclination was sometimes too strong for Reason. I concluded at length that the mere speculative Conviction that it was our interest to be completely virtuous, was not sufficient to prevent our Slipping, and that the contrary Habits must be broken, and good Ones acquired and established, before we can have any Dependence on a steady uniform Rectitude of Conduct. For this purpose I therefore contriv'd the following Method.

In the various Enumerations of the moral Virtues I had met with in my Reading, I found the Catalog more or less numerous, as different Writers included more or fewer Ideas under the same Name. Temperance, for Example, was by some confin'd to Eating and Drinking, while by others it was extended to mean the moderating every other Pleasure, Appetite, Inclination, or Passion, bodily or mental, even to our Avarice and Ambition. I propos'd to myself, for the sake of Clearness, to use rather more Names with fewer ideas annex'd to each, than a few Names with more Ideas; and I included under Thirteen Names of Virtues all that at that time occurr'd to me as necessary or desirable, and annexed to each a short Precept, which fully express'd the Extent I gave to its Meaning.

These names of virtues, with their Precepts were

Temperance.

Eat not to Dullness. Drink not to Elevation.

Silence.

Speak not but what may benefit others or yourself. Avoid trifling Conversation.

Order.

Let all your Things have their Places. Let each Part of your Business have its Time.

Resolution.

Resolve to perform what you ought. Perform without fail what you resolve.

Frugality.

Make no Expense but to do good to others or yourself: i. e. , Waste nothing.

Industry.

Lose no Time. Be always employ'd in something useful. Cut off all unnecessary Actions.

Sincerity.

Use no hurtful Deceit. Think innocently and justly; and, if you speak; speak accordingly.

Justice.

Wrong none, by doing Injuries or omitting the Benefits that are your Duty.

Moderation.

Avoid Extremes. Forbear resenting Injuries so much as you think they deserve.

Cleanliness.

Tolerate no Uncleanness in Body, Cloths or Habitation.

Tranquility.

Be not disturbed at Trifles, or Accidents common or unavoidable.

Chastity.

Rarely use Venery but for Health or Offspring; Never to Dullness, Weakness, or the Injury of your own or another's Peace or Reputation.

Humility.

Imitate Jesus and Socrates. [13]

My intention being to acquire the *Habitude* [14] of all these Virtues, I judg'd it would be well not to distract my Attention by attempting the whole at once, but to fix it on one of them at a time, and, when I should be Master of that, then to proceed to another, and so on till I should have gone thro' the thirteen; and, as the previous Acquisition of some might facilitate the acquisition of certain others, I arrang'd them with that View, as they stand above. *Temperance* first, as it tends to procure that Coolness and Clearness of Head, which is so necessary where constant Vigilance was to be kept up, and Guard maintained, against the unremitting Attraction of ancient Habits, and the Force of perpetual Temptations. This being acquir'd and establish'd, *Silence* would be more easy; and my Desire being to gain Knowledge at the same time that I improv'd in Virtue, and considering that in Conversation it was obtain'd rather by the Use of the Ears than of the Tongue, and therefore wishing to break a Habit I was getting into of Prattling, Punning, and Joking, which only made me acceptable to trifling Company, I gave *Silence* the second Place. This and the next, *Order*, I expected would allow me more time for attending to my Project and my studies; RESOLUTION once become habitual, would keep me firm in my endeavors to obtain all the subsequent Virtues; *Frugality* and *Industry* freeing me from my remaining Debt, and producing Affluence and Independence, would make more easy the practice of *Sincerity* and *Justice*, etc., etc. Conceiving then that, agreeably to the Advice of Pythagoras [15] in his Golden Verses, daily Examination would be necessary, I contrived the following Method for conducting that Examination.

I made a little Book in which I allotted a Page for each of the Virtues. I rul'd each Page with red Ink, so as to have seven Columns, one for each Day of the Week, marking each Column with a letter for the Day. I cross'd these Columns with thirteen red Lines, marking the Beginning of each Line with the first Letter of one of the Virtues, on which Line and in its proper Column I might mark by a little black Spot every Fault I found upon Examination to have been committed respecting that Virtue upon that Day.

Form of the Pages

TEMPERANCE.						
Eat not to Dulness.						
Drink not to Elevation.						

	S	M	T	W	T	F	S
T							
S	●	●	●		●	●	
O	●	●	●		●	●	●
R				●		●	
F		●			●		
I			●				
S							
J							
M							
Cl.							
T							
Ch							
H							

I determined to give a Week's strict Attention to each of the Virtues successively. Thus, in the first Week my great Guard was to avoid every the least Offence against Temperance, leaving the other Virtues to their ordinary Chance, only marking every Evening the Faults of the Day. Thus, if in the first Week I could keep my first Line, marked T clear of Spots, I suppos'd the Habit of that Virtue so much strengthen'd and its opposite weaken'd, that I might venture extending my Attention to include the next, and for the following Week keep both Lines clear of Spots. Proceeding thus to the last, I could go thro' a Course complete in Thirteen Weeks, and four Courses in a Year. And like him who, having a Garden to weed, does not attempt to eradicate all the bad Herbs at once, which would exceed his Reach and his Strength, but works on one of the Beds at a time, and, having accomplish'd the first, proceeds to a second; so I should have, (I hoped) the encouraging Pleasure of seeing on my Pages the Progress I made in Virtue, by clearing successively my Lines of their Spots, till in the End by a Number of Courses, I should he happy in viewing a clean Book after a thirteen weeks' daily Examination.

This my little Book had for its Motto these Lines from *Addison's Cato*, [16]

Here will I hold: If there's a Pow'r above us,
(And that there is, all Nature cries aloud
Thro' all her Works), he must delight in Virtue,
And that which he delights in must be happy.

Another from *Cicero*, [17]

O Vitae Philosophia Dux! O Virtutum indagatrix, expultrixque vitiorum! Unus die, bene et, ex praeceptis tuis actu, peccanti immortalitati est anteponendus.

Another from the Proverbs of Solomon speaking of Wisdom or Virtue;

Length of Days is in her right hand, and in her Left Hand Riches and Honors; Her Ways are Ways of Pleasantness, and all her Paths are Peace.

Ⅲ. 16, 17

And conceiving God to be the Fountain of Wisdom, I thought it right and necessary to solicit his Assistance for obtaining it; to this End I form'd the following little Prayer, which was prefix'd to my Tables of Examination, for daily Use.

O powerful Goodness! bountiful Father! merciful Guide! Increase in me that Wisdom which discovers my truest Interest; Strengthen my Resolutions to perform what that Wisdom dictates. Accept my kind Offices to thy other Children, as the only Return in my Power for thy continual Favors to me.

I us'd also sometimes a little Prayer which I took from *Thomson's Poems*, viz. [18],

Father of Light and Life, thou Good Supreme,
O teach me what is good, teach me thy self!
Save me from Folly, Vanity, and Vice,
From every low Pursuit; and fill my Soul
With Knowledge, conscious Peace, and Virtue pure,
Sacred, substantial, neverfading Bliss!

The precept of *Order* requiring that *every Part of my Business should have its allotted Time*, one Page in my little Book contain'd the following Scheme of Employment for the Twenty-four Hours of a natural Day.

I enter'd upon the Execution of this Plan for Self-examination, and continu'd it with occasional Intermissions for some time. I was surpris'd to find myself so much fuller of Faults than I had imagined, but I had the Satisfaction of seeing them diminish. To avoid the Trouble of renewing now and then my little Book, which by scraping out the Marks on the Paper of old Faults to make room for new Ones in a new Course, became full of Holes: I transferr'd my Tables and Precepts to the Ivory Leaves of a Memorandum Book, on which the Lines were drawn with red Ink that made a durable Stain, and on those Lines I mark'd my Faults with a black Lead Pencil, which Marks I could easily wipe out with a wet Sponge. After a while I went thro' one Course only in a Year, and afterward only one in several Years; till at length I omitted them entirely, being employ'd in Voyages and Business abroad, with a Multiplicity of Affairs, that interfered. But I always carried my little Book with me.

My Scheme of ORDER, gave me the most Trouble, and I found that, tho' it might be practicable where a Man's Business was such as to leave him the Disposition of his Time, that of a Journeyman Printer for instance, it was not possible to be exactly observ'd by a Master, who must mix with the World, and often receive People of Business at their own Hours. *Order* too, with regard to Places for Things, Papers, etc. , I found extremely difficult to acquire. I had not been early accustomed to it, and having an exceeding good Memory, I was not so sensible of the Inconvenience attending Want of Method. This Article therefore cost me so much painful Attention, and my Faults in it vex'd me so much, and I made so little Progress in Amendment, and had such frequent Relapses, that I was almost ready to give up the Attempt, and content myself with a faulty Character in that respect. Like the Man who in buying an Ax of a Smith my Neighbor, desired to have the whole of its Surface as bright as the Edge; the Smith consented to grind it bright for him if he would turn the Wheel; he turn'd, while the Smith press'd the broad Face of the Ax hard and heavily on the Stone, which made the Turning of it very fatiguing. The Man came every now and then from the Wheel to see how the Work went on; and at length would take his Ax as it was without farther Grinding. No, said the Smith, Turn on, turn on; we shall have it bright by and by; as yet, 'tis only speckled. Yes, said the Man; but I think—

The Morning Question, What Good shall I do this Day?	5	Rise, wash, and address *Powerful Goodness*; contrive Day's Business and take the Resolution of the Day; prosecute the present Study:and breakfast.—
	6	
	7	
	8	
	9	Work.
	10	
	11	
	12	Read, or overlook my Accounts, and dine.
	1	
	2	Work.
	3	
	4	
	5	
	6	Put Things in their Places, Supper, Musick, or Diversion, or Conversation, Examination of the Day.
	7	
	8	
	9	
Evening Question, What Good have I done today?	10	
	11	
	12	
	1	Sleep.—
	2	
	3	
	4	

I like a speckled Ax best. —And I believe this may have been the Case with many who having for want of some such Means as I employ'd found the Difficulty of obtaining good, and breaking bad Habits, in other Points of Vice and Virtue, have given up the Struggle, and concluded that *a speckled ax was best.* For something that pretended to be Reason was every now and then suggesting to me, that such extreme Nicety as I exacted of myself might be a kind of Foppery in Morals, which if it were known, would make me ridiculous; that a perfect Character might be attended with the Inconvenience of being envied and hated; and that a benevolent Man should allow a few Faults in himself, to keep his Friends in Countenance.

In Truth, I found myself incorrigible with respect to *Order*; and now I am grown old, and my Memory bad, I feel very sensibly the want of it. But on the whole, tho' I never arrived at the Perfection I had been so ambitious of obtaining, but fell far short of it, yet I was, by the Endeavor, a better and a happier Man than I otherwise should have been, if I had not attempted it; As those who aim at perfect Writing by imitating the engraved Copies,[19] tho' they never reach the wish'd for Excellence of those Copies, their Hand is mended by the Endeavor, and is tolerable while it continues fair and legible.

And it may be well my Posterity should be informed, that to this little Artifice, with the Blessing of God, their Ancestor ow'd the constant Felicity of his Life, down to his 79th Year in which this is written. What Reverses may attend the Remainder is in the Hand of Providence: But if they arrive, the Reflection on past Happiness enjoy'd ought to help his Bearing them with more Resignation. To *Temperance* he ascribes his long-continu'd Health, and what is still left to him of a good Constitution. To *Industry* and *Frugality*, the early Easiness of his Circumstances, and Acquisition of his Fortune, with all that Knowledge that enabled him to be a useful Citizen, and obtain'd for him some Degree of

Reputation among the Learned. To *Sincerity* and *Justice*, the Confidence
of his Country, and the honorable Employs it conferr'd upon him. And to
the joint Influence of the whole Mass of the Virtues, even in the imperfect State he was able to acquire them, all that Evenness of Temper, and
that Cheerfulness in Conversation which makes his Company still sought
for, and agreeable even to his younger Acquaintance. I hope therefore
that some of my Descendants may follow the Example and reap the Benefit.

It will be remark'd[20] that, tho' my scheme was not wholly without
Religion there was in it no Mark of any of the distinguishing Tenets of
any particular Sect. I had purposely avoided them; for being fully persuaded of the Utility and Excellency of my Method, and that it might be
serviceable to people in all Religions, and intending some time or other
to publish it, I would not have any thing in it that should prejudice any
one of any Sect against it. I purposed writing a little Comment on each
Virtue, in which I would have shown the Advantages of possessing it,
and the Mischiefs attending its opposite Vice; and I should have called
my Book *The Art of Virtue*, because it would have shown the *Means and
Manner* of obtaining Virtue; which would have distinguish'd it from the
mere Exhortation to be good, that does not instruct and indicate the
Means; but is like the Apostle's Man of verbal Charity, who only, without
showing to the Naked and Hungry *how* or where they might get Clothes or
Victuals, exhorted them to be fed and clothed. James II, 15, 16. [21]

But it so happened that my Intention of writing and publishing this
Comment was never fulfilled. I did, indeed, from time to time, put
down short Hints of the Sentiments, Reasoning, etc. , to be made use of
in it; some of which I have still by me: But the necessary close Attention
to private Business in the earlier part of Life, and public Business since,
have occasioned my postponing it. For it being connected in my Mind
with a *great and extensive Project*, that required the whole Man to exe-

cute, and which an unforeseen Succession of Employs prevented my attending to, it has hitherto remain'd unfinish'd.

In this Piece it was my Design to explain and enforce this Doctrine, that vicious Actions are not hurtful because they are forbidden, but forbidden because they are hurtful, the Nature of Man alone consider'd: That it was therefore every one's Interest to be virtuous who wish'd to be happy even in this World. And I should from this Circumstance (there being always in the World a Number of rich Merchants, Nobility, States, and Princes, who have need of honest Instruments for the Management of their Affairs, and such being so rare) have endeavored to convince young Persons that no Qualities were so likely to make a poor Man's Fortune as those of Probity and Integrity.

My List of Virtues contain'd at first but twelve: But a Quaker Friend having kindly inform'd me that I was generally thought proud; that my pride show'd itself frequently in Conversation; that I was not content with being in the right when discussing any Point, but was overbearing, and rather insolent; of which he convinc'd me by mentioning several Instances; I determined endeavoring to cure myself if I could of this Vice or Folly among the rest, and I added *Humility* to my List, giving an extensive Meaning to the Word. I cannot boast of much Success in acquiring the *Reality* of this Virtue; but I had a good deal with regard to the *Appearance* of it. I made it a Rule to forbear all direct Contradiction to the Sentiments of others, and all positive Assertion of my own. I even forbid myself, agreeably to the old Laws of our Junto, the Use of every Word or Expression in the Language that imported[22] a fix'd Opinion, such as *certainly*, *undoubtedly*, etc., and I adopted, instead of them, I *conceive*, I *apprehend*, or I *imagine* a thing to be so or so, or it so appears to me at present. When another asserted something that I thought an Error, I deny'd myself the Pleasure of contradicting him abruptly, and of showing immediately some Absurdity in his Proposition; and in answering I began by observing that in certain Cases or Circumstances his Opinion would be right, but in the present case there *appear'd* or *seem'd* to me some Difference, etc., I soon found the Advantage of this Change in my Manner. The Conversations I engag'd in went on more pleasantly. The modest way in which I propos'd my Opinions procur'd them a readier Reception and less Contradiction; I had less Mortification when I was found to be in the wrong, and I more easily prevail'd with others to give up their Mistakes and join with me when I happen'd to be in the right. And this Mode, which I at first put on with some violence to natural Inclination, became at length so easy, and so habitual to me, that perhaps for these Fifty Years past no one has ever heard a dogmatical Expression escape me. And to this Habit (after my Character of Integrity) I think it principally owing, that I had early so much Weight with my Fellow Citizens when I proposed new Institutions, or Alterations in the old; and so much Influence in public Councils when I became a Member. For I was but a bad Speaker, never eloquent, subject to much Hesitation in my choice of Words, hardly correct in Language, and yet I generally carried my Points.

In reality there is perhaps, no one of our natural Passions so hard to subdue as *Pride*. Disguise it, struggle with it, beat it down, stifle it, mortify it as much as one pleases, it is still alive, and will every now and then peep out and show itself; you will see it, perhaps, often in this History; for, even if I could conceive that I had completely overcome it, I should probably be proud of my Humility.

Thus far written at Passy, 1784.

Notes

① **Conveyancer**: an attorney who specializes in the transfer of real estate and property.

② **I had a young family**: Franklin had three children: William, born

c. 1731; Francis, born in 1732; Sarah, born in 1743.

③ "**Seest thou a man diligent in his calling, he shall stand before kings, he shall not stand before mean Men**": a quotation from Proverbs 22:29.

④ **for I have stood before five**: Franklin met these five kings during his life time: Louis XV and Louis XVI of France, George II and George III of England, and Christian VI of Denmark.

⑤ **Porringer**: bowl.

⑥ **China**: porcelain.

⑦ **Plate**: silver.

⑧ **a Presbyterian**: a member of the church adhering to a system of polity that consists of a series of four courts and elected elders.

⑨ **Election**: God's choosing who is to be saved and who is to be damned.

⑩ **Reprobation**: punishment.

⑪ **Mite**: small contribution.

⑫ **Articles of Belief and Acts of Religion**: Only the first part of Franklin's *Articles of Belief and Acts of Religion* survives. It can be found in *The Papers of Benjamin Franklin*, vol. 1, edited by Leonard W. Labaree et al. (1964).

⑬ **Socrates**: a Greek philosopher and teacher (470?-399 B. C.). Most of his mature life was devoted to philosophy. He wrote nothing. His life, thought and method are known to us chiefly through Plato and Xenophon.

⑭ **Habitude**: making these virtues an integral part of one's nature.

⑮ **Pythagoras**: a Greek philosopher and mathematician (cc. 580-c. 500 B. C.). Franklin added a note here: "Insert those Lines that direct it in a Note," and wished to include verses translated; "Let sleep not close your eyes till you have thrice examined the transactions of the day: where have I strayed, what have I done, what good have I omitted?"

⑯ ***Addison's Cato***: Joseph Addison's *Cato*, *a Tragedy* (1713; 5. 1. 15-18). Franklin also used these lines as an epigraph for his *Articles of Belief and Acts of Religion*.

⑰ **Cicero**: Marcus Tullius Cicero (1006 B. C. -1043 B. C.), Roman philosopher and orator. The quotation is from *Tusculan Disputations* (5. 2. 5), but several lines are omitted after *vitiorum*. It means: Oh, philosophy, guide of life: Oh, searcher out of virtues and expeller of vices! ... One day lived well and according to thy precepts is to be preferred to an eternity of sin.

⑱ ***Thomson's Poems***, **viz.**: James Thomson (1700-1748), a British poet who is best known for his four long meditative and descriptive poems, *The Seasons*. What Franklin quoted are "Winter" (1726), lines 218-223.

⑲ **Copies**: the models in the printed book.

⑳ **remark'd**: observed.

㉑ **James Ⅱ, 15, 16**: "If a brother or sister be naked, and destitute of daily food, And one of you say unto them, Depart in peace, be ye warmed and filled: notwithstanding ye give them not those things which are needful to the body; what doth it profit?"

㉒ **imported**: suggested.

Questions for Reading Comprehension

1. Why did Franklin set up a Public Subscription Library in Philadelphia?

2. What did the Library afford him?

3. What did he consider as a means of obtaining wealth and distinction?

4. What did Franklin regard as the essentials of every religion?

5. Make a shorthand list of the memorable anecdotes Franklin tells about himself.

6. According to the selection, why did Franklin create his "Method" for "moral perfection"?

7. Can you summarize Franklin's "Method" for "moral perfection"?

8. What surprised Franklin when he began to follow his plan for self-examination?

9. What satisfaction did he have? What gave him the most trouble?

10. At first Franklin's list contained twelve virtues. Why did he later add Humility to his list?

Discussion Questions for Appreciation

1. How would you describe Franklin's writing style?

2. What is Franklin's purpose of writing *The Autobiography*? And how does that purpose change throughout the work?

3. Franklin often struggles to strike a balance between promoting humility and promoting his accomplishments. How successful is he in maintaining this balance?

4. Discuss Franklin's optimism as a young man versus the diminished optimism he has as an adult looking back on his life. How do the two work together?

5. How does Franklin employ humor in *The Autobiography*? Find three examples of humor or worldly wisdom that help illustrate why Franklin was regarded as one of the wittiest Americans of the eighteenth century.

6. How can writing an autobiography contribute to self-knowledge? By way of example, explain what Benjamin Franklin *The Autobiographer* comes to see about Benjamin Franklin the young man.

A Question for Writing

Many critics regard *The Autobiography* as a statement about American national identity. What ideals does the book convey? And why are these ideas worth pursuing?

Chapter Two   American Romanticism and Transcendentalism

(1820-1865)

Historical Background

After the American Revolutionary War ended in 1783, America became an independent nation, and the country entered a new stage of development. From 1789 to 1865, the United States gradually formed its national identity and established its political and legal institutions. Here are some of the significant historical developments.

1. Major Wars

In 1812 a war broke out between America and Britain. The war arose from American resentment at the trade embargo imposed by France and Britain, and the British claims to search American ships for British deserters. In the end the Americans defeated the British at New Orleans. The war, which ended in 1814, strengthened American nationalism and encouraged the growth of American industry.

During the 1830, the Whites in America had a series of wars against Native Americans. The Whites defeated indigenous inhabitants (the Indians), and occupied their land.

In order to expand their territories, the Americans waged another war against Mexico and they won it. As a result, they acquired California and most of the western territory.

Although the country was rapidly expanding, it became split between an industrialized North that favored free soil and protectionism and an agricultural South that favored slavery. The election of Lincoln as president in 1860 provoked seven Southern states to secede from the Union, and they set themselves up as the Confederate States under Jefferson Davis. The American Civil War started when Confederate forces attacked Fort Sumter on 12 April, 1861. After bitter fighting, the Southern states surrendered at Appomatax on 9 April, 1865. The war cost over 600,000 lives, and many issues were left unsettled, but the Union had been preserved, and slavery had been abolished in the Emancipation of Proclamation. The war increased the political and economic dominance of the North over the South.

2. Westward Expansion

In 1803, the United States bought a large track of land (828,000 sq. miles) from France for $ 15,000,000. It comprises the western part of the Mississippi Valley, and now forms the states of Louisiana, Arkansas, Missouri, Iowa and Nebraska and part of eight other states. It is known as the Louisiana Purchase.

Another significant event was the California Gold Rush. The news of the discovery of gold in California in 1848 spread across America to Europe, and thousands of people joined in the search. It attracted many people to the West Coast, and caused a rapid push westward by pioneers. They pushed the frontier line of settlement by the Mississippi to the Great Plains and finally to the West Coast.

3. Growth of Industrialization

When the United States began to change into an industrial and urban society, the principle of assembly-line mass production was established, and technology began to bring vast material benefits to the industrialized North. But the South remained agricultural. With an increasing number of farm laborers leaving the land to work in urban businesses and factories, cities grew bigger and bigger. This period is a period of increasing prosperity in American history.

With these significant developments, the United States became a new rising nation which was rapidly expanding. The Americans were proud of their country, and a new nationalism emerged. It was justified by "Manifest Destiny", the doctrine asserting that the new nation was spiritually supreme and its expansion was Will of God. Optimism became the prevailing mood of the American people and frontier spirit became their national cultural heritage.

The Romantic period in America refers to the period between the "second revolution" of the Jacksonian Era and the close of the Civil War. It was America's first great creative period, a full flowering of the romantic impulse on American soil. In this period, American literature ceased to be primarily didactic and politically oriented. It became intense, personal and symbolic.

American Romanticism

Romanticism is characterized by a rejection of formal classical approaches to literature. It emphasizes sentiment over reason and views art as essentially an expression of the artist's thought and feeling.

Romanticism has a tendency to exalt the individual and an increasing interest in the value of the individual. It views the individual at the very center of all life and all experience and tends to place him at the center of art. It regards literature as an expression of his thought and feelings, and values its accuracy in portraying his experience. It lays emphasis on the individual's need for a freer and more personal expression, and places increasing value on spontaneity in the expression of thought and feelings.

Romanticism emphasizes the individual's natural genius and his power of imagination, seeing art as a formulation of intuitive imaginative perceptions that tend to speak a nobler truth than that of fact and logic. What the Romanticists seek is a kind of pure beauty, or supernal beauty. Some of them often use the Gothic, the remote, the grotesque, the supernatural and the terrifying as their subject matter while others prefer the natural, the commonplace and the simple, but they seek to find the absolute and the ideal by transcending the actual.

Romanticism sees nature as the revelation of God to the individual. In nature we can see a revelation of truth, the "living garment of God". So nature is a more suitable subject for true art than those aspects of the world, which is sullied by man's artifice and commerce. Romanticists are interested in the natural, primitive and uncivilized way of life because they regard nature as an escape from problems of society. They see a harmonious relationship between man and nature, and an association of human moods with the moods of nature. In this period, the desire for escape from society and a return to nature became a convention of American literature.

In the Age of Romanticism, America produced some outstanding writers of imaginative literature.

Washington Irving (1783-1859) was the first important American Romanticist and the first great American writer of imaginative literature. His most famous work is a collection of essays and tales: The Sketch Book of Geoffrey Crayon, which contains Rip Van Winkle, a tale of a man who falls asleep for twenty years and marvels at how the world has changed in his absence. The book also contains The Legend of Sleeping Hollow, a humorous story of horror and superstition.

James Fennimore Cooper (1789-1851), who wrote both novels and social criticism, is best known for his tales of frontier life and pioneer adventure, The Leatherstocking Tales. His most famous novel is *The Last of the Mohicans*. In his novels, he creates the impressive archetype of the rugged frontier woodsman. His novels are also popular for their vivid description, romantic scenes, adventurous plots and dramatic events.

One of the most important novelists of the Romantic period is **Nathaniel Hawthorne** (1804-1864), who focuses much of his work on the Puritan and transcendental themes, particularly sin and its psychological consequences. His most remarkable novel is *The Scarlet Letter*. His work tends to be rather ambiguous, highly symbolic and psychological.

Herman Melville (1819-1891) is one of the most prolific writers of the Romantic Age. He is best known for his profoundly symbolic novel *Moby Dick*. Most of his fiction is drawn from his own adventures and real-life experiences. His work makes effective use of symbolism and has profound philosophical meaning. The recurring theme in his fiction is the confrontation between innocence and evil.

Edgar Allan Poe (1809-1849) is one of the most interesting and controversial American writers of the nineteenth century. He is simultaneously a fine poet, a great writer of short stories and a highly regarded critic with his own theory of writing.

American poetry flourished during the Romantic period, which produced some poets of high renown. The best known of these poets include **Henry Wadsworth Longfellow** (1807-1882), **Walt Whitman** (1819-1892) and **Emily Dickinson** (1830-1886).

American Transcendentalism

Transcendentalism, often regarded as a philosophical romanticism, reached America a generation or two after it developed in Europe. It was based on the doctrines of ancient and modern European philosophers, particularly the German philosopher Kant, but it took on special significance in the United States in the mid-19th century where it became a literary movement and a philosophical conception.

1. Transcendentalism as a Literary Movement

This movement refers to the New England literary movement which flourished from 1835 to 1860. It started with the meetings of a small group of eminent writers and scholars who came together in a town called Concord to discuss the new thought of the time. Though they held different opinions about many issues, they seemed to generally agree that within the nature of man there was an intuitive and personal relevation that can transcend human experience. They became known as the Transcendental Club. Members of the Club included **Ralph Waldo Emerson** (1803-1882), **Henry David Thoreau** (1817-1862), **Margaret Fuller** (1810-1850) and **Nathaniel Hawthorne**. As the movement developed, it sponsored two important activities: the publication of a magazine *The Dial* and the organization of Brook Farm. It had a considerable influence on American art and literature. Key statements of its doctrine include Emerson's *Nature*, *The American Scholar*, *The Divinity School Address*, *The Transcendentalist* and "Self-Reliance" and also Thoreau's *Walden*.

2. Transcendentalism as a Philosophical Conception

Transcendentalism is also an epistemology, a way of knowing. The name and many of the ideas are derived from Kant's *Critique of Practical*

Reason (1788). Kant declared that all knowledge is transcendental and is concerned not with objects, but with our mode of knowing objects.

The ultimate characteristic of transcendentalism is "the belief that man can intuitively transcend the limits of the scenes and those of logic, and receive directly higher truths and greater knowledge which is denied to the mundane methods of knowing"[①]. Transcendentalism has been defined philosophically as the recognition in man of the capacity of knowing truth intuitively, or attaining knowledge transcending the reach of the senses.

3. The Basic Assumptions of Transcendentalism

Transcendentalism has its fundamental base a monism holding to the unity of the world and God and the immanence of God in the world. Its basic assumption is that the intuitive faculty, is the means for a conscious union of the individual psyche with the world's psyche (known as the Oversoul) and God.

God exists everywhere in the world. Because of this indwelling of divinity, everything, including every human being, in the world is a microcosm which contains within itself all the laws and meaning of existence. So in an individual we can find the clue to nature, history and ultimately the universe itself. So each individual is divine in his own right.

The individual soul can reach God without the help of the church and clergy. The soul of each individual is identical with the soul of the world, the Grand Oversoul. So man may fulfill his divine potentialities through coming into contact with the truth, beauty, and goodness embodies in nature and originating in the Oversoul.

---

① C. Hugh Holman, *A Handbook to Literature*. Indianapolis and New York: The Odyssey Press. 1972: p. 537.

Through his intuition, each individual can have direct contact with, and certain knowledge of, universal reality. Since man can intuitively transcend the limits of the senses and of logic, and receive directly higher truths and greater knowledge, man should rely on his own intuition and not any social laws, scientific understanding or empirical information that is given him by his senses to learn the real truth.

Through belief in the divine authority of man's intuition and imagination, there developed the doctrine of self-reliance and individualism. Men should trust themselves and rely on themselves. If men live according to their deepest selves, they would be living in harmony with the Oversoul. They can make their own laws and live according to their own independent principles. The new world gives each the opportunity to become a completely free and independent individual. So Transcendentalism disregards external authority, tradition and logical demonstration.

52

The ardent champion of American Transcendentalism was Emerson, who sponsored the Transcendental movement in New England. He was an essayist, a poet and a philosopher. His most important works include *Nature* (1836) and two books of essays. In many of his writings, he advocates the ideas of Transcendentalism, and stresses such values as integrity, intellectual freedom and self-reliance.

Another important Transcendentalist was Thoreau, who was a friend of Emerson. He is best known for his book *Walden* (1854), which is an account of his two-year experiment in living alone by Walden Pond where he observed the life of the woods, and devoted most of his time to study and reflection. Thoreau was also a powerful social critic. In his famous essay Civil Disobedience (1849), he explains his idea of using civil disobedience to protest government actions.

Ralph Waldo Emerson（1803-1882）

Ralph Waldo Emerson was born in Boston on May 25, 1803, a descendant from a line of preacher ancestors. When he was eight, his father died, leaving the family in financial straits. In spite of this, he went through Boston Latin School, and proceeded to Harvard in 1817 to receive a classical education. Following in his father's footsteps, Emerson was ordained a Unitarian minister in 1829, but he experienced a religious crisis after the death of his first wife, the beautiful and romantic Ellen Tucker, to whom he had been married only eighteen months.

He resigned from the Second Church and went to England in 1832, where he met the prominent British Romanticists Carlyle, Coleridge, and Wordsworth, and he learned from his English friends new ideas of German idealism and transcendentalism. In 1834 he came back to Concord, Massachusetts, and became an essayist, poet and public speaker. He also became the most eloquent spokesman of transcendentalism, advocating a direct intuition of a spiritual and immanent God in nature. He expounded his views on the mystical harmonies of man and nature, the essential perfectibility of the human spirit, the unity of the human soul with the divine Oversoul, and the values of non-conformity, intellectual and spiritual independence, and self-reliance.

Emerson gathered around him a circle of poets, reformers, artists, and thinkers who helped define a new national identity for American art—among them, Henry David Thoreau, Nathaniel Hawthorne, and Margaret Fuller. With Margaret Fuller Emerson founded *The Dial*, which published Transcendentalist literature from 1840-1844. In the years between 1837-1844 he published his most famous works *The American*

Scholar, *The Divinity School Address*, and two volumes of *Essays* (1841 & 1845), which contained the influential pieces "Self-Reliance", "The Poet", "Friendship", and "The Oversoul".

Emerson has been called "the one citizen of the New World fit to have his named uttered in the same breath with that of Plato". He is acclaimed as one of the stimulating American minds, and Transcendentalism's most seminal force. The power of Emerson comes from not only from his ideas but also from the eloquence with which he could express his ideas. Much of Emerson's style and mind can be revealed in a typically Emersonian paragraph: the sentences are not logically linked but they existed in the paragraph. Emerson also tends to repeat his ideas in various ways, sentence by sentence, paragraph by paragraph, gaining momentum as his thoughts soar.

Emerson's writings fall into two types: essays and poetry. Among his best known works are *Nature* (1836), *Essays* (1841), *Essays: Second Series* (1844), *Representing Men* (1850), *English Traits* (1856), *The Conduct of Life* (1860), and *Society and Solitude* (1870). In 1847, he published *Poems*, the fruit of his thirty years of poetic activity. Later he turned out two more volumes of poems: *May-Day and Other Pieces* (1867) and *Selected Poems* (1876).

Nature

Introduction

Considered the "gospel" of American Transcendentalism, *Nature* is a lyrical expression of the harmony Emerson felt between himself and nature. He believed that the individual soul can become the medium of the divine forces of Nature. In the "Introduction", Emerson pronounces the fundamental premise about Nature in Transcendentalism, that is, Nature is not simply the Not-Me but also the universal mind whose signs, or symbols, are visible for the individual to read, with eyes, heart and mind. The "Introduction" is followed by eight sections, each of which develops a general thesis: "Nature"; "Commodity"; "Beauty"; "Language"; "Discipline"; "Idealism"; "Spirit" and "Prospects". The following excerpt is taken from the Introduction and Chapter 1 Nature.

From *Nature*

"Nature is but an image or imitation of wisdom, the last thing of the soul; nature being a thing which doth only do, but not know."

—Plotinus[1]

Introduction

Our age is retrospective. It builds the sepulchres of the fathers. It writes biographies, histories, and criticism. The foregoing generations beheld God and nature face to face; we, through their eyes. Why should not we also enjoy an original relation to the universe? Why should not we have a poetry and philosophy of insight and not of tradition, and a religion by revelation to us, and not the history of theirs? Embosomed for a season in nature, whose floods of life stream around and through us, and invite us by the powers they supply, to action proportioned to nature, why should we grope among the dry bones of the past,[2] or put the living generation into masquerade out of its faded wardrobe? The sun shines to-day also. There is more wool and flax in the fields. There are new lands, new men, new thoughts. Let us demand our own works and laws and worship.

Undoubtedly we have no questions to ask which are unanswerable. We must trust the perfection of the creation so far, as to believe that whatever curiosity the order of things has awakened in our minds, the order of things can satisfy. Every man's condition is a solution in hiero-glyphic to those inquiries he would put. He acts it as life, before he ap-prehends it as truth. In like manner, nature is already, in its forms and tendencies, describing its own design. Let us interrogate the great appa-rition, that shines so peacefully around us. Let us inquire, to what end is nature?

All science has one aim, namely, to find a theory of nature. We have theories of races and of functions, but scarcely yet a remote ap-proach to an idea of creation. We are now so far from the road to truth, that religious teachers dispute and hate each other, and speculative men are esteemed unsound and frivolous. But to a sound judgment, the most abstract truth is the most practical. Whenever a true theory appears, it will be its own evidence. Its test is, that it will explain all phenomena. Now many are thought not only unexplained but inexplicable; as lan-guage, sleep, madness, dreams, beasts, sex.

Philosophically considered, the universe is composed of Nature and the Soul. Strictly speaking, therefore, all that is separate from us, all which Philosophy distinguishes as the NOT ME, [3] that is, both nature and art, all other men and my own body, must be ranked under this name, NATURE. In enumerating the values of nature and casting up their sum, I shall use the word in both senses; —in its common and in its philosophical import. In inquiries so general as our present one, the inaccuracy is not material; no confusion of thought will occur. *Nature*, in the common sense, refers to essences unchanged by man; space, the air, the river, the leaf. *Art* is applied to the mixture of his will with the same things, as in a house, a canal, a statue, a picture. But his opera-tions taken together are so insignificant, a little chipping, baking, patching, and washing, that in an impression so grand as that of the world on the human mind, they do not vary the result.

Chapter 1　Nature

To go into solitude, a man needs to retire as much from his chamber as from society. I am not solitary whilst I read and write, though nobody is with me. But if a man would be alone, let him look at the stars. The rays that come from those heavenly worlds, will separate between him and what he touches. One might think the atmosphere was made transparent with this design, to give man, in the heavenly bodies, the perpetual presence of the sublime. Seen in the streets of cities, how great they are! If the stars should appear one night in a thousand years, how would men believe and adore; and preserve for many generations the remembrance of the city of God which had been shown! But every night come out these envoys of beauty, and light the universe with their admonishing smile.

The stars awaken a certain reverence, because though always present, they are inaccessible; but all natural objects make a kindred impression, when the mind is open to their influence. Nature never wears a mean appearance. Neither does the wisest man extort her secret, and lose his curiosity by finding out all her perfection. Nature never became a toy to a wise spirit. The flowers, the animals, the mountains, reflected the wisdom of his best hour, as much as they had delighted the simplicity of his childhood.

When we speak of nature in this manner, we have a distinct but most poetical sense in the mind. We mean the integrity of impression made by manifold natural objects. It is this which distinguishes the stick of timber of the wood-cutter, from the tree of the poet. The charming landscape which I saw this morning, is indubitably made up of some twenty or thirty farms. Miller owns this field, Locke that, and Manning the woodland beyond. But none of them owns the landscape. There is a property in the horizon which no man has but he whose eye can integrate all the parts, that is, the poet. This is the best part of these men's farms, yet to this their warranty—deeds give no title.

To speak truly, few adult persons can see nature. Most persons do not see the sun. At least they have a very superficial seeing. The sun illuminates only the eye of the man, but shines into the eye and the heart of the child. The lover of nature is he whose inward and outward senses are still truly adjusted to each other; who has retained the spirit of infancy even into the era of manhood. [4] His intercourse with heaven and earth, becomes part of his daily food. In the presence of nature, a wild delight runs through the man, in spite of real sorrows. Nature says, — he is my creature, and maugre[5] all his impertinent griefs, he shall be glad with me. Not the sun or the summer alone, but every hour and season yields its tribute of delight; for every hour and change corresponds to and authorizes a different state of the mind, from breathless noon to grimmest midnight. Nature is a setting that fits equally well a comic or a mourning piece. In good health, the air is a cordial of incredible virtue. Crossing a bare common, in snow puddles, at twilight, under a clouded sky, without having in my thoughts any occurrence of special good fortune, I have enjoyed a perfect exhilaration. I am glad to the brink of fear. In the woods too, a man casts off his years, as the snake his slough, and at what period soever of life, is always a child. In the woods, is perpetual youth. Within these plantations of God, a decorum and sanctity reign, a perennial festival is dressed, and the guest sees not how he should tire of them in a thousand years. In the woods, we return to reason and faith. There I feel that nothing can befall me in life, —no disgrace, no calamity, (leaving me my eyes,) which nature cannot repair. Standing on the bare ground, —my head bathed by the blithe air, and uplifted into infinite space, —all mean egotism vanishes. I become a transparent eye-ball. I am nothing; I see all; the currents of the

Universal Being circulate through me; I am part or particle of God. The name of the nearest friend sounds then foreign and accidental: to be brothers, to be acquaintances, —master or servant, is then a trifle and a disturbance. I am the lover of uncontained and immortal beauty. In the wilderness, I find something more dear and connate than in streets or villages. In the tranquil landscape, and especially in the distant line of the horizon, man beholds somewhat as beautiful as his own nature.

The greatest delight which the fields and woods minister[6], is the suggestion of an occult relation between man and the vegetable. I am not alone and unacknowledged. They nod to me, and I to them. The waving of the boughs in the storm, is new to me and old. It takes me by surprise, and yet is not unknown. Its effect is like that of a higher thought or a better emotion coming over me, when I deemed I was thinking justly or doing right.

Yet it is certain that the power to produce this delight, does not reside in nature, but in man, or in a harmony of both. It is necessary to use these pleasures with great temperance. For, nature is not always tricked in holiday attire, but the same scene which yesterday breathed perfume and glittered as for the frolic of the nymphs, is overspread with melancholy today. Nature always wears the colors of the spirit. To a man laboring under calamity, the heat of his own fire hath sadness in it. Then, there is a kind of contempt of the landscape felt by him who has just lost by death a dear friend. The sky is less grand as it shuts down over less worth in the population.

Notes

① **"Nature is but an image or imitation of wisdom, the last thing of the soul; nature being a thing which doth only do, but not know"**: Emerson found the motto from the Roman philosopher Plotinus (205?-270?) in his copy of Ralph Cudworth's *The True Intellec-*

tual System of the Universe (1820).

② **,... why should we grope among the dry bones of the past**: an echo of Ezekiel 37:1-14, especially 37:4, where God tells Ezchiel to "Prophesy upon these bones, and say unto them, O ye dry bones, hear the word of the Lord." Emerson had left the ministry but was still writing as a prophet.

③ **NOT ME**: Emerson takes "not me" from Thomas Carlyle's *Sartor Resartus* (1833-1834), where it appears as a translation of the recent German philosophical term for everything but the self.

④ **Who has retained the spirit of infancy even into the era of manhood**: This is an echo of Samuel Taylor Coleridge's *Biographia Literaria*, Chapter 4, in which Coleridge defines the character and privilege of genius as the ability to carry the feelings of childhood into the powers of adulthood.

⑤ **maugre**: despite.

⑥ **minister**: give.

Questions for Reading Comprehension

1. According to paragraph 1 in the "Introduction", what does Emerson say would happen if the stars appeared one night in a thousand years?

2. According to paragraph 2, why does Emerson believe that the stars awaken a reverence in people?

3. When do natural objects make a similar impression of reverence?

4. How does Emerson describe the lover of nature?

5. What does Emerson mean when he says, "In the woods too, a man casts off his years"?

6. Why does Emerson say, "I am part particle of God"?

Discussion Questions for Appreciation

1. What is Emerson's idea about the relationship between man and na-

ture?

2. According to Emerson, what is the distinction between adult and children?

3. Where does Emerson believe the power for a true relationship between man and God comes from?

4. What Transcendental ideas does Emerson express in this essay?

A Question for Writing

What does Emerson mean when he describes himself as "a transparent eyeball" when he is in the woods? How does this state of mind affect his relationship with God?

Self-Reliance

Introduction

Self-Reliance is an essay published in Emerson's *Essays: First Series* (1841). Derived from his journals and lectures between 1836 and 1837, it contains Emerson's leading transcendental ideas.

In this essay Emerson maintains that one must trust oneself, and never imitate others. He appeals to people not to be a conformist, and suggests that the terror that scares people from self-trust is consistency. Although his philosophy and his writing seem to lack organization, his rugged individualism, noncomformist attitude, idea about self-reliance, and optimistic trust in human nature are easy to understand. Emerson's essay is an expression of the buoyant spirit of his time. It is also an ideal explanation of the conduct and activities of the American people as an expanding nation.

From **Self-Reliance**

from Essays: First Series (1841)
Ne te quaesiveris extra. [①]

> *"Man is his own star; and the soul that can*
> *Render an honest and a perfect man,*
> *Commands all light, all influence, all fate;*
>
> *Nothing to him falls early or too late.*
> *Our acts our angels are, or good or ill,*
> *Our fatal shadows that walk by us still."*

—Epilogue to Beaumont and Fletcher's[②] *Honest Man's Fortune*

Cast the bantling on the rocks,
Suckle him with the she-wolf's teat;

Wintered with the hawk and fox,
Power and speed be hands and feet.

I read the other day some verses written by an eminent painter which were original and not conventional. The soul always hears an admonition in such lines, let the subject be what it may. The sentiment they instill is of more value than any thought they may contain. To believe your own thought, to believe that what is true for you in your private heart is true for all men, —that is genius. Speak your latent conviction, and it shall be the universal sense; for the inmost in due time becomes the outmost, —and our first thought is rendered back to us by the trumpets of the Last Judgment. Familiar as the voice of the mind is to each, the highest merit we ascribe to Moses,[3] Plato, and Milton is, that they set at naught[4] books and traditions, and spoke not what men but what they thought. A man should learn to detect and watch that gleam of light which flashes across his mind from within, more than the lustre of the firmament of bards and sages. Yet he dismisses without notice his thought, because it is his. In every work of genius we recognize our own rejected thoughts: they come back to us with a certain alienated majesty. Great works of art have no more affecting lesson for us than this. They teach us to abide by our spontaneous impression with good-humored inflexibility then most when the whole cry of voices is on the other side. Else, to-morrow a stranger will say with masterly good sense precisely what we have thought and felt all the time, and we shall be forced to take with shame our own opinion from another.

There is a time in every man's education when he arrives at the con-

63

viction that envy is ignorance; that imitation is suicide; that he must take himself for better, for worse, as his portion; that though the wide universe is full of good, no kernel of nourishing corn can come to him but through his toil bestowed on that plot of ground which is given to him to till. The power which resides in him is new in nature, and none but he knows what that is which he can do, nor does he know until he has tried. Not for nothing one face, one character, one fact, makes much impression on him, and another none. This sculpture in the memory is not without preestablished harmony. The eye was placed where one ray should fall, that it might testify of that particular ray. We but half express ourselves, and are ashamed of that divine idea which each of us represents. It may be safely trusted as proportionate and of good issues, so it be faithfully imparted, but God will not have his work made manifest by cowards. A man is relieved and gay when he has put his heart into his work and done his best; but what he has said or done otherwise, shall give him no peace. It is a deliverance which does not deliver. In the attempt his genius deserts him; no muse befriends; no invention, no hope.

Trust thyself: every heart vibrates to that iron string. Accept the place the divine providence has found for you, the society of your contemporaries, the connection of events. Great men have always done so, and confided themselves childlike to the genius of their age, betraying their perception that the absolutely trustworthy was seated at their heart, working through their hands, predominating in all their being. And we are now men, and must accept in the highest mind the same transcendent destiny; and not minors and invalids in a protected corner, not cowards fleeing before a revolution, but guides, redeemers, and benefactors, obeying the Almighty effort, and advancing on Chaos and the Dark.

What pretty oracles nature yields us on this text, in the face and behaviour of children, babes, and even brutes! That divided and rebel mind, that distrust of a sentiment because our arithmetic has computed the strength and means opposed to our purpose, these have not. Their mind being whole, their eye is as yet unconquered, and when we look in their faces, we are disconcerted. Infancy conforms to nobody: all conform to it, so that one babe commonly makes four or five out of the adults who prattle and play to it. So God has armed youth and puberty and manhood no less with its own piquancy and charm, and made it enviable and gracious and its claims not to be put by, if it will stand by itself. Do not think the youth has no force, because he cannot speak to you and me. Hark! in the next room his voice is sufficiently clear and emphatic. It seems he knows how to speak to his contemporaries. Bashful or bold, then, he will know how to make us seniors very unnecessary.

The nonchalance of boys who are sure of a dinner, and would disdain as much as a lord to do or say aught to conciliate one, is the healthy attitude of human nature. A boy is in the parlour what the pit is in the playhouse; independent, irresponsible, looking out from his corner on such people and facts as pass by, he tries and sentences them on their merits, in the swift, summary way of boys, as good, bad, interesting, silly, eloquent, troublesome. He cumbers himself never about consequences, about interests: he gives an independent, genuine verdict. You must court him: he does not court you. But the man is, as it were, clapped into jail by his consciousness. As soon as he has once acted or spoken with eclat, he is a committed person, watched by the sympathy or the hatred of hundreds, whose affections must now enter into his account. There is no Lethe[5] for this. Ah, that he could pass again into his neutrality! Who can thus avoid all pledges, and having observed, observe again from the same unaffected, unbiased, unbribable, unaffrighted innocence, must always be formidable. He would utter opinions on all passing affairs, which being seen to be not private, but necessary, would sink like darts into the ear of men, and put them in fear.

These are the voices which we hear in solitude, but they grow faint and inaudible as we enter into the world. Society everywhere is in conspiracy against the manhood of every one of its members. Society is a joint-stock company, in which the members agree, for the better securing of his bread to each shareholder, to surrender the liberty and culture of the eater. The virtue in most request is conformity. Self-reliance is its aversion. It loves not realities and creators, but names and customs.

Whoso would be a man must be a nonconformist. He who would gather immortal palms must not be hindered by the name of goodness, but must explore if it be goodness. Nothing is at last sacred but the integrity of your own mind. Absolve you to yourself, and you shall have the suffrage of the world. I remember an answer which when quite young I was prompted to make to a valued adviser, who was wont to importune me with the dear old doctrines of the church. On my saying, What have I to do with the sacredness of traditions, if I live wholly from within? my friend suggested, — "But these impulses may be from below, not from above."⑥ I replied, "They do not seem to me to be such; but if I am the Devil's child, I will live then from the Devil." No law can be sacred to me but that of my nature. Good and bad are but names very readily transferable to that or this; the only right is what is after my constitution, the only wrong what is against it. A man is to carry himself in the presence of all opposition, as if every thing were titular and ephemeral but he. I am ashamed to think how easily we capitulate to badges and names, to large societies and dead institutions. Every decent and well-spoken individual affects and sways me more than is right. I ought to go upright and vital, and speak the rude truth in all ways. If malice and vanity wear the coat of philanthropy, shall that pass? If an angry bigot assumes this bountiful cause of Abolition, [7] and comes to me with his last news from Barbadoes, [8] why should I not say to him, "Go love thy infant; love thy wood-chopper: be good-natured and modest: have that grace; and never varnish your hard, uncharitable ambition with this incredible tenderness for black folk a thousand miles off. Thy love afar is spite at home." Rough and graceless would be such greeting, but truth is handsomer than the affectation of love. Your goodness must have some edge to it, —else it is none. The doctrine of hatred must be preached as the counteraction of the doctrine of love when that pules and whines. I shun father and mother and wife and brother, when my genius calls me. I would write on the lintels of the door-post, *Whim.* [9] I hope it is somewhat better than whim at last, but we cannot spend the day in explanation. Expect me not to show cause why I seek or why I exclude company. Then, again, do not tell me, as a good man did to-day, of my obligation to put all poor men in good situations. Are they *my* poor? I tell thee, thou foolish philanthropist, that I grudge the dollar, the dime, the cent, I give to such men as do not belong to me and to whom I do not belong. There is a class of persons to whom by all spiritual affinity I am bought and sold; for them I will go to prison, if need be; but your miscellaneous popular charities; the education at college of fools; the building of meeting-houses to the vain end to which many now stand; alms to sots; and the thousandfold Relief Societies; —though I confess with shame I sometimes succumb and give the dollar, it is a wicked dollar which by and by I shall have the manhood to withhold.

Virtues are, in the popular estimate, rather the exception than the rule. There is the man *and* his virtues. Men do what is called a good ac-

67

tion, as some piece of courage or charity, much as they would pay a fine in expiation of daily non-appearance on parade. Their works are done as an apology or extenuation of their living in the world, —as invalids and the insane pay a high board. Their virtues are penances. I do not wish to expiate, but to live. My life is for itself and not for a spectacle. I much prefer that it should be of a lower strain, so it be genuine and equal, than that it should be glittering and unsteady. I wish it to be sound and sweet, and not to need diet and bleeding. I ask primary evidence that you are a man, and refuse this appeal from the man to his actions. I know that for myself it makes no difference whether I do or forbear those actions which are reckoned excellent. I cannot consent to pay for a privilege where I have intrinsic right. Few and mean as my gifts may be, I actually am, and do not need for my own assurance or the assurance of my fellows any secondary testimony.

What I must do is all that concerns me, not what the people think. This rule, equally arduous in actual and in intellectual life, may serve for the whole distinction between greatness and meanness. It is the harder, because you will always find those who think they know what is your duty better than you know it. It is easy in the world to live after the world's opinion; it is easy in solitude to live after our own; but the great man is he who in the midst of the crowd keeps with perfect sweetness the independence of solitude.

The objection to conforming to usages that have become dead to you is, that it scatters your force. It loses your time and blurs the impression of your character. If you maintain a dead church, contribute to a dead Bible-society, vote with a great party either for the government or against it, spread your table like base housekeepers, —under all these screens I have difficulty to detect the precise man you are. And, of course, so much force is withdrawn from your proper life. But do your work, and I shall know you. Do your work, and you shall reinforce yourself. A man must consider what a blindman's-buff[10] is this game of conformity. If I know your sect, I anticipate your argument. I hear a preacher announce for his text and topic the expediency of one of the institutions of his church. Do I not know beforehand that not possibly can he say a new and spontaneous word? Do I not know that, with all this ostentation of examining the grounds of the institution, he will do no such thing? Do I not know that he is pledged to himself not to look but at one side, —the permitted side, not as a man, but as a parish minister? He is a retained attorney, and these airs of the bench are the emptiest affectation. Well, most men have bound their eyes with one or another handkerchief, and attached themselves to some one of these communities of opinion. This conformity makes them not false in a few particulars, authors of a few lies, but false in all particulars. Their every truth is not quite true. Their two is not the real two, their four not the real four; so that every word they say chagrins us, and we know not where to begin to set them right. Meantime nature is not slow to equip us in the prison-uniform of the party to which we adhere. We come to wear one cut of face and figure, and acquire by degrees the gentlest asinine expression. There is a mortifying experience in particular, which does not fail to wreak itself also in the general history; I mean "the foolish face of praise," the forced smile which we put on in company where we do not feel at ease in answer to conversation which does not interest us. The muscles, not spontaneously moved, but moved by a low usurping wilfulness, grow tight about the outline of the face with the most disagreeable sensation, a sensation of rebuke and warning which no brave young man will suffer twice.

For nonconformity the world whips you with its displeasure. And therefore a man must know how to estimate a sour face. The by-standers look askance on him in the public street or in the friend's parlour. If this aversion had its origin in contempt and resistance like his own, he might well go home with a sad countenance; but the sour faces of the multitude, like their sweet faces, have no deep cause, but are put on and off as the wind blows and a newspaper directs. Yet is the discontent of the multitude more formidable than that of the senate and the college. It is easy enough for a firm man who knows the world to brook the rage of the cultivated classes. Their rage is decorous and prudent, for they are timid as being very vulnerable themselves. But when to their feminine rage the indignation of the people is added, when the ignorant and the poor are aroused, when the unintelligent brute force that lies at the bottom of society is made to growl and mow, it needs the habit of magnanimity and religion to treat it godlike as a trifle of no concernment.

The other terror that scares us from self-trust is our consistency; a reverence for our past act or word, because the eyes of others have no other data for computing our orbit than our past acts, and we are loath to disappoint them.

But why should you keep your head over your shoulder? Why drag about this corpse of your memory, lest you contradict somewhat you have stated in this or that public place? Suppose you should contradict yourself; what then? It seems to be a rule of wisdom never to rely on your memory alone, scarcely even in acts of pure memory, but to bring the past for judgment into the thousand-eyed present, and live ever in a new day. In your metaphysics you have denied personality to the Deity: yet when the devout motions of the soul come, yield to them heart and life, though they should clothe God with shape and color. Leave your theory, as Joseph his coat in the hand of the harlot, and flee. [11]

A foolish consistency is the hobgoblin of little minds, adored by little statesmen and philosophers and divines. With consistency a great soul has simply nothing to do. He may as well concern himself with his shadow on the wall. Speak what you think now in hard words, and to-morrow speak what to-morrow thinks in hard words again, though it contradict every thing you said to-day. Ah, so you shall be sure to be misunderstood. Is it so bad, then, to be misunderstood? Pythagoras was misunderstood, and Socrates, and Jesus, and Luther, and Copernicus, and Galileo, and Newton, and every pure and wise spirit that ever took flesh. To be great is to be misunderstood.

I suppose no man can violate his nature. All the sallies of his will are rounded in by the law of his being, as the inequalities of Andes and Himmaleh are insignificant in the curve of the sphere. Nor does it matter how you gauge and try him. A character is like an acrostic or Alexandrian stanza;[12]—read it forward, backward, or across, it still spells the same thing. In this pleasing, contrite wood-life which God allows me, let me record day by day my honest thought without prospect or retrospect, and, I cannot doubt, it will be found symmetrical, though I mean it not, and see it not. My book should smell of pines and resound with the hum of insects. The swallow over my window should interweave that thread or straw he carries in his bill into my web also. We pass for what we are. Character teaches above our wills. Men imagine that they communicate their virtue or vice only by overt actions, and do not see that virtue or vice emit a breath every moment.

Fear never but you shall be consistent in whatever variety of actions, so they be each honest and natural in their hour. For of one will, the actions will be harmonious, however unlike they seem. These

71

varieties are lost sight of at a little distance, at a little height of thought. One tendency unites them all. The voyage of the best ship is a zigzag line of a hundred tacks. See the line from a sufficient distance, and it straightens itself to the average tendency. Your genuine action will explain itself, and will explain your other genuine actions. Your conformity explains nothing. Act singly, and what you have already done singly will justify you now. Greatness appeals to the future. If I can be firm enough to-day to do right, and scorn eyes, I must have done so much right before as to defend me now. Be it how it will, do right now. Always scorn appearances, and you always may. The force of character is cumulative. All the foregone days of virtue work their health into this. What makes the majesty of the heroes of the senate and the field, which so fills the imagination? The consciousness of a train of great days and victories behind. They shed an united light on the advancing actor. He is attended as by a visible escort of angels. That is it which throws thunder into Chatham's[13] voice, and dignity into Washington's port,[14] and America into Adams's eye. Honor is venerable to us because it is no ephemeris. It is always ancient virtue. We worship it to-day because it is not of to-day. We love it and pay it homage, because it is not a trap for our love and homage, but is self-dependent, self-derived, and therefore of an old immaculate pedigree, even if shown in a young person.

I hope in these days we have heard the last of conformity and consistency. Let the words be gazetted[15] and ridiculous henceforward. Instead of the gong for dinner, let us hear a whistle from the Spartan fife.[16] Let us never bow and apologize more. A great man is coming to eat at my house. I do not wish to please him; I wish that he should wish to please me. I will stand here for humanity, and though I would make it kind, I would make it true. Let us affront and reprimand the smooth mediocrity and squalid contentment of the times, and hurl in the face of custom, and trade, and office, the fact which is the upshot of all history, that there is a great responsible Thinker and Actor working wherever a man works; that a true man belongs to no other time or place, but is the centre of things. Where he is, there is nature. He measures you, and all men, and all events. Ordinarily, every body in society reminds us of somewhat else, or of some other person. Character, reality, reminds you of nothing else; it takes place of the whole creation. The man must be so much, that he must make all circumstances indifferent. Every true man is a cause, a country, and an age; requires infinite spaces and numbers and time fully to accomplish his design; —and posterity seem to follow his steps as a train of clients. A man Caesar is born, and for ages after we have a Roman Empire. Christ is born, and millions of minds so grow and cleave to his genius, that he is confounded with virtue and the possible of man. An institution is the lengthened shadow of one man; as, Monachism, of the Hermit Antony; the Reformation, of Luther; Quakerism, of Fox; Methodism, of Wesley; Abolition, of Clarkson. Scipio, Milton called "the height of Rome"; and all history resolves itself very easily into the biography of a few stout and earnest persons.

Let a man then know his worth, and keep things under his feet. Let him not peep or steal, or skulk up and down with the air of a charity-boy, a bastard, or an interloper, in the world which exists for him. But the man in the street, finding no worth in himself which corresponds to the force which built a tower or sculptured a marble god, feels poor when he looks on these. To him a palace, a statue, or a costly book have an alien and forbidding air, much like a gay equipage, and seem to say like that, "Who are you, Sir?" Yet they all are his, suitors for his notice, petitioners to his faculties that they will come out and take possession. The picture waits for my verdict: it is not to command me, but I am to settle its claims to praise. That popular fable of the sot who was picked up dead drunk in the street, carried to the duke's house, washed and dressed and laid in the duke's bed, and, on his waking, treated with all obsequious ceremony like the duke, and assured that he had been insane, —owes its popularity to the fact, that it symbolizes so well the state of man, who is in the world a sort of sot, but now and then wakes up, exercises his reason, and finds himself a true prince.

Our reading is mendicant and sycophantic. In history, our imagination plays us false. Kingdom and lordship, power and estate, are a gaudier vocabulary than private John and Edward in a small house and common day's work; but the things of life are the same to both; the sum total of both is the same. Why all this deference to Alfred, and Scanderbeg, and Gustavus?[17] Suppose they were virtuous; did they wear out virtue? As great a stake depends on your private act to-day, as followed their public and renowned steps. When private men shall act with original views, the lustre will be transferred from the actions of kings to those of gentlemen.

The world has been instructed by its kings, who have so magnetized the eyes of nations. It has been taught by this colossal symbol the mutual reverence that is due from man to man. The joyful loyalty with which men have everywhere suffered the king, the noble, or the great proprietor to walk among them by a law of his own, make his own scale of men and things, and reverse theirs, pay for benefits not with money but with honor, and represent the law in his person, was the hieroglyphic by which they obscurely signified their consciousness of their own right and comeliness, the right of every man.

The magnetism which all original action exerts is explained when we inquire the reason of self-trust. Who is the Trustee? What is the aboriginal Self, on which a universal reliance may be grounded? What is the nature and power of that science-baffling star, without parallax, [18] without calculable elements, which shoots a ray of beauty even into trivial and impure actions, if the least mark of independence appear? The inquiry leads us to that source, at once the essence of genius, of virtue, and of life, which we call Spontaneity or Instinct. We denote this primary wisdom as Intuition, whilst all later teachings are tuitions. In that deep force, the last fact behind which analysis cannot go, all things find their common origin. For, the sense of being which in calm hours rises, we know not how, in the soul, is not diverse from things, from space, from light, from time, from man, but one with them, and proceeds obviously from the same source whence their life and being also proceed. We first share the life by which things exist, and afterwards see them as appearances in nature, and forget that we have shared their cause. Here is the fountain of action and of thought. Here are the lungs of that inspiration which giveth man wisdom, and which cannot be denied without impiety and atheism. We lie in the lap of immense intelligence, which makes us receivers of its truth and organs of its activity. When we discern justice, when we discern truth, we do nothing of ourselves, but allow a passage to its beams. If we ask whence this comes, if we seek to pry into the soul that causes, all philosophy is at fault. Its presence or its absence is all we can affirm. Every man discriminates between the voluntary acts of his mind, and his involuntary perceptions, and knows that to his involuntary perceptions a perfect faith is due. He may err in the expression of them, but he knows that these things are so, like day and night, not to be disputed. All my wilful actions and acquisitions are but roving; —the most trivial reverie, the faintest native emotion, command my curiosity and respect. Thoughtless people contradict as readily the statement of perceptions as of opinions, or rather much more readily;

for, they do not distinguish between perception and notion. They fancy that I choose to see this or that thing. But perception is not whimsical, but fatal. If I see a trait, my children will see it after me, and in course of time, all mankind, —although it may chance that no one has seen it before me. For my perception of it is as much a fact as the sun.

The relations of the soul to the divine spirit are so pure, that it is profane to seek to interpose helps. It must be that when God speaketh he should communicate, not one thing, but all things; should fill the world with his voice; should scatter forth light, nature, time, souls, from the centre of the present thought; and new date and new create the whole. Whenever a mind is simple, and receives a divine wisdom, old things pass away, —means, teachers, texts, temples fall; it lives now, and absorbs past and future into the present hour. All things are made sacred by relation to it, —one as much as another. All things are dissolved to their centre by their cause, and, in the universal miracle, petty and particular miracles disappear. If, therefore, a man claims to know and speak of God, and carries you backward to the phraseology of some old mouldered nation in another country, in another world, believe him not. Is the acorn better than the oak which is its fulness and completion? Is the parent better than the child into whom he has cast his ripened being? Whence, then, this worship of the past? The centuries are conspirators against the sanity and authority of the soul. Time and space are but physiological colors which the eye makes, but the soul is light; where it is, is day; where it was, is night; and history is an impertinence and an injury, if it be any thing more than a cheerful apologue or parable of my being and becoming.

Man is timid and apologetic; he is no longer upright; he dares not say "I think," "I am," but quotes some saint or sage. He is ashamed before the blade of grass or the blowing rose. These roses under my window make no reference to former roses or to better ones; they are for what they are; they exist with God to-day. There is no time to them. There is simply the rose; it is perfect in every moment of its existence. Before a leaf-bud has burst, its whole life acts; in the full-blown flower there is no more; in the leafless root there is no less. Its nature is satisfied, and it satisfies nature, in all moments alike. But man postpones or remembers; he does not live in the present, but with reverted eye laments the past, or, heedless of the riches that surround him, stands on tiptoe to foresee the future. He cannot be happy and strong until he too lives with nature in the present, above time.

This should be plain enough. Yet see what strong intellects dare not yet hear God himself, unless he speak the phraseology of I know not what David, or Jeremiah, or Paul. We shall not always set so great a price on a few texts, on a few lives. We are like children who repeat by rote the sentences of grandames and tutors, and, as they grow older, of the men of talents and character they chance to see, —painfully recollecting the exact words they spoke; afterwards, when they come into the point of view which those had who uttered these sayings, they understand them, and are willing to let the words go; for, at any time, they can use words as good when occasion comes. If we live truly, we shall see truly. It is as easy for the strong man to be strong, as it is for the weak to be weak. When we have new perception, we shall gladly disburden the memory of its hoarded treasures as old rubbish. When a man lives with God, his voice shall be as sweet as the murmur of the brook and the rustle of the corn.

Notes

① **Ne te quaesiveris extra**: "Don't look for anything outside you." It is quoted from a satiric poem written by a Roman poet. Here Emerson means that man should not imitate.

② **Beaumont and Fletcher**: famous English artists and dramatists who wrote "Honest Man's Fortune" (1613) together.

③ **Moses**: a figure in *the Bible*. According to *the Old Testament* he was the head and prophet of the Israelites, and he led them out of slavery in Egypt.

④ **set at naught**: take . . . as of no account.

⑤ **Lethe**: (Greek mythology) a river in Hades. Its water causes forgetfulness when it is drunk.

⑥ **These impulses may be from below, not from above**: These impulses may be from Hell, not from Heaven.

⑦ **Abolition**: the movement against Negro slavery.

⑧ **Barbadoes**: an independent state in the Lesser Antilles, West Indies, where slavery was abolished in 1843.

⑨ **I shun father and mother and . . . , Whim**: Once my genius calls me, I'll shut all people out and take no trouble to explain the reason. I only tell them I hit upon the idea at most. (Emerson maintains that we should keep away from our parents, wives and brothers in order to answer the call of God.)

⑩ **blindman's-buff**: a game in which a blindfold player tries to catch others, who push him about.

⑪ **as Joseph his coat in the hand of the harlot, and flee**: The reference is to Joseph in Potiphar's house (Gen. xxxix). According to the account in Gensis, Joseph, sold to Potiphar as a slave, was enticed by his wife, but he refused her temptation and fled.

⑫ **an acrostic or Alexandrian stanza**: a poem or word-puzzle in which the initial, or the initial and the final, letters of the lines form a word or words.

⑬ **Chatham**: English lecturer and statesman.

⑭ **port**: manner.

⑮ **gazetted**: (usu. passive) published or announced openly. Here it means "given up openly".

⑯ **Spartan fife**: symbol of the bugle call for battle.

⑰ **Alfred, and Scanderbeg, and Gustavus**: Alfred (849-899), King of Englo-Saxons, who is often referred to as Alfred the Great. Scanderbeg (1405-1468), an Albanian national hero; Gustavus (1594-1632), King of Sweden.

⑱ **parallax**: (angular amount of) apparent displacement of object, caused by actual change of point of observation.

Questions for Reading Comprehension

1. What does the Epilogue to Beaumont and Fletcher's Honest Man's Fortune imply?

2. What, according to Emerson, is the highest merit that we ascribe to great men?

3. According to Emerson, under what conditions will man be "happy and strong"?

4. What, according to Emerson, does society require of its members?

5. According to Emerson, what will happen if we live truly?

6. What does Emerson want the American people to declare?

7. What does Emerson urge people to do?

8. What lessons do the great figures of the past teach us about the concept of self-reliance?

9. What is the central doctrine in Emerson's ethical thought?

10. Is Emerson optimistic or pessimistic about human nature and human potential?

Discussion Questions for Appreciation

1. In this essay, Emerson points out what conformity leads to, and advo-

cates self-reliance. What is the foundation of self-reliance?

2. Emerson maintains that a true individual must be willing to face the consequences of thinking individually and critically and he must not be trapped into mediocrity by his own fear of being inconsistent or not in step with his peers. Find some examples from this essay to show his individualism.

3. Today most people like traveling. But why does Emerson say that the soul is no traveler and traveling is a fool's paradise?

4. According to Emerson, society never advances. It recedes as fast on one side as it gains on the other. For everything that is given, something is taken. For instance, the civilized man has built a coach, but has lost the use of his feet. Do you agree with him? Why or why not?

5. What is Emerson's most striking stylistic quality?

6. Emerson uses many epigrams in this essay. List some examples to show the stylistic features of his writing.

A Question for Writing

To what extent can the concept of self-reliance be considered a fundamental American idea?

Henry David Thoreau (1817-1862)

Henry David Thoreau was born in Concord, Massachusetts on July 12, 1817. His father was a poor pencil-maker, while his mother was an aspiring woman who wanted her son to be well educated. He attended Concord Academy, learned surveying, and graduated from Harvard College in 1837. He took his brief fling at school teaching in his native town after graduation. He never married, spending his time alone with nature. In his own time he was regarded as an eccentric and a loafer, but from time to time he would survey for farmers in the area.

When Emerson moved to Concord, Thoreau was only seventeen. From 1841 to 1843 he lived with Emerson, who became his master, and who had a great influence on him. Actually Thoreau was Emerson's man of action. As an intimate of the members of the Transcendental Club, he worked with Emerson on *The Dial*, which was published to spread the transcendentalists' ideas. But they had different views on social reform and protest. Being more radical, Thoreau alienated himself from his master later on. He died on May 6, 1862.

Thoreau was a lover of nature, a New England mystic, a social philosopher, and a thorough transcendentalist. He rejected rationalism and conformism. In his writing, he indicated that the pursuit of material things had no value, and that he desired a life of contemplation, of being harmony with nature, and of acting on his own principles.

He was a prose stylist. "Whether with his famous aphoristic sentences, his brief fables or allegories, his thick-strewn puns, or many other rhetorical devices, Thoreau's intention always is to make the reader look beyond the obvious, routine sense of an expression to see what idea once vitalized. He ultimately wants the reader to reevaluate any institu-

81

tion, from the Christian religion to the Constitution of the United States" (Baym 711). [1]

As Emerson's disciple, Thoreau practiced the self-reflective and self-reliant Transcendentalism that Emerson preached. Today he is primarily remembered for two of his important works the book *Walden* (1854) and the essay Civil Disobedience (1849), which were written as a result of his two most extreme acts. He built himself a hut in the woods by Walden Pond, where he lived from July 4, 1845 to September 6, 1847, a period in which he wrote his most famous book *Walden*. His purpose was to get back to the naked simplicity of life and get to the very core of the universe. He wished to live a life of simplicity, independence and magnanimity without interfering with or being interfered with others. His residence at Walden Pond was interrupted by a day's imprisonment for refusal to pay a poll tax to the government that supported the Mexican War, which he considered unjust. Thoreau's experience of imprisonment inspired him to write his famous essay Civil Disobedience in 1849, which advocated his belief in passive resistance as a means of protest against social injustice. In the 20th century, this idea became the basis of Gandhi's doctrine of passive resistance, which in turn, influenced Martin Luther King.

Walden

Introduction

On July 4, 1845, Thoreau began his experiment in living alone in a hut by Walden Pond. There he deliberately lived a life of simplicity and independence, devoting his time to observations and reflections. The ex-

---

[1] Nina Baym, et al. , eds. *The Norton Anthology of American Literature*. Third Shorter Edition. New York: W. W. Norton and Company, 1989, p. 771.

periment he designed was to prove how far he could free himself from the hypocrisies and unnecessary complexities of a commercial society. He was not cut off from human communities though. There was a town he could walk to, and he also invited friends to his cabin. For Thoreau, being close to nature means being closer to the divinity manifested in/as nature's signs.

Deceptively casual, *Walden* reads like a diary of a nature lover. It is a book of essays that explores subjects concerned with nature, with the meaning of life, and with morality. *Walden* is structured on the four seasons, beginning in summer and ending in spring. It is largely narrative—with reflective digressions. Thoreau's purposes of writing this book are to make his readers evaluate the way he lived and thought, to reveal the hidden spiritual possibilities in everyone's life, and to condemn the weakness and errors of society, such as the pursuit of material things. This selection is taken from Chapter 2: Where I Lived and What I Lived for.

From *Walden*

At a certain season of our life we are accustomed to consider every spot as the possible site of a house. I have thus surveyed the country on every side within a dozen miles of where I live. In imagination I have bought all the farms in succession, for all were to be bought, and I knew their price. I walked over each farmer's premises, tasted his wild apples, discoursed on husbandry with him, took his farm at his price, at any price, mortgaging it to him in my mind; even put a higher price on it—took everything but a deed of it—took his word for his deed, for I dearly love to talk—cultivated it, and him too to some extent, I trust, and withdrew when I had enjoyed it long enough, leaving him to carry it on. This experience entitled me to be regarded as a sort of real-estate broker by my friends. Wherever I sat, there I might live, and the landscape radiated from me accordingly. What is a house but a *sedes*, a seat? —better if a country seat. I discovered many a site for a house not likely to be soon improved, which some might have thought too far from the village, but to my eyes the village was too far from it. Well, there I might live, I said; and there I did live, for an hour, a summer and a winter life; saw how I could let the years run off, buffet the winter through, and see the spring come in. The future inhabitants of this region, wherever they may place their houses, may be sure that they have been anticipated. An afternoon sufficed to lay out the land into orchard, wood-lot, and pasture, and to decide what fine oaks or pines should be left to stand before the door, and whence each blasted tree could be seen to the best advantage; and then I let it lie, fallow, perchance, for a man is rich in proportion to the number of things which he can afford to let alone.

My imagination carried me so far that I even had the refusal of several farms—the refusal was all I wanted—but I never got my fingers burned by actual possession. The nearest that I came to actual possession was when I bought the Hollowell place, and had begun to sort my seeds, and collected materials with which to make a wheelbarrow to carry it on or off with; but before the owner gave me a deed of it, his wife—every man has such a wife—changed her mind and wished to keep it, and he offered me ten dollars to release him. Now, to speak the truth, I had but ten cents in the world, and it surpassed my arithmetic to tell, if I was that man who had ten cents, or who had a farm, or ten dollars, or all together. However, I let him keep the ten dollars and the farm too, for I had carried it far enough; or rather, to be generous, I sold him the farm for just what I gave for it, and, as he was not a rich man, made him a present of ten dollars, and still had my ten cents, and seeds, and materials for a wheelbarrow left. I found thus that I had been a rich man without any damage to my poverty. But I retained the landscape, and I have since annually carried off what it yielded without a wheelbarrow. With respect to landscapes,

> "I am monarch of all I *survey*,
> My right there is none to dispute. "[①]

I have frequently seen a poet withdraw, having enjoyed the most valuable part of a farm, while the crusty farmer supposed that he had got a few wild apples only. Why, the owner does not know it for many years when a poet has put his farm in rhyme, the most admirable kind of invisible fence, has fairly impounded it, milked it, skimmed it, and got all the cream, and left the farmer only the skimmed milk.

The real attractions of the Hollowell farm, to me, were: its complete retirement, being, about two miles from the village, half a mile from the nearest neighbor, and separated from the highway by a broad field; its bounding on the river, which the owner said protected it by its fogs from frosts in the spring, though that was nothing to me; the gray color and ruinous state of the house and barn, and the dilapidated fences, which put such an interval between me and the last occupant; the hollow and lichen-covered apple trees, nawed by rabbits, showing what kind of neighbors I should have; but above all, the recollection I had of it from my earliest voyages up the river, when the house was concealed behind a dense grove of red maples, through which I heard the house-dog bark. I was in haste to buy it, before the proprietor finished getting out some rocks, cutting down the hollow apple trees, and grubbing up some young birches which had sprung up in the pasture, or, in short, had made any more of his improvements. To enjoy these advantages I was ready to carry it on; like Atlas,[②] to take the world on my shoulders—I never heard what compensation he received for that—and do all those things which had no other motive or excuse but that I might pay for it and be unmolested in my possession of it; for I knew all the

85

while that it would yield the most abundant crop of the kind I wanted, if I could only afford to let it alone. But it turned out as I have said.

All that I could say, then, with respect to farming on a large scale—I have always cultivated a garden—was, that I had had my seeds ready. Many think that seeds improve with age. I have no doubt that time discriminates between the good and the bad; and when at last I shall plant, I shall be less likely to be disappointed. But I would say to my fellows, once for all, as long as possible live free and uncommitted. It makes but little difference whether you are committed to a farm or the county jail.

Old Cato,[③] whose "De Re Rustica" is my "Cultivator," says— and the only translation I have seen makes sheer nonsense of the passage— "When you think of getting a farm turn it thus in your mind, not to buy greedily; nor spare your pains to look at it, and do not think it enough to go round it once. The oftener you go there the more it will please you, if it is good." I think I shall not buy greedily, but go round and round it as long as I live, and be buried in it first, that it may please me the more at last.

The present was my next experiment of this kind, which I purpose to describe more at length, for convenience putting the experience of two years into one. As I have said, I do not propose to write an ode to dejection, but to brag as lustily as chanticleer in the morning, standing on his roost, if only to wake my neighbors up.

When first I took up my abode in the woods, that is, began to spend my nights as well as days there, which, by accident, was on Independence Day, or the Fourth of July, 1845, my house was not finished for winter, but was merely a defence against the rain, without plastering or chimney, the walls being of rough, weather-stained boards, with wide chinks, which made it cool at night. The upright white hewn studs and freshly planed door and window casings gave it a clean and airy look, especially in the morning, when its timbers were saturated with dew, so that I fancied that by noon some sweet gum would exude from them. To my imagination it retained throughout the day more or less of this auroral character, reminding me of a certain house on a mountain which I had visited a year before. This was an airy and unplastered cabin, fit to entertain a travelling god, and where a goddess might trail her garments. The winds which passed over my dwelling were such as sweep over the ridges of mountains, bearing the broken strains, or celestial parts only, of terrestrial music. The morning wind forever blows, the poem of creation is uninterrupted; but few are the ears that hear it. Olympus[④] is but the outside of the earth everywhere.

The only house I had been the owner of before, if I except a boat, was a tent, which I used occasionally when making excursions in the summer, and this is still rolled up in my garret; but the boat, after passing from hand to hand, has gone down the stream of time. With this more substantial shelter about me, I had made some progress toward settling in the world. This frame, so slightly clad, was a sort of crystallization around me, and reacted on the builder. It was suggestive somewhat as a picture in outlines. I did not need to go outdoors to take the air, for the atmosphere within had lost none of its freshness. It was not so much within doors as behind a door where I sat, even in the rainiest weather. The Harivansa[⑤] says, "An abode without birds is like a meat without seasoning." Such was not my abode, for I found myself suddenly neighbor to the birds; not by having imprisoned one, but having caged myself near them. I was not only nearer to some of those which commonly frequent the garden and the orchard, but to those smaller and more thrilling songsters of the forest which never, or rarely, serenade a villager—the wood thrush, the veery, the scarlet tanager, the field sparrow, the whippoor-will, and many others.

I was seated by the shore of a small pond, about a mile and a half south of the village of Concord and somewhat higher than it, in the midst of an extensive wood between that town and Lincoln, and about two miles south of that our only field known to fame, Concord Battle Ground; but I was so low in the woods that the opposite shore, half a mile off, like the rest, covered with wood, was my most distant horizon. For the first week, whenever I looked out on the pond it impressed me like a tarn high up on the side of a mountain, its bottom far above the surface of other lakes, and, as the sun arose, I saw it throwing off its nightly clothing of mist, and here and there, by degrees, its soft ripples or its smooth reflecting surface was revealed, while the mists, like ghosts, were stealthily withdrawing in every direction into the woods, as at the breaking up of some nocturnal conventicle. The very dew seemed to hang upon the trees later into the day than usual, as on the sides of mountains.

This small lake was of most value as a neighbor in the intervals of a gentle rainstorm in August, when, both air and water being perfectly still, but the sky overcast, mid-afternoon had all the serenity of evening, and the wood thrush sang around, and was heard from shore to shore. A lake like this is never smoother than at such a time; and the clear portion of the air above it being, shallow and darkened by clouds, the water, full of light and reflections, becomes a lower heaven itself so much the more important. From a hill-top near by, where the wood had been recently cut off, there was a pleasing vista southward across the pond, through a wide indentation in the hills which form the shore there, where their opposite sides sloping toward each other suggested a stream flowing out in that direction through a wooded valley, but stream there was none. That way I looked between and over the near green hills to some distant and higher ones in the horizon, tinged with blue. Indeed, by standing on tiptoe I could catch a glimpse of some of the peaks of the still bluer and more distant mountain ranges in the northwest, those true-blue coins from heaven's own mint, and also of some portion of the village.

But in other directions, even from this point, I could not see over or beyond the woods which surrounded me. It is well to have some water in
your neighborhood, to give buoyancy to and float the earth. One value
even of the smallest well is, that when you look into it you see that earth
is not continent but insular. This is as important as that it keeps butter
cool. When I looked across the pond from this peak toward the Sudbury
meadows, which in time of flood I distinguished elevated perhaps by a
mirage in their seething valley, like a coin in a basin, all the earth beyond the pond appeared like a thin crust insulated and floated even by
this small sheet of interverting water, and I was reminded that this on
which I dwelt was but *dry land*.

Though the view from my door was still more contracted, I did not
feel crowded or confined in the least. There was pasture enough for my
imagination. The low shrub oak plateau to which the opposite shore arose
stretched away toward the prairies of the West and the steppes of Tarta-
ry, affording ample room for all the roving families of men. "There are
none happy in the world but beings who enjoy freely a vast horizon" —
said Damodara,[6] when his herds required new and larger pastures.

Both place and time were changed, and I dwelt nearer to those parts
of the universe and to those eras in history which had most attracted me.
Where I lived was as far off as many a region viewed nightly by astronomers. We are wont to imagine rare and delectable places in some remote
and more celestial corner of the system, behind the constellation of
Cassiopeia's Chair, far from noise and disturbance. I discovered that my
house actually had its site in such a withdrawn, but forever new and un-
profaned, part of the universe. If it were worth the while to settle in
those parts near to the Pleiades or the Hyades, to Aldebaran[7] or Altair,
then I was really there, or at an equal remoteness from the life which I
had left behind, dwindled and twinkling with as fine a ray to my nearest
neighbor, and to be seen only in moonless nights by him. Such was that

part of creation where I had squatted, —

"There was a shepherd that did live,

And held his thoughts as high

As were the mounts whereon his flocks

Did hourly feed him by."[8]

What should we think of the shepherd's life if his flocks always wandered to higher pastures than his thoughts?

Every morning was a cheerful invitation to make my life of equal simplicity, and I may say innocence, with Nature herself. I have been as sincere a worshipper of Aurora[9] as the Greeks. I got up early and bathed in the pond; that was a religious exercise, and one of the best things which I did. They say that characters were engraven on the bathing tub of King Tching Thang[10] to this effect: "Renew thyself completely each day; do it again, and again, and forever again." I can understand that. Morning brings back the heroic ages. I was as much affected by the faint hum of a mosquito making its invisible and unimaginable tour through my apartment at earliest dawn, when I was sitting with door and windows open, as I could be by any trumpet that ever sang of fame. It was Homer's requiem; itself an Iliad and Odyssey[11] in the air, singing its own wrath and wanderings. There was something cosmical about it; a standing advertisement, till forbidden, of the everlasting vigor and fertility of the world. The morning, which is the most memorable season of the day, is the awakening hour. Then there is least somnolence in us; and for an hour, at least, some part of us awakes which slumbers all the rest of the day and night. Little is to be expected of that day, if it can be called a day, to which we are not awakened by our Genius, but by the mechanical nudgings of some servitor, are not awakened by our own newly acquired force and aspirations from within, accompanied by the undulations of celestial music, instead of factory bells, and a fragrance filling the air—to a higher life than we fell asleep from; and thus the darkness bear its fruit, and prove itself to be good, no less than the light. That man who does not believe that each day contains an earlier, more sacred, and auroral hour than he has yet profaned, has despaired of life, and is pursuing a descending and darkening way. After a partial cessation of his sensuous life, the soul of man, or its organs rather, are reinvigorated each day, and his Genius tries again what noble life it can make. All memorable events, I should say, transpire in morning time and in a morning atmosphere. The Vedas[12] say, "All intelligences awake with the morning." Poetry and art, and the fairest and most memorable of the actions of men, date from such an hour. All poets and heroes, like Memnon,[13] are the children of Aurora, and emit their music at sunrise. To him whose elastic and vigorous thought keeps pace with the sun, the day is a perpetual morning. It matters not what the clocks say or the attitudes and labors of men. Morning is when I am awake and there is a dawn in me. Moral reform is the effort to throw off sleep. Why is it that men give so poor an account of their day if they have not been slumbering? They are not such poor calculators. If they had not been overcome with drowsiness, they would have performed something. The millions are awake enough for physical labor; but only one in a million is awake enough for effective intellectual exertion, only one in a hundred millions to a poetic or divine life. To be awake is to be alive. I have never yet met a man who was quite awake. How could I have looked him in the face?

We must learn to reawaken and keep ourselves awake, not by mechanical aids, but by an infinite expectation of the dawn, which does not forsake us in our soundest sleep. I know of no more encouraging fact than the unquestionable ability of man to elevate his life by a conscious endeavor. It is something to be able to paint a particular picture, or to carve a statue, and so to make a few objects beautiful; but it is far more glorious to carve and paint the very atmosphere and medium through which we look, which morally we can do. To affect the quality of the day, that is the highest of arts. Every man is tasked to make his life, even in its details, worthy of the contemplation of his most elevated and critical hour. If we refused, or rather used up, such paltry information as we get, the oracles would distinctly inform us how this might be done.

I went to the woods because I wished to live deliberately, to front only the essential facts of life, and see if I could not learn what it had to teach, and not, when I came to die, discover that I had not lived. I did not wish to live what was not life, living is so dear; nor did I wish to practise resignation, unless it was quite necessary. I wanted to live deep and suck out all the marrow of life, to live so sturdily and Spartan-like as to put to rout all that was not life, to cut a broad swath and shave close, to drive life into a corner, and reduce it to its lowest terms, and, if it proved to be mean, why then to get the whole and genuine meanness of it, and publish its meanness to the world; or if it were sublime, to know it by experience, and be able to give a true account of it in my next excursion. For most men, it appears to me, are in a strange uncertainty about it, whether it is of the devil or of God, and have *somewhat hastily* concluded that it is the chief end of man here to "glorify God and enjoy him forever."[⑭]

Still we live meanly, like ants; though the fable tells us that we were long ago changed into men; like pygmies we fight with cranes; it is error upon error, and clout upon clout, and our best virtue has for its occasion a superfluous and evitable wretchedness. Our life is frittered away by detail. An honest man has hardly need to count more than his ten fingers, or in extreme cases he may add his ten toes, and lump the rest. Simplicity, simplicity, simplicity! I say, let your affairs be as two or three, and not a hundred or a thousand; instead of a million count half a dozen, and keep your accounts on your thumb-nail. In the midst of this chopping sea of civilized life, such are the clouds and storms and quicksands and thousand-and-one items to be allowed for, that a man has to live, if he would not founder and go to the bottom and not make his port at all, by dead reckoning, and he must be a great calculator indeed who succeeds. Simplify, simplify. Instead of three meals a day, if it be necessary eat but one; instead of a hundred dishes, five; and reduce other things in proportion. Our life is like a German Confederacy,⑮ made up of petty states, with its boundary forever fluctuating, so that even a German cannot tell you how it is bounded at any moment. The nation itself, with all its so-called internal improvements, which, by the way are all external and superficial, is just such an unwieldy and overgrown establishment, cluttered with furniture and tripped up by its own traps, ruined by luxury and heedless expense, by want of calculation and a worthy aim, as the million households in the land; and the only cure for it, as for them, is in a rigid economy, a stern and more than Spartan⑯ simplicity of life and elevation of purpose. It lives too fast. Men think that it is essential that the *Nation* have commerce, and export ice, and talk through a telegraph, and ride thirty miles an hour, without a doubt, whether *they* do or not; but whether we should live like baboons or like men, is a little uncertain. If we do not get out sleepers,⑰ and forge rails, and devote days and nights to the work, but go to tinkering upon our *lives* to improve *them*, who will build railroads? And if railroads are not built, how shall we get to heaven in season? But if we stay at home and mind our business, who will want railroads? We do not ride on the railroad; it rides upon us. Did you ever think what those sleepers are that underlie the railroad? Each one is a man, an Irishman, or a Yankee man. The rails are laid on them, and they are covered with sand, and the cars run smoothly over them. They are sound sleepers, I assure you. And every few years a new lot is laid down and run over; so that, if some have the pleasure of riding on a rail, others have the misfortune to be ridden upon. And when they run over a man that is walking in his sleep, a supernumerary sleeper in the wrong position, and wake him up, they suddenly stop the cars, and make a hue and cry about it, as if this were an exception. I am glad to know that it takes a gang of men for every five miles to keep the sleepers down and level in their beds as it is, for this is a sign that they may sometime get up again.

Why should we live with such hurry and waste of life? We are determined to be starved before we are hungry. Men say that a stitch in time saves nine, and so they take a thousand stitches today to save nine tomorrow. As for *work*, we haven't any of any consequence. We have the Saint Vitus' dance,[18] and cannot possibly keep our heads still. If I should only give a few pulls at the parish bell-rope, as for a fire, that is, without setting the bell, there is hardly a man on his farm in the outskirts of Concord, notwithstanding that press of engagements which was his excuse so many times this morning, nor a boy, nor a woman, I might almost say, but would forsake all and follow that sound, not mainly to save property from the flames, but, if we will confess the truth, much more to see it burn, since burn it must, and we, be it known, did not set it on fire—or to see it put out, and have a hand in it, if that is done as handsomely; yes, even if it were the parish church itself. Hardly a man takes a half-hour's nap after dinner, but when he wakes he holds up his head and asks, "What's the news?" as if the rest of mankind had stood his sentinels. Some give directions to be waked every half-hour, doubtless for no other purpose; and then, to pay for it, they tell what they have dreamed. After a night's sleep the news is as indispensable as the breakfast. "Pray tell me anything new that has happened to a man anywhere on this globe" —and he reads it over his coffee and rolls, that a man has had his eyes gouged out this morning on the Wachito River;[19] never dreaming the while that he lives in the dark unfathomed mammoth cave of this world, and has but the rudiment of an eye himself.

For my part, I could easily do without the post-office. I think that there are very few important communications made through it. To speak critically, I never received more than one or two letters in my life—I wrote this some years ago—that were worth the postage. The penny-post is, commonly, an institution through which you seriously offer a man that penny for his thoughts which is so often safely offered in jest. And I am sure that I never read any memorable news in a newspaper. If we read of one man robbed, or murdered, or killed by accident, or one house burned, or one vessel wrecked, or one steamboat blown up, or one cow run over on the Western Railroad, or one mad dog killed, or one lot of grasshoppers in the winter—we never need read of another. One is enough. If you are acquainted with the principle, what do you care for a myriad instances and applications? To a philosopher all *news*, as it is called, is gossip, and they who edit and read it are old women over their tea. Yet not a few are greedy after this gossip. There was such a rush, as I hear, the other day at one of the offices to learn the foreign news by the last arrival, that several large squares of plate glass belonging to the establishment were broken by the pressure—news which I seriously think a ready wit might write a twelve-month, or twelve years, beforehand with sufficient accuracy. As for Spain, for instance, if you know how to throw in Don Carlos and the Infanta, and Don Pedro and Seville and Granada,[20] from time to time in the right proportions—they may have changed the names a little since I saw the papers—and serve up a bull-fight when other entertainments fail, it will be true to the letter, and give us as good an idea of the exact state or ruin of things in Spain as the most succinct and lucid reports under this head in the newspapers: and as for England, almost the last significant scrap of news from that quarter was the revolution of 1649; and if you have learned the history of her crops for an average year, you never need attend to that thing again, unless your speculations are of a merely pecuniary character. If one may judge who rarely looks into the newspapers, nothing new does ever happen in for-

95

eign parts, a French revolution not excepted.

What news! how much more important to know what that is which was never old! "Kieou-pe-yu[21] (great dignitary of the state of Wei) sent a man to Khoung-tseu to know his news. Khoung-tseu caused the messenger to be seated near him, and questioned him in these terms: What is your master doing? The messenger answered with respect: My master desires to diminish the number of his faults, but he cannot accomplish it. The messenger being gone, the philosopher remarked: What a worthy messenger! What a worthy messenger!" The preacher, instead of vexing the ears of drowsy farmers on their day of rest at the end of the week—for Sunday is the fit conclusion of an ill-spent week, and not the fresh and brave beginning of a new one—with this one other draggle-tail of a sermon, should shout with thundering voice, "Pause! Avast! Why so seeming fast, but deadly slow?"

Shams and delusions are esteemed for soundest truths, while reality is fabulous. If men would steadily observe realities only, and not allow themselves to be deluded, life, to compare it with such things as we know, would be like a fairy tale and the Arabian Nights' Entertainments. If we respected only what is inevitable and has a right to be, music and poetry would resound along the streets. When we are unhurried and wise, we perceive that only great and worthy things have any permanent and absolute existence, that petty fears and petty pleasures are but the shadow of the reality. This is always exhilarating and sublime. By closing the eyes and slumbering, and consenting to be deceived by shows, men establish and confirm their daily life of routine and habit everywhere, which still is built on purely illusory foundations. Children, who play life, discern its true law and relations more clearly than men, who fail to live it worthily, but who think that they are wiser by experience, that is, by failure. I have read in a Hindoo book, that "there was a king's son, who, being expelled in infancy from his native city, was brought up by a forester, and, growing up to maturity in that state, imagined himself to belong to the barbarous race with which he lived. One of his father's ministers having discovered him, revealed to him what he was, and the misconception of his character was removed, and he knew himself to be a prince. So soul," continues the Hindoo philosopher, "from the circumstances in which it is placed, mistakes its own character, until the truth is revealed to it by some holy teacher, and then it knows itself to be *Brahme*."[22] I perceive that we inhabitants of New England live this mean life that we do because our vision does not penetrate the surface of things. We think that that is which *appears* to be. If a man should walk through this town and see only the reality, where, think you, would the "Mill-dam" go to? If he should give us an account of the realities he beheld there, we should not recognize the place in his description. Look at a meeting-house, or a court-house, or a jail, or a shop, or a dwelling-house, and say what that thing really is before a true gaze, and they would all go to pieces in your account of them. Men esteem truth remote, in the outskirts of the system, behind the farthest star, before Adam and after the last man. In eternity there is indeed something true and sublime. But all these times and places and occasions are now and here. God himself culminates in the present moment, and will never be more divine in the lapse of all the ages. And we are enabled to apprehend at all what is sublime and noble only by the perpetual instilling and drenching of the reality that surrounds us. The universe constantly and obediently answers to our conceptions; whether we travel fast or slow, the track is laid for us. Let us spend our lives in conceiving then. The poet or the artist never yet had so fair and noble a design but some of his posterity at least could accomplish it.

Let us spend one day as deliberately as Nature, and not be thrown off the track by every nutshell and mosquito's wing that falls on the rails. Let us rise early and fast, or breakfast, gently and without perturbation;

97

let company come and let company go, let the bells ring and the children cry—determined to make a day of it. Why should we knock under and go with the stream? Let us not be upset and overwhelmed in that terrible rapid and whirlpool called a dinner, situated in the meridian shallows. Weather this danger and you are safe, for the rest of the way is down hill. With unrelaxed nerves, with morning vigor, sail by it, looking another way, tied to the mast like Ulysses.[23] If the engine whistles, let it whistle till it is hoarse for its pains. If the bell rings, why should we run? We will consider what kind of music they are like. Let us settle ourselves, and work and wedge our feet downward through the mud and slush of opinion, and prejudice, and tradition, and delusion, and appearance, that alluvion which covers the globe, through Paris and London, through New York and Boston and Concord, through Church and State, through poetry and philosophy and religion, till we come to a hard bottom and rocks in place, which we can call *reality*, and say, This is, and no mistake; and then begin, having a *point d'appui*,[24] below freshet and frost and fire, a place where you might found a wall or a state, or set a lamp-post safely, or perhaps a gauge, not a Nilometer,[25] but a Realometer, that future ages might know how deep a freshet of shams and appearances had gathered from time to time. If you stand right fronting and face to face to a fact, you will see the sun glimmer on both its surfaces, as if it were a cimeter, and feel its sweet edge dividing you through the heart and marrow, and so you will happily conclude your mortal career. Be it life or death, we crave only reality. If we are really dying, let us hear the rattle in our throats and feel cold in the extremities; if we are alive, let us go about our business.

Time is but the stream I go a-fishing in. I drink at it; but while I drink I see the sandy bottom and detect how shallow it is. Its thin current slides away, but eternity remains. I would drink deeper; fish in the sky, whose bottom is pebbly with stars. I cannot count one. I know not the first letter of the alphabet. I have always been regretting that I was not as wise as the day I was born. The intellect is a cleaver; it discerns and rifts its way into the secret of things. I do not wish to be any more busy with my hands than is necessary. My head is hands and feet. I feel all my best faculties concentrated in it. My instinct tells me that my head is an organ for burrowing, as some creatures use their snout and fore paws, and with it I would mine and burrow my way through these hills. I think that the richest vein is somewhere hereabouts; so by the divining-rod and thin rising vapors I judge; and here I will begin to mine.

Notes

① "**I am monarch of all I** *survey*, **My right there is none to dispute**": from *The Solitude of Alexander Selkirk* (italics by Thoreau—a surveyor), a poem by William Cowper (1731-1800), an English poet, hymnist.

② **Atlas**: In Greek mythology Atlas supported the heavens on his shoulders.

③ **Old Cato**: Marcus Porcius Cato (234 B. C. -149 B. C.) a Roman agricultural author.

④ **Olympus**: In Greek mythology, it is the home of the gods.

⑤ **The Harivansa**: a 5th-century Hindu epic poem.

⑥ **Damodara**: another name for the Hindu god Krishna.

⑦ **the Pleiades or the Hyades, to Aldebaran**: These are constellations.

⑧ "**There was a shepherd that did live... Did hourly feed him by**": published in 1610.

⑨ **Aurora**: in Roman mythology, the goddess of dawn.

⑩ **King Tching Thang**: another name for Confucius.

⑪ **Iliad and Odyssey**: Epic poems attributed to Homer, 8th century B. C.

⑫ **The Vedas**: Brahmin religious books.

⑬ **Memnon**: a statue in ancient Egypt said to produce music at dawn.

⑭ **"glorify God and enjoy him forever"**: from Westminster Catechism.

⑮ **a German Confederacy**: group of European states (1815-1866).

⑯ **Spartan**: like the Spartans of ancient Greece, disciplined, and austere.

⑰ **sleepers**: wooden railroad ties that support the rails.

⑱ **the Saint Vitus' dance**: chorea, a nervous disorder characterized by involuntary movements.

⑲ **the Wachito River**: a river in Arkansas and Louisiana.

⑳ **Don Carlos and the Infanta, and Don Pedro and Seville and Granada**: All these are related to Spanish and Portuguese politics in the 1830's and the 1840's.

㉑ **Kieou-pe-yu**: a character in a book by Confucius.

㉒ *Brahme*: Brahma, Hindu god of creation.

㉓ **Ulysses**: the Roman name for Odysseus, a character in Homer's epics *Iliad* and *Odyssey*.

㉔ **a *point d'appui***: a point of support.

㉕ **Nilometer**: gauge used to measure the rise of the Nile River.

Questions for Reading Comprehension

1. Where indeed did Thoreau live, both at a physical level and at a spiritual level?

2. Did Thoreau ever buy a farm? Why did he enjoy the act of buying?

3. What does Thoreau mean when he says that a poet has got all the cream, and left the farmer only the skimmed milk?

4. Why does Thoreau mention the Fourth of July as the day he began to stay in the woods?

5. Why did Thoreau think that the small lake was of most value as a

neighbor in August?

6. Why does Thoreau consider the morning the most memorable season of the day?

7. Why did he go to the woods and live there alone?

8. What, according to Thoreau, is the problem with the life of many people? And what is cure for it?

9. Does Thoreau think that men fail to live life worthily? Why?

10. Thoreau makes it very clear at the beginning of Walden that his stay in the wilderness was not a lifestyle choice but rather a temporary experiment, and he says, "At present I am a sojourner in civilized life again. " Does the short duration of Thoreau's stay at Walden undercut the importance of his project?

Discussion Questions for Appreciation

1. Thoreau's idea of civil disobedience has inspired twentieth-century leaders such as Martin Luther King and Mahatma Gandhi, but it is not certain that he has any leadership potential himself, though he often poses as a prophet for his fellowmen. Do you think he has the potential necessary for a successful political leader?

2. Thoreau occasionally gives us a series of tedious details. For example, in "House-Warming" he tells us a precise history of the freezing of Walden Pond over the past several years. Similar passages describe his farming endeavors, his home construction, and other topics. Why does he present us with these seemingly irrelevant details? How do they fit into his overall plan for *Walden*?

3. At times Thoreau is like a diarist, who narrates a flow of everyday events, as humdrum as they may be. At other times he is almost a mystic writer, who compares the topography of ponds to the shape of the human soul. And at still other times he is a social critic and moral prophet, who comments on social and moral matters. Does the

101

hodgepodge of styles in *Walden* contribute something positive to its overall meaning?

4. Thoreau is a practical man and a keen observer of nature, but he is also a fantasist who makes a lot of references to mythology. In "Economy" he mentions the Greek myth of Deucalion and Pyrrha, who created men by throwing stones over their shoulders; in "The Pond in Winter" he compares a pile of ice to Valhalla, the palace of the Scandinavian gods. In "Sounds" he describes the Fitchburg Railway train as a great mythical beast invading the calm of Walden. What is the effect of all these mythological references? Do they change the overall message of the book in any important way?

5. Thoreau repeatedly praises the simplicity and industriousness of the working poor, and comes very close to joining their ranks when he lives at subsistence level in the woods for two years. Yet in the chapter on reading he disdains popular tastes in books, implying that everyone should be able to read the Greek tragedian Aeschylus in the original, as he does. His allusions to world literature are quite lofty, including Chinese philosophers and Persian poets. Is Thoreau a snob? If so, is his democratic populism undermined by his disdain for popular culture?

A Question for Writing

Does Thoreau show any socialist tendencies, though he is writing before socialism became a recognized idea?

Edgar Allan Poe (1809-1849)

Born in Boston on January 19, 1809, Edgar Allan Poe was the son of itinerant actors. After his parents died, he was taken into the home of his godfather, John Allan, a wealthy Richmond merchant. The Allans took him to Europe, where he began his education in schools in Britain. When he returned to the United States in 1820, he continued his schooling in Richmond, and in 1826 entered the University of Virginia. He showed remarkable scholastic ability, but was forced to leave the university after only eight months because of quarrels with John Allan over his gambling debts. Poverty soon forced him to enlist in the U. S. Army. He was admitted to West Point Military Academy in 1830, but was discharged in 1831. His first book, *Tamerlane and Other Poems*, was published in 1827. It was followed by two more volumes of verse in 1829 and 1831. None of these early collections attracted critical or popular recognition.

In 1835, Poe got an editorial position on *Southern Literary Messenger* in Richmond. He contributed stories, poems, and astute literary criticism. At the age of twenty-seven, Poe married his cousin, Virginia Clemm, who was then only thirteen. The next year, he published his only novel *The Narrative of Arthur Gordon Pym* (1838). From 1838 to 1844, Poe edited *Burton's Gentleman's Magazine* (1839-1840) and *Graham's Magazine* (1841-1842). He wrote direct and incisive criticism which made him a respected and feared critic. Some of his magazine stories were collected as *Tales of the Grotesque and Arabesque* (1840). At that time he also began writing mystery stories. After his wife died in 1847, Poe found his deep sorrow difficult to bear, and he died in 1849.

During a short life of poverty, anxiety, and fantastic tragedy, Poe

103

established a new symbolic poetry, formulated the new short story in the detective and science fiction line, developed an important artistic theory, and laid foundation for analytic criticism.

In his essay "The Philosophy of Composition" (1846), Poe stresses the need to achieve a single effect when a literary work is to be read in one sitting. Poe chooses Beauty to be "the sole legitimate province of the poem". He considers sadness to be the highest manifestation of beauty. "Beauty of whatever kind in its supreme development invariably excites the sensitive soul to tears. Melancholy is thus the most legitimate of all the poetical tones". [1] He believes that the death of a beautiful woman is the most poetical topic.

Poe is a great short-story writer whose Gothic tales show, through carefully crafted symbols, complex characters in deep psychological states. Such compelling stories as "The Masque of the Red Death" (1842) and "The Fall of the House of Usher" (1839) involve the reader in a universe that is at once beautiful and grotesque, real and fantastic. His analytical mind he is evident in his famous stories of ratiocination, notably "The Murders in the Rue Morgue" (1841) and "The Purloined Letter" (1845).

In poetry, Poe is a mastet of mood. His poetry seems to illustrate his idea that the best manifestation of beauty is associated with sadness. In his famous poem "The Raven" (1845) the narrator mourns the loss of his beloved when a raven monotonously repeats the word "Nevermore". "Annabel Lee" (1849) is another poem about the loss of a beautiful woman. "Ulalume" (1847) is yet another example, written as Poe's mourning for the death of his wife.

---

[1] Edgar Allan Poe, "The Philosophy of Composition," *Graham's Magazine*, April 1846, p. 166.

The Raven

Introduction

"The Raven", which was first published in 1845 and revised several times in later publications, is considered one of Poe's best poetical works. One stormy midnight an unhappy, weary young man sits in his elaborately furnished chamber, trying to find peace from sorrow in his books and conducting a curious dialogue with a black raven that can speak the single word, "Nevermore". Tortured by grief over the loss of his beloved Lenore, he asks the bird about the possibility of meeting her in heaven, but it keeps repeating the fatal word, "Nevermore."

The poem is characterized by its dramatic variation of tone, and insistent or cumulative repetition for artistic effect. The raven's repetition of "Nevermore" reflects a rhythm that becomes stronger and more pronounced as the poem reaches its emotional climax.

The poem consists of 18 six-line stanzas. The first five lines of each stanza are in trochaic octameter, and the sixth line in trochaic tetrameter. The rime pattern is abcbbb, and the b rimes, are based on the constant refrain, "Nevermore."

The Raven

Once upon a midnight dreary, while I pondered weak and weary,
Over many a quaint and curious volume of forgotten lore,
While I nodded, nearly napping, suddenly there came a tapping,
As of some one gently rapping, rapping at my chamber door.
" 'T is some visitor," I muttered, "tapping at my chamber door
　　—Only this, and nothing more. "

Ah, distinctly I remember it was in the bleak December,

And each separate dying ember wrought its ghost upon the floor.
Eagerly I wished the morrow; —vainly I had sought to borrow
From my books surcease of sorrow - sorrow for the lost Lenore—
For the rare and radiant maiden whom the angels named Lenore—
　　Nameless here for evermore. [①]

And the silken sad uncertain rustling of each purple curtain
Thrilled me—filled me with fantastic terrors never felt before;
So that now, to still the beating of my heart, I stood repeating
" 'T is some visitor entreating entrance at my chamber door—
Some late visitor entreating entrance at my chamber door; —
　　This it is, and nothing more. "

Presently my soul grew stronger; hesitating then no longer,
"Sir," said I, "or Madam, truly your forgiveness I implore;
But the fact is I was napping, and so gently you came rapping,
And so faintly you came tapping, tapping at my chamber door,
That I scarce[②] was sure I heard you" —here I opened wide the door; —
　　Darkness there, and nothing more.

Deep into that darkness peering, long I stood there wondering, fearing,
Doubting, dreaming dreams no mortal ever dared to dream before
But the silence was unbroken, and the darkness gave no token,
And the only word there spoken was the whispered word, "Lenore!"
This I whispered, and an echo murmured back the word, "Lenore!" —
　　Merely this and nothing more.

Back into the chamber turning, all my soul within me burning,
Soon again I heard a tapping somewhat louder than before.
'Surely,' said I, 'surely that is something at my window lattice;'
Let me see then, what thereat is, and this mystery explore—
Let my heart be still a moment and this mystery explore;—
　　" 'T is the wind and nothing more!"

Open here I flung the shutter, when, with many a flirt and flutter,
In there stepped a stately raven of the saintly days of yore;
Not the least obeisance made he; not a minute stopped or stayed he;
But, with mien of lord or lady, perched above my chamber door—
Perched upon a bust of Pallas[3] just above my chamber door—
　　Perched, and sat, and nothing more.

Then this ebony bird beguiling my sad fancy into smiling,
By the grave and stern decorum of the countenance it wore,
"Though thy crest be shorn and shaven, thou," I said,　"sure no craven.
Ghastly grim and ancient raven wandering from the nightly shore—
Tell me what thy lordly name is on the Night's Plutonian shore!"[4]
　　Quoth[5] the raven, "Nevermore."

Much I marvelled this ungainly fowl to hear discourse so plainly,
Though its answer little meaning—little relevancy bore;[6]
For we cannot help agreeing that no living human being
Ever yet was blessed with seeing bird above his chamber door—
Bird or beast above the sculptured bust above his chamber door,
　　With such name as "Nevermore."

But the raven, sitting lonely on the placid bust, spoke only,

That one word, as if his soul in that one word he did outpour.
Nothing further then he uttered—not a feather then he fluttered—
Till I scarcely more than muttered "Other friends have flown before—
On the morrow will *he* leave me, as my hopes have flown before."
　　Then the bird said, "Nevermore."

Startled at the stillness broken by reply so aptly spoken,
"Doubtless," said I, "what it utters is its only stock and store,⑦
Caught from some unhappy master whom unmerciful disaster
Followed fast and followed faster till his songs one burden bore—
Till the dirges of his hope that melancholy burden bore
　　Of 'Never-nevermore.'"

But the raven still beguiling all my sad soul into smiling,
Straight I wheeled a cushioned seat in front of bird and bust and
door;
Then, upon the velvet sinking, I betook myself to linking
Fancy unto fancy, thinking what this ominous bird of yore—
What this grim, ungainly, ghastly, gaunt, and ominous bird of yore
　　Meant in croaking "Nevermore."

This I sat engaged in guessing, but no syllable expressing
To the fowl whose fiery eyes now burned into my bosom's core;
This and more I sat divining, with my head at ease reclining
On the cushion's velvet violet lining that the lamplight gloated o'er,
But whose velvet violet lining with the lamp-light gloating o'er,
　　She shall press, ah, nevermore!

Then, methought, the air grew denser, perfumed from an unseen
censer

Swung by Seraphim whose foot-falls tinkled on the tufted floor.
"Wretch," I cried, "thy God hath lent thee—by these angels he has sent thee
Respite—respite and nepenthe from thy memories of Lenore!
Quaff, oh quaff this kind nepenthe,[8] and forget this lost Lenore!"
　　Quoth the raven, "Nevermore."

"Prophet!" said I, "thing of evil! —prophet still, if bird or devil! —
Whether Tempter[9] sent, or whether tempest tossed thee here ashore,
Desolate yet all undaunted, on this desert land enchanted—
On this home by horror haunted—tell me truly, I implore—
Is there—*is* there balm in Gilead?[10]—tell me—tell me, I implore!"
　　Quoth the raven, "Nevermore."

"Prophet!" said I, "thing of evil! —prophet still, if bird or devil!
By that Heaven that bends above us—by that God we both adore—
Tell this soul with sorrow laden if, within the distant Aidenn,[11]
It shall clasp a sainted maiden whom the angels named Lenore—
Clasp a rare and radiant maiden, whom the angels named Lenore?"
　　Quoth the raven, "Nevermore."

"Be that word our sign of parting, bird or fiend!" I shrieked upstarting—
"Get thee back into the tempest and the Night's Plutonian shore!
Leave no black plume as a token of that lie thy soul hath spoken!
Leave my loneliness unbroken! —quit the bust above my door!
Take thy beak from out my heart, and take thy form from off my door!"
　　Quoth the Raven, "Nevermore."

And the raven, never flitting, still is sitting, still is sitting
On the pallid bust of Pallas just above my chamber door;
And his eyes have all the seeming[12] of a demon's that is dreaming,
And the lamplight o'er him streaming throws his shadow on the floor;
And my soul from out that shadow that lies floating on the floor
      Shall be lifted—nevermore!

Notes

① **Nameless here for evermore**: The maiden no longer has an earthy name because she has left the earth and is known in Aidenn by the name of Lenore.

② **scarce**: scarcely.

③ **Pallas**: one of the names of the Greek goddess of wisdom Athena.

④ **the Night's Plutonian shore**: the infernal regions ruled by Pluto, god of the departed spirit and the underworld.

⑤ **Quoth**: said.

⑥ **Though its answer little meaning—little relevancy bore**: Though its answer had little meaning and bore little relevancy.

⑦ **its only stock and store**: the only word it knows.

⑧ **nepenthe**: a drug thought by the ancient Greeks to relieve sorrow and pain.

⑨ **Tempter**: the Devil, Satan

⑩ **balm in Gilead**: Balm is an ointment used for soothing. Gilead is a region northeast of the Dead Sea.

⑪ **Aidenn**: a variant spelling of Eden.

⑫ **seeming**: appearance.

Questions for Reading Comprehension

1. What was the narrator doing when he first heard the tapping?

2. What did he see when he opened the door?

3. What did he see when he flung the shutter?

4. Where was the raven? And what did it look like?

5. Why did the narrator associate the raven with an agent of the supernatural?

6. What was the only word that the raven spoke?

7. Why did the narrator think that the raven spoke only one word?

8. What did he guess the word "Nevermore" meant?

9. What did he ask the bird to do toward the end of the poem?

10. Did the bird leave the narrator alone at the end of the poem?

Discussion Questions for Appreciation

1. What do you think the raven symbolizes? Why?

2. Evaluate the narrator's emotional state at the beginning of the poem, in the last but one stanza, and in the last stanza.

3. In this poem the raven steadily repeats the word "Nevermore". What do you think is the poet's intention of letting the raven repeat this word?

4. What is the theme of this poem? Is it Poe's favorite theme?

5. Poe often uses sound devices to produce a musical effect. Find out and discuss the sound devices that he uses to produce a musical effect in the poem.

A Question for Writing

Poe believes that the function of poetry is not to describe and interpret earthly experience, but to create a mood in which the soul is elevated to supernal beauty. Describe the mood of this poem, and discuss its relations with Poe's idea of the function of poetry.

Nathaniel Hawthorne（1804-1864）

Nathaniel Hawthorne was born on July 4, 1804 to a family with a long Puritan tradition in Salem, Massachusetts. One of his ancestors had been among the judges who condemned the "witches" in the Salem witchcraft trial in 1692. After his sea-captain father died in 1808, Hawthorne was raised by his mother. By his mid-teens he read extensively and determined to be a writer himself. He studied at Bowdoin College in Maine from 1821 to 1825. After graduating from college, he returned to Salem. For twelve years, Hawthorne lived in his mother's house in Salem, studying the American past, and teaching himself to write. In 1837 *Twice-Told Tales*, his first collection of stories, was published, and Hawthorne left his lonely chamber.

He worked at the Boston Customs House and then lived for a while among the Transcendental reformers and visionaries at the utopian community, Brook Farm. In 1842, he married Sophia Peabody and moved to Concord. In 1846, he published *Mosses from an Old Mansion*, another collection of stories. Unable to support himself and his wife, Hawthorne returned to Salem, where he received a political appointment as Surveyor of the Port.

Removed from office by a change of administrations, Hawthorne began writing *The Scarlet Letter*, a subtle study of guilt and retribution in Puritan Boston. Published in 1850, the novel became a sensation. He followed it with *The House of the Seven Gables*. When his college friend Franklin Piece（1804-1869）became the 14th U. S. President, Hawthorne was appointed American Consul at Liverpool, England. After many years in Europe, he returned to America but, with the exception of *The Marble Faun*（1860）, he was unable to complete any major work during his later years.

Hawthorne's fiction deals with the themes of guilt and secrecy, and shows his constant preoccupation with the effects of Puritanism in New England. Different from his ancestors, Hawthorne had a feeling of Puritanism as being intolerant and cruel. When he read the accounts about his American ancestors, he was reported to have read them with fascination and horror. Although he was appalled by the Puritan injustice, he was convinced that there was both good and evil in Puritanism.

Hawthorne's *The Scarlet Letter* is often considered the first great American novel. The story, set about two hundred years earlier in the Boston area, tells the story of the adulterous love between Arthur Dimmesdale, a Puritan minister, and Hester Prynne, a married woman in his congregation. But it is the *consequence* of the adultery and the respective struggles of the two lovers that get us involved. The novel's focus is on the complex moral implications of the affair.

113

At his best, Hawthorne was a master of psychological insight. His novels were perhaps the deepest and most psychological in the 19th century because he was interested in "the moral and psychological consequences that manifested themselves in human beings as a result of their pride". His stories display a psychological insight into moral isolation and human emotion. His interest in the moral and the religious is primarily subjective and psychological. He was fond of using symbols to reveal the psychology of his characters. He used masks, veils, shadows, emblems to give dramatic forms to the universal dilemmas of humanity. His style is soft, flowing, and almost feminine. But his observation is always somber. The ambiguity in his stories keeps the reader in a world of uncertainty.

The Minister's Black Veil

Introduction

This short story was published in *The Token* in 1836, and in Twice-Told Tales in 1837. One Sunday morning, a New England Puritan minister, the Reverend Mr. Hooper, ascends his pulpit and delivers his sermon with his face covered by a black veil. When the sermon is over, people begin to gossip about the veil. They guess that he may have committed an unpardonable sin or have kept a secret guilt in his heart. Yet he refuses to explain his action to his horrified congregation. The next day his fiancée Elizabeth begs him to put aside the veil, but he refuses, explaining that he is hiding his face either for sorrow or for a secret sin. Then Elizabeth leaves him. Then he goes through life with his face concealed by the veil, which makes him a stranger to other people. However, with the passage of time he becomes a much-respected minister, winning many converts and sympathizing wonderfully with sinners. Before he dies, a neighboring minister asks him again to put aside the black veil, but again he refuses, saying that the veil is a symbol, and that he will not remove it until friends show their inmost heart to each other and men shrink not from the eye of his Creators. In the end he dies, and is buried with his black veil on.

The Minister's Black Veil
A Parable[①]

The Sexton stood in the porch of Milford meeting-house, pulling busily at the bell-rope. The old people of the village came stooping along the street. Children, with bright faces, tripped merrily beside their parents, or mimicked a graver gait, in the conscious dignity of their Sunday clothes. Spruce bachelors looked sidelong at the pretty maidens, and fancied that the Sabbath sunshine made them prettier than on week days. When the throng had mostly streamed into the porch, the sexton began to toll the bell, keeping his eye on the Reverend Mr. Hooper's door. The first glimpse of the clergyman's figure was the signal for the bell to cease its summons.

"But what has good Parson Hooper got upon his face?" cried the sexton in astonishment.

All within hearing immediately turned about, and beheld the semblance[②] of Mr. Hooper, pacing slowly his meditative way towards the meeting-house. With one accord they started, expressing more wonder than if some strange minister were coming to dust the cushions of Mr. Hooper's pulpit.

"Are you sure it is our parson?" inquired Goodman Gray[③] of the sexton.

"Of a certainty it is good Mr. Hooper," replied the sexton. "He was to have exchanged pulpits with Parson Shute, of Westbury; but Parson Shute sent to excuse himself yesterday, being to preach a funeral sermon."

The cause of so much amazement may appear sufficiently slight. Mr. Hooper, a gentlemanly person, of about thirty, though still a bachelor, was dressed with due clerical neatness, as if a careful wife had starched his band, and brushed the weekly dust from his Sunday's garb. There was but one thing remarkable in his appearance. Swathed about his forehead, and hanging down over his face, so low as to be shaken by his breath, Mr. Hooper had on a black veil. On a nearer view it seemed to consist of two folds of crape, which entirely concealed his features, except the mouth and chin, but probably did not intercept his sight, further than to give a darkened aspect to all living and inanimate things. With this gloomy shade before him, good Mr. Hooper walked onward, at a slow and quiet pace, stooping somewhat, and looking on the ground, as is customary with abstracted men, yet nodding kindly to those of his parishioners who still waited on the meeting-house steps. But so wonder-struck were they that his greeting hardly met with a return.

"I can't really feel as if good Mr. Hooper's face was behind that piece of crape," said the sexton.

"I don't like it," muttered an old woman, as she hobbled into the meeting-house. "He has changed himself into something awful, only by hiding his face."

"Our parson has gone mad!" cried Goodman Gray, following him across the threshold.

A rumor of some unaccountable phenomenon had preceded Mr. Hooper into the meeting-house, and set all the congregation astir. Few could refrain from twisting their heads towards the door; many stood up-right, and turned directly about; while several little boys clambered up-on the seats, and came down again with a terrible racket. There was a general bustle, a rustling of the women's gowns and shuffling of the men's feet, greatly at variance with that hushed repose which should at-tend the entrance of the minister. But Mr. Hooper appeared not to notice the perturbation of his people. He entered with an almost noiseless step, bent his head mildly to the pews on each side, and bowed as he passed his oldest parishioner, a white-haired great-grandsire, who occupied an arm-chair in the centre of the aisle. It was strange to observe how slowly this venerable man became conscious of something singular in the ap-pearance of his pastor. He seemed not fully to partake of the prevailing wonder, till Mr. Hooper had ascended the stairs, and showed himself in the pulpit, face to face with his congregation, except for the black veil. That mysterious emblem was never once withdrawn. It shook with his measured breath, as he gave out the psalm; it threw its obscurity be-tween him and the holy page, as he read the Scriptures;[④] and while he prayed, the veil lay heavily on his uplifted countenance. Did he seek to hide it from the dread Being[5] whom he was addressing?

Such was the effect of this simple piece of crape, that more than one woman of delicate nerves was forced to leave the meeting-house. Yet perhaps the pale-faced congregation was almost as fearful a sight to the minister, as his black veil to them.

Mr. Hooper had the reputation of a good preacher, but not an energetic one: he strove to win his people heavenward by mild, persuasive influences, rather than to drive them thither by the thunders of the Word.[6] The sermon which he now delivered was marked by the same characteristics of style and manner as the general series of his pulpit oratory. But there was something, either in the sentiment of the discourse itself, or in the imagination of the auditors, which made it greatly the most powerful effort that they had ever heard from their pastor's lips. It was tinged, rather more darkly than usual, with the gentle gloom of Mr. Hooper's temperament. The subject had reference to secret sin, and those sad mysteries which we hide from our nearest and dearest, and would fain conceal from our own consciousness, even forgetting that the Omniscient[7] can detect them. A subtle power was breathed into his words. Each member of the congregation, the most innocent girl, and the man of hardened breast, felt as if the preacher had crept upon them, behind his awful veil, and discovered their hoarded iniquity[8] of deed or thought. Many spread their clasped hands on their bosoms. There was nothing terrible in what Mr. Hooper said, at least, no violence; and yet, with every tremor of his melancholy voice, the hearers quaked. An unsought pathos came hand in hand with awe. So sensible were the audience of some unwonted attribute in their minister, that they longed for a breath of wind to blow aside the veil, almost believing that a stranger's visage would be discovered, though the form, gesture, and voice were those of Mr. Hooper.

At the close of the services, the people hurried out with indecorous

117

confusion, eager to communicate their pent-up amazement, and conscious of lighter spirits the moment they lost sight of the black veil. Some gathered in little circles, huddled closely together, with their mouths all whispering in the centre; some went homeward alone, wrapt in silent meditation; some talked loudly, and profaned the Sabbath day with ostentatious laughter. A few shook their sagacious heads, intimating that they could penetrate the mystery; while one or two affirmed that there was no mystery at all, but only that Mr. Hooper's eyes were so weakened by the midnight lamp, as to require a shade. After a brief interval, forth came good Mr. Hooper also, in the rear of his flock. Turning his veiled face from one group to another, he paid due reverence to the hoary heads⑨, saluted the middle aged with kind dignity as their friend and spiritual guide, greeted the young with mingled authority and love, and laid his hands on the little children's heads to bless them. Such was always his custom on the Sabbath day. Strange and bewildered looks repaid him for his courtesy. None, as on former occasions, aspired to the honor of walking by their pastor's side. Old Squire Saunders, doubtless by an accidental lapse of memory, neglected to invite Mr. Hooper to his table, where the good clergyman had been wont to bless the food, almost every Sunday since his settlement.⑩ He returned, therefore, to the parsonage, and, at the moment of closing the door, was observed to look back upon the people, all of whom had their eyes fixed upon the minister. A sad smile gleamed faintly from beneath the black veil, and flickered about his mouth, glimmering as he disappeared.

"How strange," said a lady, "that a simple black veil, such as any woman might wear on her bonnet, should become such a terrible thing on Mr. Hooper's face!"

"Something must surely be amiss with Mr. Hooper's intellects," observed her husband, the physician of the village. "But the strangest part of the affair is the effect of this vagary, even on a sober-minded man like myself. The black veil, though it covers only our pastor's face, throws its influence over his whole person, and makes him ghostlike from head to foot. Do you not feel it so?"

"Truly do I," replied the lady; "and I would not be alone with him for the world. I wonder he is not afraid to be alone with himself!"

"Men sometimes are so," said her husband.

The afternoon service was attended with similar circumstances. At its conclusion, the bell tolled for the funeral of a young lady. The relatives and friends were assembled in the house, and the more distant acquaintances stood about the door, speaking of the good qualities of the deceased, when their talk was interrupted by the appearance of Mr. Hooper, still covered with his black veil. It was now an appropriate emblem. The clergyman stepped into the room where the corpse was laid, and bent over the coffin, to take a last farewell of his deceased parishioner. As he stooped, the veil hung straight down from his forehead, so that, if her eyelids had not been closed forever, the dead maiden might have seen his face. Could Mr. Hooper be fearful of her glance, that he so hastily caught back the black veil? A person who watched the interview between the dead and living, scrupled not to affirm, that, at the instant when the clergyman's features were disclosed, the corpse had slightly shuddered, rustling the shroud and muslin cap, though the countenance retained the composure of death. A superstitious old woman was the only witness of this prodigy. From the coffin Mr. Hooper passed into the chamber of the mourners, and thence to the head of the staircase, to make the funeral prayer. It was a tender and heart-dissolving prayer, full of sorrow, yet so imbued with celestial hopes, that the music of a heavenly harp, swept by the fingers of the dead, seemed faintly to be heard among the saddest accents of the minister. The people trembled, though they but darkly understood him when he prayed that they, and himself, and all of mortal race, might be ready, as he trusted this young maiden had been, for the dreadful hour that should snatch the veil from their faces. The bearers went heavily forth, and the mourners followed, saddening all the street, with the dead before them, and Mr. Hooper in his black veil behind.

"Why do you look back?" said one in the procession to his partner.

I had a fancy, " replied she, " that the minister and the maiden's spirit were walking hand in hand. "

"And so had I, at the same moment," said the other.

That night, the handsomest couple in Milford village were to be joined in wedlock. Though reckoned a melancholy man, Mr. Hooper had a placid cheerfulness for such occasions, which often excited a sympathetic smile where livelier merriment would have been thrown away. There was no quality of his disposition which made him more beloved than this. The company at the wedding awaited his arrival with impatience, trusting that the strange awe, which had gathered over him throughout the day, would now be dispelled. But such was not the result. When Mr. Hooper came, the first thing that their eyes rested on was the same horrible black veil, which had added deeper gloom to the funeral, and could portend nothing but evil to the wedding. Such was its immediate effect on the guests that a cloud seemed to have rolled duskily from beneath the black crape, and dimmed the light of the candles. The bridal pair stood up before the minister. But the bride's cold fingers quivered in the tremulous hand of the bridegroom, and her deathlike paleness caused a whisper that the maiden who had been buried a few hours before was come from her grave to be married. If ever another wedding were so dismal, it was that famous one where they tolled the wedding knell. After performing the ceremony, Mr. Hooper raised a glass of wine to his lips, wishing happiness to the new-married couple in a strain of mild pleasantry that ought to have brightened the features of the guests, like a cheerful gleam from the hearth. At that instant, catching a glimpse of his figure in the looking-glass, the black veil involved his own spirit in the horror with which it overwhelmed all others. His frame shuddered, his lips grew white, he spilt the untasted wine upon the carpet, and rushed forth into the darkness. For the Earth, too, had on her Black Veil.

The next day, the whole village of Milford talked of little else than Parson Hooper's black veil. That, and the mystery concealed behind it, supplied a topic for discussion between acquaintances meeting in the street, and good women gossiping at their open windows. It was the first item of news that the tavern-keeper told to his guests. The children babbled of it on their way to school. One imitative little imp covered his face with an old black handkerchief, thereby so affrighting his playmates that the panic seized himself, and he well-nigh lost his wits by his own waggery. ⑪

It was remarkable that of all the busybodies and impertinent people in the parish, not one ventured to put the plain question to Mr. Hooper, wherefore he did this thing. Hitherto, whenever there appeared the slightest call for such interference, he had never lacked advisers, nor shown himself adverse to be guided by their judgment. If he erred at all, it was by so painful a degree of self-distrust, that even the mildest censure would lead him to consider an indifferent action as a crime. Yet, though so well acquainted with this amiable weakness, no individual among his parishioners chose to make the black veil a subject of friendly remonstrance. There was a feeling of dread, neither plainly confessed nor carefully concealed, which caused each to shift the responsibility upon another, till at length it was found expedient to send a deputation of the church, in order to deal with Mr. Hooper about the mystery, before it should grow into a scandal. Never did an embassy so ill discharge its duties. The minister received them with friendly courtesy, but became silent, after they were seated, leaving to his visitors the whole burden of introducing their important business. The topic, it might be supposed, was obvious enough. There was the black veil swathed round Mr. Hooper's forehead, and concealing every feature above his placid mouth, on which, at times, they could perceive the glimmering of a melancholy smile. But that piece of crape, to their imagination, seemed to hang down before his heart, the symbol of a fearful secret between him and them. Were the veil but cast aside, they might speak freely of it, but not till then. Thus they sat a considerable time, speechless, confused, and shrinking uneasily from Mr. Hooper's eye, which they felt to be fixed upon them with an invisible glance. Finally, the deputies returned abashed to their constituents, pronouncing the matter too weighty to be handled, except by a council of the churches, if, indeed, it might not require a general synod. [12]

But there was one person in the village unappalled by the awe with which the black veil had impressed all beside herself. When the deputies returned without an explanation, or even venturing to demand one, she, with the calm energy of her character, determined to chase away the strange cloud that appeared to be settling round Mr. Hooper, every moment more darkly than before. As his plighted wife, [13] it should be her privilege to know what the black veil concealed. At the minister's first visit, therefore, she entered upon the subject with a direct simplicity, which made the task easier both for him and her. After he had seated himself, she fixed her eyes steadfastly upon the veil, but could discern nothing of the dreadful gloom that had so overawed the multitude: it was but a double fold of crape, hanging down from his forehead to his mouth, and slightly stirring with his breath.

"No," said she aloud, and smiling, "there is nothing terrible in this piece of crape, except that it hides a face which I am always glad to look upon. Come, good sir, let the sun shine from behind the cloud. First lay aside your black veil: then tell me why you put it on."

Mr. Hooper's smile glimmered faintly.

"There is an hour to come," said he, "when all of us shall cast aside our veils. Take it not amiss,⑭ beloved friend, if I wear this piece of crape till then."

"Your words are a mystery⑮, too," returned the young lady. "Take away the veil from them, at least."

"Elizabeth, I will," said he, "so far as my vow may suffer me. Know, then, this veil is a type and a symbol, and I am bound to wear it ever, both in light and darkness, in solitude and before the gaze of multitudes, and as with strangers, so with my familiar friends. No mortal eye will see it withdrawn. This dismal shade must separate me from the world: even you, Elizabeth, can never come behind it!"

"What grievous affliction hath befallen you," she earnestly

inquired, "that you should thus darken your eyes forever?"

"If it be a sign of mourning," replied Mr. Hooper, "I, perhaps, like most other mortals, have sorrows dark enough to be typified by a black veil. "

"But what if the world will not believe that it is the type of an innocent sorrow?" urged Elizabeth. "Beloved and respected as you are, there may be whispers that you hide your face under the consciousness of secret sin. For the sake of your holy office, do away this scandal!"

The color rose into her cheeks as she intimated the nature of the rumors that were already abroad in the village. But Mr. Hooper's mildness did not forsake him. He even smiled again—that same sad smile, which always appeared like a faint glimmering of light, proceeding from the obscurity beneath the veil.

"If I hide my face for sorrow, there is cause enough," he merely replied; "and if I cover it for secret sin, what mortal might not do the same?"

And with this gentle, but unconquerable obstinacy did he resist all her entreaties. At length Elizabeth sat silent. For a few moments she appeared lost in thought, considering, probably, what new methods might be tried to withdraw her lover from so dark a fantasy, which, if it had no other meaning, was perhaps a symptom of mental disease. Though of a firmer character than his own, the tears rolled down her cheeks. But, in an instant, as it were, a new feeling took the place of sorrow: her eyes were fixed insensibly[16] on the black veil, when, like a sudden twilight in the air, its terrors fell around her. She arose, and stood trembling before him.

"And do you feel it then, at last?" said he mournfully.

She made no reply, but covered her eyes with her hand, and turned to leave the room. He rushed forward and caught her arm.

"Have patience with me, Elizabeth!" cried he, passionately. "Do not desert me, though this veil must be between us here on earth. Be mine, and hereafter there shall be no veil over my face, no darkness between our souls! It is but a mortal veil—it is not for eternity! O! you know not how lonely I am, and how frightened, to be alone behind my black veil. Do not leave me in this miserable obscurity forever!"

"Lift the veil but once, and look me in the face," said she.

"Never! It cannot be!" replied Mr. Hooper.

"Then farewell!" said Elizabeth.

She withdrew her arm from his grasp, and slowly departed, pausing at the door, to give one long shuddering gaze, that seemed almost to penetrate the mystery of the black veil. But, even amid his grief, Mr. Hooper smiled to think that only a material emblem had separated him from happiness, though the horrors, which it shadowed forth, must be drawn darkly between the fondest of lovers.

From that time no attempts were made to remove Mr. Hooper's

black veil, or, by a direct appeal, to discover the secret which it was supposed to hide. By persons who claimed a superiority to popular prejudice, it was reckoned merely an eccentric whim, such as often mingles with the sober actions of men otherwise rational, and tinges them all with its own semblance of insanity. But with the multitude, good Mr. Hooper was irreparably a bugbear. He could not walk the street with any peace of mind, so conscious was he that the gentle and timid would turn aside to avoid him, and that others would make it a point of hardihood to throw themselves in his way. The impertinence of the latter class compelled him to give up his customary walk at sunset to the burial ground; for when he leaned pensively over the gate, there would always be faces behind the gravestones, peeping at his black veil. A fable went the rounds[17] that the stare of the dead people drove him thence. It grieved him, to the very depth of his kind heart, to observe how the children fled from his approach, breaking up their merriest sports, while his melancholy figure was yet afar off. Their instinctive dread caused him to feel more strongly than aught else, that a preternatural horror was interwoven with the threads of the black crape. In truth, his own antipathy to the veil was known to be so great, that he never willingly passed before a mirror, nor stooped to drink at a still fountain, lest, in its peaceful bosom, he should be affrighted by himself. This was what gave plausibility to the whispers, that Mr. Hooper's conscience tortured him for some great crime too horrible to be entirely concealed, or otherwise than so obscurely intimated. Thus, from beneath the black veil, there rolled a cloud into the sunshine, an ambiguity of sin or sorrow, which enveloped the poor minister, so that love or sympathy could never reach him. It was said that ghost and fiend consorted with him there. With self-shudderings and outward terrors, he walked continually in its shadow, groping darkly within his own soul, or gazing through a medium that saddened the whole world. Even the lawless wind, it was believed, respec-

126

ted his dreadful secret, and never blew aside the veil. But still good Mr. Hooper sadly smiled at the pale visages of the worldly throng as he passed by.

Among all its bad influences, the black veil had the one desirable effect, of making its wearer a very efficient clergyman. By the aid of his mysterious emblem—for there was no other apparent cause—he became a man of awful power over souls that were in agony for sin. His converts always regarded him with a dread peculiar to themselves, affirming, though but figuratively, that, before he brought them to celestial light, they had been with him behind the black veil. Its gloom, indeed, enabled him to sympathize with all dark affections. Dying sinners cried aloud for Mr. Hooper, and would not yield their breath till he appeared; though ever, as he stooped to whisper consolation, they shuddered at the veiled face so near their own. Such were the terrors of the black veil, even when Death had bared his visage! Strangers came long distances to attend service at his church, with the mere idle purpose of gazing at his figure, because it was forbidden them to behold his face. But many were made to quake ere they departed! Once, during Governor Belcher's[18] administration, Mr. Hooper was appointed to preach the election sermon. Covered with his black veil, he stood before the chief magistrate, the council, and the representatives, and wrought so deep an impression that the legislative measures of that year were characterized by all the gloom and piety of our earliest ancestral sway.

In this manner Mr. Hooper spent a long life, irreproachable in outward act, yet shrouded in dismal suspicions; kind and loving, though unloved, and dimly feared; a man apart from men, shunned in their health and joy, but ever summoned to their aid in mortal anguish. As years wore on, shedding their snows above his sable veil, he acquired a name throughout the New England churches, and they called him Father Hooper. Nearly all his parishioners, who were of mature age when he was settled, had been borne away by many a funeral: he had one congregation in the church, and a more crowded one in the churchyard; and having wrought so late into the evening, and done his work so well, it was now good Father Hooper's turn to rest.

Several persons were visible by the shaded candle-light, in the death chamber of the old clergyman. Natural connections[19] he had none. But there was the decorously grave, though unmoved physician, seeking only to mitigate the last pangs of the patient whom he could not save. There were the deacons, and other eminently pious members of his church. There, also, was the Reverend Mr. Clark, of Westbury, a young and zealous divine, who had ridden in haste to pray by the bedside of the expiring minister. There was the nurse, no hired handmaiden of death, but one whose calm affection had endured thus long in secrecy, in solitude, amid the chill of age, and would not perish, even at the dying hour. Who, but Elizabeth! And there lay the hoary head of good Father Hooper upon the death pillow, with the black veil still swathed about his brow, and reaching down over his face, so that each more difficult gasp of his faint breath caused it to stir. All through life that piece of crape had hung between him and the world: it had separated him from cheerful brotherhood and woman's love, and kept him in that saddest of all prisons, his own heart; and still it lay upon his face, as if to deepen the gloom of his darksome chamber, and shade him from the sunshine of eternity.

For some time previous, his mind had been confused, wavering doubtfully between the past and the present, and hovering forward, as it were, at intervals, into the indistinctness of the world to come. There had been feverish turns,[20] which tossed him from side to side, and wore away what little strength he had. But in his most convulsive struggles, and in the wildest vagaries of his intellect, when no other thought retained its sober influence, he still showed an awful solicitude lest the black veil should slip aside. Even if his bewildered soul could have forgotten, there was a faithful woman at his pillow, who, with averted eyes, would have covered that aged face, which she had last beheld in the comeliness of manhood. At length the death-stricken old man lay quietly in the torpor of mental and bodily exhaustion, with an imperceptible pulse, and breath that grew fainter and fainter, except when a long, deep, and irregular inspiration seemed to prelude the flight of his spirit.

The minister of Westbury approached the bedside.

"Venerable Father Hooper," said he, "the moment of your release[21] is at hand. Are you ready for the lifting of the veil that shuts in time from eternity?"

Father Hooper at first replied merely by a feeble motion of his head; then, apprehensive, perhaps, that his meaning might be doubtful, he exerted himself to speak.

"Yea," said he, in faint accents, "my soul hath a patient weariness until that veil be lifted."

"And is it fitting," resumed the Reverend Mr. Clark, "that a man so given[22] to prayer, of such a blameless example, holy in deed and thought, so far as mortal judgment may pronounce; is it fitting that a father in the church should leave a shadow on his memory, that may seem to blacken a life so pure? I pray you, my venerable brother, let not this thing be! Suffer us to[23] be gladdened by your triumphant aspect as you go to your reward. Before the veil of eternity be lifted, let me cast aside this black veil from your face!"

And thus speaking, the Reverend Mr. Clark bent forward to reveal the mystery of so many years. But, exerting a sudden energy, that made all the beholders stand aghast, Father Hooper snatched both his hands from beneath the bedclothes, and pressed them strongly on the black veil, resolute to struggle, if the minister of Westbury would contend with a dying man.

"Never!" cried the veiled clergyman. "On earth, never!"

"Dark old man!" exclaimed the affrighted minister, "with what horrible crime upon your soul are you now passing to the judgment?"[24]

Father Hooper's breath heaved; it rattled in his throat; but, with a mighty effort, grasping forward with his hands, he caught hold of life, and held it back till he should speak. He even raised himself in bed; and there he sat, shivering with the arms of death around him, while the black veil hung down, awful at that last moment, in the gathered terrors of a lifetime. And yet the faint, sad smile, so often there, now seemed to glimmer from its obscurity, and linger on Father Hooper's lips.

"Why do you tremble at me alone?" cried he, turning his veiled face round the circle of pale spectators. "Tremble also at each other! Have men avoided me, and women shown no pity, and children screamed and fled, only for my black veil? What, but the mystery which it obscurely typifies, has made this piece of crape so awful? When the friend shows his inmost heart to his friend; the lover to his best beloved; when man does not vainly shrink from the eye of his Creator, loathsomely treasuring up the secret of his sin; then deem me a monster, for the symbol beneath which I have lived, and die! I look around me, and, lo! on every visage a Black Veil!"

While his auditors shrank from one another, in mutual affright, Father Hooper fell back upon his pillow, a veiled corpse, with a faint smile lingering on the lips. Still veiled, they laid him in his coffin, and a veiled corpse they bore him to the grave. The grass of many years has sprung up and withered on that grave, the burial stone is moss-grown, and good Mr. Hooper's face is dust; but awful is still the thought that it mouldered beneath the Black Veil!

Notes

① **Parable**: A story designed to teach a moral or religious principle. According to Hawthorne's own note, "Another clergyman in New England, Mr. Joseph Moody, of York, Maine, who died about eighty years since, made himself remarkable by the same eccentricity that is here related of the Reverend Mr. Hooper. In his case, however, the symbol had a different import. In early life he had accidentally killed a beloved friend; and from that day till the hour of his own death, he hid his face from men".

② **semblance**: willfully deceptive appearance.

③ **Goodman Gray**: Mr. Gray. "Goodman" is a title of address similar to "Mr."

④ **the Scriptures**: the Bible.

⑤ **the dread Being**: God.

⑥ **the Word**: the Word of God, or the Bible as the revelation of God.

⑦ **the Omniscient**: God.

⑧ **hoarded iniquity**: hidden wickedness.

⑨ **the hoary heads**: the old people.

⑩ **since his settlement**: since he was officially put in his position as a minister.

⑪ **waggery**: mischievous jesting.

⑫ **synod**: a consultative council of clergy.

⑬ **his plighted wife**: his fiancée.

⑭ **Take it not amiss**: Don't take offence at it.

⑮ **"Your words are a mystery"**: "I do not understand what you say".

⑯ **insensibly**: callously.

⑰ **went the rounds**: went round.

⑱ **Governor Belcher**: Jonathan Belcher, Governor of Massachusetts and New Hampshire (1730-1741).

⑲ **Natural connections**: Relatives.

⑳ **turns**: attacks of illness.

㉑ **release**: death.

㉒ **given**: devoted.

㉓ **Suffer us**: allow us.

㉔ **the judgment**: God's final judgment of man.

Questions for Reading Comprehension

1. How does the black veil, when the minister first wears it, affect his parishioners?

2. How does the black veil affect the minister's sermons that Sunday morning?

3. What is the villagers' response to the minister's black veil?

4. What happens in the afternoon when the minister bends over the coffin of a young lady?

5. What happens during the wedding of a handsome couple that night?

6. Why do the deputies fail in their attempt to remove the minister's black veil?

7. Elizabeth thinks that the veil might well be a "symptom of mental disease". What is the specific nature of the disease? What evidence is there to suggest that she might be right?

8. "Among all its bad influences, the black veil had the one desirable effect of making its wearer a very efficient clergyman." Explain what this desirable effect is?

9. Why does the Reverend Mr. Clark persuade Father Hooper to remove his black veil before he dies?

10. When the minister is dying, he says: "I look around me, and, lo! On every visage a Black Veil!!" What does he imply?

Discussion Questions for Appreciation

1. "All through life that piece of crape had hung between him and the world; it had separated from cheerful brotherhood and woman's love, and kept him in that saddest of all prisons, his own heart." What effect does the veil have on Mr. Hooper's life?

2. Mr. Hooper dislikes the black veil himself. His antipathy to the veil is known to be so great that he never willingly passes before a mirror, nor stoops to drink at a still fountain. Why does he persist in wearing it?

3. The black veil is the major symbol in the story. What do you think is its function in the story?

4. Does Hawthorne believe that everyone seems to cover up his innermost "evil" in the way the minister tries to convince his people with his black veil? If he does, do you agree with him?

5. Hawthorne and Emerson are contemporaries and they are both members of the Transcendental Club, but they have different views of man and the world. Discuss the differences between these two writers.

A Question for Writing

Intellectually intrigued by the prospect of evil, Hawthorne's fiction is noted for its pessimistic reflection of a world dominated by Puritanism. Does he recognize a decadence inherent in Puritanism and the oppressing guilt and secrecy to which it inevitably leads?

Henry Wadsworth Longfellow（1807-1882）

Henry Wadsworth Longfellow was born of a well-to-do New England family on February 27, 1807 in Portland, Maine. He attended Bowdoin College in 1822, where one of his classmates was Nathaniel Hawthorne. Longfellow went to Europe to study language, against the wish of his father, who thought that his son should become a lawyer. After four years of study in France, Spain, Italy, Germany, and England, he became so skilled in languages that later he taught a variety of languages and literatures, and even wrote his own language textbooks. In 1836 he became Professor of Modern Languages at Harvard University. He held this position until his retirement in 1854. The last twenty-eight years of his life were spent in writing, studying and travel. As a result of his attachment to languages and his broad knowledge of European literature, and through his work as a teacher, anthologist, and poet, he did much to bring European culture to America.

Longfellow wrote poems on a wide range of subjects, contemporary and historical, and he used many different verse forms and meters with great technical skill. His most famous works, however, are those that bring to life stories from the American past: *Evangeline* (1847), *The Courtship of Miles Standish* (1858), and "Paul Revere'd Ride" (1861). Late in life, grieving over his wife's death, Longfellow translated Dante's *The Divine Comedy*. Throughout his life Longfellow wrote noble and elevated verse built around romanticized characters and heroic sentiments. His versatility and enthusiasm won him a large audience, but, more important, he helped to popularize poetry itself in America.

Longfellow had the gift of easy rhyme. He wrote poetry with natural grace and melody. Read or heard once or twice, his rhyme and meters cling to the mind long after the sense may be forgotten. His poetry expresses a spirit of optimism and faith in the goodness of life which evokes immediate response in the emotions of his readers.

A Psalm of Life

Introduction

"A Psalm of Life" was first published in 1839 and included in Longfellow's first book of poems, *Voices of the Night*. It consists of nine quatrains of alternately rimed trochaic tetrameters. It was very popular when it was published because it fitted the spirit of enterprise and energy of the times.

A Psalm of Life
What The Heart Of The Young Man Said To The Psalmist

Tell me not, in mournful numbers,
Life is but an empty dream! —
For the soul is dead that slumbers,
And things are not what they seem.

Life is real— Life is earnest—
And the grave is not its goal;
Dust thou art, to dust returnest,
Was not spoken of the soul.

Not enjoyment, and not sorrow,
Is our destined end or way;
But to *act*, that each to-morrow
Find us farther than to-day.

Art is long, and time is fleeting,
And our hearts, though stout and brave,
Still, like muffled drums, are beating
Funeral marches to the grave.

In the world's broad field of battle,
In the bivouac of Life,
Be not like dumb, driven cattle!
Be a hero in the strife!

Trust no Future, howe'er pleasant!
Let the dead Past bury its dead!
Act, —act in the living Present!
Heart within, and God o'er head!

Lives of great men all remind us
We can make *our* lives sublime,
And, departing, leave behind us
Footprints on the sands of time;

Footprints, that perhaps another,
Sailing o'er life's solemn main,
A forlorn and shipwreck'd brother,
Seeing, shall take heart again.

Let us, then, be up and doing,
With a heart for any fate;
Still achieving, still pursuing,
Learn to labor and to wait.

Questions for Reading Comprehension

1. Why does the speaker ask the psalmist not to tell him "Life is but an empty dream"?
2. What is the speaker's opinion about life?
3. According to Stanza 3, what is "our destined end or way"?
4. Why is the image of a "field of battle" in stanza 5 appropriate for the presentation of the speaker's view of life?
5. What do we learn from the lives of the great, according to stanza 7?
6. What kind of person is the speaker of this poem?

Discussion Questions for Appreciation

1. How, according to the speaker, can we help future generations?
2. According to the speaker, how should our lives be led to overcome the fact that each day brings us nearer to death?
3. Interpret the metaphor of "Footprints on the sand of time". To what, specifically, might this image refer?
4. In what way does the poem echo Emerson's idea of self-reliance?
5. Is this poem a didactic one? Why or why not?

A Question for Writing

Longfellow wrote "A Psalm of Life" when he was young. Do you think that the poem represents the visions and ideals of a young person?

Herman Melville (1819-1891)

Herman Melville was born in New York City on August 1, 1819. His father was a prosperous merchant, but later he invested unwisely and went bankrupt. His family moved from New York to Albany. He dropped out of school shortly after his father's death and went to work at the age of fifteen in a variety of trades, and then he decided to become a seaman.

In 1839 he signed on a British merchant ship, the *St. Lawrence*, bound for Liverpool and back. This shipboard experience became the basis for his novel *Redburn* (1849). In 1841 he signed on a whaler, the *Acushnet*, which was bound for the South Seas where he gained the information about whaling that he later used in his novel *Moby Dick* (1851). But after nineteen months of hardships Melville jumped ship at Nukuhiva in the Marquesas Islands in 1842. There, Melville was the captive of a cannibal tribe for a month before he escaped aboard an Australian whaler. Later he wrote about these experiences in his novels *Typee* (1846) and *Mardi* (1849). In 1843 he served as seaman, and was discharged in 1844. He married Elizabeth Shaw, daughter of Chief Justice Shaw of Boston in 1847. From 1850 till 1863, he and his wife lived on a farm near Pittsfield, Massachusetts. Later in his life, Melville worked as a Customs Inspector (1866-1885). He died in 1891.

In many ways Melville is a modern novelist. His work is now widely recognized for its rich imagery, its super incantatory prose and its intricate exploration of human psychology. The best known of Melville's novels is *Moby Dick or The Whale*. His major works also include *Typee* (1846), *Billy Budd* (1924), "Bartleby the Scrivener" (1853) and "Benito Cereno" (1855).

Typee is Melville's fictionalized biography based on his experience of living among a primitive tribe when he had deserted the *Acushnet*. The book describes Melville's captivity as being benevolent and the Marquesan "cannibals" as pleasure-loving. The account conveys the irony that a civilized man cannot return to paradise.

Billy Budd, a posthumous novella written during the last years of Melville's life, represents his persistent concern over man's place in a naturally indifferent and hostile world made worse by laws of human society and the industrial revolution. It is psychologically profound, and strikingly modern in its use of narrative strategies that duplicate the themes of the novella.

In Melville's short story "Bartleby the Scrivener: a Story of Wall Street", the central character Bartleby is a clerk in the Dead Letter Office who copies legal documents. His tomblike office against the background of Wall Street represents a world uncongenial to human life. The simple repetition of copying things that are themselves repetition of jargons does not require any creativity. One day Bartleby rebels against this pathetic existence and says "I would prefer not to" any request. Gradually his complacent employer gradually becomes sympathetic with his protest and learns the great commandment to love his fellow man.

Moby Dick

Introduction

The novel, which was published in 1851, is the realistic account of a whaling voyage within which is set a symbolic account of the conflict between man and his fate. Ishmael, the narrator, who finds life on shore grim, decides to go to sea. He signs aboard the whaling ship named *Pequod*. Its captain, Ahab, is a tall, broad man with a white leg, made from the jaw of a sperm whale. His own leg has been torn away by Moby Dick—a huge white whale. After losing his leg, he is determined to pursue the whale and kill it. He hangs a doubloon on the mast as a reward for anyone who sights it first. Eventually the white whale appears, and the *Pequod* begins its fight against it. On the third day, Ahab and his crew manage to harpoon the whale, but it carries the ship along with it to its doom. All on board get drowned except Ishmael, who survives to tell the story.

The following selection is part of Chapter 135 of the novel. On the third day, Starbuck begins to feel panic for helping Ahab, wondering if he does "disobey his God" by doing so. The crew remains tense at the suspense until Ahab finally spies the whale's spout again. Before Ahab sets out on a third attempt against the whale, he tells Starbuck that "some ships sail from their ports and ever afterwards are missing" and the two shake hands. As Ahab leaves, Starbuck calls for him to come back, for he sees sharks, but Ahab cannot hear him. When Ahab and the crew reach Moby Dick, the whale seems "combinedly possessed by all the angels that fell from heaven." Ahab can see the corpse of Fedallah still attached to the whale by the line. Ahab is able to stab the whale with his harpoon, but when Moby Dick writhes in pain, it tips Ahab's boat over. Ahab orders his men to return to the ship as the whale chases them, but it smashes the ship, which begins to sink. In a possible act of suicide, Ahab throws his harpoon, becomes entangled in its line and goes along with it. As the Pequod goes down, Tashtego attempts to nail a flag to the ship, but a sky-hawk is caught in the flag and it goes down with the ship as well.

From ***Moby Dick***

Chapter CXXXV

The Chase—Third Day

The morning of the third day dawned fair and fresh, and once more the solitary night-man at the fore-mast-head was relieved by crowds of the daylight look-outs, who dotted every mast and almost every spar.

"D'ye see him[①]?" cried Ahab; but the whale was not yet in sight.

"In his infallible wake, though; but follow that wake, that's all. Helm there; steady, as thou goest, and hast been going. What a lovely day again! were it a new-made world, and made for a summer-house to the angels, and this morning the first of its throwing open to them, a fairer day could not dawn upon that world. Here's food for thought, had Ahab time to think[②]; but Ahab never thinks; he only feels, feels, feels; *that's* tingling enough for mortal man, to think's audacity. God only has that right and privilege. Thinking is, or ought to be, a coolness and a calmness; and our poor hearts throb, and our poor brains beat too much for that. And yet, I've sometimes thought my brain was very calm—frozen calm[③], this old skull cracks so, like a glass in which the contents turned to ice, and shiver it. And still this hair is growing now; this moment growing, and heat must breed it; but no, it's like that sort of common grass that will grow anywhere, between the earthy clefts of Greenland ice or in Vesuvius lava. How the wild winds blow it; they whip it about me as the torn shreds of split sails lash the tossed ship they cling to. A vile wind that has no doubt blown this through prison corridors and cells, and wards of hospitals, and ventilated them, and now comes blowing hither as innocent as fleeces. Out upon it[④]! —it's tainted. Were I the wind, I'd blow no more on such a wicked, miserable world. I'd crawl somewhere to a cave, and slink there. And yet, 'tis a noble and heroic thing, the wind! who ever conquered it? In every fight it has the last and bitterest blow. Run tilting at it, and you but run through it. Ha! a coward wind that strikes stark naked men, but will not stand to receive a single blow. Even Ahab is a braver thing—a nobler thing than *that*. Would now the wind but had a body; but all the things that most exasperate and outrage mortal man, all these things are bodiless, but only bodiless as objects, not as agents[⑤]. There's a most special, a most cunning, oh, a most malicious difference! And yet, I say again, and swear it now, that there's something all glorious and gracious in the wind. These warm Trade Winds, at least, that in the clear heavens blow straight on, in strong and steadfast, vigorous mildness; and veer not from their mark, however the baser currents of the sea may turn and tack, and mightiest Mississippies of the land[6] swift and swerve about, uncertain where to go at last. And by the eternal Poles! these same Trades that so directly blow my good ship on; these Trades, or something like them—something so unchangeable, and full as strong, blow my keeled soul[7] along! To it[8]! Aloft there! What d'ye see?"

"Nothing, sir. "

"Nothing! and noon at hand! The doubloon goes a-begging! See the sun! Aye, aye, it must be so. I've oversailed him. How, got the start[9]? Aye, he's chasing *me* now; not I, *him*[10]—that's bad; I might have known it, too. Fool! the lines—the harpoons he's towing. Aye, aye, I have run him by last night. About[11]! about! Come down, all of ye, but the regular look outs! Man the braces!"

Steering as she had done, the wind had been somewhat on the Pequod's[12] quarter, so that now being pointed in the reverse direction, the braced ship sailed hard upon the breeze as she rechurned the cream in her own white wake.

"Against the wind he now steers for the open jaw," murmured Starbuck[13] to himself, as he coiled the new-hauled main-brace upon the rail. "God keeps us, but already my bones feel damp within me, and from the inside wet my flesh. I misdoubt me that I disobey my God in obeying him!"

"Stand by to sway me up!" cried Ahab, advancing to the hempen basket. "We should meet him soon. "

"Aye, aye, sir," and straightway Starbuck did Ahab's bidding, and once more Ahab swung on high[14].

143

A whole hour now passed; gold-beaten out to ages[15]. Time itself now held long breaths with keen suspense. But at last, some three points off the weather bow, Ahab descried the spout again, and instantly from the three mast-heads three shrieks went up as if the tongues of fire[16] had voiced it.

"Forehead to forehead I meet thee, this third time, Moby Dick! On deck there! —brace sharper up; crowd her into the wind's eye. He's too far off to lower yet[17], Mr. Starbuck. The sails shake! Stand over that helmsman with a top-maul! So, so; he travels fast, and I must down. But let me have one more good round look aloft here at the sea; there's time for that. An old, old sight, and yet somehow so young; aye, and not changed a wink since I first saw it, a boy, from the sand-hills of Nantucket[18]! The same! —the same! —the same to Noah as to me. There's a soft shower to leeward. Such lovely leewardings! They must lead somewhere—to something else than common land, more palmy than the palms. Leeward! the white whale goes that way; look to windward, then; the better if the bitterer quarter. But good bye, good bye, old mast-head! What's this? —green? aye, tiny mosses in these warped cracks. No such green weather[19] stains on Ahab's head! There's the difference now between man's old age and matter's. But aye, old mast, we both grow old together; sound in our hulls[20], though, are we not, my ship? Aye, minus a leg, that's all. By heaven this dead wood has the better of my live flesh every way. I can't compare with it; and I've known some ships made of dead trees outlast the lives of men made of the most vital stuff of vital fathers. What's that he said? he should still go before me, my pilot[21]; and yet to be seen again? But where? Will I have eyes at the bottom of the sea, supposing I descend those endless stairs? and all night I've been sailing from him, wherever he did sink to. Aye, aye, like many more thou told'st direful truth as touching thyself, O Parsee; but, Ahab, there thy shot fell short. Good-bye, mast-head—keep a good eye upon the whale, the while I'm gone. We'll talk to-morrow, nay, to-night, when the white whale lies down there, tied by head and tail."

He gave the word; and still gazing round him, was steadily lowered through the cloven blue air to the deck.

In due time the boats were lowered; but as standing in his shallop's stern, Ahab just hovered upon the point of the descent, he waved to the mate, —who held one of the tackle-ropes on deck—and bade him pause.

"Starbuck!"

"Sir?"

"For the third time my soul's ship starts upon this voyage, Starbuck."

"Aye, sir, thou wilt have it so."

"Some ships sail from their ports, and ever afterwards are missing, Starbuck!"

"Truth, sir: saddest truth."

"Some men die at ebb tide; some at low water; some at the full of the flood; —and I feel now like a billow that's all one crested comb, Starbuck. I am old; —shake hands with me, man."

Their hands met; their eyes fastened; Starbuck's tears the glue[22].

"Oh, my captain, my captain! —noble heart—go not—go not! —see, it's a brave man that weeps; how great the agony of the persuasion then!"

"Lower away!" —cried Ahab, tossing the mate's arm from him. "Stand by the crew!"

In an instant the boat was pulling round close under the stern.

"The sharks! the sharks!" cried a voice from the low cabin-window there; "O master, my master, come back!"

But Ahab heard nothing; for his own voice was high-lifted then;

and the boat leaped on.

Yet the voice spake true; for scarce had he pushed from the ship, when numbers of sharks, seemingly rising from out the dark waters beneath the hull, maliciously snapped at the blades of the oars, every time they dipped in the water; and in this way accompanied the boat with their bites. It is a thing not uncommonly happening to the whale-boats in those swarming seas; the sharks at times apparently following them in the same prescient way that vultures hover over the banners of marching regiments in the east. But these were the first sharks that had been observed by the Pequod since the White Whale had been first descried; and whether it was that Ahab's crew were all such tiger-yellow barbarians, and therefore their flesh more musky to the senses of the sharks—a matter sometimes well known to affect them, —however it was, they seemed to follow that one boat without molesting the others.

"Heart of wrought steel!" murmured Starbuck gazing over the side, and following with his eyes the receding boat— "canst thou yet ring boldly to that sight? —lowering thy keel among ravening sharks, and followed by them, open-mouthed to the chase; and this the critical third day? —For when three days flow together in one continuous intense pursuit; be sure the first is the morning, the second the noon, and the third the evening and the end of that thing—be that end what it may. Oh! my God! what is this that shoots through me, and leaves me so deadly calm, yet expectant, —fixed at the top of a shudder! Future things swim before me, as in empty outlines and skeletons; all the past is somehow grown dim. Mary, girl! thou fadest in pale glories behind me; boy! I seem to see but thy eyes grown wondrous blue. Strangest problems of life seem clearing; but clouds sweep between—Is my journey's end coming[23]? My legs feel faint; like his who has footed it all day[24]. Feel thy heart, —beats it yet? Stir thyself, Starbuck! —stave it off[25]— move, move! speak aloud! —Mast-head there! See ye my boy's hand on the hill? —Crazed; —aloft there! —keep thy keenest eye upon the boats: —mark well the whale! —Ho! again! —drive off that hawk! see! he pecks—he tears the vane"—pointing to the red flag flying at the main-truck— "Ha! he soars away with it! —Where's the old man now? see'st thou that sight, oh Ahab! —shudder, shudder!"

The boats had not gone very far, when by a signal from the mast-heads—a downward pointed arm, Ahab knew that the whale had sounded; but intending to be near him at the next rising, he held on his way a little sideways from the vessel[26]; the becharmed crew maintaining the profoundest silence, as the head-beat waves hammered and hammered against the opposing bow.

"Drive, drive in your nails, oh ye waves! to their uttermost heads[27] drive them in! ye but strike a thing without a lid; and no coffin and no hearse can be mine: —and hemp only can kill me! Ha! ha!"

Suddenly the waters around them slowly swelled in broad circles; then quickly upheaved, as if sideways sliding from a submerged berg of ice, swiftly rising to the surface. A low rumbling sound was heard; a subterraneous hum; and then all held their breaths; as bedraggled with trailing ropes, and harpoons, and lances, a vast form shot lengthwise, but obliquely from the sea. Shrouded in a thin drooping veil of mist, it hovered for a moment in the rainbowed air; and then fell swamping back into the deep. Crushed thirty feet upwards, the waters flashed for an instant like heaps of fountains, then brokenly sank in a shower of flakes, leaving the circling surface creamed like new milk round the marble trunk of the whale.

"Give way!" cried Ahab to the oarsmen, and the boats darted forward to the attack; but maddened by yesterday's fresh irons that corroded in him, Moby Dick seemed combinedly possessed by all the angels that fell from heaven. The wide tiers of welded tendons overspreading his broad white forehead, beneath the transparent skin, looked knitted together; as head on, he came churning his tail among the boats; and once more flailed them apart; spilling out the irons and lances from the two mates' boats, and dashing in one side of the upper part of their bows, but leaving Ahab's almost without a scar.

While Daggoo and Queequeg were stopping the strained planks; and as the whale swimming out from them, turned, and showed one entire flank as he shot by them again; at that moment a quick cry went up. Lashed round and round to the fish's back; pinioned in the turns upon turns in which, during the past night, the whale had reeled the involutions of the lines around him, the half torn body of the Parsee was seen[28]; his sable raiment frayed to shreds; his distended eyes turned full upon old Ahab.

The harpoon dropped from his hand.

"Befooled, befooled!"—drawing in a long lean breath—"Aye, Parsee! I see thee again.—Aye, and thou goest before; and this, *this* then is the hearse that thou didst promise[29]. But I hold thee to the last letter of thy word. Where is the second hearse? Away, mates, to the ship! those boats are useless now; repair them if ye can in time, and return to me; if not, Ahab is enough to die—Down, men! the first thing that but offers to jump from this boat I stand in, that thing I harpoon. Ye are not other men, but my arms and my legs; and so obey me.—Where's the whale? gone down again?"

But he looked too nigh the boat; for as if bent upon escaping with the corpse he bore, and as if the particular place of the last encounter had been but a stage in his leeward voyage, Moby Dick was now again steadily swimming forward; and had almost passed the ship,—which thus far had been sailing in the contrary direction to him, though for the present her headway had been stopped. He seemed swimming with his utmost velocity, and now only intent upon pursuing his own straight path in the sea.

"Oh! Ahab," cried Starbuck, "not too late is it, even now, the third day, to desist. See! Moby Dick seeks thee not. It is thou, thou, that madly seekest him!"

Setting sail to the rising wind, the lonely boat was swiftly impelled to leeward, by both oars and canvas. And at last when Ahab was sliding by the vessel, so near as plainly to distinguish Starbuck's face as he leaned over the rail, he hailed him to turn the vessel about, and follow him, not too swiftly, at a judicious interval. Glancing upwards, he saw Tashtego, Queequeg, and Daggoo, eagerly mounting to the three mast-heads; while the oarsmen were rocking in the two staved boats which had but just been hoisted to the side, and were busily at work in repairing them. One after the other, through the port-holes, as he sped, he also caught flying glimpses of Stubb and Flask, busying themselves on deck among bundles of new irons and lances. As he saw all this; as he heard the hammers in the broken boats; far other[30] hammers seemed driving a nail into his heart. But he rallied. And now marking that the vane or flag was gone from the main-mast-head, he shouted to Tashtego, who had just gained that perch, to descend again for another flag, and a hammer and nails, and so nail it to the mast.

Whether fagged by the three days' running chase, and the resistance to his swimming in the knotted hamper he bore; or whether it was some latent deceitfulness and malice in him: whichever was true, the White Whale's way now began to abate, as it seemed, from the boat so rapidly nearing him once more; though indeed the whale's last start had not been so long a one as before. And still as Ahab glided over the waves the unpitying sharks accompanied him; and so pertinaciously stuck to the boat; and so continually bit at the plying oars, that the blades became jagged and crunched, and left small splinters in the sea, at almost every dip.

"Heed them not! those teeth but give new rowlocks to your oars.

Pull on! 'tis the better rest[31], the shark's jaw than the yielding water. "

"But at every bite, sir, the thin blades grow smaller and smaller!"

"They will last long enough! pull on! —But who can tell" —he muttered— "whether these sharks swim to feast on the whale or on Ahab[32]? —But pull on! Aye, all alive, now—we near him. The helm! take the helm! let me pass," —and so saying two of the oarsmen helped him forward to the bows of the still flying boat.

At length as the craft was cast to one side, and ran ranging along with the White Whale's flank, he seemed strangely oblivious of its advance—as the whale sometimes will—and Ahab was fairly within the smoky mountain mist, which, thrown off from the whale's spout, curled round his great, Monadnock[33] hump; he was even thus close to him; when, with body arched back, and both arms lengthwise high-lifted to the poise, he darted his fierce iron, and his far fiercer curse into the hated whale. As both steel and curse sank to the socket, as if sucked into a morass, Moby Dick sideways writhed; spasmodically rolled his nigh flank against the bow, and, without staving a hole in it, so suddenly canted the boat over, that had it not been for the elevated part of the gunwale to which he then clung, Ahab would once more have been tossed into the sea. As it was, three of the oarsmen—who foreknew not the precise instant of the dart, and were therefore unprepared for its effects—these were flung out; but so fell, that, in an instant two of them clutched the gunwale again, and rising to its level on a combing wave, hurled themselves bodily inboard again; the third man helplessly dropping astern, but still afloat and swimming.

Almost simultaneously, with a mighty volition of ungraduated, instantaneous swiftness, the White Whale darted through the weltering sea. But when Ahab cried out to the steersman to take new turns with the line, and hold it so; and commanded the crew to turn round on their seats, and tow the boat up to the mark; the moment the treacherous line felt that double strain and tug, it snapped in the empty air!

"What breaks in me? Some sinew cracks! —'tis whole again; oars! oars! Burst in upon him!"

Hearing the tremendous rush of the sea-crashing boat, the whale wheeled round to present his blank forehead at bay; but in that evolution[34], catching sight of the nearing black hull of the ship; seemingly seeing in it the source of all his persecutions; bethinking it—it may be— a larger and nobler foe; of a sudden, he bore down upon its advancing prow, smiting his jaws amid fiery showers of foam.

Ahab staggered; his hand smote his forehead. "I grow blind; hands! stretch out before me that I may yet grope my way. Is't night?"

"The whale! The ship!" cried the cringing oarsmen.

"Oars! oars! Slope downwards to thy depths, O sea, that ere it be for ever too late, Ahab may slide this last, last time upon his mark! I see: the ship! the ship! Dash on, my men! Will ye not save my ship?"

But as the oarsmen violently forced their boat through the sledge-hammering seas, the before whale-smitten bow-ends of two planks burst through, and in an instant almost, the temporarily disabled boat lay nearly level with the waves; its half-wading, splashing crew, trying hard to stop the gap and bale out the pouring water.

Meantime, for that one beholding instant, Tashtego's mast-head hammer remained suspended in his hand; and the red flag, half-wrapping him as with a plaid, then streamed itself straight out from him, as his own forward-flowing heart; while Starbuck and Stubb, standing upon the bowsprit beneath, caught sight of the down-coming monster just as soon as he.

"The whale, the whale! Up helm, up helm! Oh, all ye sweet powers of air, now hug me close! Let not Starbuck die, if die he must, in a woman's fainting fit. Up helm, I say—ye fools, the jaw! the jaw! Is this the end of all my bursting prayers? all my life-long fidelities? Oh, Ahab,

Ahab, lo, thy work[35]. Steady! helmsman, steady. Nay, nay! Up helm again! He turns to meet us! Oh, his unappeasable brow drives on towards one, whose duty tells him he cannot depart. My God, stand by me now!"

"Stand not by me, but stand under me, whoever you are that will now help Stubb; for Stubb, too, sticks here. I grin at thee, thou grinning whale! Who ever helped Stubb, or kept Stubb awake, but Stubb's own unwinking eye? And now poor Stubb goes to bed upon a mattress[36] that is all too soft; would it were stuffed with brushwood! I grin at thee, thou grinning whale! Look ye, sun, moon, and stars! I call ye assassins of as good a fellow as ever spouted up his ghost[37]. For all that, I would yet ring glasses with ye[38], would ye but hand the cup! Oh, oh! oh, oh! thou grinning whale, but there'll be plenty of gulping soon! Why fly ye not[39], O Ahab! For me, off shoes and jacket to it; let Stubb die in his drawers! A most mouldy and over salted death, though; —cherries! cherries! cherries! Oh, Flask, for one red cherry ere we die!"

"Cherries? I only wish that we were where they grow. Oh, Stubb, I hope my poor mother's drawn my part-pay ere this; if not, few coppers will now come to her, for the voyage is up."

From the ship's bows, nearly all the seamen now hung inactive; hammers, bits of plank, lances, and harpoons, mechanically retained in their hands, just as they had darted from their various employments; all their enchanted eyes intent upon the whale, which from side to side strangely vibrating his predestinating head, sent a broad band of overspreading semicircular foam before him as he rushed. Retribution, swift vengeance, eternal malice were in his whole aspect, and spite of all that mortal man could do, the solid white buttress of his forehead smote the ship's starboard bow, till men and timbers reeled. Some fell flat upon their faces. Like dislodged trucks, the heads of the harpooners aloft shook on their bull-like necks. Through the breach, they heard the waters pour, as mountain torrents down a flume.

"The ship! The hearse! —the second hearse!" cried Ahab from the boat; "its wood could only be American!"

Diving beneath the settling ship[40], the whale ran quivering along its keel; but turning under water, swiftly shot to the surface again, far off the other bow, but within a few yards of Ahab's boat, where, for a time, he lay quiescent.

"I turn my body from the sun. What ho, Tashtego! let me hear thy hammer. Oh! ye three unsurrendered spires of mine; thou uncracked keel; and only god-bullied hull; thou firm deck, and haughty helm, and Pole-pointed prow, —death-glorious ship! must ye then perish, and without me? Am I cut off from the last fond pride of meanest shipwrecked captains? Oh, lonely death on lonely life! Oh, now I feel my topmost greatness lies in my topmost grief. Ho, ho! from all your furthest bounds, pour ye now in, ye bold billows of my whole foregone life, and top this one piled comber of my death! Towards thee I roll, thou all-destroying but unconquering whale; to the last I grapple with thee; from hell's heart I stab at thee; for hate's sake I spit my last breath at thee. Sink all coffins and all hearses to one common pool! and since neither can be mine, let me then tow to pieces[41], while still chasing thee, though tied to thee, thou damned whale! *Thus*, I give up the spear!"

The harpoon was darted; the stricken whale flew forward; with igniting velocity the line ran through the grooves; —ran foul. Ahab stooped to clear it; he did clear it; but the flying turn caught him round the neck, and voicelessly as Turkish mutes bowstring their victim, he was shot out of the boat, ere the crew knew he was gone. Next instant, the heavy eye-splice in the rope's final end flew out of the stark-empty tub, knocked down an oarsman, and smiting the sea, disappeared in its depths.

For an instant, the tranced boat's crew stood still; then turned.

"The ship? Great God, where is the ship?" Soon they through dim, bewildering mediums saw her sidelong fading phantom, as in the gaseous Fata Morgana; only the uppermost masts out of water; while fixed by infatuation, or fidelity, or fate, to their once lofty perches, the pagan harpooners[42] still maintained their sinking lookouts on the sea. And now, concentric circles seized the lone boat itself, and all its crew, and each floating oar, and every lance-pole, and spinning, animate and inanimate, all round and round in one vortex, carried the smallest chip of the Pequod out of sight.

But as the last whelmings intermixingly poured themselves over the sunken head of the Indian[43] at the mainmast, leaving a few inches of the erect spar yet visible, together with long streaming yards of the flag, which calmly undulated, with ironical coincidings, over the destroying billows they almost touched; —at that instant, a red arm and a hammer hovered backwardly uplifted in the open air, in the act of nailing the flag faster and yet faster to the subsiding spar. A sky-hawk that tauntingly had followed the main-truck downwards from its natural home among the stars, pecking at the flag, and incommoding Tashtego there; this bird now chanced to intercept its broad fluttering wing between the hammer and the wood; and simultaneously feeling that etherial thrill, the submerged savage beneath, in his death-gasp, kept his hammer frozen there; and so the bird of heaven, with archangelic shrieks, and his imperial beak thrust upwards, and his whole captive form folded in the flag of Ahab, went down with his ship, which, like Satan, would not sink to hell till she had dragged a living part of heaven along with her, and helmeted herself with it.

Now small fowls flew screaming over the yet yawning gulf; a sullen white surf beat against its steep sides; then all collapsed, and the great shroud of the sea rolled on as it rolled five thousand years ago.

Notes

① **D'ye see him**？：Do you see him? Him refers to the white whale Moby Dick.

② **Here's food... to think**：Food refers to what Ahab might think about in his spare time.

③ **frozen calm**：clear mind.

④ **Out upon it**：Out upon you.

⑤ **agents**：opposite to objects, supernatural power.

⑥ **mightiest Mississippies of the land**：rivers like Mississippi.

⑦ **my keeled soul**：my ship.

⑧ **To it**：Bring the ship to it. It refers to the wind.

⑨ **How, got the start**：How did we get the start?

⑩ **not I, _him_**：not I'm chasing him. Him refers to the white whale Moby Dicky.

⑪ **About**：Turn over.

⑫ **Pequod**：name of the whaler.

⑬ **Starbuck**：the first mate of the Pequod.

⑭ **Ahab swung on high**：Ahab was swung on high.

⑮ **gold-beaten out to ages**：(the whole hour) was gold-beaten out to ages.

⑯ **the tongues of fire**：their voices are as fast as the tongues of fire.

⑰ **He's too far off to lower yet**：He refers to the white whale.

⑱ **Nantucket**：an island in the southeast of Massachusetts, which was famous for its whaling industry at that time. In the novel, it is the hometown of Ahab.

⑲ **green weather**：green moss.

⑳ **sound in our hulls**：Both of us are strong and healthy. Ahab assimilates his body to the hulls of a ship.

㉑ **Pilot**：Fedallah, one of the sailors Ahab took aboard in private. He is a mysterious prophet by Ahab's sides.

㉒ **Starbuck's tears the glue**: Starbuk's tears were like glue, which attracts Ahab's attention.

㉓ **Is my journey's end coming**: "Journey" is a pun, referring to the journey of the whaler and to his own life journey.

㉔ **like his who has footed it all day**: like the legs of those who have walked all day.

㉕ **stave it off**: ward off. It refers to the death.

㉖ **vessel**: the whaler *Pequod*.

㉗ **heads**: the heads of nails.

㉘ **the half torn body... was seen**: The Parsee refers to Fedallah.

㉙ *this* **then is the hearse that thou didst promise**: This refers to the body of the white whale.

㉚ **far other**: many other.

㉛ **'tis the better rest**: It is the better death.

㉜ **feast on the whale or on Ahab**: Feast is a metaphor here. The shark could have either Ahab or the whale as a feast, no matter who wins the fight.

㉝ **Monadnock**: A hill in the southwest of New Hemisphere. Here it refers to the huge back of the white whale.

㉞ **evolution**: revolution, which means turning around.

㉟ **lo, thy work**: look, what you have done!: "Work" refers to the dangerous situation which was caused by Ahab's vengeful mentality.

㊱ **mattress**: sea.

㊲ **spouted up his ghost**: gave up his ghost, died.

㊳ **ring glasses with ye**: "Ye" refers to the sun, the moon and stars.

㊴ **Why fly ye not**: Why don't you escape?

㊵ **the settling ship**: the sinking ship.

㊶ **let me then tow to pieces**: let me be towed to pieces.

㊷ **the pagan harpooners**: the three harpooners who don't believe in

Christianity.

㊸ **the Indian**: Stubb's harpooner.

Questions for Reading Comprehension

1. Describe Ahab's physical appearance and discuss how this adds to the readers' impression of the character.
2. What kind of man is Ahab?
3. Why does Ahab want to kill the White Whale?
4. Do you think circumstances conspire against Ahab?
5. Why is the ship compared to Satan?

Discussion Questions for Appreciation

1. What do you think of the character Ahab?
2. What is Fedallah's role in the novel?
3. What does the white whale Moby Dick symbolize?
4. What is the symbolic significance of Ahab's fight against Moby Dick?
5. How is the concept of fate used to organize the narrative?

A Question for Writing

What themes does Melville explore in his novel *Moby Dick*?

Walt Whitman（1819-1892）

Walt Whitman was born on Long Island, New York, into a Quaker family. His father was a politically radical farmer and carpenter. The family moved to Brooklyn in 1822. Whitman did not have much formal education, but he taught himself by reading and writing and by learning from life. He left school at the age of eleven; and worked his way from office boy to editor of a New York newspaper, *The Brooklyn Eagle.* In 1844, a political disagreement with his publisher led him to leave his job. Later, he taught in country schools. In 1855 he published at his own expenses the first edition of *Leaves of Grass* which contained only twelve poems. In 1862, Whitman went to Virginia in order to nurse his brother George, who was wounded in combat. He also worked with the wounded in camp hospitals during the Civil War. After the war, Whitman got a position working as a clerk in the Department of Interior, but was dismissed on charges that *Leaves of Grass* was an immoral volume. He was then hired in the Attorney General's office. He worked there till 1873 when the death of his mother triggered his paralysis. He lived his final decades in increasing poor health but with growing fame as he produced larger and larger versions of his *Leaves of Grass.*

One of Whitman's contributions to American literature is his use of free verse, which has no regular meter, rhythm, or line length. He creates a rhythm that depends on natural speech rhythms. He develops an original poetic style, which is devoid of conventional rhyme and meter. He writes long lines which flow with a pulsing energy. The great majority of his poems depend on parallelism and other reiterative devices for its structure and cadence. His diction is frank, sensuous, and sibilant.

Whitman was one of the most original and inspiring American poets of the nineteenth century and a central influence on the direction of modern poetry. Today he is remembered chiefly for his one great book *Leaves of Grass*. There are more than 400 poems in the book, which was published in his lifetime in nine expanded and re-arranged editions (from 1855 to 1892). Its themes are multiple. Whitman's rich experiences and his insights enabled him to probe into many fields of social life, and the various philosophies that he was acquainted with. Whitman expresses in his book his democratic ideas. Besides, his sings of science, labor, and nature. He establishes his democratic outlook on the basis of his love and admiration for, and his faith in, the common people.

"Song of Myself" is considered the most significant poem of the volume, and a repertory of Whitman's thought. From a blade of "curling grass" he sees into the mystery of death and birth. Whitman extols the ideals of democracy and equality and celebrates the dignity, and the joy of the common man. The poem reveals a world without rank and hierarchy, illustrating the principle of democracy and equality. Hence "Song of Myself" is really a song of everybody, especially a song of the common man.

When I Heard the Learn'd Astronomer

Introduction

"When I Heard the Learn'd Astronomer" was first published in 1865. It falls visually into one unit but we can see that it can actually be divided into two units. The first unit describes what the speaker hears in the lecture room while the second is about the reaction he has. So the relationship between these two units is, in a sense, one of cause and effect.

When I Heard the Learn'd Astronomer

When I heard the learn'd astronomer,

When the proofs, the figures, were ranged in columns before me,

When I was shown the charts, the diagrams, to add, divide, and measure them,

When I sitting heard the learned astronomer where he lectured with much applause in the lecture room,

How soon unaccountable I became tired and sick,

Till rising and gliding out I wander'd off by myself,

In the mystical moist night-air, and from time to time,

Look'd up in perfect silence at the stars.

Questions for Reading Comprehension

1. What aids does the astronomer use during his lecture?
2. What does the speaker feel about the lecture as he listens?
3. Where does the speaker go when he wanders off?
4. What does the speaker do after he leaves the lecture room?
5. What is the difference between the astronomer and the speaker?

Discussion Questions for Appreciation

1. What wisdom does the speaker find that the astronomer and his audience do not have?
2. What is the rhythmic pattern of the poem? What does this pattern imply?
3. What poetic devices are employed in this poem? And what is the effect?
4. What does this poem have in common with Romantic or Transcendentalist poetry that you have read? In what way is it different?

Cavalry Crossing a Ford

Introduction

"Cavalry Crossing a Ford" is one of Whitman's famous Civil War poems. It was first published in 1865. In some way it resembles the poetry of the Imagists. It presents such a striking central image that it is like a realistic painting.

Cavalry Crossing a Ford

A line in long array where they wind betwixt green islands,

They take a serpentine course, their arms flash in the sun—hark to the musical clank,

Behold the silvery river, in it the splashing horses loitering stop to drink,

Behold the brown-faced men, each group, each person a picture, the negligent rest on the saddles,

Some emerge on the opposite bank, others are just entering the ford—while,

Scarlet and blue and snowy white,

The guidon flags flutter gayly in the wind.

Questions for Reading Comprehension

1. What is the central image in the poem?
2. What are the four parts of the image?
3. What adjectives does the poet use to paint this verse picture?
4. What do lines 3 and 4 imply?
5. Do the soldiers really care about the war?

Discussion Questions for Appreciation

1. What functions does the central image perform in the poem?

2. What atmosphere does the poem create?

3. What is the poet's attitude toward the war?

4. Comment on the poet's attitude toward the war.

Come Up from the Fields, Father

Introduction

"Come Up from the Fields, Father" is another Civil War poem. It does not present us with a scene of the war. Instead, it tells us about the death of a soldier who has died in a battle and more importantly, about the shattering effect of the thought of his death has on his family, especially his mother.

Come Up from the Fields, Father

1

Come up from the fields, father, here's a letter from our Pete;

And come to the front door, mother—here's a letter from thy dear son.

2

Lo, 'tis autumn;

Lo, where the trees, deeper green, yellower and redder,

Cool and sweeten Ohio's villages, with leaves fluttering in the moderate wind;

Where apples ripe in the orchards hang, and grapes on the trellis'd vines;

(Smell you the smell of the grapes on the vines?

Smell you the buckwheat, where the bees were lately buzzing?)

Above all, lo, the sky, so calm, so transparent after the rain, and with wondrous clouds;

Below, too, all calm, all vital and beautiful—and the farm prospers well.

3

Down in the fields all prospers well;

But now from the fields come, father—come at the daughter's call;

And come to the entry, mother—to the front door come, right away.

Fast as she can she hurries—something ominous—her steps trembling;

She does not tarry to smooth her hair, nor adjust her cap.

Open the envelope quickly;

O this is not our son's writing, yet his name is sign'd;

O a strange hand writes for our dear son—O stricken mother's soul!

All swims before her eyes—flashes with black—she catches the main words only;

Sentences broken— "gun-shot wound in the breast, cavalry skirmish, taken to hospital,

At present low, but will soon be better. "

4

Ah, now, the single figure to me,

Amid all teeming and wealthy Ohio, with all its cities and farms,

Sickly white in the face, and dull in the head, very faint,

By the jamb of a door leans.

"Grieve not so, dear mother" , (the just-grown daughter speaks through her sobs;

The little sisters huddle around, speechless and dismay'd;)

"See, dearest mother, the letter says Pete will soon be better. "

5

Alas, poor boy, he will never be better, (nor may-be needs to be better, that brave and simple soul;)
While they stand at home at the door, he is dead already;
The only son is dead.

But the mother needs to be better;
She, with thin form, presently drest in black;
By day her meals untouch'd—then at night fitfully sleeping, often waking,
In the midnight waking, weeping, longing with one deep longing,
O that she might withdraw unnoticed—silent from life, escape and withdraw,
To follow, to seek, to be with her dear dead son.

Questions for Reading Comprehension

1. Who receives the letter and calls the father and mother to the front door?
2. What is the mother's reaction to receiving the letter?
3. What has happened to the son?
4. Why does the poet describe the prosperous farm in Ohio?
5. What is the effect of the news on the mother?

Discussion Questions for Appreciation

1. What contrast does the poem build?
2. What is its effect of this contrast on the reader?
3. What idea does the poem present?
4. Why does the poet use the word "better" three times in the poem?

Out of the Cradle Endlessly Rocking

Introduction

This poem was first published as a Child's Reminiscence in the New York Saturday Press in 1859 and incorporated in 1860 into the third edition of *Leaves of Grass* as "A Word Out of the Sea", and was given the title in 1871. It describes what happens when a boy in Long Island steals out of his home one night and listens to the calls of two mocking birds by the sea.

Out of the Cradle Endlessly Rocking

Out of the cradle endlessly rocking

Out of the mocking-bird's throat, the musical shuttle,

Out of the Ninth-month midnight,

Over the sterile sands and the fields beyond, where the child leaving his bed wander'd alone,

bareheaded, barefoot

Down from the shower'd halo,

Up from the mystic play of shadows twining and twisting as if they were alive,

Out from the patches of briers and blackberries,

From the memories of the bird that chanted to me,

From your memories sad brother, from the fitful risings and fallings I heard,

From under that yellow half-moon late-risen and swollen as if with tears,

From those beginning notes of yearning and love there in the mist,

From the thousand responses of my heart never to cease,

From the myriad thence-arous'd words,

From the word stronger and more delicious than any,

From such as now they start the scene revisiting,
As a flock, twittering, rising, or overhead passing,
Borne hither, ere all eludes me, hurriedly,
A man, yet by these tears a little boy again,
Throwing myself on the sand, confronting the waves,
I, chanter of pains and joys, uniter of here and hereafter,
Taking all hints to use them, but swiftly leaping beyond them,
A reminiscence sing.

Once Paumanok[①],
When the lilac-scent was in the air and Fifth-month grass was growing,
Up this seashore in some briers,
Two feather'd guests[②] from Alabama, two together,
And their nest, and four light-green eggs spotted with brown,
And every day the he-bird to and fro near at hand,
And every day the she-bird crouch'd on her nest, silent, with bright eyes,
And every day I, a curious boy, never too close, never disturbing them,
Cautiously peering, absorbing, translating.

Shine! shine! shine!
Pour down your warmth, great sun!
While we bask, we two together.

Two together!
Winds blow south, or winds blow north,
Day come white, or night come black,
Home, or rivers and mountains from home,
Singing all time, minding no time,
While we two keep together.

Till of a sudden,
May-be kill'd, unknown to her mate,
One forenoon the she-bird crouch'd not on the nest,
Nor return'd that afternoon, nor the next,
Nor ever appear'd again.

And thenceforward all summer in the sound of the sea,
And at night under the full of the moon in calmer weather,
Over the hoarse surging of the sea,
Or flitting from brier to brier by day
I saw, I heard at intervals the remaining one, the he-bird,
The solitary guest from Alabama.

Blow! blow! blow!
Plow up sea-winds along Paumanok's shore;
I wait and I wait till you blow my mate to me.

Yes, when the stars glisten'd,
All night long on the prong of a moss-scallop'd stake,
Down almost amid the slapping waves,
Sat the lone singer wonderful causing tears.

He call'd on his mate
He pour'd forth the meanings which I of all men know.
Yes my brother I know,
The rest might not, but I have treasur'd every note
For more than once dimly down to the beach gliding
Silent, avoiding the moonbeams, blending myself with the shadow
Recalling now the obscure shapes, the echoes, the sounds and sights af-

ter their sorts
The white arms out in the breakers tirelessly tossing
I, with bare feet, a child, the wind wafting my hair
Listen'd long and long.

Listen'd to keep, to sing, now translating the notes
Following you my brother

Soothe! soothe! soothe!
Close on its wave soothes the wave behind,
And again another behind embracing and lapping, every one close,
But my love soothes not me, not me.

Low hangs the moon, it rose late,
It is lagging—I think it is heavy with love, with love.

O madly the sea pushes upon the land,
With love, with love.

O night! do I not see my love fluttering out among the breakers?
What is that little black thing I see there in the white?

Loud! loud! loud!
Loud I call to you, my love!
High and clear I shoot my voice over the waves,
Surely you must know who is here, is here,
You must know who I am, my love.

Low-hanging moon!
What is that dusky spot in your brown yellow?

O it is the shape, the shape of my mate!
O moon do not keep her from me any longer.

Land! land! O land!
Whichever way I turn, O I think you could give me my mate back again if
you only would,
For I am almost sure I see her dimly whichever way I look.

O rising stars!
Perhaps the one I want so much will rise, will rise with some of you.

O throat! O trembling throat!
Sound clearer through the atmosphere!
Pierce the woods, the earth,
Somewhere listening to catch you must be the one I want.

Shake out carols!
Solitary here, the night's carols!
Carols of lonesome love! death's carols!
Carols under that lagging, yellow, waning moon!
O under that moon where she droops almost down into the sea!
O reckless despairing carols.
But soft! sink low!
Soft! let me just murmur,
And do you wait a moment you husky-nois'd sea,
For somewhere I believe I heard my mate responding to me,
So faint, I must be still, be still to listen,
But not altogether still, for then she might not come immediately to me.

Hither my love!

Here I am! here!
With this just-sustain'd note I announce myself to you,
This gentle call is for you my love, for you.

Do not be decoy'd elsewhere,
That is the whistle of the wind, it is not my voice,
That is the fluttering, the fluttering of the spray,
Those are the shadows of leaves.

O darkness! O in vain!
O I am very sick and sorrowful.

O brown halo in the sky near the moon, drooping upon the sea!
O troubled reflection in the sea!
O throat! O throbbing heart!
And I singing uselessly, uselessly all the night.

O past! O happy life! O songs of joy!
In the air, in the woods, over fields,
Loved! loved! loved! loved! loved!
But my mate no more, no more with me!
We two together no more.

The aria sinking,
All else continuing, the stars shining,
The winds blowing, the notes of the bird continuous echoing,
With angry moans the fierce old mother incessantly moaning,
On the sands of Paumanok's shore gray and rustling,
The yellow half-moon enlarged, sagging down, drooping, the face of the
sea almost touching,

The boy ecstatic, with his bare feet the waves, with his hair the atmosphere dallying,

The love in the heart long pent, now loose, now at last tumultuously bursting,

The aria's meaning, the ears, the soul, swiftly depositing,

The strange tears down the cheeks coursing,

The colloquy there, the trio, each uttering,

The undertone, the savage old mother incessantly crying,

To the boy's soul's questions sullenly timing, some drown'd secret hissing,

To the outsetting bard.

Demon or bird! (said the boy's soul,)

Is it indeed toward your mate you sing? or is it really to me?

For I, that was a child, my tongue's use sleeping, now I have heard you,

Now in a moment I know what I am for, I awake,

And already a thousand singers, a thousand songs, clearer, louder and more sorrowful than yours,

A thousand warbling echoes have started to life within me, never to die.

O you singer solitary, singing by yourself, projecting me,

O solitary me listening, never more shall I cease perpetuating you,

Never more shall I escape, never more the reverberations,

Never more the cries of unsatisfied love be absent from me,

Never again leave me to be the peaceful child I was before what there in the night,

By the sea under the yellow and sagging moon,

The messenger there arous'd, the fire, the sweet hell within,

The unknown want, the destiny of me.

O give me the clew! (it lurks in the night here somewhere,)
O if I am to have so much, let me have more!

A word then, (for I will conquer it,)
The word final, superior to all,
Subtle, sent up—what is it? —I listen—
Are you whispering it, and have been all the time, you sea waves?
Is that it from your liquid rims and wet sands?

Whereto answering, the sea,
Delaying not, hurrying not,
Whisper'd me through the night, and very plainly before daybreak,
Lisp'd to me the low and delicious word death,
And again death, death, death, death,
Hissing melodious, neither like the bird nor like my arous'd child's heart,
But edging near as privately for me rustling at my feet,
Creeping thence steadily up to my ears and laving me softly all over,
Death, death, death, death, death.

Which I do not forget,
But fuse the song of my dusky demon and brother,
That he sang to me in the moonlight on Paumanok's gray beach,
With the thousand responsive songs at random,
My own songs awaked from that hour,
And with them the key, the word up from the waves,
The word of the sweetest song and all songs,
That strong and delicious word which, creeping to my feet,
(Or like some old crone rocking the cradle, swathed in sweet garments,
bending aside,)

The sea whisper'd me.

Notes
① **Paumanok**：Long Island.
② **Two feather'd guests**：two birds.

Questions for Reading Comprehension

1. What is the effect of the use of the repeated preposition such as out, over, down, up, from?
2. Describe the plot line of this poem.
3. What happens to the two birds in the poem?
4. What does the sea symbolize?
5. What does the sea show the boy?

Discussion Questions for Appreciation

1. How does this poem link Whitman to the Romantics?
2. Describe Whitman's account of his development as a poet.
3. What is Whitman's attitude toward "death"?
4. Why does the speaker say "My own songs awaked from that hour"?

A Question for Writing

What is uniquely American about Whitman's poetry? Consider both his theme and style.

Emily Dickinson（1830-1886）

Emily Dickinson was born in Amherst, Massachusetts, on December 10, 1830. Her family was well-known for educational and political activity. Her father, an orthodox Calvinist, was a lawyer and businessman and also served in Congress. Her grandfather was one of the founders of the Amherst College, from which she graduated. Then she attended the Mount Holyoke Female Seminary in South Hadley, and visited Boston, Washington, and Philadelphia when she was young. As she grew older, she communicated with fewer and fewer people. She was described during her adolescent years as a shy, demure, neatly dressed young woman. She led a seemingly uneventful life, but her neighbors knew that there was something extraordinary about this radiant yet isolated woman. At the age of fifty-six Dickinson died in the house in which she had been born.

Dickinson was never married. However, she cultivated intense intellectual companionships with several men in succession. Benjamin F. Newton, who encouraged her to write poems, improved her literary and cultural tastes and influenced her ideas on religion. Charles Wadsworth, who was a married minister, provided her with intellectual challenge and contact with the outside world. Thomas Higginson (1823-1911), an intelligent and sympathetic critic, gave Dickinson his comment and advice on her poems.

Dickinson wrote many poems, but did not intend to publish them. Only seven of her poems were published in the newspapers during her lifetime. Yet after her death people found in her home many small packages of her poems. Some of the poems had been carefully revised and neatly tied with ribbons; others had been scrawled on scraps of paper. In all, 1775 poems were preserved. After Dickinson's death, Higginson worked with her niece to produce six volumes of her poems. Since Dickinson had never put a date on her own poem, the editors numbered her poems. In 1950 Harvard University bought all her copyright. A complete collection, *The Poems of Emily Dickinson*, came out in 1955.

Dickinson's poems are written in a wry voice, with sharp, unusual images and punctuation. The range of Dickinson's poetry suggests not her limited experiences but the power of her creativity and imagination. Although Dickinson lived in the flood of the romantic revolution, she seems to have nothing in common with the leading writers of the time. She was wholly original, taking the stuff of her poetry merely from her personal experiences in order to express what she felt about love, nature, friendship, death, and immortality. She developed her own poetic form with many peculiar features, such as the abundant use of dashes, and irregular and often idiosyncratic punctuation and capitalization. Her mode of expression is characterized by clear-cut and delicately original imagery, precise diction, and fragmentary and enigmatic metrical pattern.

Wild Nights—Wild Nights!

Introduction

In the poem "Wild Nights—Wild Nights!" the speaker reveals all her innermost feelings to her lover. Love is expressed in an unabashed manner. So some people think that it is the most candidly erotic of Dickinson's poems. It relies heavily on symbols. In the poem, both the boat and the sea are used as symbols.

25

Wild Nights—Wild Nights!

Were I with thee

Wild Nights should be

Our luxury!

Futile—the Winds—

To a Heart in port—

Done with the Compass—

Done with the Chart!

Rowing in Eden

Ah, the Sea!

Might I but moor—Tonight—

In Thee!

Questions for Reading Comprehension

1. What do wild nights refer to?

2. What does "our luxury" mean?

3. What do the boat and the sea symbolize?

4. Does "Rowing in Eden—" complete the idea of safe harborage which begins in lines 5 and 6: "Futile—the Winds—/ To a Heart in port"? Or does the line initiate a new idea and action?

5. Does "Ah, the Sea!" imply that the speaker is moving from sheltered paradisical waters toward the sea, by rowing? Or does the speaker simply see the sea and exult in the sight? Or does she long to leave Eden behind and go to sea?

Discussion Questions for Appreciation

1. Is this a poem of unrestrained sexual passion?

2. Some people say that this poem is the portrayal of a religious experience? Do you agree?

A Bird Came down the Walk—

Introduction

In the poem "A Bird Came down the Walk—", the speaker observes the bird in the garden as it eats a worm, pecks at the grass, hops sidewise to let a beetle pass. When the speaker offers it a crumb, it is frightened and flies away. The bird becomes an emblem for the quick, lively, ungraspable wild essence that distances nature from human beings who desire to appropriate or tame it. But the most remarkable feature of this poem is the imagery of its final stanza, in which Dickinson provides one of the most breath-taking descriptions of flying in poetry.

328

A Bird came down the Walk—
He did not know I saw—
He bit an Angleworm in halves
And ate the fellow, raw,

And then he drank a Dew
From a convenient Grass—
And then hopped sidewise to the Wall
To let a Beetle pass—

He glanced with rapid eyes
That hurried all around—
They looked like frightened Beads, I thought—
He stirred his Velvet Head

Like one in danger, Cautious,

I offered him a Crumb

And he unrolled his feathers

And rowed him softer home—

Than Oars divide the Ocean,

Too silver for a seam—

Or Butterflies, off Banks of Noon

Leap, plashless as they swim.

Questions for Reading Comprehension

1. What does the bird eat in the natural world?

2. Why does the bird hop sidewise to let a beetle pass? Does the bird fear the beetle?

3. What does the speaker do in stanza 4?

4. Is the bird frightened by the speaker? Why?

5. What does the speaker compare the bird's movement to in stanza 5?

Discussion Questions for Appreciation

1. What kind of atmosphere do the first two stanzas create?

2. Interpret the implied meaning of line 2: "He did not know I saw—".

3. What effect does the comparison in stanza 5 impose on the poem?

4. What is Dickinson's attitude toward nature?

I Died for Beauty—But Was Scarce

Introduction

"I died for Beauty—but was scarce" is about two dead people having a conversation about their lives. Dickinson associates beauty and truth in this poem, which echoes Keats' idea that Beauty is Truth, Truth

Beauty. This poem creates a scene that is, by turns, grotesque and compelling, frightening and comforting.

449

I died for Beauty—but was scarce
Adjusted in the Tomb
When One who died for Truth, was lain
In an adjoining Room①—

He questioned softly "Why I failed"?
"For Beauty", I replied—
"And I—for Truth—Themself② are One—
We Brethren, are", He said—

And so, as Kinsmen, met a Night③—
We talked between④ the Rooms—
Until the Moss had reached our lips⑤—
And covered up—our names—

Notes
① **Room**: Tomb.
② **Themself** = Themselves = They.
③ **a Night**: one night.
④ **between**: across
⑤ **Until the Moss had reached our lips**: "Lips" refer to the lips of the dead, and to the tombstone.

Questions for Reading Comprehension
1. Why does the first speaker "I" say that he was scarcely adjusted?
2. Why does the second speaker "he" ask, "Why I failed"?
3. The second speaker says, "We Brethren are". What does he mean?

4. What happens to the two speakers toward the end of the poem? And what does it imply?

Discussion Questions for Appreciation

1. What is the theme of the poem?
2. Does this poem have anything to do with Dickinson's principle of poetic composition?

Because I Could Not Stop for Death—

Introduction

"Because I Could Not Stop for Death" is one of Dickinson's most popular poems. It is a dramatic representation of the passage from the world of the living to the afterlife. In this poem, Death comes as a "gentleman" for the speaker, his intended "lady". They drive in a carriage in the country. They pass the school, the fields of gazing grain and the setting sun. In the last stanza, the "gentleman" disappears. The "lady" feels that she has been tricked and abandoned. So in the depiction of Death as the courtly suitor and as the fraudulent seducer, the poem reflects a basic ambiguity about death and immortality. A famous poet Allen Tate says that this poem is one of the greatest in the English language.

712

Because I could not stop for Death—
He kindly stopped for me—
The Carriage held but just Ourselves—
And Immortality.

We slowly drove—He knew no haste

180

And I had put away
My labor and my leisure too,
For His Civility—

We passed the School, where Children strove
At Recess—in the Ring—
We passed the Fields of Gazing Grain—
We passed the Setting Sun—

Or rather—He passed Us—
The Dews drew quivering and chill—
For only Gossamer, my Gown—
My Tippet—only Tulle—

We paused before a House that seemed
A Swelling of the Ground—
The Roof was scarcely visible—
The Cornice—in the Ground—

Since then—'tis Centuries—and yet
Feels shorter than the Day
I first surmised the Horses' Heads
Were toward Eternity—

Questions for Reading Comprehension

1. What does Death's carriage hold?

2. What are the three things that the speaker and Death pass in stanza 3?

3. What is the "House" in the ground in stanza 5? Is this the speaker's final destination?

4. Is the speaker in this poem alive or dead? What day is she describing?

5. Why does the day seem so long to the speaker?

Discussion Questions for Appreciation

1. What do lines 1 to 2 suggest about human behavior?

2. What might the three things the speaker pass in stanza 3 represent?

3. What is Dickinson's idea about death and immortality?

A Question for Writing

What are the features of Dickinson's poetry that impress you most?

Chapter Three   American Realism and American Naturalism

(1865-1914)

Historical Background

The Civil War was a watershed marking the transformation of the United States from an agrarian country to an industrialized one. Consistent with the changes in economic system, the second half of the 19th century also witnessed great changes in social system, in ideology and in cultural and moral values. The War, lasting over a period of four years from 1861 to 1864, cost US$ 8 billion and claimed 600, 000 lives[①]. It exerted such an influence on American society that it can never escape the discussion of the literary achievements in this period.

The Civil War was the result of the growing contradictions between the South and the North concerning political, economic, social and cultural institutions. The War ended with the victory on the Northern side. "The industrial North had triumphed over the agrarian South, and from that victory came a society based on mass labor and

---

① Nina Baym, ed. *The Norton Anthology of American Literature* (New York: W. W. Norton & Company, 1998), 5th edition, vol. 2, 1.

mass consumption. "① The transcontinental railway (which was completed in 1869 and had developed four lines by 1885), the extensive use of electricity, the invention of new means of communication (telephone and telegraph), and the discovery and the extraction of such natural resources as coal, oil, gold and silver worked together to increase industrial and agricultural productivity and to drive the country toward a prosperous and wealthy one. The growth of population (doubled from 1870 to 1890) brought forth large cities and towns②. At the same time, the national income quadrupled. By mid-1890s, about 4,000 millionaires appeared, including Cornelius Vanderbilt, John D. Rockefeller, Andrew Carnegie and J. P. Morgan who dominated the American industry to a large extent until the early half of the 20th century. As a result of the population's flocking to cities and the rise of large-scale industries, the relationship between employers and employees became more impersonal. The power of traditional political groups was challenged by the appearance of new political groups that spoke for the laboring class. At the same time, the power of the federal government expanded, encouraging the exploitation of natural resources but invoking racial and ethnic conflicts.

With wealth and power concentrated in the hands of only a few, the gulf between the rich and the poor was widened and social contradictions were sharpened. The spread of industrialization inevitably created extremes of wealth and poverty. Slum areas like Bowery, New York ap-

---

① George McMichael, ed. *Anthology of American Literature* (New York: Macmillan Publishing Company, 1980), 3rd edition, vol. 2, 1.

② The population of New York city, for example, rose from 500,000 to nearly 3.5 million, and that of Chicago grew from 20,000 to more than 2 million during these 50 years or so. Please see Nina Baym, ed. *The Norton Anthology of American Literature* (New York: W. W. Norton & Company, 1998), 5th edition, vol. 2, 2.

peared where crimes, murder, diseases, and violence found their way. For the countless ordinary people, life became a struggle for survival.

Toward the end of this century, the Westward Movement that had brought people constant hope for a better life half a century before was no longer inspiring since the frontier was about to close. Farmers were still going westward, but not much land was waiting to be cultivated. A sense of suffering, unhappiness, disillusionment and pessimism began to prevail. "The Gilded Age" (Mark Twain) came instead of the golden one which people had expected. This is "an age of extremes": "of decline and progress, of poverty and dazzling wealth, of gloom and buoyant hope"[1]. The national spirit changed to admiration for driving ambition, a lust for money and power. Farmers had to depend on the transcontinental railway to transport their products; therefore railway became a giant "octopus" (Frank Norris) holding in its grips the fate of farmers.

The spread of Darwin's theory of evolution—the theories of "survival by social selection" and "survival of the fittest" —changed people's ideology. Living in an indifferent, cold and Godless world, man was no longer free. People's outlook toward life became pessimistic. The assumptions shared by the Transcendentalists such as Ralph Waldo Emerson were now interrogated. People began to realize that God was not benevolent as they had expected, human nature was not born good as they believed, the attempt for an individual to cultivate himself to achieve perfection was not as easily fulfilled as they had anticipated, and the relationship between man and nature was not as harmonious as they had imagined. "The worth of the American dream, the idealized, romantic view of man and his life in the New World, began to lose its hold on the

185

---

① George McMichael, ed. *Anthology of American Literature* (New York: Macmillan Publishing Company, 1980), 3rd edition, vol. 2, 2.

imagination of the people. "①

The rapid growth of economy along with large-scale immigration demanded widespread public education. Higher education was no longer restricted to the children of the middle and upper-classes. Public "land-grant" universities were established on millions of acres of federal land given to the states. With the decline of New England culture, New York replaced Boston as the nation's literary center. The appearance of low-cost magazines and the ever important newspapers strove to cater to the tastes of a variety of readers. The translation of European literary masters, including Thomas Hardy, Emile Zola, Leo Tolstoy, Anton Chekhov and Henrik Ibsen, added to the nation's interest in literary writings. People from all social groups were drawn to the literary circle, most notably women who became "the nation's dominant cultural force"② as a result of women's education and their acute observation of social problems.

American Realism

Realism was originated in France as *réalisme*, a literary doctrine that called for "reality and truth" in the depiction of ordinary life. It soon spread to other countries in Europe. Zola, Flaubert, Balzac, Tolstoy and Dostoyevsky were among the outstanding representatives. This "notoriously overused term"③ is often employed to characterize a literary writing style that was popular with some European countries and the U.

---

① Chang Yaoxin, *A Survey of American Literature* (Tianjin: Nankai University Press, 2003), 2nd edition, 117.

② George McMichael, ed. *Anthology of American Literature* (New York: Macmillan Publishing Company, 1980), 3rd edition, vol. 2, 4.

③ Nina Baym, ed. *The Norton Anthology of American Literature* (New York: W. W. Norton & Company, 1998), 5th edition, vol. 2, 6.

S. from the 1830s to the end of the 19th century. William Dean Howells defines realism as "nothing more and nothing less than the truthful treatment of material."

Realism reacts against romanticism and sentimentalism. It expresses the concern for the commonplace, and for the familiar and the low. "In matters of style, there was contrast between the genteel and graceful prose on the one hand, and vernacular diction and rough and ready frontier humor on the other." [1] Possessing what Henry James called "a powerful impulse to mirror the unmitigated realities of life," realistic writers seek to portray American life as it really is, insisting that the ordinary and the local are most suitable for artistic representation. They select representative and ordinary characters from daily life, describe the setting in which these characters live in a faithful way, and try to avoid authorial intrusion into the judgment of either the characters or their behaviors.

To summarize, American realism has the following salient features:

1. verisimilitude of detail derived from observation;

2. a reliance on the representative in plot, setting and character;

3. an objective rather than an idealized view of human nature and experience.

Realism first appeared in America in the literature of local color, "an amalgam of romantic plots and realistic descriptions of things immediately observable: the dialects, customs, sights, and sounds of regional America" [2]. Local color writing reached its peak in the 1880s and began

---

① Chang Yaoxin, *A Survey of American Literature* (Tianjin: Nankai University Press, 2003), 2nd edition, 118.

② Nina Baym, ed. *The Norton Anthology of American Literature* (New York: W. W. Norton & Company, 1998), 5th edition, vol. 2, 5.

to decline by the turn of the century. Although these local colorists tend to idealize and the tall-tale humor prevalent among the frontier pioneers finds its way into many local color writings, these writers still retain their truthful representation of the local life that they are familiar with.

Some representative local colorists include:

Bret Harte (1836-1902), the first American writer of local color to achieve wide popularity. His major concern is the western mining towns in the pioneering days. His "The Luck of Roaring Camp", "The Outcasts of Poker Flat", and "Tennessee's Partner" are among the best stories ever written by an American.

Harriet Beecher Stowe (1811-1896), a woman writer whose object is "to interpret to the world the New England life and character in that particular time of history which may be called the seminal period". Her representative writings include *Oldtown Folks* (1869) and *Uncle Tom's Cabin* (1852).

Kate Chopin (1850-1904), another notable woman writer who is concerned with the preservation of the American South. She is famous for *Bayou Folk* (1894), *A Night in Acadie* (1897) and *The Awakening* (1899). She is particularly interested in presenting women's living conditions, and *The Awakening* is regarded as one of the most important writings about women's awakening to their oppression and miseries.

Mary E. W. Freeman (1852-1930), whose "A New England Nun" contemplates on the decline of New England culture.

Charles W. Chesnutt (1858-1932), a writer who keeps an eye on the blacks living on the plantations.

Hamlin Garland (1860-1940), a writer who invents the word "veritism" for his own style of realism. He is remembered for *Main-Traveled Roads* (1891) and *Crumbling Idols* (1904), truthful representation of the farm life in the American West.

Edith Wharton (1862-1937), a woman writer whose outstanding literary achievement represented by *Souls Belated* (1899), *The House of Mirth* (1905) and *The Custom of the Country* (1913) remains a mirror to the New York high society.

Mary Austin (1868-1934), whose *The Walking Woman* (1907) writes about the deserts in Southern California and invites a feminist reading.

Mark Twain (1835-1910), a local colorist in his earlier career but later immersing himself into the bigger currents of realism. His major works include: *The Adventures of Tom Sawyer* (1876), *The Adventures of Huckleberry Finn* (1884), *Life on the Mississippi* (1883), and *The Gilded Age* (1873). Mark Twain has the gifted talent of transforming colloquial humor into written form, and his *The Adventures of Huckleberry Finn* remains a perfect example of the colloquial style that is not only characteristically Mark Twainian but also finds its way into the writings of later writers such as Ernest Hemingway.

American Realism produces three great masters. Ranking with Mark Twain, William Dean Howells and Henry James cannot escape our attention.

189

William Dean Howells (1837-1920) finds his subject matter in the experiences of the middle class by sustaining an objective point of view. His experience of working as the editor-in-chief of *The Atlantic Monthly* for more than 10 years safeguards his position as the arbiter of American literary realism. His works include *The Rise of Silas Lapham* (1885) and *Criticism and Fiction* (1891). As the "dean" of American literature for many decades, he naturally becomes the first president of the American Academy of Arts and Letters.

Henry James (1843-1916) probes deeply into the individual psychology of his characters, writing in a rich and intricate style which corresponds to the complex human experience he describes. His *Daisy Miller* (1878), *The Wings of the Dove* (1902) and *The Ambassadors*

(1903) show his concern about American innocence in contact and contrast with European sophistication and decadence. For the Americans, this is a process of growth from innocence to maturity. James is also a literary critic. His *The Art of Fiction* (1884) remains an important literary theoretical work ever written.

American Naturalism

Naturalism, "an extraordinarily elastic term"[1], is a new and harsher realism. It develops on the basis of realism but goes a step further in portraying social reality. Under the influence of Charles Darwin's evolution theory and Herbert Spencer's application of Darwin's theory in social relations, naturalists are especially concerned with how human beings strive to find meaning in their experiences, how people fight against environment and other external forces, and what elements make people who and what they are.

Thematically, naturalistic writers write "detailed descriptions of the lives of the downtrodden and of the abnormal"[2] by frankly treating human passion and sexuality to show the animalistic nature of human beings. They are interested in finding out how men and women are overwhelmed by the forces of environment and by the forces of heredity. Technically, naturalistic writers make detailed documentation of life. The gloomy and pessimistic atmosphere in many naturalistic writings mark naturalism more naked and wicked than realism in its representation of social reality.

---

① Annette T. Rubinstein, *American Literature: Root and Flower* (Beijing: Foreign Language Teaching and Research Press, 1988), 226.

② George McMichael, ed. *Anthology of American Literature* (New York: Macmillan Publishing Company, 1980), 3rd edition, vol. 2, 6.

However, it is dangerous to make a sweeping generalization about naturalists concerning their "pessimistic" attitude toward life. R. W. Horton believes, "American naturalists could not accept the deterministic attitude of the complete helplessness of man and the view of an amoral and predatory universe and adopt a thoroughgoing scientific attitude in the portrayal of the American scene. "[1] Since man is governed by his instincts and desires, he has no free will to control his fate. Holding this attitude, naturalistic writers do not attempt "to make moral judgments"[2].

American Naturalism first came into existence in *Maggie, a Girl of the Streets* by Stephen Crane, then displayed its manifesto in *McTeague* by Frank Norris, and later came to its maturity in *Sister Carrie* by Theodore Dreiser.

Stephen Crane (1871-1900) is brought to fame by his *The Red Badge of Courage* (1895). War ceases to be a symbol of courage and heroism in the story; instead, it turns out to be a slaughter house and a ruthless machine. *Maggie, a Girl of the Streets* (1893), the first naturalistic novel by an American, is based on the writer's observation of the Bowery life. The downfall and destruction of the heroine shows that environment is a shaping influence in the life of an insignificant human being.

Frank Norris (1870-1902) exerts general influences on such later writers as Faulkner and Steinbeck, but he is not much read today for his excessive sentiment and philosophical inconsistencies. *McTeague* (1899), a textbook and manifesto of American naturalism, writes about

191

---

[1] R. W. Horton, *Backgrounds of American Literary Thought* (Englewood Cliffs, N. J. : Prentice-Hall, Inc. , 1974), 267-268.

[2] James D. Hart, *The Oxford Companion to American Literature* (New York: Oxford University Press, 1965), 4th edition, 585.

the forces of environment controlling the destiny of human beings. Norris'
trilogy, comprising of *The Octopus* (1901), *The Pit* (1903) and *The
Wolf* (never written), is about the fate of the American farmers caught
in the grip of the railway company.

Theodore Dreiser (1871-1945) is the greatest American literary
naturalist. He believes that "man was merely a mechanism moved by
chemical and physical forces beyond his control", and that man was
"merely an animal driven by greed and lust in a struggle for existence".
His works are powerful in the portrayal of the American life, but his style
is crude with inexact expressions and clichés. Nevertheless, it is in
Dreiser's works that American naturalism is said to have come of age.
Sister Carrie (1900) remains a masterpiece of naturalistic writing for its
frank representation of the rise and fall of a country girl in a metropolis.
Dreiser's sympathy with the heroine goes throughout the story.

Ambrose Bierce (1842-1914) is not only remembered for his short
stories but also for his "cynical and scathing"[①] newspaper articles. His
belief that man is trapped in the endless struggle against fate is best represented in the stories collected in *Tales of Soldiers and Civilians*
(1892).

Edwin Arlington Robinson (1860-1935) achieves reputation as a
poet in the first decade of the 20th century. His outlook toward an indifferent God, meaningless life and helpless man, exemplified in such brilliant poems as "Man Against the Sky", "Richard Cory", "Miniver Che-
evy", marks him a naturalist in vision.

O. Henry (1862-1910, pseudonym of William Sidney Porter) has
a fine sense of humour and is adept at depicting social life, especially
that of ironic circumstances. His characters are often plain and simple

---

① George McMichael, ed. *Anthology of American Literature* (New York:
Macmillan Publishing Company, 1980), 3rd edition, vol. 2, 718.

and the plots usually depend on the surprise ending. "The Gift of the Magi", "The Last Leaf" and "The Whirligig of Life" are some of his most renowned stories.

Willa Cather (1873-1947) mainly writes about how people try to find meaning in life against adversity. Her best works include *The Troll Garden* (1905), *O Pioneers!* (1913), *The Song of the Lark* (1915) and *My Antonia* (1918).

Jack London (1876-1916) reads extensively against a wandering life experience. Writing more than 50 books, he finally indulges himself in alcoholism and mental disintegration. The influence of Nietzche is found in the super man in *The Sea Wolf* (1904) and the superdog in *The Call of the Wild* (1903). *Martin Eden* (1909), an autobiographical novel, is also a powerful literary work of London. London's writings bear the imprints of his critical attitude toward the American materialistic society.

Samuel Langhorne Clemens (1835-1910)

Samuel Langhorne Clemens, better known for his pen name of Mark Twain, grew up in the Mississippi River frontier town of Hannibal, Missouri, which he later fictionalized as St. Petersburg in *The Adventures of Tom Sawyer* (1876) and *The Adventures of Huckleberry Finn* (1884). "Mark Twain" is the phrase Mississippi boatmen used to signify two fathoms (3.6 meters) of water, the depth needed for a boat's safe passage.

Mark Twain got his education through experience and keen observation of people and events. After his father's death, he went to work for his brother's print shop at the age of fifteen. Since then, he wandered for three years eastward as far as New York. Attracted by the river life of the Mississippi, Mark Twain worked as a licensed steamboat pilot until 1861, when the Civil War disrupted Mississippi River traffic. In the following years, he succumbed to the silver mining fever in Nevada and made yet lost more than one fortune. He earned his first recognition as a writer with his short story "The Celebrated Jumping Frog of Calaveras County" (1865), which was based on the stories he had heard in the California mining camps. After a trip to Europe in 1869, Mark Twain produced *The Innocents Abroad* (1869), a humorous narrative that ridicules foreign sights and manners from the point of view of the American democrat.

In 1870 he married Olivia Langdon and settled down in Hartford, Connecticut, where he built a $ 100,000 mansion with his royalties. There he wrote his two masterpieces, *The Adventures of Tom Sawyer*, and *The Adventures of Huckleberry Finn*. In 1895, at the age of sixty, Mark Twain lost all his money through unwise investments. To clear the debts, he set out on a lecturing tour around the world. During this period, his daughter died, his wife suffered nervous breakdown, and his own health was falling. As a result, his later writings revealed the deep grief over his personal losses, and reflected deep cynicism and disillusionment with the world. "The Man That Corrupted Hadleyburg" (1900), "What Is Man" (1906), and "The Mysterious Stranger" (1916) all exuded an air of savage despair. At the age of seventy-two, Mark Twain was awarded the degree of Doctor of Literature by Oxford University. Three years later, he died in Connecticut on April 21, 1910.

Mark Twain's works can be divided into four types. The first type is the "personalized fiction" which refers to works that fictionalize people and events that Mark Twain was familiar with. These works include *The Adventures of Tom Sawyer*, *The Adventures of Huckleberry Finn*, *The Gilded Age: A Tale of Today* (1873). The second type may be called "travel fiction" and these works include *The Innocents Abroad*, *Roughing It* (1873), *A Tramp Abroad* (1880), *Life on the Mississippi* (1883), and *Following the Equator* (1897). The third type may be named "historical romances" which show Mark Twain's familiarity with the romance tradition and his ability to subvert its conventionalized implications. These works include *The Prince and Pauper* (1882), *A Connecticut Yankee in King Arthur's Court* (1889), and *Personal Recollections of Joan of Arc by the Sieur Louis Conte* (1896). The fourth type are short stories and "tall tales", which suggest Mark Twain's connection with the frontier spirit and his fondness of local color. Two of his best known stories are "The Celebrated Jumping Frog of Calaveras County" and "The Man That Corrupted Hadleyburg". "

Mark Twain's famous novel *The Adventures of Tom Sawyer* revolves around the youthful adventures of the novel's schoolboy protagonist, Thomas Sawyer, who lives with his Aunt Polly in the quaint town of St. Petersburg, just off the shore of the Mississippi River. In this novel,

Mark Twain creates a myth of endless childhood pleasures. However, Tom is presented as the embodiment of over-sentimentality, a problem with the society of that time.

The Adventures of Huckleberry Finn, which was completed in 1883, has often been considered to be Mark Twain's masterpiece for its combination of raw humor with startlingly mature material, and its direct attacks on many of the southern traditions. Huck and a runaway slave named Jim meet and raft south on the Mississippi River. They nurture friendship during their journey, and Huck renounces his upbringing in the South in order to continue to help Jim to escape, but he is never free of the socially prevalent racial prejudices. The book with its carefully controlled point of view, with its implicit ironies expressed through the voice of a semiliterate boy, its masterful use of dialects; its balancing of nostalgic romanticism and realism, humor and pathos, innocence and evil, all united for a journey down the river, has instructed and moved people of all ages.

Mark Twain, who started his writing career by telling tall tales, is the first American author to write great books using a genuinely colloquial and native American speech. The magnificent yet deceptive, constantly changing river is the main feature of his imaginative landscape. He tends to represent social life through the portrayal of local places. He foresees the coming of the "Great American novel," to which he has a considerable share. Ernest Hemingway says that all of American literature comes from one great book, that is, Twain's *Adventures of Huckleberry Finn*.

Mark Twain is also an outstanding humorist and satirist. He has a genuine hatred for hypocrisy and pretentiousness, and expresses it in a humorous manner. This, combined with his "deadpan" technique of delivery, keeps his writing fresh and appealing.

The Celebrated Jumping Frog of Calaveras County

Introduction

"The Celebrated Jumping Frog of Calaveras County" is Mark Twain's most famous western tale. It was first published in the New York Saturday Press in 1865 as "Jim Smiley and His Jumping Frog", and reprinted two years later as the title piece of his first book. The story was revised several times. Another version of the story bears the title "The Notorious Jumping Frog of Calaveras County." The story is set in a gold-mining camp in Calaveras County, California, and has its origins in the folklore of the Gold Rush era. It was one of Twain's earliest writings and helped establish his reputation as a humorist. The story is a story within a frame story: The first narrator introduces us to a second narrator, Simon Wheeler, who then tells the tale of Jim Smiley, whose frog can outjump any frogs in the Calaveras County. But a stranger who comes to the County stuffs the champion frog with bird shot and wins the bet with Jim Smiley with an average frog from the swamp. The story is regarded as an example of tall tale. Twain's use of humor and exaggeration is remarkable, so is the tale's satirical focus on existing cultural differences between the western and eastern regions of the United States.

The Celebrated Jumping Frog of Calaveras County

In compliance with the request of a friend of mine, who wrote me from the East, I called on good-natured, garrulous old Simon Wheeler, and inquired after my friend's friend, Leonidas W. Smiley, as requested to do, and I hereunto append the result[①]. I have a lurking suspicion that Leonidas W. Smiley is a myth; that my friend never knew such a personage; and that he only conjectured that, if I asked old Wheeler about him, it would remind him of his infamous Jim Smiley, and he would go to work and bore me nearly to death with some infernal reminiscence of him as long and tedious as it should be useless to me. If that was the design, it certainly succeeded.

I found Simon Wheeler dozing comfortably by the bar-room stove of the old, dilapidated tavern in the ancient mining camp of Angel's, and I noticed that he was fat and bald-headed, and had an expression of winning gentleness and simplicity upon his tranquil countenance. He roused up and gave me good-day. I told him a friend of mine had commissioned me to make some inquiries about a cherished companion of his boyhood named Leonidas W. Smiley Rev. Leonidas W. Smiley a young minister of the Gospel, who he had heard was at one time a resident of Angel's Camp. I added that, if Mr. Wheeler could tell me any thing about this Rev. Leonidas W. Smiley, I would feel under many obligations to him.

Simon Wheeler backed me into a corner and blockaded me there with his chair, and then sat me down and reeled off[2] the monotonous narrative which follows this paragraph. He never smiled, he never frowned, he never changed his voice from the gentle-flowing key to which he tuned the initial sentence, he never betrayed the slightest suspicion of enthusiasm[3]; but all through the interminable narrative there ran a vein of impressive earnestness and sincerity, which showed me plainly that, so far from his imagining that there was any thing ridiculous or funny about his story, he regarded it as a really important matter, and admired its two heroes as men of transcendent genius in finesse. To me, the spectacle of a man drifting serenely along through such a queer yarn without ever smiling, was exquisitely absurd. As I said before, I asked him to tell me what he knew of Rev. Leonidas W. Smiley, and he replied as follows. I let him go on in his own way, and never interrupted him once:

There was a feller[4] here once by the name of Jim Smiley, in the winter of '49 or may be it was the spring of '50 I don't recollect exactly, somehow, though what makes me think it was one or the other is because I remember the big flume wasn't finished when he first came to the camp; but anyway, he was the curiousest man about always betting on any thing that turned up you ever see, if he could get any body to bet on the other side; and if he couldn't, he'd change sides. Any way that suited the other man would suit him any way just so's he got a bet, he was satisfied. But still he was lucky, uncommon lucky; he most always come out winner. He was always ready and laying for a chance; there couldn't be no solittry thing mentioned but that feller'd offer to bet on it, and take any side you please, as I was just telling you. If there was a horse-race, you'd find him flush, or you'd find him busted⑤ at the end of it; if there was a dog-fight, he'd bet on it; if there was a cat-fight, he'd bet on it; if there was a chicken-fight, he'd bet on it; why, if there was two birds setting on a fence, he would bet you which one would fly first; or if there was a camp-meeting, he would be there reg'lar, to bet on Parson Walker, which he judged to be the best exhorter about here, and so he was, too, and a good man. If he even seen a straddle-bug start to go any wheres, he would bet you how long it would take him to get wherever he was going to, and if you took him up, he would foller⑥ that straddle-bug to Mexico but what he would find out where he was bound for and how long he was on the road. Lots of the boys here has seen that Smiley, and can tell you about him. Why, it never made no difference to him he would bet on any thing the dangdest feller. Parson Walker's wife laid very sick once, for a good while, and it seemed as if they warn's going to save her; but one morning he come in, and Smiley asked how she was, and he said she was considerable better thank the Lord for his infinite mercy and coming on so smart that, with the blessing of Providence⑦, she'd get well yet; and Smiley, before he thought, says, "Well, I'll risk two-and-a-half that she don't, any way."

Thish-yer Smiley had a mare the boys called her the fifteen-minute nag, but that was only in fun, you know, because, of course, she was faster than that and he used to win money on that horse, for all she was so slow and always had the asthma, or the distemper, or the consumption, or something of that kind. They used to give her two or three hundred yards start, and then pass her under way; but always at the fag-end of the race she'd get excited and desperate-like, and come cavorting and straddling up[8], and scattering her legs around limber, sometimes in the air, and sometimes out to one side amongst the fences, and kicking up m-o-r-e dust, and raising m-o-r-e racket with her coughing and sneezing and blowing her nose and always fetch up at the stand just about a neck ahead, as near as you could cipher it down[9].

And he had a little small bull pup, that to look at him you'd think he wan's worth a cent, but to set around and look ornery, and lay for a chance to steal something. But as soon as money was up on him, he was a different dog; his underjaw'd begin to stick out like the fo'castle of a steamboat, and his teeth would uncover, and shine savage like the furnaces. And a dog might tackle him, and bully-rag him, and bite him, and throw him over his shoulder two or three times, and Andrew Jackson[10] which was the name of the pup, Andrew Jackson would never let on but what he was satisfied, and hadn't expected nothing else and the bets being doubled and doubled on the other side all the time, till the money was all up; and then all of a sudden he would grab that other dog jest by the j'int[11] of his hind leg and freeze on it not chew, you understand, but only jest grip and hang on till they thronged up the sponge, if it was a year. Smiley always come out winner on that pup, till he harnessed a dog once that didn't have no hind legs[12], because they'd been sawed off by a circular saw, and when the thing had gone along far enough, and the money was all up, and he come to make a snatch for his pet bolt, he saw in a minute how he'd been imposed on, and how the other dog had him in the door, so to speak, and he 'peered surprised, and then he looked sorter discouraged-like, and didn't try no more to win the fight, and so he got shucked out bad. He give Smiley a look, as much as to say his heart was broke, and it was his fault, for putting up a dog that hadn't no hind legs for him to take bolt of, which was his main dependence in a fight, and then he limped off a piece and laid down and died. It was a good pup, was that Andrew Jackson, and would have made a name for hisself if he'd lived, for the stuff was in him, and he had genius I know it, because he hadn't had no opportunities to speak of, and it don't stand to reason that a dog could make such a fight as he could under them circumstances, if he hadn't no talent. It always makes me feel sorry when I think of that last fight of his'n, and the way it turned out.

Well, thish-yer Smiley had rat-terriers, and chicken cocks, and tom-cats, and all of them kind of things, till you couldn't rest, and you couldn't fetch nothing for him to bet on but he'd match you. He ketched[13] a frog one day, and took him home, and said he cal'klated to edercate[14] him; and so he never done nothing for three months but set in his back yard and learn that frog to jump. And you bet you he did learn him, too. He'd give him a little punch behind, and the next minute you'd see that frog whirling in the air like a doughnut see him turn one summerset, or may be a couple, if he got a good start, and come down flat-footed and all right, like a cat. He got him up so in the matter of catching flies, and kept him in practice so constant, that he'd nail a fly every time as far as he could see him. Smiley said all a frog wanted was education, and he could do most any thing and I believe him. Why, I've seen him set Dan'l Webster[15] down here on this floor Dan'l Webster was the name of the frog and sing out, "Flies, Dan'l, flies!" and quicker'n you could wink, he'd spring straight up, and snake a fly off 'n the counter there, and flop down on the floor again as solid as a gob of mud, and fall to scratching the side of his head with his hind foot as indifferent as if he hadn't no idea he'd been doin' any more'n any frog might do[16]. You never see a frog so modest and straightforward as he was, for all he was so gifted. And when it come to fair and square jumping on a dead level, he could get over more ground at one straddle than any animal of his breed you ever see. Jumping on a dead level was his strong suit, you understand; and when it come to that, Smiley would ante up[17] money on him as long as he had a red. Smiley was monstrous proud of his frog, and well he might be, for fellers that had traveled and been everywheres, all said he laid over[18] any frog that ever they see.

Well, Smiley kept the beast in a little lattice box, and he used to fetch him down town sometimes and lay for a bet. One day a feller a stranger in the camp, he was come across him with his box, and says:

"What might it be that you've got in the box?"

And Smiley says, sorter indifferent like, "It might be a parrot, or it might be a canary, may be, but it an't it's only just a frog."

And the feller took it, and looked at it careful, and turned it round this way and that, and says, "H'm so 'tis[19]. Well, what's he good for?"

"Well," Smiley says, easy and careless, "He's good enough for one thing, I should judge he can outjump any frog in Calaveras County."

The feller took the box again, and took another long, particular look, and give it back to Smiley, and says, very deliberate, "Well, I don't see no p'ints about that frog that's any better'n any other frog."

"May be you don't," Smiley says. "May be you understand frogs, and may be you don't understand 'em; may be you've had experience, and may be you an't only a amature, as it were. Anyways, I've got my opinion, and I'll risk forty dollars that he can outjump any frog in Calaveras County."

And the feller studied a minute, and then says, kinder sad like, "Well, I'm only a stranger here, and I an't got no frog; but if I had a frog, I'd bet you."

And then Smiley says, "That's all right that's all right if you'll hold my box a minute, I'll go and get you a frog." And so the feller took the box, and put up his forty dollars along with Smiley's, and set down to wait.

So he set there a good while thinking and thinking to hisself, and then he got the frog out and prized his mouth open and took a tea-spoon and filled him full of quail shot[20] filled him pretty near up to his chin and set him on the floor. Smiley he went to the swamp and slopped around in the mud for a long time, and finally he ketched a frog, and fetched him in, and give him to this feller, and says:

"Now, if you're ready, set him alongside of Dan'l, with his forepaws just even with Dan'l, and I'll give the word." Then he says, "One two three jump!" and him and the feller touched up the frogs from behind, and the new frog hopped off, but Dan'l give a heave, and hysted up his shoulders so like a Frenchman, but it wan's no use he couldn't budge[21]; he was planted as solid as an anvil, and he couldn't no more stir than if he was anchored out. Smiley was a good deal surprised, and he was disgusted too, but he didn't have no idea what the matter was, of course.

The feller took the money and started away; and when he was going out at the door, he sorter jerked his thumb over his shoulders this way at Dan'l, and says again, very deliberate, "Well, I don't see no p'ints about that frog that's any better'n any other frog."

Smiley he stood scratching his head and looking down at Dan'l a long time, and at last he says, "I do wonder what in the nation that frog throw'd off for I wonder if there an't something the matter with him he 'pears to look mighty baggy, somehow." And he ketched Dan'l by the nap of the neck, and lifted him up and says, "Why, blame my cats, if he don't weigh five pound!" and turned him upside down, and he belched out a double handful of shot. And then he see how it was, and he was the maddest man he set the frog down and took out after that fel-ler, but he never ketchd him. And-

[Here Simon Wheeler heard his name called from the front yard, and got up to see what was wanted.] And turning to me as he moved away, he said: "Just set where you are, stranger, and rest easy I an't going to be gone a second."

But, by your leave, I did not think that a continuation of the history of the enterprising vagabond Jim Smiley would be likely to afford me much information concerning the Rev. Leonidas W. Smiley, and so I started away.

At the door I met the sociable Wheeler returning, and he button-holed me and recommenced:

"Well, thish-yer Smiley had a yeller one-eyed cow that didn't have no tail, only jest a short stump like a bannanner, and "

"Oh! hang Smiley and his afflicted cow!" I muttered, good-na-turedly, and bidding the old gentleman good-day, I departed.

Notes

① **append the result**: attach the result; add the result to this piece of writing.

② **reeled off**: repeated a lot of information quickly and easily.

③ **he never changed his voice from the gentle-flowing key to which he tuned the initial sentence, he never betrayed the slightest sus-picion of enthusiasm**: His voice never changed from the initial gen-tle-flowing way of delivering the speech, and he never showed the slightest enthusiasm about the story in his voice.

④ **feller**: fellow

⑤ **you'd find him flush, or you'd find him busted**: you'd find him red in the face because he had won the bet, or you'd find him penni-less because he had lost the bet.

⑥ **foller**：follow

⑦ **Providence**：God's grace.

⑧ **cavorting and straddling up**：jumping up and over something with high spirit.

⑨ **cipher it down**：notice.

⑩ **Andrew Jackson**：The seventh president of the United States from 1829 to 1837. Unlike previous presidents, Jackson was born into a poor family. His election to the presidency shifted the balance of power in the country from wealthy, East Coast interests to those of the farmers and small-business owners in the West. He is also famous for his strong will and toughness.

⑪ **j'int**：joint.

⑫ **didn't have no hind legs**：did not have hind legs.

⑬ **ketched**：the past tense of *catch* in slang.

⑭ **edercate**：educate.

⑮ **Dan'l Webster**：Daniel Webster, American politician and lawyer. He gained fame as one of the best-known orators of his time. He argued numerous cases before the Supreme Court, served in the Congress of the United States, and twice served as secretary of state (1841-1843 and 1850-1852). A vigorous advocate of a strong national government, Webster championed the continued unity of the United States in the pre-Civil War era.

⑯ **as if he hadn't no idea he'd been doin' any more'n any frog might do**：as if he had no idea that he had been doing more than any frog might do.

⑰ **ante up**：to pay an amount of money in order to be able to be involved in (a bet).

⑱ **laid over**：won over.

⑲ **h'm so 'tis**：hmm, so it is.

⑳ **shot**: small metal ball.

㉑ **budge**: move.

Questions for Reading Comprehension

1. Why does the first narrator call on Simon Wheeler?

2. Whom does Simon Wheeler talk about? Why does he talk about him?

3. Where is the narrator from? Is he educated?

4. Where do you think old Simon Wheeler lives?

5. Did Simon Wheeler have a good education? Why or why not?

6. Why does the writer name the pup and the frog after two American politicians?

7. Why is Jim Smiley's frog defeated by the stranger's?

8. Do you think Simon Wheeler is a good story-teller?

9. How does the first narrator respond to the story of Jim Smiley?

10. How does Simon Wheeler counteract the ridiculousness of the story about Jim Smiley?

Discussion Questions for Appreciation

1. What are the differences in character and cultural background between the first narrator and the second narrator Simon Wheeler?

2. How do these differences contribute to the humor of the story?

3. How does the first narrator's language differ from that of the second? How do the differences contribute to the reliability of their narration?

4. Conflicts arise when the East meets the West. How does Mark Twain present the two sides involved in the conflict?

5. As a typical western hoax, the story tells about how the weak succeed in "hoaxing" the strong. In what way does the story reflect the reality in the California Mining camps?

A Question for Writing

Mark Twain once said, "I see no great difference between a man and a watch, except that a man is conscious and a watch is not." How does Mark Twain view human nature? How does the story reflect the writer's view of hum nature?

Henry James (1843-1916)

Henry James was born on April 15, 1843 in New York City. His family enjoyed upper middle-class prosperity as the result of shrewd land purchases by his grandfather, an Irish immigrant. His father was an eminent philosopher and reformer. The James children were educated in a variety of unorthodox circumstances: sometimes at schools, sometimes with private tutors, always with access to books and new experiences. In 1855 the James family embarked on a three-year trip to Geneva, London, and Paris—an experience that made Henry James aware of the sophistication of European culture.

Upon their return from Europe, the family moved to Cambridge, where they had contacts with prominent writers and thinkers, including Ralph Waldo Emerson, Henry David Thoreau, and Bronson Alcott. Henry James soon discontinued his lessons, turning instead to writing. From 1862 to 1863 he attended Harvard Law School, where he read French novelists and critics such as Balzac and George Sand instead of law. He also read intensively George Eliot and Hawthorne. At first James tried to live and work as an art and drama critic in New York, but found the materialistic bent of American life and its lack of culture and sophistication intolerable, so he settled down in London in 1876 and spent most of his adult life there. James became a British subject in 1915, a year before his death at seventy-three. He remained a bachelor throughout life.

Henry James wrote twenty novels and more than one hundred short stories and novellas, as well as literary criticism, plays, travelogues, autobiographies and reviews. He was influenced by such European and American writers. as George Eliot, Turgenev, Flaubert and Hawthorne.

Leon Edel, James' biographer, divides Henry James' mature career into three periods. [1] In the first period, *The American* (1877), *Daisy Miller* (1879), and *Washington Square* (1881), helped him win international fame. Works of this period also include *The Portrait of a Lady* (1881), one of the greatest books James ever wrote. In the second period (1882-1900) of his writing career, James experimented with diverse themes and forms—initially with novels dealing explicitly with the social and political currents of the 1870s and 1880s, then with writing for the theater, and finally with shorter fictions that explore the relationship between artists and society—as in *The Great Good Place* (1900), and the troubled psychology of oppressed children and haunted or obsessed men and women. In his third period, James revived his theme of innocence in a corrupted world. Famous works of this period include *The Turn of the Screw* (1898), *The Wings of the Dove* (1902), *The Best in the Jungle* (1903), *The Ambassadors* (1903), and *The Golden Bowl* (1904). He is known for using a particular method which he termed as "point of view" to illuminate situation and characters through one or several minds, and people observe events through the consciousness of the characters. "James increasingly removed himself as controlling narrator; in T. S. Eliot's phrase, he became invisible in his work. "[2] In a sense, Henry James is the predecessor of the technique of "the stream of consciousness", which was later developed by James Joyce, Virginia Woolf and other writers.

Besides, Henry James is a master of handling "the international theme" —American innocence in contrast with European sophistication.

---

[1] Nina Baym, ed. *The Norton Anthology of American Literature* (New York: W. W. Norton & Company, 1998), the fifth edition, 282.

[2] Ibid. , 283.

However, there are disputes regarding James' own stance in the conflict. Some say that he rejects his native land and wishes to acquire the sophistication and culture he identified with Europeans, whereas others think that the strength and innocence exhibited by his American characters emerge as the ultimate values of his fiction.

Henry James contributes immensely to literary criticism. In his essay "The Art of Fiction" (1988), a highly significant statement of his fictional principles, he declares that the aim of novel is to represent life, and says that "the province of art is all life; all observation, all vision."[①]

Daisy Miller

Introduction

Daisy Miller was first published in the Cornhill Magazine 37 (June to July 1878), and later dramatized by the author in 1883. It is a novel about American innocence defeated by the traditional values of Europe. The striking contrast between American innocence and European sophistication presented in the novel is typical of James' fiction and that of many realist writers who examine the interplay between innocence and experience.

The novella can be divided into two parts. The first part is about Daisy's activity in Vevey. Winterbourne, a young American expatriate who meets Daisy from New York in the watering resort of Vevey, is somewhat attracted by her youthful freshness. Having no perception of the complex code that underlies behavior in European society, Daisy becomes the subject of gossip in Vevey because of her free and intimate

---

① Chang Yaoxin, *A Survey of American Literature* (Tianjin: Nankai University Press, 1990), 175.

manners with their courier. She goes on a castle tour with Winterbourne, which goes against the European tradition that a young woman should go out in the company of men without a chaperon. So Winterbourne is warned by his aunt and patroness to keep away from Daisy. Part Two is about Daisy's activities in Rome. Several months later, Winterbourne meets the Miller family in Rome, where he finds that Daisy has become a scandal among the Americans in Europe for she goes openly in the street with young men, and is involved in a romance with a young Italian adventurer. In the end, Daisy catches influenza after going out at night with Mr. Govanelli, an Italian man, and dies a week afterwards. It is at Daisy's funeral that Winterbourne realizes that she is really innocent, and her apparent immorality is only the unfortunate result of her American spirit of freedom, but it is misinterpreted by the Europeans and Europeanized Americans. The following excerpt is taken from Part II.

From *Daisy Miller*

Winterbourne, who had returned to Geneva the day after his excursion to Chillon, went to Rome toward the end of January. His aunt had been established there for several weeks, and he had received a couple of letters from her. "Those people you were so devoted to last summer at Vevey have turned up here, courier and all," she wrote. "They seem to have made several acquaintances, but the courier continues to be the most intimate. The young lady, however, is also very intimate with some third-rate Italians, with whom she rackets about[①] in a way that makes much talk. Bring me that pretty novel of Cherbuliez's—Paule Mere—and don't come later than the 23rd."

......

"He's an Italian," Daisy pursued with the prettiest serenity. "He's a great friend of mine; he's the handsomest man in the world—except Mr. Winterbourne! He knows plenty of Italians, but he wants to know some Americans. He thinks ever so much of Americans. He's tremendously clever. He's perfectly lovely!"

It was settled that this brilliant personage should be brought to Mrs. Walker's party, and then Mrs. Miller prepared to take her leave. "I guess we'll go back to the hotel," she said.

"You may go back to the hotel, Mother, but I'm going to take a walk," said Daisy.

"She's going to walk with Mr. Giovanelli," Randolph proclaimed.

"I am going to the Pincio," said Daisy, smiling.

"Alone, my dear—at this hour?" Mrs. Walker asked. The afternoon was drawing to a close—it was the hour for the throng of carriages and of contemplative pedestrians. "I don't think it's safe, my dear," said Mrs. Walker.

"Neither do I," subjoined Mrs. Miller. "You'll get the fever, as sure as you live. Remember what Dr. Davis told you!"

"Give her some medicine before she goes," said Randolph.

The company had risen to its feet; Daisy, still showing her pretty teeth, bent over and kissed her hostess. "Mrs. Walker, you are too perfect," she said. "I'm not going alone; I am going to meet a friend."

"Your friend won't keep you from getting the fever," Mrs. Miller observed.

"Is it Mr. Giovanelli?" asked the hostess.

Winterbourne was watching the young girl; at this question his attention quickened. She stood there, smiling and smoothing her bonnet ribbons; she glanced at Winterbourne. Then, while she glanced and smiled, she answered, without a shade of hesitation, "Mr. Giovanelli—the beautiful Giovanelli."

"My dear young friend," said Mrs. Walker, taking her hand pleadingly, "don't walk off to the Pincio at this hour to meet a beautiful Italian."

"Well, he speaks English," said Mrs. Miller.

"Gracious me!" Daisy exclaimed, "I don't to do anything improper. There's an easy way to settle it." She continued to glance at Winterbourne. "The Pincio is only a hundred yards distant; and if Mr. Winterbourne were as polite as he pretends, he would offer to walk with me!"

Winterbourne's politeness hastened to affirm itself, and the young girl gave him gracious leave to accompany her. They passed downstairs before her mother, and at the door Winterbourne perceived Mrs. Miller's carriage drawn up, with the ornamental courier whose acquaintance he had made at Vevey seated within. "Goodbye, Eugenio!" cried Daisy; "I'm going to take a walk." The distance from the Via Gregoriana to the beautiful garden at the other end of the Pincian Hill is, in fact, rapidly traversed. As the day was splendid, however, and the concourse of vehicles, walkers, and loungers numerous, the young Americans found their progress much delayed. This fact was highly agreeable to Winterbourne, in spite of his consciousness of his singular situation. The slow-moving, idly gazing Roman crowd bestowed much attention upon the extremely pretty young foreign lady who was passing through it upon his arm; and he wondered what on earth had been in Daisy's mind when she proposed to expose herself, unattended, to its appreciation. His own mission, to her sense, apparently, was to consign her to the hands of Mr. Giovanelli; but Winterbourne, at once annoyed and gratified, resolved that he would do no such thing. . . .

When they had passed the gate of the Pincian Gardens, Miss Miller began to wonder where Mr. Giovanelli might be. "We had better go straight to that place in front," she said, "where you look at the view."

"I certainly shall not help you to find him," Winterbourne declared.

"Then I shall find him without you," cried Miss Daisy.

"You certainly won't leave me!" cried Winterbourne.

She burst into her little laugh. "Are you afraid you'll get lost—or run over? But there's Giovanelli, leaning against that tree. He's staring at the women in the carriages: did you ever see anything so cool?"

Winterbourne perceived at some distance a little man standing with folded arms nursing his cane. He had a handsome face, an artfully poised hat, a glass in one eye, and a nosegay in his buttonhole. Winterbourne looked at him a moment and then said, "Do you mean to speak to that man?"

"Do I mean to speak to him? Why, you don't suppose I mean to communicate by signs?"

"Pray understand, then," said Winterbourne, "that I intend to remain with you. "

Daisy stopped and looked at him, without a sign of troubled consciousness in her face, with nothing but the presence of her charming eyes and her happy dimples. "Well, she's a cool one!" thought the young man.

"I don't like the way you say that," said Daisy. "It's too imperious. "

"I beg your pardon if I say it wrong. The main point is to give you an idea of my meaning. "

The young girl looked at him more gravely, but with eyes that were prettier than ever. "I have never allowed a gentleman to dictate to me, or to interfere with anything I do. "

"I think you have made a mistake," said Winterbourne. "You should sometimes listen to a gentleman—the right one. "

Daisy began to laugh again. "I do nothing but listen to gentlemen!" she exclaimed. "Tell me if Mr. Giovanelli is the right one?"

The gentleman with the nosegay in his bosom had now perceived our two friends, and was approaching the young girl with obsequious rapidity. He bowed to Winterbourne as well as to the latter's companion; he had a brilliant smile, an intelligent eye; Winterbourne thought him not a bad-looking fellow. But he nevertheless said to Daisy, "No, he's not the right one."

Daisy evidently had a natural talent for performing introductions; she mentioned the name of each of her companions to the other. She strolled alone with one of them on each side of her; Mr. Giovanelli, who spoke English very cleverly—Winterbourne afterward learned that he had practiced the idiom upon a great many American heiresses—addressed her a great deal of very polite nonsense; he was extremely urbane, and the young American, who said nothing, reflected upon that profundity of Italian cleverness which enables people to appear more gracious in proportion as they are more acutely disappointed. Giovanelli, of course, had counted upon something more intimate; he had not bargained for a party of three. But he kept his temper in a manner which suggested far-stretching intentions. Winterbourne flattered himself that he had taken his measure. "He is not a gentleman," said the young American; "he is only a clever imitation of one. He is a music master, or a penny-a-liner, or a third-rate artist. Damn his good looks!" Mr. Giovanelli had certainly a very pretty face; but Winterbourne felt a superior indignation at his own lovely fellow countrywoman's not knowing the difference between a spurious[2] gentleman and a real one. Giovanelli chattered and jested and made himself wonderfully agreeable. It was true that, if he was an imitation, the imitation was brilliant. "Nevertheless," Winterbourne said to himself, "a nice girl ought to know!" And then he came back to the question whether this was, in fact, a nice girl. Would a nice girl, even allowing for her being a little American flirt, make a rendezvous[3] with a presumably low-lived foreigner? The rendezvous in this case, indeed, had been in broad daylight and in the most crowded corner of Rome, but was it not impossible to regard the choice of these circumstances as a proof of extreme cynicism? Singular though it may

215

seem, Winterbourne was vexed that the young girl, in joining her amoroso, should not appear more impatient of his own company, and he was vexed because of his inclination. It was impossible to regard her as a perfectly well-conducted young lady; she was wanting in a certain indispensable delicacy. It would therefore simplify matters greatly to be able to treat her as the object of one of those sentiments which are called by romancers "lawless passions." That she should seem to wish to get rid of him would help him to think more lightly of her, and to be able to think more lightly of her would make her much less perplexing. But Daisy, on this occasion, continued to present herself as an inscrutable[④] combination of audacity and innocence.

She had been walking some quarter of an hour, attended by her two cavaliers, and responding in a tone of very childish gaiety, as it seemed to Winterbourne, to the pretty speeches of Mr. Giovanelli, when a carriage that had detached itself from the revolving train drew up beside the path. At the same moment Winterbourne perceived that his friend Mrs. Walker—the lady whose house he had lately left—was seated in the vehicle and was beckoning to him. Leaving Miss Miller's side, he hastened to obey her summons. Mrs. Walker was flushed; she wore an excited air. "It is really too dreadful," she said. "That girl must not do this sort of thing. She must not walk here with you two men. Fifty people have noticed her."

Winterbourne raised his eyebrows. "I think it's a pity to make too much fuss about it."

"It's a pity to let the girl ruin herself!"

"She is very innocent," said Winterbourne.

"She's very crazy!" cried Mrs. Walker. "Did you ever see anything so imbecile[⑤] as her mother? After you had all left me just now, I could not sit still for thinking of it. It seemed too pitiful, not even to attempt to save her. I ordered the carriage and put on my bonnet, and came here as quickly as possible. Thank Heaven I have found you!"

"What do you propose to do with us?" asked Winterbourne, smiling.

"To ask her to get in, to drive her about here for half an hour, so that the world may see she is not running absolutely wild, and then to take her safely home."

"I don't think it's a very happy thought," said Winterbourne; "but you can try."

Mrs. Walker tried. The young man went in pursuit of Miss Miller, who had simply nodded and smiled at his interlocutor in the carriage and had gone her way with her companion. Daisy, on learning that Mrs. Walker wished to speak to her, retraced her steps with a perfect good grace and with Mr. Giovanelli at her side. She declared that she was delighted to have a chance to present this gentleman to Mrs. Walker. She immediately achieved the introduction, and declared that she had never in her life seen anything so lovely as Mrs. Walker's carriage rug.

"I am glad you admire it," said this lady, smiling sweetly. "Will you get in and let me put it over you?"

"Oh, no, thank you," said Daisy. "I shall admire it much more as I see you driving round with it."

"Do get in and drive with me!" said Mrs. Walker.

"That would be charming, but it's so enchanting just as I am!" and Daisy gave a brilliant glance at the gentlemen on either side of her.

"It may be enchanting, dear child, but it is not the custom here," urged Mrs. Walker, leaning forward in her victoria, with her hands devoutly clasped.

"Well, it ought to be, then!" said Daisy. "If I didn't walk I should expire[6]."

"You should walk with your mother, dear," cried the lady from Geneva, losing patience.

"With my mother dear!" exclaimed the young girl. Winterbourne saw that she scented interference. "My mother never walked ten steps in her life. And then, you know," she added with a laugh, "I am more than five years old."

"You are old enough to be more reasonable. You are old enough, dear Miss Miller, to be talked about."

Daisy looked at Mrs. Walker, smiling intensely. "Talked about? What do you mean?"

"Come into my carriage, and I will tell you."

Daisy turned her quickened glance again from one of the gentlemen beside her to the other. Mr. Giovanelli was bowing to and fro, rubbing down his gloves and laughing very agreeably; Winterbourne thought it a most unpleasant scene. "I don't think I want to know what you mean," said Daisy presently. "I don't think I should like it."

Winterbourne wished that Mrs. Walker would tuck in her carriage rug and drive away, but this lady did not enjoy being defied, as she afterward told him. "Should you prefer being thought a very reckless girl?" she demanded.

"Gracious!" exclaimed Daisy. She looked again at Mr. Giovanelli, then she turned to Winterbourne. There was a little pink flush in her cheek; she was tremendously pretty. "Does Mr. Winterbourne think," she asked slowly, smiling, throwing back her head, and glancing at him from head to foot, "that, to save my reputation, I ought to get into the carriage?"

Winterbourne colored; for an instant he hesitated greatly. It seemed so strange to hear her speak that way of her "reputation." But he himself, in fact, must speak in accordance with gallantry. The finest gallantry, here, was simply to tell her the truth; and the truth, for Winterbourne, as the few indications I have been able to give have made him known to the reader, was that Daisy Miller should take Mrs. Walker's advice. He looked at her exquisite prettiness, and then he said, very gently, "I think you should get into the carriage."

Daisy gave a violent laugh. "I never heard anything so stiff! If this is improper, Mrs. Walker," she pursued, "then I am all improper, and you must give me up. Goodbye; I hope you'll have a lovely ride!" and, with Mr. Giovanelli, who made a triumphantly obsequious salute, she turned away.

Mrs. Walker sat looking after her, and there were tears in Mrs. Walker's eyes. "Get in here, sir," she said to Winterbourne, indicating the place beside her. The young man answered that he felt bound to accompany Miss Miller, whereupon Mrs. Walker declared that if he refused her this favor she would never speak to him again. She was evidently in earnest. Winterbourne overtook Daisy and her companion, and, offering the young girl his hand, told her that Mrs. Walker had made an imperious claim upon his society. He expected that in answer she would say something rather free, something to commit herself still further to that "recklessness" from which Mrs. Walker had so charitably endeavored to dissuade her. But she only shook his hand, hardly looking at him, while Mr. Giovanelli bade him farewell with a too emphatic flourish of the hat.

Winterbourne was not in the best possible humor as he took his seat in Mrs. Walker's victoria. "That was not clever of you," he said candidly, while the vehicle mingled again with the throng of carriages.

"In such a case," his companion answered, "I don't wish to be clever; I wish to be earnest!"

"Well, your earnestness has only offended her and put her off."

"It has happened very well," said Mrs. Walker. "If she is so perfectly determined to compromise herself, the sooner one knows it the better; one can act accordingly."

"I suspect she meant no harm," Winterbourne rejoined.

"So I thought a month ago. But she has been going too far."

"What has she been doing?"

"Everything that is not done here. Flirting with any man she could pick up; sitting in corners with mysterious Italians; dancing all the evening with the same partners; receiving visits at eleven o'clock at night. Her mother goes away when visitors come."

"But her brother," said Winterbourne, laughing, "sits up till midnight."

"He must be edified by what he sees. I'm told that at their hotel everyone is talking about her, and that a smile goes round among all the servants when a gentleman comes and asks for Miss Miller."

"The servants be hanged!" said Winterbourne angrily. "The poor girl's only fault," he presently added, "is that she is very uncultivated."

"She is naturally indelicate," Mrs. Walker declared.

"Take that example this morning. How long had you known her at Vevey?"

"A couple of days."

"Fancy, then, her making it a personal matter that you should have left the place!"

Winterbourne was silent for some moments; then he said, "I suspect, Mrs. Walker, that you and I have lived too long at Geneva!" And he added a request that she should inform him with what particular design she had made him enter her carriage.

"I wished to beg you to cease your relations with Miss Miller—not to flirt with her—to give her no further opportunity to expose herself—to let her alone, in short."

"I'm afraid I can't do that," said Winterbourne. "I like her extremely."

"All the more reason that you shouldn't help her to make a scandal."

"There shall be nothing scandalous in my attentions to her. "

"There certainly will be in the way she takes them. But I have said what I had on my conscience," Mrs. Walker pursued. "If you wish to rejoin the young lady I will put you down. Here, by the way, you have a chance. "

The carriage was traversing that part of the Pincian Garden that overhangs the wall of Rome and overlooks the beautiful Villa Borghese. It is bordered by a large parapet, near which there are several seats. One of the seats at a distance was occupied by a gentleman and a lady, toward whom Mrs. Walker gave a toss of her head. At the same moment these persons rose and walked toward the parapet. Winterbourne had asked the coachman to stop; he now descended from the carriage. His companion looked at him a moment in silence; then, while he raised his hat, she drove majestically away. Winterbourne stood there; he had turned his eyes toward Daisy and her cavalier. They evidently saw no one; they were too deeply occupied with each other. When they reached the low garden wall, they stood a moment looking off at the great flat-topped pine clusters of the Villa Borghese; then Giovanelli seated himself, familiarly, upon the broad ledge of the wall. The western sun in the opposite sky sent out a brilliant shaft through a couple of cloud bars, whereupon Daisy's companion took her parasol out of her hands and opened it. She came a little nearer, and he held the parasol over her; then, still holding it, he let it rest upon her shoulder, so that both of their heads were hidden from Winterbourne. This young man lingered a moment, then he began to walk. But he walked—not toward the couple with the parasol; toward the residence of his aunt, Mrs. Costello.

...

221

Notes

① **racket about**: hang around like a whore.

② **spurious**: fake.

③ **rendezvous**: appointment.

④ **inscrutable**: not understandable.

⑤ **imbecile**: stupid.

⑥ **expire**: die.

Questions for Reading Comprehension

1. Does Mrs. Costello's view of Daisy influence Winterbourne in any way? How do you know?

2. When Winterbourne meets Daisy at Mrs. Walker's house, Daisy blames him for being "mean", and Mrs. Walker seems to feel very quaint at Daisy's remarks. Why?

3. What does this scene tell us about Daisy's character?

4. How does Mrs. Miller think of Daisy, who knows a lot of gentlemen in Rome?

5. What is Mrs. Walker response when Daisy says she is going to walk out with Mr. Giovaneli?

6. When Winterbourne first meets Mr. Giovaneli, he "reflected on the depth of Italian subtlety, so strangely opposed to Anglo-Saxon simplicity, which enables people to show a smoother surface in proportion as they're more acutely displeased." What is Winterbourne's first impression of Mr. Giovaneli?

7. What does Winterbourne's first impression reveal about Mr. Giovaneli?

8. Winterbourne gets on the carriage, but later asks Mrs. Walker to drop him. What does this indicate about his character? When he gets off the carriage, he does not go to meet Daisy and Mr. Giovaneli. Why doesn't he do so?

Discussion Questions for Appreciation

1. Why do you think James chooses to call his heroine "Daisy Miller"?

Do the names "Winterbourne," "Mrs. Walker," and "Giovanelli" seem significant or perhaps ironic in any way?

2. In the story Winterbourne shows contradictory attitudes towards Daisy. He tries to decide whether she is a flirt or a naïve girl. Illustrate his attitudes by citing some examples from the reading.

3. Does Daisy's relationship with Mr. Giovaneli differ from her relationship with Winterbourne? What's the most impressive feature of Mr. Giovaneli? What does this represent?

4. Daisy defies European convention and falls a victim to her own innocence. Discuss the character of Daisy. Some of James' contemporaries thought that his portrait of Daisy was insulting to Americans. Do you share this opinion?

5. In his whole writing career, James is concerned with "point of view", which is the center of his aesthetics of fiction writing. Through whose eyes do we see most of the events in *Daisy Miller*? Comment on this "point of view".

A Question for Writing

James' fame rests largely on his handling of "the international theme" —American innocence in contrast with European sophistication. Comment on his handling of this theme in the novel *Daisy Miller*.

Edith Wharton (1862-1937)

Edith Wharton was born on January 24, 1862 in New York, into a wealthy and socially prominent family. She was educated by tutors and governesses. For a girl of her social class, the purpose of life is to find a marriage partner with similar background. Therefore, since her adolescence, she was required to attend balls and large parties, and to pay much attention to fashion and etiquette. However, Wharton rejected these values and spent as much time as she could in her father's library at home and in similar libraries of her friends. She started to compose poems in her teens and also finished secretly a novella. In 1885 she married Edward Wharton, a Boston banker, who was twelve years her senior. Wharton's role as a wife with social responsibilities and her writing ambitions resulted in her nervous collapse. She was advised that writing might help her recover. So, in the 1890s Wharton started to contribute to *Scribner's Magazine.* Her first collection of short stories appeared in the late 1890s. Her first book *The Decoration of Houses* appeared in 1897.

Wharton gained her first literary success with her book *The House of Mirth* (1905), the story of a beautiful but poor woman, Lily Bart, who is trained to be a decorative upper-class wife but who is unable to sell herself into an upper-class family. *The Custom of the Country* (1913) is a story about a young ambitious woman, Undine Spragg from Ohio, who makes her way up the social ladder, stepping on Americans and Europeans alike in her pursuit of money and power. Wharton's most famous novel is *The Age of Innocence* (1920), which was awarded the Pulitzer Prize. Her other major works include the long tale *Ethan Frome* (1911), which is set in impoverished rural New England, and *The Reef*

(1912). The novel *Hudson River Bracketed* (1929) and its sequel *The Gods Arrive* (1932) compare the cultures of Europe and the sections of the U. S. she knew. Wharton also wrote poems, essays, travel books and an autobiography, *A Backward Glance* (1934).

Though Edith Wharton and her husband lived together for twenty-eight years, their marriage was not happy. From 1906 to 1909, Wharton had an affair with an American journalist Morton Fullerton. The Whartons were divorced in 1913 and Edith spent the rest of her life in France.

During World War I, Wharton wrote reports for American newspapers. She also assisted in organizing relief efforts for refugees and children displaced by German advance. She was also active in fund-raising activities, and participated in the production of an illustrated anthology of war writings by prominent authors and artists. Wharton died in France on August 11, 1937.

Wharton received a Pulitzer Prize in 1921. Two years later, she became the first woman to receive a Doctor of Letters Degree from Yale University. Her central subject is the conflict between social obligations and individual fulfillment. She has also written extensively on New York families with old money in struggle with social climbers. Her fiction belongs to the novel of manners tradition. Her prose is elegant and her plots are tightly constructed.

225

Ethan Frome

Introduction

The story of *Ethan Frome* is set in a small town named Starkfield. The protagonist Ethan Frome has to drop out of college to take care of his sick mother, and Zeena is the nurse to help him. After his mother's death, Ethan marries Zeena out of fear for loneliness. But the marriage is never happy. Ethan wants to sell the mill and leaves Starkfiled for a big city so as to fulfill his dream of becoming an engineer. But Zeena, out of her fear for big-city life, prolongs her illness in order to stay in Starkfiled. Mattie, a relative of Zeena, stays with the Fromes, helping with their household chores. Ethan is much attracted by Mattie's liveliness. He struggles between whether to leave Zeena and elope with Mattie or to stay in Starkfiled and live the rest of his life taking care of his sick and cold wife. However, in a sober evaluation of his financial situation, Ethan comes to realize the impossibility of running away. When Zeena determines to drive Mattie away, Ethan and Mattie come to the idea of dying together on their way to the railway station. The following excerpts include the Epilogue, when the narrator, who comes to Starkfield as an engineer, visits the Fromes twenty years after the suicide event on the way to the railway station.

The conflict between social obligations and individual fulfillment has always been a subject for Wharton. Again and again, Wharton displays the hold that social convention has on Ethan's passion for Mattie. Also, Wharton seems to reveal the helplessness of man, his insignificance in a cold world, and his lack of dignity in face of the crushing forces of environment and heredity. In the story, not only does bleak, oppressive cold shape Starkfield's physical landscape; it penetrates the characters' psychic landscapes as well.

From *Ethan Frome*

The Querulous Drone[1] ceased as I entered Frome's kitchen, and of the two women sitting there I could not tell which had been the speaker.

One of them, on my appearing, raised her tall bony figure from her seat, not as if to welcome me—for she threw me no more than a brief glance of surprise—but simply to set about preparing the meal which Frome's absence had delayed. A slatternly calico wrapper hung from her shoulders and the wisps of her thin grey hair were drawn away from a high forehead and fastened at the back by a broken comb. She had pale opaque eyes which revealed nothing and reflected nothing, and her narrow lips were of the same sallow colour as her face.

The other woman was much smaller and slighter. She sat huddled in an armchair near the stove, and when I came in she turned her head quickly toward me, without the least corresponding movement of her body. Her hair was as grey as her companion's, her face as bloodless and shrivelled, but amber-tinted, with swarthy shadows sharpening the nose and hollowing the temples. Under her shapeless dress her body kept its limp immobility, and her dark eyes had the bright witch-like stare that disease of the spine sometimes gives.

Even for that part of the country the kitchen was a poor-looking place. With the exception of the dark-eyed woman's chair, which looked like a soiled relic of luxury bought at a country auction, the furniture was of the roughest kind. Three coarse china plates and a broken-nosed milk-jug had been set on a greasy table scored with knife-cuts, and a couple of straw-bottomed chairs and a kitchen dresser of unpainted pine stood meagrely against the plaster walls.

"My, it's cold here! The fire must be 'most out," Frome said, glancing about him apologetically as he followed me in.

The tall woman, who had moved away from us toward the dresser, took no notice; but the other, from her cushioned niche, answered complainingly, in a high thin voice. "It's on'y just been made up this very minute. Zeena fell asleep and slep' ever so long, and I thought I'd be frozen stiff before I could wake her up and get her to 'tend to it."

I knew then that it was she who had been speaking when we entered.

Her companion, who was just coming back to the table with the remains of a cold mince-pie in a battered pie-dish, set down her unappetising burden without appearing to hear the accusation brought against her.

Frome stood hesitatingly before her as she advanced; then he looked at me and said: "This is my wife, Mis' Frome." After another interval he added, turning toward the figure in the arm-chair: "And this is Miss Mattie Silver..."

Note

① **The Querulous Drone**: The Endless Complaint

Questions for Reading Comprehension

1. "One of them, on my appearing, raised her tall bony figure from her seat, not as if to welcome me—for she threw me no more than a brief glance of surprise—but simply to set about preparing the meal which Frome's absence had delayed." Whom does this excerpt describe, Mattie or Ethan's wife? How do you know?
2. What impresses the narrator when he comes to Ethan's house?
3. Who does the narrator find complaining when he enters Ethan's house?
4. Who is about to prepare the dinner for Ethan? Is it surprising to you?
5. Why does Mattie have to stay with the Fromes?

Discussion Questions for Appreciation

1. The imagery of *Ethan Frome* is built around cold, ice and snow, and hues of white. The characters constantly complain about the cold. How does the description of Ethan's house reinforce the theme of *Ethan Frome*?
2. In the story, the only decision Ethan makes is to commit suicide with Mattie. Is this decision an active or a passive one?
3. What does this decision reveal about Ethan's character?
4. What are the changes in Mattie's appearance and character?

A Question for Writing

Wharton's central subject is the conflict between social obligations and individual fulfillment. Discuss if this is true with *Ethan Frome* and justify yourself.

Stephen Crane (1871-1900)

Stephen Crane was born in Newark, New Jersey, on November 1, 1871, as the fourteenth child of a Methodist minister. He started to write stories at the age of eight and at sixteen he was writing articles for the *New York Tribune*. In 1888 he began his higher education at Hudson River Institute and Claverack College. Claverack, a military school, served in developing Crane's interests in Civil War studies and military training—knowledge he would later use in his writing of *The Red Badge of Courage* (1895). After his mother's death in 1890—his father had died earlier—Crane moved to New York, where he lived a bohemian life, and worked as a free-lance writer and journalist.

While supporting himself by writing, he lived among the poor in the Bowery slums to work on his first novel *Maggie: A Girl of the Streets* (1893), which was a milestone in the development of literary naturalism. It tells the story of a good woman's downfall in a slum environment. Just as Crane points out, "it tries to show that environment is a tremendous thing in the world and frequently shapes lives regardless."[①] However, since *Maggie* painted an unabashed picture of the bitter life of the slum-dwellers, it was rejected by editors and publishers at that time. Crane had to print the book at his own expense, borrowing the money from his brother.

Crane's second novel, *The Red Badge of Courage* brought him international fame. It depicts the American Civil War from the point of view of an ordinary soldier. It has been called the first modern war novel.

---

① Dennis Poupard, ed., *Twentieth-Century Literary Criticism*, 11 vols. (Detroit: Gale Research Company, 1983), 121.

Henry Fleming, the protagonist, portrays a first hand account of the personal and psychological effects that war may have on a person in battle. While Crane inadvertently criticizes the futility of combat throughout the narrative, the essence of the piece lies less in the war and more in the specific development and changes undergone by the character Henry. As Poupard says, " Often compared to Impressionist painting, *The Red Badge of Courage* is a series of vivid episodes in which a young soldier, Henry Fleming, confronts a gamut of emotions—fear, courage, pride, and humility—in his attempt to understand battlefield experiences; in this respect, Fleming represents the 'Everyman' of war". [1]

Crane's collection of poems *The Black Rider* also came out in 1895. These books brought Crane better reporting assignments. He traveled to Greece, Cuba, Texas and Mexico, reporting mostly on war events. His short story "The Open Boat" is based on his shipwreck experience on the journey to Cuba in 1896. With a small party of other passengers, Crane spent several days drifting in an open boat before being rescued. This experience impaired his health permanently.

231

As his marriage to a lady who had run a sporting house in Florida outraged many of his countrymen, Crane settled in Sussex, England, where he became friends with Joseph Conrad, H. G. Wells, and Henry James. During these restless years he refined his use of realism to expose social evils. In 1899 Crane returned to Cuba to cover the Spanish-American War. Due to poor health he was obliged to return to England. He died of tuberculosis on June 5, 1900 at Badenweiler in Germany.

Crane is a representative of American naturalism. His fictional world is a naturalistic one in which man is deprived of free will and expects no help from any quarter. True to naturalism, Crane shows his

---

[1] Dennis Poupard, ed. , *Twentieth-Century Literary Criticism*, 11 vols. (Detroit: Gale Research Company, 1983), 119.

characters trapped in situations which they cannot control. Still, these characters show courage and valor in the face of insurmountable adversities.

Crane was much influenced by impressionistic painters from whom he learned the importance of feeling and the way of choosing parts of reality. He gave the readers just those objects which create the real impression, and his writings put less emphasis on action and more emphasis on the feelings that exist in immediate experience.

Crane is a master of irony. Besides verbal and dramatic irony, he uses situational irony that emphasizes the discrepancy between what we assume it will be and what actually happens. Crane's power with words and his ability to live with paradox make his writing interesting.

The Red Badge of Courage

Introduction

The Red Badge of Courage has been called a "flowering of pure naturalism." The story is in essence a psychological study of the mind of a youth, Henry Fleming. The protagonist is an average teenager who comes from a small New York farming family. He is forever wrestling with his own internal dilemmas concerning courage, fear, and manhood. Some critics have argued that the book ends with Henry's psychological maturation, while others have suggested that Henry remains as vain and deluded at the end of the book as he is at the beginning.

The book is chiefly concerned with chronicling Henry's anxieties, moods, thoughts and impressions as he progresses through the series of episodes that make up the book. The focus of the book is on the effect of war and actions on the mind and emotions of a young man swinging wildly between confidence and fear, between understanding and bewilderment. Crane filters many of the experiences through the mind of Henry

Fleming, thus creating a literary style called Impressionism. Impressionism is a style of writing that presents an author's or a character's impression of an experience rather than a more realistic description of it.

The plot of the novel can be divided into five parts: 1) Henry before the battle; 2) Henry during the first fighting; 3) Henry's flight; 4) Henry's wound and his return to his regiment; 5) Henry in battle again.

From *The Red Badge of Courage*
Chapter 12

The column that had butted stoutly at the obstacles in the roadway was barely out of the youth's sight before he saw dark waves of men come sweeping out of the woods and down through the fields. He knew at once that the steel fibers had been washed from their hearts[①]. They were bursting from their coats and their equipments as from entanglements[②]. They charged down upon him like terrified buffaloes.

Behind them blue smoke curled and clouded above the treetops, and through the thickets he could sometimes see a distant pink glare. The voices of the cannon were clamoring in interminable chorus.

The youth was horrors-tricken. He stared in agony and amazement. He forgot that he was engaged in combating the universe. He threw aside his mental pamphlets on the philosophy of the retreated and rules for the guidance of the damned.

The fight was lost. The dragons were coming with invincible strides. The army, helpless in the matted thickets and blinded by the overhanging night, was going to be swallowed. War, the red animal, war, the blood-swollen god, would have bloated fill.

Within him something bade to cry out. He had the impulse to make a rallying speech, to sing a battle hymn, but he could only get his tongue to call into the air: "Why—why—what—what's th' matter?"

233

Soon he was in the midst of them. They were leaping and scampering all about him. Their blanched faces shone in the dusk. They seemed, for the most part, to be very burly men. The youth turned from one to another of them as they galloped along. His incoherent questions were lost. They were heedless of his appeals. They did not seem to see him.

They sometimes gabbled insanely. One huge man was asking of the sky: "Say, where de plank road? Where de plank road!" It was as if he had lost a child. He wept in his pain and dismay.

Presently, men were running hither and thither in all ways. The artillery booming, forward, rearward, and on the flanks made jumble of ideas of direction. Landmarks had vanished into the gathered gloom. The youth began to imagine that he had got into the center of the tremendous quarrel, and he could perceive no way out of it. From the mouths of the fleeing men came a thousand wild questions, but no one made answers.

The youth, after rushing about and throwing interrogations at the heedless bands of retreating infantry, finally clutched a man by the arm. They swung around face to face.

"Why—why—" stammered the youth struggling with his balking tongue.

The man screamed: "Let go me! Let go me!" His face was livid and his eyes were rolling uncontrolled. He was heaving and panting. He still grasped his rifle, perhaps having forgotten to release his hold upon it. He tugged frantically, and the youth being compelled to lean forward was dragged several paces.

"Let go me! Let go me!"

"Why—why—" stuttered the youth.

"Well, then!" bawled the man in a lurid rage. He adroitly and fiercely swung his rifle. It crushed upon the youth's head. The man ran on.

The youth's fingers had turned to paste upon the other's arm. The energy was smitten from his muscles. He saw the flaming wings of lightning flash before his vision. There was a deafening rumble of thunder within his head.

Suddenly his legs seemed to die. He sank writhing to the ground. He tried to arise. In his efforts against the numbing pain he was like a man wrestling with a creature of the air.

There was a sinister struggle.

Sometimes he would achieve a position half erect, battle with the air for a moment, and then fall again, grabbing at the grass. His face was of a clammy pallor. Deep groans were wrenched from him.

At last, with a twisting movement, he got upon his hands and knees, and from thence, like a babe trying to walk, to his feet. Pressing his hands to his temples he went lurching over the grass.

He fought an intense battle with his body. His dulled senses wished him to swoon and he opposed them stubbornly, his mind portraying unknown dangers and mutilations if he should fall upon the field. He went tall soldier fashion. He imagined secluded spots where he could fall and be unmolested. To search for one he strove against the tide of pain.

Once he put his hand to the top of his head and timidly touched the wound. The scratching pain of the contact made him draw a long breath through his clinched teeth. His fingers were dabbled with blood. He regarded them with a fixed stare.

Around him he could hear the grumble of jolted cannon as the scurrying horses were lashed toward the front. Once, a young officer on a besplashed charger nearly ran him down. He turned and watched the mass of guns, men, and horses sweeping in a wide curve toward a gap in a fence. The officer was making excited motions with a gauntleted hand. The guns followed the teams with an air of unwillingness, of being dragged by the heels.

235

Some officers of the scattered infantry were cursing and railing like fishwives. Their scolding voices could be heard above the din. Into the unspeakable jumble in the roadway rode a squadron of cavalry. The faded yellow of their facings shone bravely. There was a mighty altercation.

The artillery were assembling as if for a conference.

The blue haze of evening was upon the field. The lines of forest were long purple shadows. One cloud lay along the western sky partly smothering the red.

As the youth left the scene behind him, he heard the guns suddenly roar out. He imagined them shaking in black rage. They belched and howled like brass devils guarding a gate. The soft air was filled with the tremendous remonstrance. With it came the shattering peal of opposing infantry. Turning to look behind him, he could see sheets of orange light illumine the shadowy distance. There were subtle and sudden lightnings in the far air. At times he thought he could see heaving masses of men.

He hurried on in the dusk. The day had faded until he could barely distinguish place for his feet. The purple darkness was filled with men who lectured and jabbered. Sometimes he could see them gesticulating against the blue and somber sky. There seemed to be a great ruck of men and munitions spread about in the forest and in the fields.

The little narrow roadway now lay lifeless. There were overturned wagons like sun-dried bowlders. The bed of the former torrent was choked with the bodies of horses and splintered parts of war machines.

It had come to pass that his wound pained him but little. He was afraid to move rapidly, however, for a dread of disturbing it. He held his head very still and took many precautions against stumbling. He was filled with anxiety, and his face was pinched and drawn in anticipation of the pain of any sudden mistake of his feet in the gloom.

His thoughts, as he walked, fixed intently upon his hurt. There was a cool, liquid feeling about it and he imagined blood moving slowly down under his hair. His head seemed swollen to a size that made him think his neck to be inadequate.

The new silence of his wound made much worriment. The little blistering voices of pain that had called out from his scalp were, he thought, definite in their expression of danger. By them he believed he could measure his plight. But when they remained ominously silent he became frightened and imagined terrible fingers that clutched into his brain.

Amid it he began to reflect upon various incidents and conditions of the past. He bethought him of certain meals his mother had cooked at home, in which those dishes of which he was particularly fond had occupied prominent positions. He saw the spread table. The pine walls of the kitchen were glowing in the warm light from the stove. Too, he remembered how he and his companions used to go from the school-house to the bank of a shaded pool. He saw his clothes in disorderly array upon the grass of the bank. He felt the swash of the fragrant water upon his body. The leaves of the overhanging maple rustled with melody in the wind of youthful summer.

237

He was overcome presently by a dragging weariness. His head hung forward and his shoulders were stooped as if he were bearing a great bundle. His feet shuffled along the ground.

He held continuous arguments as to whether he should lie down and sleep at some near spot, or force himself on until he reached a certain haven. He often tried to dismiss the question, but his body persisted in rebellion and his senses nagged at him like pampered babies.

......

Chapter 13

The youth went slowly toward the fire indicated by his departed friend. As he reeled, he bethought him of the welcome his comrades would give him. He had a conviction that he would soon feel in his sore heart the barbed missiles of ridicule. He had no strength to invent a tale; he would be a soft target.

He made vague plans to go off into the deeper darkness and hide, but they were all destroyed by the voices of exhaustion and pain from his body. His ailments, clamoring, forced him to seek the place of food and rest, at whatever cost.

He swung unsteadily toward the fire. He could see the forms of men throwing black shadows in the red light, and as he went nearer it became known to him in some way that the ground was strewn with sleeping men.

Of a sudden he confronted a black and monstrous figure. A rifle barrel caught some glinting beams. "Halt! halt!" He was dismayed for a moment, but he presently thought that he recognized the nervous voice. As he stood tottering before the rifle barrel, he called out: "Why, hello, Wilson, you—you here?"

The rifle was lowered to a position of caution and the loud soldier came slowly forward. He peered into the youth's face. "That you, Henry?"

"Yes, it's—it's me."

"Well, well, ol' boy," said the other, "by ginger, I'm glad t' see yeh! I give yeh up fer a goner. I thought yeh was dead sure enough." There was husky emotion in his voice.

The youth found that now he could barely stand upon his feet. There was a sudden sinking of his forces. He thought he must hasten to produce his tale to protect him from the missiles already on the lips of his redoubtable comrades. So, staggering before the loud soldier, he began: "Yes, yes. I've—I've had an awful time. I've been all over. Way over on th' right. Ter'ble fightin' over there. I had an awful time. I got separated from the reg'ment. Over on th' right, I got shot. In th' head. I never see sech fightin'. Awful time. I don't see how I could a' got separated from th' reg'ment. I got shot, too. "

His friend had stepped forward quickly. "What? Got shot? Why didn't yeh say so first? Poor ol' boy, we must—hol' on a minnit; what am I doin'. I'll call Simpson. "

Another figure at that moment loomed in the gloom. They could see that it was the corporal. "Who yeh talkin' to, Wilson?" he demanded. His voice was anger-toned. "Who yeh talkin' to? Yeh th' derndest sentinel—why—hello, Henry, you here? Why, I thought you was dead four hours ago! Great Jerusalem, they keep turnin' up every ten minutes or so! We thought we'd lost forty-two men by straight count, but if they keep on a-comin' this way, we'll git th' comp'ny all back by mornin' yit. Where was yeh?"

"Over on th' right. I got separated" —began the youth with considerable glibness.

But his friend had interrupted hastily. "Yes, an' he got shot in th' head an' he's in a fix, an' we must see t' him right away. " He rested his rifle in the hollow of his left arm and his right around the youth's shoulder.

"Gee, it must hurt like thunder!" he said.

The youth leaned heavily upon his friend. "Yes, it hurts—hurts a good deal," he replied. There was a faltering in his voice.

"Oh," said the corporal. He linked his arm in the youth's and drew him forward. "Come on, Henry. I'll take keer 'a yeh. "

As they went on together the loud private called out after them: "Put 'im t' sleep in my blanket, Simpson. An'—hol' on a minnit—here's my canteen. It's full 'a coffee. Look at his head by th' fire an' see how it looks. Maybe it's a pretty bad un. When I git relieved in a couple 'a minnits, I'll be over an' see t' him. "

The youth's senses were so deadened that his friend's voice sounded

239

from afar and he could scarcely feel the pressure of the corporal's arm. He submitted passively to the latter's directing strength. His head was in the old manner hanging forward upon his breast. His knees wobbled.

The corporal led him into the glare of the fire. "Now, Henry," he said, "let's have look at yer ol' head."

The youth sat obediently and the corporal, laying aside his rifle, began to fumble in the bushy hair of his comrade. He was obliged to turn the other's head so that the full flush of the fire light would beam upon it. He puckered his mouth with a critical air. He drew back his lips and whistled through his teeth when his fingers came in contact with the splashed blood and the rare wound.

"Ah, here we are!" he said. He awkwardly made further investigations. "Jest as I thought," he added, presently. "Yeh've been grazed by a ball. It's raised a queer lump jest as if some feller had lammed yeh on th' head with a club. It stopped a-bleedin' long time ago. Th' most about it is that in th' mornin' yeh'll fell that a number ten hat wouldn't fit yeh. An' your head'll be all het up an' feel as dry as burnt pork. An' yeh may git a lot 'a other sicknesses, too, by mornin'. Yeh can't never tell. Still, I don't much think so. It's jest a damn' good belt on th' head, an' nothin' more. Now, you jest sit here an' don't move, while I go rout out th' relief. Then I'll send Wilson t' take keer 'a yeh."

The corporal went away. The youth remained on the ground like a parcel. He stared with a vacant look into the fire.

After a time he aroused, for some part, and the things about him began to take form. He saw that the ground in the deep shadows was cluttered with men, sprawling in every conceivable posture. Glancing narrowly into the more distant darkness, he caught occasional glimpses of visages that loomed pallid and ghostly, lit with a phosphorescent glow. These faces expressed in their lines the deep stupor of the tired soldiers. They made them appear like men drunk with wine. This bit of forest might have appeared to an ethereal wanderer as a scene of the result of some frightful debauch.

On the other side of the fire the youth observed an officer asleep, seated bolt upright, with his back against a tree. There was something perilous in his position. Badgered by dreams, perhaps, he swayed with little bounces and starts, like an old, toddy-stricken grandfather in a chimney corner. Dust and stains were upon his face. His lower jaw hung down as if lacking strength to assume its normal position. He was the picture of an exhausted soldier after a feast of war.

He had evidently gone to sleep with his sword in his arms. These two had slumbered in an embrace, but the weapon had been allowed in time to fall unheeded to the ground. The brass-mounted hilt lay in contact with some parts of the fire.

Within the gleam of rose and orange light from the burning sticks were other soldiers, snoring and heaving, or lying deathlike in slumber. A few pairs of legs were stuck forth, rigid and straight. The shoes displayed the mud or dust of marches and bits of rounded trousers, protruding from the blankets, showed rents and tears from hurried pitchings through the dense brambles.

The fire cackled musically. From it swelled light smoke. Overhead the foliage moved softly. The leaves, with their faces turned toward the blaze, were colored shifting hues of silver, often edged with red. Far off to the right, through a window in the forest could be seen a handful of stars lying, like glittering pebbles, on the black level of the night.

Occasionally, in this low-arched hall, a soldier would arouse and turn his body to a new position, the experience of his sleep having taught him of uneven and objectionable places upon the ground under him. Or, perhaps, he would lift himself to a sitting posture, blink at the fire for an unintelligent moment, throw a swift glance at his prostrate companion, and then cuddle down again with a grunt of sleepy content.

The youth sat in a forlorn heap until his friend the loud young soldier came, swinging two canteens by their light strings. "Well, now, Henry, ol' boy," said the latter, "we'll have yeh fixed up in jest about a minnit."

He had the bustling ways of an amateur nurse. He fussed around the fire and stirred the sticks to brilliant exertions. He made his patient drink largely from the canteen that contained the coffee. It was to the youth a delicious draught. He tilted his head afar back and held the canteen long to his lips. The cool mixture went caressingly down his blistered throat. Having finished, he sighed with comfortable delight.

The loud young soldier watched his comrade with an air of satisfaction. He later produced an extensive handkerchief from his pocket. He folded it into a manner of bandage and soused water from the other canteen upon the middle of it. This crude arrangement he bound over the youth's head, tying the ends in a queer knot at the back of the neck.

"There," he said, moving off and surveying his deed, "yeh look like th' devil, but I bet yeh feel better."

The youth contemplated his friend with grateful eyes. Upon his aching and swelling head the cold cloth was like a tender woman's hand.

"Yeh don't holler ner say nothin'," remarked his friend approvingly. "I know I'm a blacksmith at takin' keer 'a sick folks, an' yeh never squeaked. Yer a good un, Henry. Most 'a men would a' been in th' hospital long ago. A shot in th' head ain't foolin' business."

The youth made no reply, but began to fumble with the buttons of his jacket.

"Well, come, now," continued his friend, "come on. I must put yeh t' bed an' see that yeh git a good night's rest."

The other got carefully erect, and the loud young soldier led him among the sleeping forms lying in groups and rows. Presently he stooped and picked up his blankets. He spread the rubber one upon the ground and placed the woolen one about the youth's shoulders.

"There now," he said, "lie down an' git some sleep."

The youth, with his manner of doglike obedience, got carefully down like a crone stooping. He stretched out with a murmur of relief and comfort. The ground felt like the softest couch.

But of a sudden he ejaculated: "Hol' on a minnit! Where you goin' t' sleep?"

His friend waved his hand impatiently. "Right down there by yeh."

"Well, but hol' on a minnit," continued the youth. "What yeh goin' t' sleep in? I've got your—"

The loud young soldier snarled: "Shet up an' go on t' sleep. Don't be makin' a damn' fool 'a yerself," he said severely.

After the reproof the youth said no more. An exquisite drowsiness had spread through him. The warm comfort of the blanket enveloped him and made a gentle langour. His head fell forward on his crooked arm and his weighted lids went softly down over his eyes. Hearing a splatter of musketry from the distance, he wondered indifferently if those men sometimes slept. He gave a long sigh, snuggled down into his blanket, and in a moment was like his comrades.

243

Notes

① **... the steel fibers had been washed from their hearts**: the strong psychological defense which was taught by the army no longer existed in their hearts.

② **They are bursting from their coats and their equipments as from entanglements**: They are trying all they can to get away from their coats and their equipments.

Questions for Reading Comprehension

1. How is the battle scene described in the excerpt?

2. What does this description imply about the nature of war?

3. What does Henry feel during the battlefield?

4. How are the other soldiers portrayed in the excerpt?

5. "Amid it he began to reflect upon various incidents and conditions of the past. He bethought him of certain meals his mother had cooked at home, in which those dishes of which he was particularly fond had occupied prominent positions. He saw the spread table. The pine walls of the kitchen were glowing in the warm light from the stove. Too, he remembered how he and his companions used to go from the school-house to the bank of a shaded pool. He saw his clothes in disorderly array upon the grass of the bank. He felt the swash of the fragrant water upon his body. The leaves of the overhanging maple rustled with melody in the wind of youthful summer". Why does the writer describe Henry's reflection on various incidents and conditions of the past during his flight?

6. How does Henry get wounded? How does he explain his wound to Wilson?

7. Is Henry questioned further about his whereabouts in the war? Why or why not?

8. When the corporal sees Henry, he exclaims, "Why, I thought you was dead four hours ago! Great Jerusalem, they keep turnin' up every ten minutes or so! We thought we'd lost forty-two men by straight count, but if they keep on a-comin' this way, we'll git th' comp'ny all back by mornin' yit. Where was yeh?" What does his exclamation imply about the situation with his regime?

Discussion Questions for Appreciation

1. The description of the battle scene has nothing to do with glory and bravery. Is it what you expected when you read the title of the novel—*The Red Badge of Courage*?

2. After returning to his regime, Henry is well taken after because of his wound. Does this counteract the naturalistic view that the universe is indifferent to man's sufferings? Justify yourself.

3. What does Stephen Crane feel about war? What is his attitude towards war?

4. One of the most important themes of the novel is that nature is indifferent to man. How does the story convey this theme?

5. What are some of the most important symbols in the novel?

A Question for Writing

The term "Pathetic Fallacy" is often used to describe the human belief that nature mirrors human emotions and behavior. "Pathetic" comes from "Pathos," the Greek word for "feeling." Why would a naturalist call this belief a "Pathetic Fallacy"? Quote evidence from the novel to justify your understanding.

Theodore Dreiser （1871-1945）

Theodore Dreiser was born in Sullivan, Indiana, the son of a German immigrant. He grew up in poverty, and his schooling was erratic as the family moved from town to town. He left home when he was sixteen and worked at whatever jobs he could find. With the help of his former teacher, he was able to spend a year at the University of Indiana. He was, however, a voracious reader of such writers as Hawthorne, Poe, Balzac, and Freud, who influenced his thought and his reaction against organized religion. He also read Charles Darwin, Ernest Haeckel, Thomas Huxley, and Herbert Spencer, and these late-nineteenth-century scientists and social scientists all supported the view that nature and society have no divine sanction, and that human being, just as much as other life forms, are participants in an evolutionary process in which only those who adapt successfully to their environments survive. As a result, the tension between determinism and the potential for friendship and the improvement of social institutions appears in Dreiser's fiction.

In 1892 Dreiser started to write for the *Chicago Globe*, and moved to a better position with the *St. Louis Globe-Democrat*. In 1898 he married a Missouri schoolteacher, but the marriage was unhappy. Dreiser separated permanently from his wife in 1909, but never earnestly sought a divorce.

Dreiser started his career as a novelist with *Sister Carrie* (1900), a powerful account of a young working girl's rise to success and her slow decline. Carrie Meeber, a young country girl from Wisconsin who comes to Chicago, is attracted by the prospect of excitement that rapidly growing urban centers hold out for so many young people in the late eighteenth century. There she is seduced first by a traveling salesman, then by a married middle-aged manager, who then flees with her to New York, where he slowly declines while she begins a successful career on the stage. The president of the publishing company, disapproved of this work, and in attempt was made to promote it. However, *Sister Carrie* was reissued in 1907, and it became one of the most famous novels in American literary history.

Then family troubles drove Dreiser to the verge of suicide, but he recovered with the help of his brother Paul. He worked at a variety of literary jobs, and as an editor-in-chief of three women's magazines until 1910, when he resigned to write *Jennie Gerhardt* (1911), the story of Jennie, a girl who is seduced by a senator. She bears a child out of wedlock but sacrifices her own interests to avoid harming her lover's career. It was followed by a novel based on the life of the American transportation magnate, Charles T. Jerkes—*The Financier* (1912), then followed by *The Titan* (1914), which showed the influence of the evolutionary ideas of Herbert Spencer and Nietzsche's concept of the Übermensch. And the last volume of the trilogy, *The Stoic*, was finished in 1945.

247

The publication of *An American Tragedy* in 1925 brought Dreiser great fame. The story was based on a murder in upper New York State in 1906. Clyde Griffiths, a poor boy who dreams of a life of luxury and status, plans to murder Roberta Alden, a factory worker who gets pregnant from him when he sees the opportunity to marry the wealthy Sondra Finchley. The identification of power with money is at the heart of this novel.

In 1927, Dreiser visited Russia and became an advocate of socialism. He published *Dreiser Looks at Russia* in 1928 to express his left-oriented views. Shortly before his death, he joined the Communist Party.

Dreiser has been a controversial figure in American literary history. His works are powerful in their portrayal of the changing American life, but his style is considered crude. His interest is often in human motives and behavior and in the particularities of the environments that help to shape them. As a leading figure of American Naturalism, he portrays the world as a Godless one in which man is thrown upon himself to keep alive at the best he can against the overwhelming odds of the cold, indifferent environment. Nevertheless, Dreiser has a warm heart, for his sympathies are always with the oppressed and the weak, even though his famous determinism is essentially sentimental at root.

Old Rogaum and His Theresa

Introduction

This short story was first published as "Butcher Rogaum's Door" in *Ready's Mirror* 2 (December 12, 1901). Dreiser revised it as "Old Rogaum and His Theresa" for inclusion in *Free and Other Stories* (1918), the source of the present text. "Old Rogaum and His Theresa" dramatizes the tensions within newly arrived immigrant families between the legacy of Old World values and a new generation coming of age in America's big cities.

Old Rogaum and His Theresa

In all Bleecker Street[①] was no more comfortable doorway than that of the butcher Rogaum, even if the first floor was given over to meat market purposes. It was to one side of the main entrance, which gave ingress to the butcher shop, and from it led up a flight of steps, at least five feet wide, to the living rooms above. A little portico stood out in front of it, railed on either side, and within was a second or final door, forming, with the outer or storm door, a little area, where Mrs. Rogaum and her children sat of a summer's evening. The outer door was never locked, owing to the inconvenience it would inflict on Mr. Rogaum, who had no other way of getting upstairs. In winter, when all had gone to bed, there had been cases in which belated travelers had taken refuge there from snow and sleet. One or two newsboys occasionally slept there, until routed out by Officer Maguire, who, seeing it half open one morning at two o'clock, took occasion to look in. He jogged the newsboys sharply with his stick, and then, when they were gone, tried the inner door, which was locked.

You ought to keep that outer door locked, Rogaum, " he observed to the phlegmatic butcher the next evening, as he was passing, " People might get in. A couple o' kids was sleepin' in there last night.

"Ach, dot iss no difference," answered Rogaum pleasantly. "I haf der inner door locked, yet. Let dem sleep. Dot iss no difference. "

"Better lock it," said the officer, more to vindicate his authority than anything else. "Something will happen there yet. "

The door was never locked, however, and now of a summer evening Mrs. Rogaum and the children made pleasant use of its recess, watching the rout of streetcars and occasionally belated trucks go by. The children played on the sidewalk, all except the budding Theresa (eighteen just turning) , who, with one companion of the neighborhood, the pretty Kenrihan girl, walked up and down the block, laughing, glancing and watching the boys. Old Mrs. Kenrihan lived in the next block, and there, sometimes the two stopped. There, also, they most frequently pretended to be when talking with the boys in the intervening side street. Young "Connie" Almerting and George Goujon were the bright particular mashers[2] who held the attention of the maidens in this block. These two made their acquaintance in the customary bold, boyish way, and thereafter the girls an urgent desire to be out in the street together after eight, and to linger where the boys could see and overtake them.

Old Mrs. Rogaum never knew. She was a particularly fat, old German lady, completely dominated by her liege and portly lord, and at nine o'clock regularly, as he had long ago deemed meet her fit, she was wont to betake her way upward and so to bed. Old Rogaum himself, at that hour, closed the market and went to his chamber.

Before that all the children were called sharply, once from the door-step below, and once from the window above, only Mrs. Rogaum did it first and Rogaum last. It had come, because of the shade of lenience, not wholly apparent in the father's nature, that the older of the children needed two callings and sometimes three. Theresa, now that she had "got in" with the Kenrihan maiden, needed that many calls and even more.

She was just at the age for which mere thoughtless, sensory life holds its greatest charm. She loved to walk up and down in the as yet bright street where were voices and laughter, and occasionally moonlight streaming down. What a nuisance it was to be called at nine, anyhow. Why should one have to go in then, anyhow. What old fogies her parents were, wishing to go to bed so early. Mrs. Kenrihan was not so strict with her daughter. It made her pettish when Rogaum insisted calling as he often did in German, "Come you now," in a very hoarse and belligerent voice.

She came, eventually, frowning and wretched, all the moonlight calling her, all the voices of the night urging her to come back. Her innate opposition due to her urgent youth made her coming later and later, however, until now, by August of this, her eighteenth year, it was nearly ten when she entered, and Rogaum was almost invariably angry.

"I vill lock you oudt," he declared, in strongly accented English, while she tried to slip by him each time. "I vill show you. Du sollst[3] come ven I say, yet. Hear now."

"I'll not," answered Theresa, but was always under her breath.

Poor Mrs. Rogaum troubled at hearing the wrath in her husband's voice. It spoke of harder and fiercer times, which had been with her. Still she was not power enough in the family councils to put in a weighty word. So Rogaum fumed unrestricted.

There were other nights, however, many of them, and now that the young sparks of the neighborhood had enlisted the girls attention, it was a more trying time than ever. Never did a street seem more beautiful. Its shabby red walls, dusty pavements and protruding store steps and iron railings seemed bits of the ornamental paraphernalia of Heaven itself. These lights, the cars, the moon, the street lamp! Theresa had a tender eye for the dashing Almerting, a young idler and loafer of the district, the son of a stationer farther up the street. What a fine fellow he was, indeed! What a handsome nose and chin! What eyes! What authority! His cigarette was always cocked at a high angle, in her presence, and his hat had the least suggestion of being set to one side. He had a shrewd way of winking one eye, taking her boldly by the arm, hailing her as, "Hey, Pretty!" and was strong and athletic and worked (when he worked) in a tobacco factory. His was a trade, indeed, nearly acquired, as he said, and his jingling pockets attested that he had money of his own. Altogether, he was very captivating.

"Aw, whaddy ya want to go in for?" he used to say to her, tossing his head gayly on one side to listen and holding her by the arm, as old Rogaum called. "Tell um yuh didn't hear."

"No, I've got to go," said the girl, who was soft and plump and fair—a Rhine maiden type.

"Well, yuh don't have to go just yet. Stay another minute. George, what was the fellow's name that tried to sass us the other day?"

"Theresa!" roared Rogaum forcefully. "If you don't now come! Ve vill see!"

"I've got to go," said Theresa with a faint effort toward starting. "Can't you hear? Don't hold me. I haf to."

"Aw, whaddy ya want to be such a coward for? Y' don't have to go. He won't do nothin' tuh yuh. My old man was always hollerin' like that up tuh a coupla years ago. Let him holler! Say, kid, but yuh got sweet eyes! They're as blue! An' your mouth,"

"Now stop! You hear me!" Theresa would protest softly, as, swiftly, he would slip an arm about her waist and draw her to him, sometimes in vain, sometimes in a successful effort to kiss her.

As a rule she managed to interpose an elbow between her face and his, but even then he would manage to touch an ear or a cheek or her neck-sometimes her mouth, full and warm—before she would develop sufficient energy to push him away and herself free. Then she would protest mock earnestly or sometimes run away.

"Now, I'll never speak to you any more, if that's the way you're going to do. My father don't allow me to kiss boys, anyhow," and then she would run, half ashamed, half smiling to herself as he would stare after her, or if she lingered, develop a kind of anger and even rage.

"Aw, cut it! Whaddy ya want to be so shy for? Dontcha like me? What's getting into yuh anyhow? Hey?"

"In the meantime George Goujon and Myrtle Kenrihan, their companions, might be sweeting and going through similar contest, perhaps a hundred feet up the street, or near at hand. The quality of old Rogaum voice would by now become so raucous, however, that Theresa would have lost all comfort in the scene and, becoming frightened, hurry away. Then it was often that both Almerting and Goujon as well as Myrtle Kenrihan would follow her to the corner, almost in sight of the irate butcher.

"Let him call" young Almerting would insist, laying a final hold on her soft white fingers and causing her to quiver thereby.

"Oh, no," she would gasp nervously. "I can't."

"Well, go on, then," he would say, and with a flip of his heel would turn back, leaving Theresa to wonder whether she had alienated him forever or no. Then she would hurry to her father's door.

"Muss ich all my time spenden calling, mit you on de streeds oudt?" old Rogaum would roar wrathfully, the while his fat hand would descend on her back. "Take dot now. Vy don'd you come ven I call? In now, I vill show you. Und come you yussed vunce more at dis time—ve vill see if I am the boss in my own house, aber! Komst du vun minute nach[④] ten tomorrow und you vill see vot you vill get. I vill der door lock. Du sollst not in kommen. Mark! Oudt sollst du stayen-oudt!" and he would glare wrathfully at her retreating figure.

Sometimes Theresa would whimper, sometimes cry or sulk. She almost hated her father for his cruelty, "the big, fat, rough thing," and just because she wanted to stay out in the bright streets, too. Because he was old and stout and wanted to go to bed at ten, he thought everyone else did. And outside was the dark sky with its stars, the street lamps, the tinkle and laughter of eternal life.

"Oh!" she would sigh as she undressed and crawled into her small neat bed. To think that she had to live like this all of her days! At the same time, old Rogaum was angry, and equally determined. It was not so much that he imagined his Theresa was in bad company as yet, but he wished to forefend against any possible danger. This was not a good neighborhood by any means. The boys around here were tough. He wanted Theresa to pick some nice sober youth from among the other Germans he and his wife knew here and there—at the Lutheran Church, for instance. Otherwise she shouldn't marry. He knew she only walked from his shop to the door of the Kenrihan's and back again. Had not his wife told him so? If he had thought upon what far pilgrimage her feet had already ventured, or had even seen the dashing Almerting hanging near, then had there been wrath indeed. As it was, his mind was more or less at ease.

On many, many evenings it was much the same. Sometimes she got in on time, sometimes not, but more and more "Connie" Almerting claimed her for his "steady" and bought her ice-cream. In the range of the short block and its confining corners it was done, lingering by the curbstone and strolling a half block either way in the side streets, until she had offended seriously at home, and the threat was repeating anew. He often tried to persuade her to go on picnics or outings of various kinds, but this, somehow, was not to be thought of at her age—at least with him. She knew her father would never endure the thought, and never even had the courage to mention it, let alone run away. Mere lingering with him at the adjacent street corners brought stronger and stronger admonishments—even more blows and the threat that she should not get in at all.

Well enough she meant to obey, but on one radiant night late in June the time fled too fast. The moon was so bright, the air so soft. The feel of far summer things was in the wind and even in the dusty street. Theresa, in a newly starched white summer dress, had been loitering up and down with Myrtle when as usual they encountered Almerting and Goujon. Now it was ten, and the regular calls were beginning.

"Aw, wait a minute," said "Connie." "Stand still. He won't lock yuh out."

"But he will, though," said Theresa. "You don't know him."

"Well, if he does, come on back to me. I'll take care of yuh. I'll be here. But he won't though. If you stayed out a little while he'd letcha in all right. That's the way my old man used to try to do me but it didn't work with me. I'd stay out an' he'd let me in, just the same. Don'tcha let him kidja." He jingles some loose change in his pocket.

Never in his life had he had a girl on his hands at any unseasonable hour, but it was nice to talk big, and there was a club to which he belonged. The Varick Street Roosters, and to which he had a key. It would be closed and empty at this hour, and she could stay there until morning, if need be or with Myrtle Kenrihan. He would take her there if she insisted. There was a sinister grin on the youth's face.

By now Theresa's affections had carried her far. This youth with his slim body, his delicate strong hands, his fine chin, straight mouth and hard dark eyes—how wonderful he seemed! He was but nineteen to her eighteen but cold, shrewd, and daring. Yet how tender he seemed to her, how well worth having! Always, when he kissed her now, she trembled in the balance. There was something in the iron grasp of his fingers that went through her like fire. His glance held hers at times when she could scarcely endure it.

"I'll wait, anyhow," he insisted.

Longer and longer she lingered, but now for once no voice came.

She began to feel that something was wrong—a greater strain than if old Rogaum's voice had been filling the whole neighborhood.

"I've got to go," she said.

"Gee, but you're a coward, yuh are!" said he derisively. "What'r yuh always so scared about? He always says he'll lock yuh out, but he never does."

"Yes, but he will," she insisted nervously. "I think he has this time. You don't know him. He's something awful when he gets real mad. Oh, Connie, I must go!" For the sixth or seventh time she moved, and once more he caught her arm and waist and tried to kiss her, but she slipped away from him.

"Ah, yuh!" he exclaimed. "I wish he would lock yuh out!"

At her own doorstep, she paused momentarily, more to soften he progress than anything. The outer door was open as usual, but not the inner. She tried it, but it would not give. It was locked! For a moment she paused, cold fear racing over her body, and then knocked.

No answer.

Again she rattled the door, this time nervously, and was about to cry.

Still no answer.

At last she heard her father's voice, hoarse and indifferent, not addressed to her at all, to her mother.

"Let her go, now," it said savagely, from the front room where he supposed she could not hear. "I vill her a lesson teach."

"Hadn't you better let her in now, yet?" pleaded Mrs. Rogaum faintly.

"No," insisted Mr. Rogaum. "Nefer! Let her go now. If she vill alvays stay oudt, let her stay now. Ve vill see how she likes dot."

His voice was rich in wrath, and he was saving up a good beating for her into the bargain, that she knew. She would have to wait and wait and plead, and when she was thoroughly wretched and subdued he would let her in and beat her—such a beating as she had never received in all her born days.

Again the door rattled and she still got no answer. Not even her call brought a sound.

Now, strangely, a new element, not heretofore apparent in her nature but nevertheless wholly there, was called into life, springing in action as Diana⑤, full formed. Why should he always be so harsh? She hadn't don anything but stay out a little later than usual. He was always so anxious to keep her in and subdue her. For once the cold chills of her girlish fears left her, and she answered angrily.

"All right," she said, some old German stubbornness springing up, "I won't knock. You don't let me in, then."

A suggestion of tears was in her eyes, but she backed firmly out into the stoop and sat down, hesitating. Old Rogaum saw her, lowering down from the lattice, but said nothing. He would teach her for once what were proper hours!

At the corner, standing, Almerting also saw her. He recognized the simple white dress, and paused steadily, a strange thrill racing over him. Really they had locked her out! Gee, this was new. It was great, in a way. There she was, white, quiet, shut out, waiting at her father's doorstep.

Sitting thus, Theresa pondered a moment, her girlish rashness and anger dominating her. Her pride was hurt and she felt revengeful. They would shut her out, would they? All right, she would go out and they should look to it how they would get her back—the old curmudgeons. For the moment the home of Myrtle Kenrihan came to her as possible refuge, but he decided that she need not go there yet. She had better wait a while and see—or walk and frighten them. He would beat her, would he? Well maybe he would, and maybe he wouldn't. She might come back, but still that was a thing afar off. Just now it didn't matter so much. "Connie" was still there on the corner. He loved her dearly. She felt it.

Getting up, she stepped to the now quieting sidewalk and strolled up the street. It was a rather nervous procedure, however. There were street cars still, and stores lighted and people passing, but soon these would not be, and she was locked out. The streets were already more than long silent walks and gleaming rows of lamps.

At the corner her youthful lover almost pounced upon her.

"Locked out, are yuh?" he asked, his eyes shining.

For the moment she was delighted to see him, for a nameless dread had already laid hold of her. Home meant so much. Up to now it had been her whole life.

"Yes," she answered feebly.

"Well, let's stroll on a little," said the boy. He had not as yet quite made up his mind what to do, but the night was young. It was so fine to have with him—his.

At the farther corner they passed Officers Maguire and Delahanty, idly swinging their clubs and discussing politics.

" 'Tis a shame," Officer Delahanty was saying, "the way things are run now," but he paused to add, "Ain't that old Rogaum's girl over there with young Almerting?"

"It is," replied Maguire looking after her.

"Well, I'm thinkin' he'd better be keepin' an eye on her," said the former.

"She's too young to be runnin' around with the likes o' him."

Maguire agreed. "He's a young tough," he observed. "I never liked him. He's too fresh. He works over here in Myer's tobacco factory, and belongs to the Roosters. He's up to no good, I'll warrant that."

"Teach 'em a lesson, I would," Almerting was saying to Theresa as they strolled on. "We'll walk around a while an' make 'em think yuh mean business. They won't lock yuh out any more. If they don't let yuh in when we come back I'll find yuh a place, all right."

His sharp eyes were gleaming as he looked around into her own. Already he had made up his mind that she should not go back if he could help it. He knew a better place than home for this night, anyhow—the club room of the Roosters, if nowhere else. They could stay there for a time, anyhow.

By now old Rogaum, who had seen her walking up the street alone, was marveling at her audacity, but thought she would soon come back. It was amazing that she could exhibit such temerity, but he would teach her! Such a whipping! At half-past ten, however, he stuck his head out of the open window and saw nothing of her. At eleven, the same! Then he walked the floor.

At first wrathful, then nervous, then nervous and wrathful, he finally ended all nervous, without a scintilla of wrath. His stout wife sat up in bed and began to wring her hands.

"Lie down!" he commanded. "You make me sick. I know vot I am doing!"

"Is she still at der door?" pleaded the mother.

"No," he said. "I don't tink so. She should come ven I call."

His nerves were weakening, however, and now they finally collapsed.

"She vent de stread up," he said anxiously after a time. "I vill go after."

Slipping on his coat, he went down the stairs and out into the night. It was growing late, and the stillness and gloom of midnight were nearing. Nowhere in sight was Theresa. First one way and then another he went, looking here, there, everywhere, finally groaning.

"Ach, Gott!" he said, the sweat bursting out on his brow, "vot in Teufal's⑥ name iss dis?"

He thought he would seek a policeman, but there was none. Officer Maguire had long since gone for a quiet game in one of the neighboring saloons. His partner had temporarily returned to his own beat. Still old Rogaum hunted on, worrying more and more.

Finally he bethought him to hasten home again, for she must have got back. Mrs. Rogaum, too, would be frantic if she had not. If she were not there he must go to the police. Such a night! And his Theresa— This thing could not go on.

As he turned into his own corner he almost ran, coming up to the little portico wet and panting. At a puffing step he turned, and almost fell over a white body at his feet, a prone and writhing woman.

"Ach, Gott!" he cried aloud, almost shouting in his distress and excitement. "Theresa, vot iss dis? Wilhelmina, a light now. Bring a light now, I say, for himmel's sake! Theresa hat sich *umgebracht*⑦. Help!"

He had fallen to his knees and was turning over the writhing, groaning figure. By the pale light of the street, however, he could make out that it was not his Theresa, fortunately, as he had at first feared, but another and yet there was something very like her in the figure.

"Um!" said the stranger weakly. "Ah!"

The dress was grey, not white as was his Theresa's, but the body was round and plump. It cut the fiercest cords of his intensity, this thought of death to a young woman, but there was something else about the situation which made him forget his own troubles.

Mrs. Rogaum, loudly admonished, almost tumbled down the stairs. At the foot she held the light she had brought—a small glass oil-lamp— and then nearly dropped it. A fairly attractive figure, more girl than woman, rich in all her physical charms that characterize a certain type, lay hear to dying. Her soft hair had fallen back over a good forehead, now quite white. Her pretty hands, well decked with rings, were clutched tightly in an agonized grip. At her neck a blue silk shirtwaist and a light lace collar were torn away where she had clutched herself, and on the white flesh was a yellow stain as of one who had been burn-ed. A strange odor reeked in the area, and in one corner was a spilled bottle.

"Ach, Gott!" exclaimed Mrs. Rogaum. "It iss a vooman! She haf herself gekilt. Run for der police! Oh my! Oh my!"

Rogaum did not kneel for more than moment. Somehow, this creature's fate seemed in some psychic way identified with that of his own daughter. He bounded up, and jumping out his front door, he began to call lustily for the police. Officer Maguire, at a social game nearby, heard the very first cry and came running.

"What's the matter here, now?" he exclaimed, rushing up full and ready for murder, robbery, fire, or indeed, anything in the whole roster of human calamities. "A vooman!" said Rogaum excitedly. "She haf herself *umgebracht*. She iss dying. Ach, Gott! in my own doorstep, yet!"

"Vere iss der hospital?" put in Mrs. Rogaum, thinking clearly of an ambulance, but not being able to express it. "She iss gekilt, sure. Oh! Oh!" and banding over her the poor motherly soul stroked the tightened hands, and trickled tears upon the blue shirtwaist. "Ach, vy did you do dot?" she said. "Ach, for vy?"

Officer Maguire was essentially a man of action. He jumped to the sidewalk, amid the gathering company, and beat aloud with his club upon the stone flagging. Then he ran to the nearest police phone, returning to aid in another way he might. A milk wagon passing on its way from the Jersey ferry with a few tons of fresh milk aboard, he held it up and demanded a helping.

"Give us quart there, will you?" he said authoritatively. "A woman's swallowed acid in here. "

"Sure," said the driver, anxious to learn the cause of the excitement. "Got a glass, anybody?"

Maguire ran back and returned bearing a measure. Mrs. Rogaum stood looking nervously on, while the stocky officer raised the golden head and poured the milk.

"Here, now, drink this," he said. "Come on. Try an' swallow it. "

The girl, a blonde of a type the world too well knows, opened her eyes, and looked, groaning a little.

"Drink it," shouted the officer fiercely. "Do you want to die? Open your mouth!"

Used to a fear of the law in all her days, she obeyed now, even in death.

The lips parted, the fresh milk was drained to the end, some spilling on neck and cheek.

While they were working old Rogaum came back and stood looking on, by the side of his wife. Also Officer Delahanty, having heard the peculiar wooden ring of the stick upon the stone in the night, had come up.

"Ach, ach," exclaimed Rogaum rather distractedly, "und she iss oudt yet. I could not find her. Oh, oh!"

There was a clang of a gong up the street as the racing ambulance turned in rapidly. A young hospital surgeon dismounted, and seeing the woman's condition, ordered immediate removal. Both officers and Rogaum, as well as the surgeon, helped place her in the ambulance. After a moment the lone bell, ringing wildly in the night, was all the evidence remaining that tragedy had been here.

"Do you know how she came here?" asked officer Delahanty, coming back to get Rogaum's testimony for the police.

"No, no," answered Rogaum wretchedly. "She vass here alretty. I vass for my daughter loog. Ach, himmel, I haf my daughter lost. She iss avay."

Mrs. Rogaum also chattered, the significance of Theresa's absence all the more painfully emphasized this.

The officer did not at first get the import of this. He was only interested in the facts of the present case.

"You say she was here when you come. Where was you?"

"I vass for my daughter loog. I come here, und der vooman vass here now alretty."

"Yes. What time was this?"

"Only now yet. Yussed a half-hour."

Officer Maguire had strolled up, after chasing away a small crowd that had gathered with fierce and unholy threats. For the first time now he noticed the peculiar perturbation of the usually placid German couple.

"What about your daughter?" he asked, catching a word as to that.

Both old people raised their voices at once.

"She haf gone. She haf run avay. Ach, himmel, ve must for her loog. Quick—she could not get in. Ve had der door shut."

"Locked her out, eh?" inquired Maguire after a long time, hearing much of the rest of the story.

"Yes," explained Rogaum. "It was to schkare her a liddle. She vould not come ven I called."

"Sure, that's the girl we saw walkin' with young Almerting, do ye mind? The one in the white dress," said Delahanty to Maguire.

"White dress, yah!" echoed Rogaum, and then the fact of her walking with someone had come home like a blow.

"Did you hear dot?" he exclaimed even as Mrs. Rogaum did likewise. " *Mein Gott, hast du das gehoert?*[⑧] "

He fairly jumped as he said it. His hands flew up to his stout and ruddy head.

"Whaddy ya want to let her out for nights?" asked Maguire roughly, catching the drift of the situation. "That's no time for young girls to be out, anyhow, and with these toughs around here. Sure, I saw her, nearly two hours ago."

"Ach," groaned Rogaum. "Two hours yet. Ho, ho, ho!" His voice was quite histeric.

"Well, go on in," said Officer Delahanty. "There's no use in yelling out here. Give us a description of her an' we'll send out an alarm. You won't be able to find her walkin' around."

Her parents described exactly. The two men turned to the nearest police box and then disappeared, leaving the old German couple in the throws of distress. A time-worn old church-clock nearby now chimed out one and then two. The note cut like knives. Mrs Rogaum began fearfully to cry. Rogaum walked and blustered to himself.

"It's a queer case, that," said officer Delahanty to Maguire after having reported the matter of Theresa, but referring solely to the outcast of the doorway so recently sent away and in whose fate they were much more interested. She was being a part of the commercialized vice of the city, they were curios as to the cause of her suicide. "I think I know

263

that woman. I think I know where she came from. You do, too—Adele's around the corner, eh? She didn't come into that doorway by herself, either. She was put there. You know how they do. "

"You're right," said Maguire. "She was put there, all right, and that's just where she came from, too. "

The two of them now tipped up there noses and cocked their eyes significantly.

"Let's go around," added Maguire.

They went, the significant red light over the transom at 68 telling its own story. Strolling leisurely up, they knocked. At the very first sound a painted denizen of the half-world opened the door.

"Where's Adele?" asked Maguire as the two, hats on as usual, stepped in.

"She's gone to bed. "

"Tell her to come down. "

They seated themselves deliberately in the gaudy mirrored parlor and waited, conversing between themselves in whispers. Presently a sleepy-looking woman of forty in a gaudy robe of a heavy texture, and slippered in red appeared.

"We're here about the suicide case you had tonight. What about it? Who she was? How'd she come to be in the doorway around the corner? Come now," Maguire added, as the madam assumed an air of mingled injured and ignorant innocence, "you know. Can that stuff! How did she come to take poison? "

"I don't know what you're talking about," said the woman with the utmost air of innocence. "I never heard of any suicide. "

"Aw, come now," insisted Delahanty, "the girl around the corner. You know. We know you've got a pull, but we've got to know about this case, just the same. Come across now. It won't be published. What made her take the poison?"

Under the steady eyes of the officers the woman hesitated, but finally weakened.

"Why—why—her lover went back on her—that's all. She got so blue, we just couldn't do anything with her. I tried to, but she wouldn't listen."

"Lover, eh?" put in Maguire as thought that were the most unheard—of thing in the world. "What is his name?"

"i don't know. You can never tell that."

"What was her name—Annie?" asked Delahanty wisely, as though he knew but was merely inquiring for form's sake.

"No—Emily."

"Well, how did she come to get over there, anyhow?" inquired Maguire most pleasantly.

"George took her," she replied, referring to a man-of-all-work about the place.

Then little by little as they sat there the whole miserable story came out, miserable as all the wilfulness and error and suffering in the world.

"How old was she?"

"Oh, twenty-one."

"Well, where'd she come from?"

"Oh, here in New York. Her family locked her out one night, I think."

Something in the way the woman said this last brought old Rogaum and his daughter back to the policeman's minds. They had forgotten all about her by now, although they had turned in alarm. Fearing to interfere too much with this well-known and politically controlled institution, the two men left, but outside they to talking of the other case.

"We ought to tell old Rogaum about her some time," said Maguire to Delahanty cynically. "He locked his kid out to-night."

"Yes, it might be a good thing for him to hear that," replied the other. "We'd better go round there an' see if his girl's back yet. She may be back by now," and so they returned but a little disturbed by the joint miseries.

At Rogaum's door they once more knocked loudly.

"Is your daughter back again?" asked Maguire when a reply was had.

"Ach, no," replied Mrs. Rogaum, who was quite alone now. "My husband he haf gone oudt again to loog vunce more. Oh, my! Oh, my!"

"Well, that's what you get for lockin' her out," returned Maguire loftily, the other story was fresh in his mind. "That other girl downstairs her tonight was locked out too, once." He chanced to have a girl-child of his own and somehow he was in the mood for pointing out moral. "you oughtn't to do anything like that. Where d'yuh expect she's goin' to if you lock her out?"

Mrs Rogaum groaned. She explained it was not her fault, but anyhow it was carrying coals to Newcastle to talk to her so. The advice was better for her husband.

The pair finally returned to the station to see if the call had been attended to.

"Sure," said the sergeant, "certainly. Whaddy ya think?" and he heard from the blotter before him:

" 'Look out for girl, Theresa Rogaum. Aged 18; height, about 5, 3; light hair, blue eyes, white cotton dress, trimmed with blue ribbon. Lat seen with lad named Almerting, about 19 years of age, about 5, 9; weight 135 pounds. '"

There were more details even more pointed out and conclusive. For over an hour now, supposedly, policemen from the Battery to Harlem, and far beyond, had been scanning long streets and dim shadows for a girl in a white dress with a youth of nineteen—supposedly.

Officer Halsey, another of this region, which took in a portion of Washington Square, has seen a many couple this pleasant summer evening since the description of Theresa and Almerting had been read to him over the telephone, but non that answered to these. Like Maguire and Delahanty, he was more or less indifferent to all such cases, but idling on a corner near the park at about three a. m., a brother officer, one Paisly by name, came up and casually mentioned the missing pair also.

"I bet I saw that couple, not over an hour ago. She was dressed in white, and looked to me as if she didn't want to be out. I didn't happen to think at the time, but now I remember. They acted sort o' funny. She did, anyhow. They went in this park down at the Fourth street end there."

"Supposing we beat it, then," suggested Halsey, weary for something to do.

"Sure," said the other quickly, and together they began a careful search, kicking around in te moonlight under the trees. The moonlight was leaning moderately toward the west, and all the branches were silvered with light and dew. Among the flowers, past clumps of bushes, near the fountain, they searched, each one going his was alone. At last, the wondering Halsey pushed beside a thick clump of flaming bushes, ruddy, slightly, even in the light. A murmur of voices greeted him, and something was very much like the sound of a sob.

"What's that?" he said mentally, drawing near and listening.

"Why don't you come on now?" said the first of the voices heard. "They won't let you in anymore. You're with me, ain't you? What's the use cryin'?"

No answer to this, but no sobs. She must have been crying silently.

"Come on. I can take care of yuh. We can live in Hoboken[9]. I know a place we can go to-night. That's all right."

There was a movement as if the speaker were patting her on the shoulder.

"What's the use of cryin'? Don't you believe I love yuh?"

The officer who had stolen quietly around to get a better view now came closer. He wanted to see for himself. In the moonlight, from a comfortable distance, he could see them seated. The tall bushes were almost all about the bench. In the arms of the youth was the girl in white, held very close. Leaning over to get a better view, he saw him kiss her and hold her—hold her in such a way that she could but yield to him, whatever her slight disinclination.

It was a common affair at earlier hours, but rather interesting now. The officer was interested. He crept nearer.

"What are you two doin' here?" he suddenly inquired, rising before them, as though he had not seen.

The girl tumbled out of her compromising position, speechless and blushing violently. The young man stood up, nervous, but defiant.

"Aw, we were just sittin' here," he replied.

"Yes? Well, say, what's your name? I think we're lookin' for you two, anyhow. Almerting?"

"That's me," said the youth.

"And yours?" he adds, addressing Theresa.

"Theresa Rogaum," replied the latter brokenly, beginning to cry.

"Well, you two'll have to come along with me," he added laconically. "The Captain wants to see both of you," and he marched them solely away.

"What for?" young Almerting ventured to inquire after a time, blanched with fright.

"Never mind," replied the policeman irritably. "Come along, you'll find out at the station house. We want you both. That's enough."

At the other end of the park Paisly joined them, and, at the station-house, the girl was given a chair. She was all tears and melancholy with a modicum possibly of relief at being thus rescued from the world. Her companion, for all his youth, was defiant if circumspect, a natural animal defeated of its aim.

"Better go for her father," commented the sergeant, and by four in the morning old Rogaum, who had still been up walking the floor, was rushing stationward. From the earlier rage he had passed to an almost killing grief, but now at the thought that he might possibly see his daughter alive and well once more he was overflowing with a mingled emotion which contained fear, rage, sorrow, and a number of other things. What should he do to her if she were alive? Beat her? Kiss her? Or what? Arrived at the station, however, and seeing his fair Theresa in the hands of the police, and this young stranger lingering near, also detained, he was beside himself with fear, rage, and affection.

"You! You!" he exclaimed at once, glaring at the imperturbable Almerting, when told that the young man was found with his girl. Then, seized with a sudden horror, he added, turning to Theresa, "Vot haf you done? Oh, oh! You! You!" he repeated again to Almerting angrily now that he felt his daughter was safe. "Come not near my tochter any more! I vill preak your effery pone, du teufel, du!"

He made a move toward the incarcerated lover, but here the sergeant interfered.

"Stop that, now," he said calmly. "Take you daughter out of her and go home, or I'll lock you both up. We don't want any fighting in here. D'ye hear? Keep your daughter off the streets hereafter, then she won't get into trouble. Don't let her run around with such young toughs as this." Almerting winced. "Then there won't anything happen to her. We'll do whatever punishing'sa to be done."

"Aw, what's eatin' him!" commented Almerting dourly, now that he felt himself reasonably say from a personal encounter. "What have I done? He locked her out, didn't he? I was just keepin' her company till morning."

"Yes, we know all about that," said the sergeant, "and about you, too. You shut up, or you'll go downtown to Special Sessions. I want no guff out o' you." Still he ordered the butcher angrily to be gone.

Old Rogaum heard nothing. He had his daughter. He was taking her home. She was not dead—not even morally injured in so far as he could learn. He was a compound of wondrous feelings. What to do was beyond him.

At the corner near the butcher shop they encountered the wakeful Maguire, still idling, as they passed. He was pleased to see that Rogaum had his Theresa once more. It raised him to a high, moralizing height.

"Don't lock her out any more," he called significantly. "That's what brought the other girl to your door, you know!"

"Vot iss dot?"[10] said Rogaum.

"I say the other girl was locked out. That's why she committed suicide."

"Ach, I know," said the husky German under his breath, but he had no intention of locking her out. He did not what he would do until they were in the presence of his crying wife, who fell upon Theresa, weeping. Then he decided to be reasonably lenient.

"She vass like you," said the old mother to the wandering Theresa, ignorant of the seeming lesson brought to their very door. "She vass loog like you."

"I vill not vip you now," said the old butcher solemnly, too delighted to think of punishment after having feared every horror under the sun, "aber, go not oudt any more. Keep off the streets so late. I von't hav it. Dot loafer, aber—let him yussed come here for some more! I fix him!"

"No, no," said the fat mother tearfully, smoothing her daughter's hair. "She vouldn't run avay no more yet, no, no." Old Mrs. Rogaum was all mother.

"Well, you wouldn't let me in," insists Theresa, "and I didn't have any place to go. What do you want me to do? I'm not going to stay in the house all the time."

"I fix him!" roared Rogaum, unloading all his rage now on the recreant lover freely. "Yussed let him come some more! Der penitentiary he should haf!①

"Oh, he's not so bad," Theresa told her mother, almost a heroine now that she was home and safe. "He's Mr. Almerting, the stationer's boy. They live here in the next block."

"Don't you ever bother that girl again," the sergeant was saying to young Almerting as he turned him loose an hour later. "If you do, we'll get you, and you won'd get off under six moths. Y'hear me, do you?"

"Aw, I don't want 'er," replied the boy truculently and cynically. "Let him have his old daughter. What'd he want to lock'er out for? They'd better not lock'er out again though, that's all I say. I don't want'er."

"Beat it!" replied the sergeant, and away he went.

Notes

① **Bleecker Street**: A street in Greenwich Village in New York City. Dreiser lived in Greenwich Village from 1917 to 1918 while he revised this story.

② **mashers**: male flirts. Charles Drouet in the novel *Sister Carrie* is initially described as a masher, a man "whose dress or manners are calculated to elicit the admiration of susceptible young women."

③ **Du soollst**: You shall.

④ **Komst du vun minute nach**: Come you one minute after.

⑤ **Diana**: a Roman deity, goddess of the moon, hunting, and women in childbirth.

⑥ **Teufal's**：The Devil's.

⑦ **Theresa hat sich *umgebracht***：Theresa has killed herself.

⑧ ***Mein Gott, hast du das gehoert***?：My God, did you hear that?

⑨ **Hoboken**：A seaport in Northeastern New Jersey, opposite New York City.

⑩ **Vot iss dot**?：What is that?

⑪ **Der penitentiary he should haf**!：He should be put into the penitentiary!"

Questions for Reading Comprehension

1. Where do Old Rogaum and his Theresa live?

2. What does Old Rogaum do? What do you know about him?

3. What kind of a woman is Mrs. Rogaum?

4. What kind of a girl is Theresa?

5. What is the conflict between Rogaum and Theresa?

6. How is the conflict between them resolved?

7. What do you know about Connie Almerting? What's the drive behind his relationship with Theresa? What does the story say about youth?

8. What does the story suggest about death?

9. What is the author's attitude towards women and human beings in general?

10. What do you think of Dreiser's writing style?

Discussion Questions for Appreciation

1. Old Rogaum speaks English with a strong German dialect, while Theresa speaks relatively standard English. What possible conclusion can you draw from their ways of speaking?

2. What is the function of Emily's story in "Old Rogaum and His Theresa"?

3. "Old Rogaum and His Theresa" is set in lower Manhattan, in aneighborhood of recent immigrants, mostly German and Irish. How are people there described? Where does the narrator seem to situate himself with regard to this cast of characters?

4. Some say "Old Rogaum and His Theresa" is in some ways about the situation of women at the turn of the century. Describe this predicament. Is it explored or exploited in this story?

5. In what ways does the plot of "Old Rogaum and His Theresa" suggest a fable or a parable? Or in other words, what lessons does the story teach?

A Question for Writing

Naturalists believe that man is at the mercy of uncontrollable forces and desires. How is this naturalistic idea presented in the story?

Jack London (1876-1916)

John Griffith London was born in San Francisco on January 12, 1876, an illegitimate son. He took his stepfather's name and grew up in poverty. His circumstances of birth became a lifelong source of anxious curiosity for him, and found their way into many of his short stories and longer works. From his early youth, he did odd jobs to support himself, experiencing the struggle for survival. However, he determined to educate himself and managed to become a special student at the University of California. But because he went short of money, he had to leave the university after one semester. Then he joined the Oakland chapter of the Socialist Labor Party and became an active member, embracing both Marxism and the darker views of Nietzsche and Darwinism. As a result, London believed in both the inevitable triumph of the working class and the evolutionary necessity of the survival of the strongest. Some of his works, such as *The People of the Abyss* (1903), *War of the Classes* (1905), *The Iron Heel* (1908), and *Revolution* (1910) reflect his involvement in the socialist movement, yet some others, such as *The Call of the Wild* (1903) and *The Sea Wolf* (1904), dramatize his belief in the law of survival and the will to power. And the tension between his competing beliefs is most vividly projected in his autobiographical novel *Martin Eden* (1909).

Martin Eden depicts the inner stresses that London experienced during his rise from obscure poverty to wealth and fame. Eden, an impoverished but intelligent and hardworking sailor and laborer, is determined to become a writer. Eventually, his writing makes him rich and famous, but he realizes that the woman he loves cares for nothing but his money and fame. His despair over her inability to love causes him to lose faith in human nature. He also suffers from class alienation, for he no longer belongs to the working class. But he rejects the materialistic values of the wealthy, whom he works so hard to join. In the end he sails for the South Pacific and commits suicide by jumping into the sea.

London, who wrote fervently, in part for money, initiated his practice of writing at least a thousand words every day; and he threw his money about when he became one of the best-paid writers of his day. His first collection of stories, *The Son of the Wolf* (1900), is set largely in the Klondike region of Alaska and the Canadian Yukon. His other bestsellers include *The Call of the Wild* and *The Sea-Wolf*. Wolf Larsen, the ruthless, amoral protagonist of the latter book, best realizes London's ideal of a Nietschzian "superman." London also wrote many popular stories involving the primitive struggle of strong and weak individuals in the context of irresistible natural forces such as the wild sea or the Arctic. Among such stories, "To Build a Fire" has been recognized as classic. It combines the tragic drama of human pride and the crushing power of nature.

Later in his life he suffered from gonorrhea, insomnia, a severe skin condition, and pyorrhea. He regularly took both arsenic and morphine to relieve the pain. To make matters worse, he continued to drink heavily despite repeated warnings. On November 22, 1916, he died at the age of forty, of a self-injected overdose of morphine.

Jack London is a prolific writer whose fiction explores three geographies and their cultures: the Yukon, California, and the South Pacific. He experiments with many literary forms, from conventional love stories and dystopias to science fantasy. London is also fascinated by the way violence tests and defines character as his contemporaries Stephen Crane and Frank Norris do.

There is a general determinist overtone in London's themes: men and women are more evolved animals whose behavior is determined by laws of nature. In life, the fittest thrive and individual claims on life must be subjected to the survival of the human species. For the purpose of survival, animals, inclusive of humans, can regress from the level of their current evolution to more primitive levels. His contradictory beliefs in both Marxism and Darwinism are surely imprinted in his works. Yet some critics point out that the conflict between individual demand and social demand within London cause him to feel despair, which is inevitably reflected in his works.

The Law of Life

Introduction

This story was first printed in *McClure's Magazine* in March, 1901, and was later included in *Children of the Frost* (1902). It was one of the earliest stories by London. In the story, London presents the Indian custom of leaving the old alone to die for the sake of the survival of the tribe. "The Law of Life" is a reflection of London's determinist view and the despair he feels hence.

The Law of Life

Old Koskoosh listened greedily. Though his sight had long since faded, his hearing was still acute, and the slightest sound penetrated to the glimmering intelligence which yet abode behind the withered forehead, but which no longer gazed forth upon the things of the world[①]. Ah! that was Sit-cum-to-ha, shrilly anathematizing the dogs as she cuffed and beat them into the harnesses. Sit-cum-to-ha was his daughter's daughter, but she was too busy to waste a thought upon her broken grandfather, sitting alone there in the snow, forlorn and helpless. Camp must be broken. The long trail waited while the short day refused to linger. Life called her, and the duties of life, not death. And he was very close to death now.

The thought made the old man panicky[2] for the moment, and he stretched forth a palsied hand which wandered tremblingly over the small heap of dry wood beside him. Reassured that it was indeed there, his hand returned to the shelter of his mangy furs, and he again fell to listening[3]. The sulky crackling of half-frozen hides[4] told him that the chief's moose-skin lodge had been struck, and even then was being rammed and jammed into portable compass. The chief was his son, stalwart and strong, head man of the tribesmen, and a mighty hunter. As the women toiled with the camp luggage, his voice rose, chiding them for their slowness. Old Koskoosh strained his ears. It was the last time he would hear that voice. There went Geehow's lodge[5]! And Tusken's! Seven, eight, nine; only the shaman's could be still standing. There! They were at work upon it now. He could hear the shaman grunt as he piled it on the sled. A child whimpered, and a woman soothed it with soft, crooning gutturals. Little Koo-tee, the old man thought, a fretful child, and not overstrong. It would die soon, perhaps, and they would burn a hole through the frozen tundra and pile rocks above to keep the wolverines away. Well, what did it matter? A few years at best, and as many an empty belly as a full one. And in the end, Death waited, ever-hungry and hungriest of them all.

What was that? Oh, the men lashing the sleds and drawing tight the thongs. He listened, who would listen no more. The whip-lashes snarled and bit among the dogs. Hear them whine! How they hated the work and the trail! They were off! Sled after sled churned slowly away into the silence. They were gone. They had passed out of his life, and he faced the last bitter hour alone. No. The snow crunched beneath a moccasin[6]; a man stood beside him; upon his head a hand rested gently. His son was good to do this thing. He remembered other old men whose sons had not waited after the tribe. But his son had. He wandered away into the past, till the young man's voice brought him back.

"Is it well with you?" he asked.

And the old man answered, "It is well."

"There be wood beside you," the younger man continued, "and the fire burns bright. The morning is gray, and the cold has broken. It will snow presently. Even now is it snowing."

"Ay, even now is it snowing."

"The tribesmen hurry. Their bales are heavy, and their bellies flat with lack of feasting. The trail is long and they travel fast. I go now. It is well?"

"It is well. I am as a last year's leaf, clinging lightly to the stem. The first breath that blows, and I fall. My voice is become like an old woman's. My eyes no longer show me the way of my feet, and my feet are heavy, and I am tired. It is well."

He bowed his head in content till the last noise of the complaining snow had died away, and he knew his son was beyond recall. Then his hand crept out in haste to the wood. It alone stood between him and the eternity that yawned in upon him. At last the measure of his life was a handful of fagots. One by one they would go to feed the fire, and just so, step by step, death would creep upon him. When the last stick had surrendered up its heat, the frost would begin to gather strength. First his feet would yield, then his hands; and the numbness would travel, slowly, from the extremities to the body. His head would fall forward upon his knees, and he would rest. It was easy. All men must die.

He did not complain. It was the way of life, and it was just. He had been born close to the earth, close to the earth had he lived, and the law thereof was not new to him. It was the law of all flesh. Nature was not kindly to the flesh. She had no concern for that concrete thing called the individual. Her interest lay in the species, the race. This was the deepest abstraction⑦ old Koskoosh's barbaric mind was capable of, but he grasped it firmly. He saw it exemplified in all life. The rise of the sap, the bursting greenness of the willow bud, the fall of the yellow leaf—in this alone was told the whole history. But one task did Nature set the individual. Did he not perform it, he died. Did he perform it, it was all the same, he died. ⑧ Nature did not care; there were plenty who were obedient, and it was only the obedience in this matter, not the obedient, which lived and lived always. The tribe of Koskoosh was very old. The old men he had known when a boy, had known old men before them. Therefore it was true that the tribe lived, that it stood for the obedience of all its members, way down into the forgotten past, whose very resting-places were unremembered. They did not count; they were episodes. They had passed away like clouds from a summer sky. He also was an episode, and would pass away. Nature did not care. To life she set one task, gave one law. To perpetuate was the task of life, its law was death. A maiden was a good creature to look upon, full-breasted and strong, with spring to her step and light in her eyes. But her task was yet before her. The light in her eyes brightened, her step quickened, she was now bold with the young men, now timid, and she gave them of her own unrest. And ever she grew fairer and yet fairer to look upon, till some hunter, able no longer to withhold himself, took her to his lodge to cook and toil for him and to become the mother of his children. And with the coming of her offspring her looks left her. Her limbs dragged and shuffled, her eyes dimmed and bleared, and only the little children found joy against the withered cheek of the old squaw by the fire. Her task was done. But a little while, on the first pinch of famine or the first long trail, and she would be left, even as he had been left, in the snow, with a little pile of wood. Such was the law. He placed a stick carefully upon the fire and resumed his meditations. It was the same everywhere, with all things. The mosquitoes vanished with the first frost. The little tree-squirrel crawled away to die. When age settled upon the rabbit it became slow and heavy, and could no longer outfoot its enemies. Even the big bald-face grew clumsy and blind and quarrelsome, in the end to be dragged down by a handful of yelping huskies. He remembered how he had abandoned his own father on an upper reach of the Klondike one winter, the winter before the missionary came with his talkbooks and his box of medicines. Many a time had Koskoosh smacked his lips over the recollection of that box, though now his mouth refused to moisten. The "painkiller" had been especially good. But the missionary was a bother after all, for he brought no meat into the camp, and he ate heartily, and the hunters grumbled. But he chilled his lungs[9] on the divide by the Mayo, and the dogs afterwards nosed the stones away and fought over his bones.

Koskoosh placed another stick on the fire and harked back deeper into the past. There was the time of the Great Famine, when the old men crouched empty-bellied to the fire, and let fall from their lips dim traditions of the ancient day when the Yukon ran wide open for three winters, and then lay frozen for three summers. He had lost his mother in that famine. In the summer the salmon run had failed, and the tribe looked forward to the winter and the coming of the caribou. Then the winter came, but with it there were no caribou. Never had the like been known, not even in the lives of the old men. But the caribou did not come, and it was the seventh year, and the rabbits had not replenished[10], and the dogs were naught but bundles of bones. And through the long darkness the children wailed and died, and the women, and the old men; and not one in ten of the tribe lived to meet the sun when it came back in the spring. That was a famine!

But he had seen times of plenty, too, when the meat spoiled on their hands, and the dogs were fat and worthless with overeating—times when they let the game go unkilled, and the women were fertile, and the lodges were cluttered with sprawling men-children and women-children. Then it was the men became high-stomached[11], and revived ancient quarrels, and crossed the divides[12] to the south to kill the Pellys, and to the west that they might sit by the dead fires of the Tananas[13]. He remembered, when a boy, during a time of plenty, when he saw a moose pulled down by the wolves. Zing-ha lay with him in the snow and watched—Zing-ha, who later became the craftiest of hunters, and who, in the end, fell through an air-hole on the Yukon. They found him, a month afterward, just as he had crawled halfway out and frozen stiff to the ice.

But the moose. Zing-ha and he had gone out that day to play at hunting after the manner of their fathers. On the bed of the creek they struck the fresh track of a moose, and with it the tracks of many wolves. "An old one," Zing-ha, who was quicker at reading the sign, said— "an old one who cannot keep up with the herd. The wolves have cut him out from his brothers, and they will never leave him." And it was so. It was their way. By day and by night, never resting, snarling on his heels, snapping at his nose, they would stay by him to the end. How Zing-ha and he felt the blood-lust quicken! The finish would be a sight to see!

Eager-footed, they took the trail, and even he, Koskoosh, slow of sight and an unversed[14] tracker, could have followed it blind, it was so wide. Hot were they on the heels of the chase, reading the grim tragedy, fresh-written, at every step. Now they came to where the moose had made a stand. Thrice the length of a grown man's body, in every direction, had the snow been stamped about and uptossed. In the midst were the deep impressions of the splay-hoofed game, and all about, everywhere, were the lighter footmarks of the wolves. Some, while their brothers harried the kill, had lain to one side and rested. The full-stretched impress of their bodies in the snow was as perfect as though made the moment before. One wolf had been caught in a wild lunge of the maddened victim and trampled to death. A few bones, well picked, bore witness.

Again, they ceased the uplift of their snowshoes at a second stand. Here the great animal had fought desperately. Twice had he been dragged down, as the snow attested, and twice had he shaken his assailants clear and gained footing once more. He had done his task long since, but none the less was life dear to him. Zing-ha said it was a strange thing, a moose once down to get free again; but this one certainly had. The shaman would see signs and wonders in this when they told him.

And yet again, they come to where the moose had made to mount the bank and gain the timber. But his foes had laid on from behind, till he reared and fell back upon them, crushing two deep into the snow. It was plain the kill was at hand, for their brothers had left them untouched. Two more stands were hurried past, brief in time-length and very close together. The trail was red now, and the clean stride of the great beast had grown short and slovenly. Then they heard the first sounds of the battle—not the full-throated chorus of the chase, but the short, snappy bark which spoke of close quarters and teeth to flesh[15]. Crawling up the wind, Zing-ha bellied it through the snow, and with him crept he, Koskoosh, who was to be chief of the tribesmen in the years to come. Together they shoved aside the under branches of a young spruce and peered forth. It was the end they saw.

The picture, like all of youth's impressions, was still strong with him, and his dim eyes watched the end played out as vividly as in that far-off time. Koskoosh marvelled at this, for in the days which followed, when he was a leader of men and a head of councillors, he had done great deeds and made his name a curse in the mouths of the Pellys, to say naught[16] of the strange white man he had killed, knife to knife, in open fight.

For long he pondered on the days of his youth, till the fire died down and the frost bit deeper. He replenished it with two sticks this time, and gauged his grip on life[17] by what remained. If Sit-cum-to-ha had only remembered her grandfather, and gathered a larger armful, his hours would have been longer. It would have been easy. But she was ever a careless child, and honored not her ancestors from the time the Beaver, son of the son of Zing-ha, first cast eyes upon her. Well, what mattered it? Had he not done likewise in his own quick youth? For a while he listened to the silence. Perhaps the heart of his son might soften, and he would come back with the dogs to take his old father on with the tribe to where the caribou ran thick and the fat hung heavy upon them.

He strained his ears, his restless brain for the moment stilled. Not a stir, nothing. He alone took breath in the midst of the great silence. It was very lonely. Hark! What was that? A chill passed over his body. The familiar, long-drawn howl broke the void, and it was close at hand. Then on his darkened eyes was projected the vision of the moose—the old bull moose—the torn flanks and bloody sides, the riddled mane, and the great branching horns, down low and tossing to the last. He saw the flashing forms of gray, the gleaming eyes, the lolling tongues, the slavered fangs. And he saw the inexorable circle close in till it became a dark point in the midst of the stamped snow.

A cold muzzle thrust against his cheek[18], and at its touch his soul leaped back to the present. His hand shot into the fire and dragged out a burning faggot. Overcome for the nonce by his hereditary fear of man, the brute[19] retreated, raising a prolonged call to his brothers; and greedily they answered, till a ring of crouching, jaw-slobbered gray was stretched round about. [20] The old man listened to the drawing in[21] of this circle. He waved his brand wildly, and sniffs turned to snarls; but the panting brutes refused to scatter. Now one wormed his chest forward, dragging his haunches after, now a second, now a third; but never a one drew back. Why should he cling to life? he asked, and dropped the blazing stick into the snow. It sizzled and went out. The circle grunted uneasily, but held its own. Again he saw the last stand of the old bull moose, and Koskoosh dropped his head wearily upon his knees. What did it matter after all? Was it not the law of life?

Notes

① **and the slightest sound penetrated to the glimmering intelligence which yet abode behind the withered forehead, but which no longer gazed forth upon the things of the world**: referring to the old man, whose existing intelligence abiding behind the withered forehead is still acute to the slightest sound, but no longer looking forward to the future things in the world.

② **panicky**: in panic, uneasy.

③ **fell to listening**: turned to listening.

④ **hides**: animals' skin, especially when it has been removed to be used for leather.

⑤ **There went Geehow's lodge**: Geehow's tent was torn down, preparing to leave.

⑥ **moccasin**: a flat comfortable shoe made of soft leather.

⑦ **abstraction**: concept; philosophy.

⑧ **But one task did Nature set the individual. Did he not perform it, he died. Did he perform it, it was all the same, he died**: Nature set the individual only one task. The individual who didn't perform it died. The individual who did perform it, died as well.

⑨ **chilled his lungs**: froze his lungs, meaning catching a cold.

⑩ **replenished**: filled with something again; refilled.

⑪ **high-stomached**: with a full stomach.

⑫ **divides**: the border lines between Indian tribes.

⑬ **Tananas**: the name of an Indian tribe.

⑭ **unversed**: inexperienced.

⑮ **not the full-throated chorus of the chase, but the short, snappy bark which spoke of close quarters and teeth to flesh**: not the full sound uttered when chasing the moose, but the short clear sound indicating that the wolves have come to close contact with the moose, and have their teeth ready for flesh.

⑯ **naught**: nothing, here in the context, not mentioning.

⑰ **gauged his grip on life**: measured his cling to life.

⑱ **A cold muzzle thrust against his neck**: The muzzle of the moose thrust against his neck.

⑲ **the brute**: the brutal moose.

⑳ **till a ring of crouching, jaw-slobbered gray was stretched round about**: "a ring of gray" in the sentence refers to a group of gray moose circle around the old man, crouching, with their mouth watering.

㉑ **draw in**: the ring or the circle formed by the group of moose gets smaller and smaller.

Questions for Reading Comprehension

1. Who is the narrator of the story?

2. In which season does the story take place? And who are those people in the story?

3. Why is Old Koskoosh deserted by his people?

4. Why does Old Koskoosh give up fighting for his life?

5. How does Old Koskoosh justify the fact of being deserted?

6. What do you think would happen to Old Koskoosh in the end?

7. How does Old Koskoosh's death echo his hunting trip during his energetic youth?

8. What, according to the story, is the law of life?

Discussion Questions for Appreciation

1. While sitting there, Old Koskoosh recollects many things, including the famine days, the plenty days, and his hunting trip. How do his recollections contribute to the theme of the story?

2. What does the title "The Law of Life" suggest?

3. What do you think of the Indian tradition of "deserting the old", taking into consideration the harsh circumstances at the time of the story?

4. How does the author view the relationship between man and nature?

5. What are the naturalistic views revealed in this story?

A Question for Writing

London once told Charmian, his second wife, "To me the idea of death is sweet. Think of it—to lie down and go into the dark out of all the struggle and pain of living—to go to sleep and rest, always to be resting... When I come to die, I will be smiling at death, I promise you." How does London's attitude toward death find its way into this story?

Chapter Four American Modernism

(1914-1945)

Historical Background

The 20th century did not actually begin until the second decade, the first being just a continuation of the previous century. This period of 30-odd years caught between the two world wars was characterized by social transformation, economic upheavals and downfalls and the corresponding changes in people's outlook on life. World War Ⅰ was a dividing line between the 19th century and modern America, whereas World War Ⅱ was another dividing line separating America from the contemporary period. However, the 1910s, the 1920s and the 1930s, blocked off from the other periods in American history by a world war at either end, were very different from each other, displaying distinguished features and producing writers of different styles.

These decades witnessed great literary achievement, which was notably highlighted by six writers who won the Nobel Prize for Literature: Sinclair Lewis (1930), Eugene O'Neill (1936), T. S. Eliot (1948), William Faulkner (1949), Ernest Hemingway (1954) and John Steinbeck (1962).

1910s

WWI was the biggest event of the time. People went into it with extreme enthusiasm, inspired by the ideal of making the world safe for democracy. The War really made United States one of the world's major powers. Mass production and modern technology marked its industry after the war years. At the same time, old moral values broke down. Young people wore bobbed hair and short skirts. Women took to drinking and smoking.

A tremendous disillusionment prevailed among people because nothing had changed after the War as people had expected. The participation in the War brought about "the senses of a great civilization being destroyed or destroying itself, of social breakdown, and of individual powerlessness"[1]. There was a popular contempt for the law—the prohibition of alcohol, bootleggers, etc. People's dream for peace was shattered and the country was building up economic troubles toward disaster. A loss of faith began with the widespread of Darwin's theories of evolution and Nietzsche's claim of the death of God. "Without faith man could no longer keep his feeling and thought whole; hence the sense of life being fragmented, chaotic and disjunctive. And without faith, man no longer felt secure and happy and hopeful in his world. Hence the feeling of gloom and despair."[2]

---

[1] Nina Baym, ed., *The Norton Anthology of American Literature* (New York: W. W. Norton & Company, 1998), 5th edition, 2: 911.

[2] Chang Yaoxin, *A Survey of American Literature* (Tianjin: Nankai university press, 2003), 2nd edition, 156.

Modernism

Modernism was an international literary and artistic movement which originated in Europe and later spread to other parts of the world. It gained expression in many related fields of art, such as painting (Pablo Picasso, Juan Gris, Georges Braque, Marcel Duchamp and other painters associated with Dadaism), music (Igor Stravinsky), sculpture, fiction (James Joyce's *Ulysses*, Virginia Woolf's *To the Lighthouse* and *Mrs. Dalloway*, Marcel Proust's *Remembrance of Things Past*, Thomas Mann's *The Magic Mountain*), and poetry (William Butler Yeats). Many artists interpreted modernity as an experience of loss; therefore, they were actually anti-modern in their artistic outlook.

American literature and art at the beginning of the 20th century were in this trend. Writers, artists and architects adopted "a variety of avant-garde doctrines so revolutionary as to exhaust the traditional vocabulary of the arts and require the creation of new descriptive terms: futurism, expressionism, post-impressionism, Dadaism, imagism, and surrealism."[1] Museum of Modern Art (New York) was founded in 1929. Skyscrapers became the landmark of modernistic architecture. T. S. Eliot's *The Waste Land* (1922), disclosing the spiritual wasteland of modern people, established the modern tradition in the American literary scene. By 1920s, modernism became part of everyday vocabulary of the Americans.

Many modernistic writers believe that "the previously sustaining structures of human life... had been either destroyed or shown up as

289

① George McMichael, ed., *Anthology of American Literature* (New York: Macmillan Publishing Company, 1985), 3rd edition, 2: 969.

falsehood or fantasies"①. The subject matter of a modernistic writing often became the work itself since the writer was obsessed with the interrelationship between literature and life. A modernistic writing will seem "to begin arbitrarily, to advance without explanation, and to end without resolution, consisting of vivid segments juxtaposed without cushioning or integrating transitions."② Fragments and fragmentation dominated human experience as well as artistic writing. No matter what modernistic techniques were employed, the search for meaning—the meaning of life, the meaning of literature—remained the ultimate purpose of many modernistic writers.

Imagism

The Imagist Movement began in London and later spread to the US. It flourished from 1909 to 1917. *Poetry: A Magazine of Verse*, founded in Chicago by Harriet Monroe in 1912, became the chief carrier of Imagist poems. It provided a channel for young poets to publish their experimental verses.

Imagism underwent three major phases in its development③:

1. 1908-1909

An Englishman, T. E. Hulme, founded a Poets' Club in 1908,

---

① Nina Baym, ed., *The Norton Anthology of American Literature* (New York: W. W. Norton & Company, 1998), 5th edition, 2: 915.

② Ibid., 2: 916.

③ For detailed analysis of the development of Imagist Movement, please see William Pratt, *The Imagist Poem* (New York: E. P. Dutton & Co. Inc., 1963) and Stanley Coffman, *Imagism, A Chapter for the History of Modern Poetry* (New York: Farrar, Strauss, and Groux, 1972).

which met in Soho every Wednesday evening to discuss poetry. He believed that the most effective means to express the momentary impressions is through "the use of one dominant image". The image must enable one "to dwell and linger upon a point of excitement, to achieve the impossible and convert a point into a line". Hulme went into World War I and later died in it. Other poets carried on with what he had been doing.

2. 1912-1914

Ezra Pound took over the movement. He defined image as "that which presents an intellectual and emotional complex in an instant of time". Richard Aldington believed that the exact word must bring the effect of the object before the reader as it had presented itself to the poet's mind at the time of writing. In 1912, these poets published a collection of poems, entitled *Des Imagistes*, which contained the poems of Hilda Doolittle (known as H. D.), Richard Aldington, F. S. Flint, Amy Lowell, William Carlos Williams and Ezra Pound, and in which a manifesto of Imagism came into being. This manifesto included three writing principles:

a. Direct treatment of the "thing", whether subjective or objective;

b. To use absolutely no word that does not contribute to the presentation;

c. As regarding rhythm, to compose in the sequence of the musical phrase, not in the sequence of a metronome.

These principles, brevity and conciseness in expression, free verse and frank treatment of the object, showed the rebellion of these poets against the Victorian poetic tradition. Free verse is not free, as T. S.

291

Eliot said, "No *vers is libre* for the man who wants to do a good job."
Realizing the limitations of the poetic principles of Imagism and attempting
to experiment with other writing techniques, Ezra Pound left the Movement
for Vorticism.

3. 1914-1917

Amy Lowell took over the movement and developed it into "Amy-
gism" (Pound's phrase). In 1915, 1916, 1917, three volumes of *Some
Imagist Poets* came out, containing six principles of poetic composition
which were based on the original three. After 1917, Imagism ceased to
be a movement.

The Imagist Movement drew from a variety of poetic traditions—
Greek, Provencal, Japanese and Chinese poetry. The ideographic and
pictographic nature of Chinese language, and "virile laconism and austere pregnancy"[①] which characterize ancient Chinese poetry particularly
fascinated the Imagists.

However, a dominant image is incapable of sustaining a longer poetic effort. Thus no great poetry came out. Nevertheless, the movement
offered a new way of expressing experiences with a new life. It became a
training school for many young poets who started their career by writing
Imagist poems.

An outstanding representative of Imagist poems is Ezra Pound's two-
line poem, "In a Station of the Metro". Other well-known Imagist poems
include William Carlos Williams' "The Red Wheelbarrow", Amy
Lowell's "Wind and Silver", Hilda Doolittle's "Oread", T. E. Hulme's
"Autumn" and F. S. Flint's "The Swan".

---

① Chang Yaoxin, *A Survey of American Literature* (Tianjin: Nankai university prsee, 2003), 2nd edition, 161.

1920s

This is a time of "carefree prosperity, isolated from the world's problems, bewildering social change and a feverish pursuit of pleasure"[1], a time of selfish frivolity and abandonment of social customs.

1. Industrialization and urbanization. The middle class engaged themselves in pursuing individual success, which was hallmarked by financial profit and personal enjoyment. People moved into cities in great numbers. By 1925, half of the America population lived in cities and suburbs[2]. Highways joined cities together so that people's geographical notion changed. Industries such as automobile, electricity, iron and steel, architecture rose in such rapid speed that America became one of the richest countries in the world.

2. Women's liberation. Thanks to the Nineteenth Amendment to the Constitution passed in August 1920, women finally gained the right to vote. Many started working by themselves and insisted on "their right to a personhood that was identical to men's."[3] Traditions regarding courtship, marriage and child-rearing underwent tremendous changes. Women began to challenge the long-cherished division of labor.

3. Mass media and luxuries. The appearance of cars, radios, movies, advertising, etc. brought America into a consuming society. The development of the assembly-lines finally made automobiles cheap enough for ordinary Americans. People lived beyond their means, gam-

---

① Elisabeth B. Booz, *A Brief Introduction to Modern American Literature* (Shanghai: Shanghai Foreign Language Education Press, 1982), 1.

② Ibid. , 2.

③ Nina Baym, ed. , *The Norton Anthology of American Literature* (New York: W. W. Norton & Company, 1998), 5th edition, 2: 913.

bling and making profits illegally. Some even went into debt in order to catch up with the Jones. The Eighteenth Amendment to the Constitution which prohibited the manufacture, sale and transportation of liquor was widely ignored. Gangsters who were connected with bootlegging organized crimes so horrible that they completely destroyed people's sense of safety.

4. Disillusionment. Young people took part in the War with great enthusiasm, believing that this war was "the war to end wars". After the War, President Woodrow Wilson declared that "Americans had gained everything for which they had fought"[1]; however, people were astounded at the catastrophes and sacrifices they had experienced. They saw at last their ideals for a better world were "bargained away for power and profit"[2]. People began to question government and lost confidence in the political leaders.

The Lost Generation

This is a term "applied to the disillusioned intellectuals and aesthetes of the years following the First World War, who rebelled against former ideals and values, but could replace them only by despair or a cynical hedonism."[3] These intellectuals were especially "disillusioned by their war experiences and alienated by what they perceived as the

---

[1] George McMichael, ed., *Anthology of American Literature* (New York: Macmillan Publishing Company, 1985), 3rd edition, 2: 970.

[2] Elisabeth B. Booz, *A Brief Introduction to Modern American Literature* (Shanghai: Shanghai Foreign Language Education Press, 1982), 3.

[3] James D. Hart, *The Oxford Companion to American Literature* (New York: Oxford University Press, 1965), 4th edition, 495.

crassness of American culture and its 'puritanical' repressions. "[1] They became expatriates, living in European cities such as London and Paris, standing aside and writing about what they saw—the failure of the American society. They believed that the American bourgeois society was hypocritical, vulgar and crude, concerning only with making money. It was a society where individual thought and individual expression were crushed. These intellectuals include F. Scott Fitzgerald (1896-1940), Ernest Hemingway (1899-1961), e. e. cummings (1894-1962), Sinclair Lewis (1885-1951), H. L. Mencken (1880-1956), and Sherwood Anderson (1876-1941). The term came from Gertrude Stein's comment to Hemingway, "You are all a lost generation. "

Harlem Renaissance

Harlem Renaissance was a term to describe the revival of the literary and artistic achievement in the 1920s by Afro-American writers. As a result of the mass production in big cities, the Afro-Americans migrated from the South to the North in the hope of experiencing a new life style. The change from rural to urban way of living created social problems in the first place until the social conflicts were eased as a result of economic increase. The Jazz music of the American Negro became gradually accepted by the most elite audiences.

The writers who were associated with Harlem Renaissance include Countee Cullen (1903-1946), Langston Hughes (1902-1967), Claude McKay (1890-1948), Sterling Brown (1901-1989), Jean Toomer

---

[1] M. H. Abrams, *A Glossary of Literary Terms* (New York: Harcourt Brace College Publishers, 1999), 7th edition, 208.

(1894-1967), Jessie Fauset (1884-1961), Wallace Thurman (1902-1934), James Weldon Johnson (1871-1938), and Marcus Garvey (1887-1940). Their artistic endeavor paved the way for the emergence of later black writers, which include Richard Wright (1908-1960), Ralph Ellison (1914-1994), Gwendolyn Brooks (1917-2000), James Baldwin (1924-1986), Alex Haley (1921-1992), Imamu Amiri Baraka (LeRoi Jones, 1934-   ), Alice Walker (1944-   ), and Toni Morrison (1931-   ).

The 1920s produced a large number of great literary men. In the field of fiction writing, the most notable writer of the period was Sinclair Lewis who criticizes American vulgarity in *Main Street* (1920) and who became the first in American literary history to win the Nobel Prize for literature. Sherwood Anderson, preoccupied with the sympathy for the underprivileged, produced such collections of short stories as *Winesburg, Ohio* (1919) and *Death in the Woods* (1933). Willa Cather's (1873-1947) *O Pioneers*! (1913) and *My Antonia* (1918) secured her place in American literary history. Ernest Hemingway, although the Nobel Prize for literature came to him rather late, remained a chief spokesman for the Lost Generation. F. Scott Fitzgerald, with his *The Great Gatsby* (1925) and a number of other writings, stood as the cornerstone for the roaring 1920s, or the Jazz Age.

In the field of poetry writing, the most distinguished poet that America produced in the 1920s was T. S. Eliot (1888-1965) whose *The Waste Land* (1922) vividly represents the spiritual wasteland of the mo-dern man and has thus become a hallmark of modernistic writing. Poets who were associated with Imagism, Ezra Pound, William Carlos Williams and e. e. cummings, continued to write poetry but did not restrict themselves with Imagist principles.

1930s

This is a time of poverty, unemployment, bleakness, important social and political movements, a new social consciousness and social upheavals.

1. The Crash and the Depression. The collapse of the Stock Market in 1929 suddenly ended the prosperity in the previous decade. Workers were unemployed[1], engaging themselves in strikes and protests in the hope of securing a proper place in society; whereas the farmers were driven off the land by drought and debts. Black people were especially conscious of the social hierarchy. Capital was further concentrated in the hands of a few monopolizing tycoons. All the contradictions inherent in the capitalist system were intensified. By 1933, America was ready to collapse.

2. The New Deal. Franklin Roosevelt, who became the U. S. President in 1933 and who held the position until 1945, launched the New Deal, a series of measures—social security, welfare, unemployment insurance and acts securing job opportunities in public sectors— "to restore people's confidence and start the nation toward recovery"[2]. Improvements and changes were seen to benefit the ordinary people.

3. The Leftists. The expatriates came back from Paris, taking an active part in the political and social movements in America. They used words as weapons to express their sympathy with the oppressed. They

---

[1] "More than 14 million workers got bogged down in unemployment." Please see 胡荫桐、刘树森主编，《美国文学教程》（南开大学出版社，1995 年），第 328 页。

[2] Elisabeth B. Booz, *A Brief Introduction to Modern American Literature* (Shanghai: Shanghai Foreign Language Education Press, 1982), 7.

hoped that their writing would play a decisive role in bringing about so-cial changes. Therefore, they advocated new ways of writing and reforms in language. The Communist Party "enjoyed a significant increase in membership and prestige"[①] in this period. Some of the Party members looked to Russia as an example of a better, more secure social system. Unfortunately, after the joint Russo-German invasion of Poland, the country was soon swept into World War II.

The most outstanding novelist in the 1930s is John Steinbeck (1902-1968) whose *Of Mice and Men* (1937) and *The Grapes of Wrath* (1939) truthfully represent the poverty of the American farmers. Similar to Steinbeck, John Dos Passos (1896-1970) expresses his concern with the people living in the Depression years in his trilogy, *U. S. A.* (1930-1936). William Faulkner (1897-1962), with his series of novels set against a fictional Yoknapatawpha County, establishes himself as a Southern writer. Katherine Ann Porter (1890-1980), Eudora Welty (1909-2001) and Carson McCullers (1917-1967) further add the sing-ing strength for the South. Among the Afro-American writers in the peri-od, the most important is Richard Wright (1908-1960) whose *Native Son* (1940) and a number of short stories remain significant in Afro-American literary history.

In poetry writing, Ezra Pound, T. S. Eliot and e. e. cummings con-tinued to contribute to the poetic voice of the nation, and other poets who joined them include Robert Frost (1874-1963), Carl Sandburg (1878-1967), Wallace Stevens (1879-1955) and Marianne Moore (1887-1972).

This period witnessed the appearance of a number of great play-wrights, together with Eugene O'Neill (1888-1953) whose outstanding

298

---

① Nina Baym, ed. , *The Norton Anthology of American Literature* (New York: W. W. Norton & Company, 1998), 5th edition, 2: 913.

achievement won him the Nobel Prize for literature in 1936 and whose dramatic canon remained unsurpassed by later writers. Clifford Odets (1906-1963) is remembered as a Left writer for his *Waiting for Lefty* (1935). Thornton Wilder (1897-1975) writes about the town people's lives in *Our Town* (1933) and *The Skin of Our Teeth* (1942). Lillian Hellman (1905-1984), with her *The Children's Hour* (1934) and *The Little Foxes* (1939), was the most important woman playwright at the time.

Ezra Pound（1885-1972）

Ezra Pound decisively affected the course of twentieth-century American literature. His assertion "Make it new" served as a rallying cry for many writers of his time, and was the driving force behind Modernist literature.

Pound was born in Hailey, Idaho. When he was still an infant, his family settled in a comfortable suburb near Philadelphia. Pound determined that by age thirty he would know more about poetry than anyone else living, so he attended Hamilton College and the University of Pennsylvania, where he earned an M. A. in 1906. Encouraged by his college friend William Carlos Williams and Hilda Doolittle (H. D.), Pound began a comprehensive study of poetry in English, Spanish, French, Italian, Provencal, Latin and Greek (and later, Chinese).

From 1908 to 1920, he resided in London, where he associated with many writers, including William Butler Yeats, for whom he worked as a secretary, and T. S. Eliot, whose *Waste Land* he drastically edited and improved. Many of his critical essays were later collected and published in books. He was also a contributing editor to Harriet Monroe's important Chicago magazine *Poetry*.

In 1915 Pound began writing his great work *The Cantos*, which spanned from 1917 to 1959. He started a new school of poetry known as Imagism, which advocated a clear, highly visual presentation. He also experimented with the dramatic monologue, a poetic form developed by the English Victorian poet Robert Browning.

Since Pound's extreme political positions offended members of the British literary establishment, he had to leave Britain for Paris. His survey of history persuaded him that the ideal society was a hierarchy with a

300

strong leader and an agricultural economy, thus he greeted the Italian fascist dictator Benito Mussolini as a deliverer, and voluntarily served the Italian government by making many English radio broadcasts in which he vilified the Jews, President Roosevelt and American society in general, foolishly thinking that he was contributing to peace and to a better world. After the war, he was arrested and imprisoned in Pisa, an experience reflected in what is perhaps his greatest poetic achievement, *The Pisan Cantos*. Judged mentally incapable of standing the trial, Pound spent thirteen years in a hospital for the insane, where he continued to write some of his finest work. In 1948 *The Pisan Cantos* (LXX-IV-LXXXIV) won the Library of Congress' newly established Bollingen Prize for poetry, an event that provoked tremendous debate about Pound's stature as a poet as well as a citizen.

With the help of many literary men, Pound finally gained his release from the mental hospital. He returned to Italy, where he died at the age of eighty-seven.

301

Pound's major works include *Personae* (1926), *Hugh Selwyn* (1920), and *The Cantos*. *The Cantos* were separate poems of varying lengths, combing reminiscence, meditation, description, and transcriptions from books Pound was reading. It is a vast epic in free verse narrated by several personae. Part of *The Cantos* is based on Pound's translation from Confucius; Cantos LII through LXI list in detail the succession of Chinese dynasties, which, in their rise and fall, seems to support Pound's concept of how an usurious economy corrupts. By tracing the rise and fall of western and eastern empires, he analyzes the destruction of human civilization caused by materialization.

Pound is most frequently associated with the Imagist movement. Rather than describing something—an object or situation—and then generalizing about it. Imagist poets attempt to present the object directly, any significance to be derived from the image has to appear inherent in its spare, clean presentation. Also, this new poetry tends to work in non-syntactical fragments. Although imagism as a formal poetic movement lasted only briefly, much subsequent twentieth-century poetry bears its influence.

In a Station of the Metro

Introduction

"In a Station of the Metro" is a classic Imagist poem, presenting a quick, sharp image of people seen in the darkness of the Paris subway (the Metro). One day in 1913, the poet was struck by the beautiful faces of some women and children against the wet and dark background in a Paris subway station. His effort to express this experience ended in a 130-odd-line poem which the poet tore into pieces since he was not satisfied with it. A year later, the poet presented a two-line poem as we see here today.

In a Station of the Metro

The apparition of these faces in the crowd;
Petals on a wet, black bough.

Questions for Reading Comprehension

1. Where does the narrator see the "faces"?
2. What are the "faces" compared to?
3. What adjectives does the narrator use to describe the "bough"? How does the description foreground the "petals"?
4. What are the two images juxtaposed in the poem?

Discussion Questions for Appreciation

1. Does the poet supply you with any information about how you should think or feel about the poem?

2. Why does the poet use the word "apparition" rather than the word "appearance"?

3. Pound himself mentions the following Japanese haiku (a two-line couplet with rhymes) in an essay. Compare "In the Station of the Metro" with this haiku and discuss their similarities and differences.

    > The footsteps of the cat upon the snow
    > are like the plum blossoms.

4. What are the advantages and disadvantages of Imagist poetry, using this poem as an illustration?

A Question for Writing

In what way does this poem reflect Imagist poetry?

Robert Frost（1874-1963）

Although Robert Frost is often identified with New England, he was born in California and lived there until his father's death. When Frost was eleven, he moved to New England farm country where his mother supported the family by teaching at school. She also introduced him to the works of the English romantic writers and the New England Transcendentalists.

Frost graduated from high school in 1891 in Lawrence, Massachusetts, sharing the post of valedictorian with Elinor White, whom he married three years later. Frost was enrolled at Dartmouth College in 1892, and later at Harvard, but never earned a formal degree. He drifted through a string of occupations after leaving school, working as a teacher, a cobbler, an editor and a farmer. His first professional poem "My Butterfly" was published on November 8, 1894, in the New York newspaper *The Independent*. Being unable to support himself by writing poetry and cultivating a farm, Frost decided to sell his farm and take his family to England. It was in London that Frost met such contemporary British poets as Edward Thomas, Rupert Brooke, and Robert Graves. While in England, Frost also established a friendship with Ezra Pound, who reviewed his first book, *A Boy's Will* (1913) favorably, and helped promote the publication of his second book, *North of Boston* (1914), which was well received by critics in America and England.

The favorable reception of his books persuaded Frost to return home. He bought another farm in New Hampshire and prospered through teaching and lecturing at various colleges. By the 1920s, he was the most celebrated poet in America, and with each new book—including *New Hampshire* (1923), *A Further Range* (1936), *Steeple Bush*

(1947), and *In the Clearing* (1962) —his fame and honors increased. For the rest of his lives, he lived and taught in Massachusetts and Vermont.

Frost won the Pulitzer Prize four times and received commendations by the American Academy of Arts and Letters and the Poetry Society of America in 1938 and in 1941 respectively. Honors from forty-four institutions were awarded to him. When invited to read his poem at President Kennedy's inauguration in 1961, Frost seemed to have become the nation's unofficial Poet Laureate. However, the success he enjoyed for the rest of life did not seem to reduce the bitterness left by the suicide of his son and the mental collapse of his daughter. Frost died in Boston on January 29, 1963.

The Norton Anthology of American Literature classifies Frost's poetry into the following four categories:

1. nature lyrics which describes and comments on a scene or event, like "The Tuft of Flowers," "The Road Not Taken," "Mending Wall," "Birches," and "Stopping by Woods on a Snowy Evening."

2. dramatic narratives in blank verse which are about the grieves of country people, like "A Servant to Servants", "The Death of a Hired Man", and "Home Burial".

3. satirical poems which criticizes the indifference and isolation among modern people, like "Departmental" and "A Considerable Speck".

4. philosophical poems which are generally short, abstract and thought-provoking, like "Design", "Acceptance" and "Nothing Gold Can Stay".

Most of Frost's poems are set in the New England country, which revitalizes the tradition of New England regionalism, yet Frost is by no means a merely regional poet. He is noted for his clarity of diction, the simplicity of images and the use of folksy speaker, which make his poems look natural and simple. But beneath the surface simplicity of his poetry, there is a profound understanding of life and the world.

Most of his poems are in traditional verse forms and metrics, yet he manages to bring a distinctive voice on the regularity of these forms, thus creating designed rhythmic tensions.

Frost's often dark meditations on universal themes, his adherence to language as it is actually spoken, the psychological complexity of his portraits, the distinct flavour he gives to traditional form and subject matter, as well as the layers of ambiguity and irony in his works, have made him essentially a modern poet.

The Road Not Taken

Introduction

The poem, included in *Mountain Interval* (1916), was written in Feb., 1915, just before Frost was ready to return to the United States. Frost felt sorrowful about his friend Edward Thomas' going into the First World War, and recalled his experience four years earlier in a New Hampshire forest. "The Road Not Taken" depicts a choice made—a choice we all make—that "made all the difference." However, the similarity of the two choices and the difficulty of the selection have made the readers aware that to choose means to give up another alternative.

The Road Not Taken

Two roads diverged in a yellow wood,
And sorry I could not travel both
And be one traveler, long I stood
And looked down one as far as I could
To where it bent in the undergrowth;

Then took the other, as just as fair,

And having perhaps the better claim,

Because it was grassy and wanted wear;

Though as for that the passing there

Had worn them really about the same,

And both that morning equally lay

In leaves no step had trodden black.

Oh, I kept the first for another day!

Yet knowing how way leads on to way,

I doubted if I should ever come back.

I shall be telling this with a sigh

Somewhere ages and ages hence:

Two roads diverged in a wood, and I—

I took the one less traveled by,

And that has made all the difference.

Questions for Reading Comprehension

1. Why does the speaker feel sorry in the first stanza?

2. Why does the speaker think that the second road may have the better claim?

3. Which road does he take? Why?

4. Why does the speaker say that he will be telling this story with a sign "ages and ages hence"?

5. Does the speaker think he has made the wrong choice? Why or why not?

Discussion Questions for Appreciation

1. What do the two roads represent?
2. What does the speaker's choice tell about him?
3. Are the two roads the same or different? What do their similarities or differences suggest?
4. Why is the poem entitled "The Road Not Taken"?
5. What rhythmical devices does the poet use in the poem?

A Question for Writing

What philosophy of life is implied in the poem? Have you met with any dilemmas in your life comparable to the speaker's?

Fire and Ice

308

Introduction

The poem "Fire and Ice" was published in 1920, immediately after the First World War. According to Frost, the poem "begins in delight, and ends in wisdom."

Fire and Ice

Some say the world will end in fire,
Some say in ice.
From what I've tasted of desire
I hold with those who favor fire.
But if it had to perish twice,
I think I know enough of hate
To know that for destruction ice

Is also great

And would suffice.

Questions for Reading Comprehension

1. What are the two things that some people say the world will end in?

2. What emotion does the speaker associate with fire and ice?

3. What does the poet suggest that the two emotions have in common?

4. What does the speaker seem to agree with concerning the end of the world?

Discussion Questions for Appreciation

1. What other kinds of destruction besides destruction of the world might the poem be talking about?

2. What is the complex idea that is expressed in the poem?

3. How do you understand the last word of the poem, "suffice"?

4. Is this poem written in free verse? Justify yourself.

Mending Wall

Introduction

The poem is collected in *North of Boston*. By symbolizing the wall as a barrier between people, the poet tries to show that people need to be separate individuals as well as members of a community.

Mending Wall

Something there is that doesn't love a wall,

That sends the frozen-ground-swell [①] under it,

And spills[②] the upper boulders in the sun;

And makes gaps even two can pass abreast.

The work of hunters is another thing:

I have come after them and made repair

Where they have left not one stone on a stone,

But they would have the rabbit out of hiding,

To please the yelping dogs. The gaps I mean,

No one has seen them made or heard them made,

But at spring mending-time we find them there.

I let my neighbour know beyond the hill;

And on a day we meet to walk the line

And set the wall between us once again.

We keep the wall between us as we go.

To each the boulders that have fallen to each.

And some are loaves and some so nearly balls

We have to use a spell to make them balance:

"Stay where you are until our backs are turned!"

We wear our fingers rough with handling them.

Oh, just another kind of out-door game,

One on a side. It comes to little more:

There where it is we do not need the wall:

He is all pine and I am apple orchard.

My apple trees will never get across

And eat the cones under his pines, I tell him.

He only says, "Good fences make good neighbours."

Spring is the mischief in me, and I wonder

If I could put a notion in his head:

"Why do they make good neighbours? Isn't it

Where there are cows? But here there are no cows.

Before I built a wall I'd ask to know

What I was walling in or walling out,

And to whom I was like to give offence.

Something there is that doesn't love a wall,

That wants it down. " I could say "Elves" to him,[3]

But it's not elves exactly, and I'd rather

He said it for himself. I see him there

Bringing a stone grasped firmly by the top

In each hand, like an old-stone savage armed.

He moves in darkness as it seems to me,

Not of woods only and the shade of trees.

He will not go behind his father's saying,

And he likes having thought of it so well

He says again, "Good fences make good neighbours. "

Notes

① **sends the frozen-ground-swell**: make the frozen ground swell. Freezing expands the damp earth, and shoves the earth up, which causes the stone wall to crumble.

② **spill**: (make the upper boulder) to fall

③ **could say "Elves" to him**: could tell him that the fairies knocked down the wall.

Questions for Reading Comprehension

1. How many characters are there in the poem? Who are they?

2. What is the thing that "doesn't love a wall" (line 1)?

3. What happens as a result of the fact that "Something there is that

doesn't love a wall"? What other kind of destruction to the wall is described in Lines 5 to 9?

4. How do the speaker and his neighbor go about fixing the wall at spring mending-time (Lines 12 to 22)?

5. What is the central issue or subject matter in the poem?

Discussion Questions for Appreciation

1. What kind of darkness surrounds his neighbor? And why is the neighbor compared to a savage?

2. Why does the speaker say that the wall stays always where we do not need it (Line 23)?

3. What does the wall symbolize? What do people wall in and wall out?

4. How is the speaker's attitude towards the wall different from his neighbor's?

5. What do the speaker and his neighbor represent respectively?

A Question for Writing

How do you understand "Good fences make good neighbors" (Line 27)?

Stopping by Woods on a Snowy Evening

Introduction

The poem first appeared in *New Hampshire*. It is a lyric poem in iambic tetrameter quatrain. It is about a weary journeyer stopping by the woods to contemplate over death on the "darkest evening of the year." Through the analogy between the traveler's actions in the poem and a person's journey through life, the poet reveals that in the hard struggle of life people may feel tired and desire to have a momentary relief from the obligations of life. The journeyer's complex feelings for death are summarized in three simple words: "lovely, dark, deep."

Stopping by Woods on a Snowy Evening

Whose woods these are I think I know.
His house is in the village though;
He will not see me stopping here
To watch his woods fill up with snow.

My little horse must think it queer
To stop without a farmhouse near
Between the woods and frozen lake
The darkest evening of the year.

He gives his harness bells a shake
To ask if there is some mistake.
The only other sound's the sweep
Of easy wind and downy flake.

The woods are lovely, dark and deep.
But I have promises to keep,
And miles to go before I sleep,
And miles to go before I sleep.

Questions for Reading Comprehension

1. Why is the owner of the woods unable to see the speaker stopping by his woods?
2. What causes the speaker to stop?
3. What is the horse's response when the speaker stops?
4. When and where does the event in the poem take place?
5. Why does the speaker find the woods lovely?

6. What must the speaker do before he goes to sleep?

Discussion Questions for Appreciation

1. What is the function of the horse in the second and third stanzas?

2. What internal conflict does the speaker experience when he decides to leave the woods?

3. What might the incident by the woods represent?

4. Why does the poet repeat the line "And miles to go before I sleep"? Does the meaning of the word "sleep" alter in any way?

5. What is the rhyme scheme of the poem? What effect does this rhyme scheme create? Or how is the poem "knit" to a close?

Thomas Stearns（T. S.）Eliot（1888-1965）

T. S. Eliot was born in Saint Louis, Missouri on September 26, 1888. His mother involved herself in cultural and charitable activities and wrote poetry; his father was a successful businessman, and his grandfather was the founder of Washington University. Eliot was educated at Harvard and did graduate work in philosophy at the Sorbonne in Paris, and at Oxford from 1915-1916. He read Dante, his most admired poet, and Jules Laforgue, the French poet brilliant in portraying modern city-scope with unusual wit and visual imagery. Eliot began writing traditional poetry when he was at college. In 1908, however, Arthur Symons's book *The Symbolist Movement in Literature* (1899) exerted profound influence on him and altered his view of poetry. He also explored the poetry of the seventeenth century metaphysical poets like John Donne and later acknowledged his indebtedness to them.

315

Eliot settled in London in 1914. He worked first as a teacher, then as a clerk while writing poetry in his spare time. His wife's continuous illnesses and his father's disapproval and subsequent death led Eliot to an emotional breakdown. After recovering, Eliot founded, and edited the literary journal, *Criterion*. He also served as director for London publisher, Faber & Faber, from 1925 until his death in 1965. In 1927 he took British citizenship and joined the Anglican Church, actions that had profound effects on the content and scope of his poetry. In 1948, Eliot was awarded the Nobel Prize for literature. Eliot and his first wife Vivian separated in 1932. At age sixty-eight, he married his long-time secretary, Valerie Fletcher. Eliot died in 1965, and his ashes were buried in the church at East Coker.

T. S. Eliot is surely one of the most influential poets of the 20th century. His poetry and critical works helped shape modern literature. In 1917, encouraged by his friend and mentor, he published his first major poem "The Love Song of J. Alfred Prufrock." It is narrated in the form of soliloquy and reveals Eliot's early style, mixing humor and pessimism. Then, he published his most famous poem "The Waste Land" (1922) which expresses his horror at the spiritual turmoil of modern Europe. It combines fragments of the literature of the past, shoring them against the ruins of contemporary society. To many, the poem seems to catch precisely the state of culture and society after the First World War. It contains many technical innovations and has exerted great influence on modern poetry. Eliot's "Ash Wednesday" (1930) is more traditional. Actually, it was written after his conversion to Anglicanism. With its religious emphasis, it is more hopeful than his previous work.

Eliot also wrote several plays including *Murder in the Cathedral* (1935), and *The Family Reunion* (1939). When the Second World War disrupted theatre performances, he wrote non-dramatic poetry again. Three of his poems used the same structure and themes—time and eternity, memory and history—and he named this group of poems *Four Quartets* (1943). After *Four Quartets*, Eliot again turned to writing verse plays, of which the most successful was *The Cocktail Party* (1950).

Eliot contributes a lot to literary criticism. The basic themes of his criticism concern the relationship between tradition and individual talent, and between the past, the present, and the future. In his influential essay "Tradition and Individual Talents" he defines the Western poetic tradition as an organic whole: "Literature is not a collection of the writing of individuals, but of ' organic wholes ' ". [1] This approach to literature has a major influence on the practices of New Criticism.

---

[1] Frank Kermode, ed. , *Selected Prose of T. S. Eliot* (London: Faber & Faber, 1987), 68.

Eliot's poetry is difficult to read, for he follows his belief that poetry should aim at a representation of the complexities of modern civilization in language and that such representation necessarily leads to difficult poetry. The difficulty of his poetry lies in the abundance of seemingly disconnected images and symbols as well as his learned quotations and allusions. For Eliot, The only way of expressing emotion in the form of art is by finding an "objective correlative"; and symbols and images would be the best "objective correlatives" which serve to evoke emotion.

The Love Song of J. Alfred Prufrock

Introduction

The poem "The Love Song of J. Alfred Prufrock" was written when T. S. Eliot was at Harvard. It depicts a timid middle-aged man thinking of going to propose marriage to a lady but hesitating all the way there. It is a dramatic monologue spoken by J. Alfred Prufrock, whose very name seems to combine the dignity and absurdity of his public and private selves. These two selves are probably the "you and I" of the first line—a person who is outwardly a "proper" member of the "best" society, but who, inwardly, is lost, lonely, and suffering. In the poem, Prufrock sees himself as Lazarus coming back from the dead, but can not break through his deadness. He sees himself as John the Baptist, that vigo-rous, dynamic, committed human being that he is by all standards not, for he only wastes his life in a purposeless social environment in an aimless, silly, repetitive way. The latter part of the poem captures his sense of defeat for failing to act courageously. "Unable to bring himself and his world together, to build a base for meaningful action, Prufrock represents the spiritual impotence of archetypal modern man. What is redeeming is probably his self-perception: he sees his own absurdity." [1]

The Love Song of J. Alfred Prufrock

S'io credesse che mia risposta fosse
A persona che mai tornasse al mondo,
Questa fiamma staria senza piu scosse.
Ma percioche giammai di questo fondo
Non torno vivo alcun, s'i'odo il vero,
Senza tema d'infamia ti rispondo. [1]

Let us go then, you and I,
When the evening is spread out[2] against the sky
Like a patient etherized upon a table;
Let us go, through certain half-deserted streets,
The muttering retreats
Of restless nights in one-night cheap hotels
And sawdust restaurants with oyster-shells:
Streets that follow like a tedious argument
Of insidious intent
To lead you to an overwhelming question . . .
Oh, do not ask, "What is it?"
Let us go and make our visit.

In the room the women come and go
Talking of Michelangelo. [3]

---

① Chang Yaoxin, *A Survey of American Literature* (Tianjin: Nankai University Press, 1990), 247.

The yellow fog that rubs its back upon the window-
panes,
The yellow smoke that rubs its muzzle on the window-
panes,
Licked its tongue into the corners of the evening,
Lingered upon the pools that stand in drains,
Let fall upon its back the soot that falls from chimneys,
Slipped by the terrace, made a sudden leap,
And seeing that it was a soft October night,
Curled once about the house, and fell asleep.

And indeed there will be time[④]
For the yellow smoke that slides along the street,
Rubbing its back upon the window-panes;
There will be time, there will be time
To prepare a face to meet the faces that you meet;
There will be time to murder and create,
And time for all the works and days of hands[⑤]
That lift and drop a question on your plate;
Time for you and time for me,
And time yet for a hundred indecisions,
And for a hundred visions and revisions,
Before the taking of a toast and tea.

In the room the women come and go
Talking of Michelangelo.

And indeed there will be time
To wonder, "Do I dare?" and, "Do I dare?"
Time to turn back and descend the stair,

With a bald spot in the middle of my hair—

(They will say: "How his hair is growing thin!")

My morning coat, my collar mounting firmly to the chin,

My necktie rich and modest, but asserted by a simple pin—

(They will say: "But how his arms and legs are thin!")

Do I dare

Disturb the universe?

In a minute there is time

For decisions and revisions which a minute will reverse.

For I have known them all already, known them all:

Have known the evenings, mornings, afternoons,

I have measured out my life with coffee spoons;

I know the voices dying with a dying fall[6]

Beneath the music from a farther room.

So how should I presume?

And I have known the eyes already, known them all—

The eyes that fix you in a formulated phrase,

And when I am formulated, sprawling on a pin,[7]

When I am pinned and wriggling on the wall,

Then how should I begin

To spit out all the butt-ends[8] of my days and ways?

And how should I presume?

And I have known the arms already, known them all—

Arms that are braceleted and white and bare

(But in the lamplight, downed with light brown hair!)

Is it perfume from a dress

That makes me so digress?

Arms that lie along a table, or wrap about a shawl.

And should I then presume?

And how should I begin?

Shall I say, I have gone at dusk through narrow streets

And watched the smoke that rises from the pipes

Of lonely men in shirt-sleeves, leaning out of windows? ...

I should have been a pair of ragged claws[9]

Scuttling across the floors of silent seas.

And the afternoon, the evening, sleeps so peacefully!

Smoothed by long fingers,

Asleep ... tired ... or it malingers,

Stretched on the floor, here beside you and me.

Should I, after tea and cakes and ices,

Have the strength to force the moment to its crisis?

But though I have wept and fasted, wept and prayed,

Though I have seen my head (grown slightly bald)

brought in upon a platter,[10]

I am no prophet—and here's no great matter;

I have seen the moment of my greatness flicker,

And I have seen the eternal Footman hold my coat,

and snicker,

And in short, I was afraid.

And would it have been worth it, after all,

After the cups, the marmalade, the tea,

Among the porcelain, among some talk of you and me,

Would it have been worth while,

To have bitten off the matter with a smile,

To have squeezed the universe into a ball[11]

To roll it towards some overwhelming question,

To say: "I am Lazarus[12], come from the dead,

Come back to tell you all, I shall tell you all" —

If one, settling a pillow by her head

Should say: "That is not what I meant at all;

That is not it, at all."

And would it have been worth it, after all,

Would it have been worth while,

After the sunsets and the dooryards and the sprinkled streets,

After the novels, after the teacups, after the skirts that trail along the floor—

And this, and so much more? —

It is impossible to say just what I mean!

But as if a magic lantern threw the nerves in patterns on a screen:

Would it have been worth while

If one, settling a pillow or throwing off a shawl,

And turning toward the window, should say:

"That is not it at all,

That is not what I meant, at all."

No! I am not Prince Hamlet[13], nor was meant to be;
Am an attendant lord[14], one that will do
To swell a progress[15], start a scene or two,
Advise the prince; no doubt, an easy tool,
Deferential, glad to be of use,
Politic, cautious, and meticulous;
Full of high sentence[16], but a bit obtuse;
At times, indeed, almost ridiculous—
Almost, at times, the Fool[17].

I grow old ... I grow old ...
I shall wear the bottoms of my trousers rolled.
Shall I part my hair behind?[18] Do I dare to eat a
peach?
I shall wear white flannel trousers, and walk upon the
beach.
I have heard the mermaids singing, each to each[19].

I do not think that they will sing to me.

I have seen them riding seaward on the waves
Combing the white hair of the waves blown back
When the wind blows the water white and black.
We have lingered in the chambers of the sea
By sea-girls wreathed with seaweed red and brown
Till human voices wake us, and we drown.

Notes

① ***The meaning of this epigraph is as follows***："If I thought that my
reply was made to someone who would return to the world, this flame

[of my tongue] would no longer tremble. But since nobody has ever returned from these depths alive, if what I have heard is true, I'll answer you without fear of infamy. " These words are spoken by Guido da Montefeltro (1212-1298) in Dante's *Inferno*, XXVII, 61-66. Guido, with other deceitful counse-lors, is punished in a single prison of flame for the treacherous advice he gave to Pope Boniface.

② **When the evening is spread out**: This metaphor occurs many times in Henri Bergson's *Time and Free Will* (1889) to bolster the idea of "duration". While at Harvard, Eliot frequently referred to this book in his writings about Bergson.

③ **In the room the women come and go... Michelangelo** (13-14, 35-36): French Symbolist (an heavy influence on Eliot) Jules Laforgue has a similar line about the masters of the Sienne school. Eliot parodies Laforgue but creates a realistic scene of intellectual gossip. Michelangelo was a Renaissance Italian sculptor, painter, and poet.

④ **And indeed there will be time**: Cf. "Had we but world enough and time," from Metaphysical poet Andrew Marvell's "To His Coy Mistress." The speaker of the poem argues to his "coy mistress" that they could take their time in courtship games only if they were immortal; ironically, Prufrock deludes himself into thinking there will be time to court his lady or ladies.

⑤ **the works and days of hands**: "Works and Days" is a poem about the farming year by the Greek poet Hesiod (8th century B. C.). The ironic divide is between utilitarian farm labor and the "works and days of hands" in empty social gestures.

⑥ **dying fall**: In Shakespeare's *Twelfth Night* Duke Orsino asks for an encore of melancholy music: "That strain again! It had a dying fall" (1. 1. 4).

⑦ **sprawling on a pin**: Insect specimens are pinned into place for scientific study. Prufrock's comparison to an animal of some kind is the second of three in the poem (the first is the cat in the third stanza, the third is the crab claws [Lines 73-74]).

⑧ **butt-ends**: the ends of smoked cigarettes.

⑨ **a pair of ragged claws**: self-pitying remark that he would have been better as a crab at the bottom of the ocean. Cf. *Hamlet* 2. 2. 205-206. Hamlet mocks the unwitting and aging Polonius, saying that Polonius could become young like Hamlet only if he somehow went back in time: "for you yourself, sir, should be old as I am, if, like a crab, you could go backward."

⑩ **Though I have seen my head... brought in upon a platter**: Matthew 14: 3-11, Mark 6: 17-29 in the Bible, the death of John the Baptist. A dancing girl named Salome requested the head of John the Baptist on a silver platter from King Herod. Prufrock's observation of his "(grown slightly bald)" head parodies the event and gives it the flavor of mock-heroism found throughout the poem.

325

⑪ **To have squeezed the universe into a ball**: Cf. Andrew Marvell "To His Coy Mistress" (41-44): "Let us roll all our strength and all / Our sweetness up into one ball, / And tear our pleasures with rough strife / Thorough the iron gates of life." The imagery is suggestive of phallic penetration of the hymen.

⑫ **Lazarus**: Luke 16: 19-31 in the Bible. In the parable, Lazarus, a beggar, went to Heaven, while Dives, a rich man, went to Hell. Dives wanted to warn his brothers about Hell and appeased to Abraham (unsuccessfully) for Lazarus to be sent back to tell them. The parable is perhaps suggestive of the Dante-Guido da Montefeltro allusion in the epigraph; both concern themselves with the possibility of returning from the afterlife.

⑬ **Prince Hamlet**: Shakespeare's most famous character, from *Hamlet*. Hamlet, like Prufrock, is indecisive and anxious about future consequences. Prufrock echoes Hamlet's famous saying "to be or not to be" (3.1.66) at the end of this line ("nor was meant to be"), a line that is about wondering whether it is worth existing ("to exist or not to exist") and couches itself in the passive tense ("to be").

⑭ **attendant lord**: Prufrock does not believe he is a hero, like Hamlet, but an "attendant lord" (in this case, the implication is doddering father Polonius from *Hamlet*), a mere auxiliary character.

⑮ **To swell a progress**: an Elizabethan state journey made by a royal or noble person. Elizabethan plays sometimes showed full-blown "progresses" crossing the stage.

⑯ **high sentence**: older meanings: "opinions," "sententiousness."

⑰ **Fool**: standard character in Elizabethan drama, such as a court jester who entertains the nobility and speaks wise nonsense (the Fool in *King Lear* is perhaps the best example).

⑱ **I shall wear the bottoms of my trousers rolled. / Shall I part my hair behind**: At the time, both styles were considered bohemian; the middle-aged Prufrock pathetically wonders if he can reverse his aging by embracing such youthful fashion.

⑲ **I have heard the mermaids singing, each to each**: Cf. John Donne's "Song," with its "Teach me to hear mermaids singing." Arhtur Symons' *The Symbolist Movement in Literature* (London: Heinemann, 1899) quotes "El Desdichado" ("The Disinherited") by Gérard de Nerval(1808-1855): "J'ai rêvé dans la grotte où nage la sirène" ("I have dreamed in the cave where the siren swims"; p. 37).

Questions for Reading Comprehension

1. Why does the poet begin the poem with a quotation from Dante's Inferno?

2. What are "you and I" going out to do? Where do the streets lead to?

3. What does the simile in Line 3 suggest about Prufrock's mood or feel-

ings?

4. In Lines 15 to 22, the yellow fog seems animated. What kind of animal in particular do you think Prufrock has in mind? Is the yellow fog able to come into the house? What does this indicate? The fog goes from window-panes to the ground. What does this order of progression indicate?

5. Why does Prufrock say there will be time in Line 27 and Lines 32 to 34?

6. According to Lines 37 to 46, what would Prufrock "disturb" if he dares to ask his question?

7. How does Prufrock portray himself [Lines 39 to 44]?

8. How do you understand the word "presume" in Line 54? What's the irony in the use of the word "presume" in Line 54?

9. Why doesn't Prufrock "force the moment to its crisis" (Lines 75 to 86)?

10. Who does Prufrock say he is and is not in Lines 111 to 119?

11. Eliot has Prufrock ask the question in Line 122, "Do I dare to eat a peach?" What's Eliot's intention here if we compare this question with Hamlet's famous question "to be or not to be..."? Does "Peach" bear any symbolic significance?

12. Whom has Prufrock heard singing in Lines 124 to 131? What does he think these creatures will not do?

13. Why is it significant that Prufrock hears the mermaids? Why will they not sing for him?

14. In Lines 1 to 14, Prufrock's imagery progresses from a general look at the skyline to the streets, to a hotel room and then to sawdust-covered floors in restaurants. What do the images suggest about Prufrock's personality? What does this order of progression indicate?

15. "And indeed there will be time" (23, 37) is an allusion to Metaphysical poet Andrew Marvell's "To His Coy Mistress" ("Had we

but world enough, and time") , in which the speaker urges his lady to speed up their courtship. For what does Prufrock say there will be time? What is Prufrock trying to avoid?

Discussion Questions for Appreciation

1. Why would Prufrock think of himself as "you and I," or "we"?

2. What do the opening quotation, Lines 51, 73 to 74, 82 and 85 reveal about Prufrock's view of his life and his self-image?

3. What do the images in Lines 121 to 123 suggest about the future Prufrock foresees for himself? Is this future different from his past?

4. How is the city portrayed in the poem? Does this sense of the city bear any relation to Prufrock's character and his dilemma? How is the picture of modern life presented in the poem?

5. Does the name "Prufrock" bear any symbolic significance? What is it?

6. The rhythm of the lines in the poem is deliberately irregular. What does this rhyme scheme indicate?

7. The poem is an interior, dramatic monologue. Is it a love song in any traditional sense?

8. Some critics say that Prufrock's propensity to move backward and downward is suggestive of his nearness to death, of his back-pedaling down into Hell. Please quote evidence from the poem to justify Prufrock's propensity to move backward and downward.

A Question for Writing

Eliot says in his article "Tradition and Individual Talents", "The only way of expressing emotion in the form of art is by finding an ' objective correlative'; in other words, a set of objects, a situation, a chain of events which shall be the formula of that particular emotion; such that when the external facts, which must terminate in sensory experience, are given, the emotion is immediately evoked." Has this literary principle penetrated into the writing of this poem ? Please justify yourself.

Sherwood Anderson (1876-1941)

Sherwood Anderson was born in Camden, Ohio. His father declined from the harness business. So the family led a transient life, moving from one place to another after work. Anderson attended school only intermittently because he had to help to support his family by working as a newsboy, housepainter, stock handler, and stable groom. When he was sixteen, the family finally settled down in Clyde, Ohio, which later became the model for his famous book *Winesburg Ohio*. In 1896, he moved to Chicago, where he worked as a warehouse laborer and attended business classes at night. During the Spanish-American War he fought in Cuba and returned after the war to Ohio, for a final year of schooling at Wittenberg College, Springfield.

Anderson and his first wife settled in Ohio where Anderson managed a mail-order house as well as two paint firms. But he increasingly felt that his need to write conflicted with his business career. Then he made a dramatic change in his life. He left his wife and moved to Chicago. There he took a job in advertising and joined the so-called Chicago Group, which included such writers as Theodore Dreiser, Edgar Lee Masters and Carl Sandburg.

Anderson's first two novels were *Windy Macpherson's Son* (1916), the story of a man who runs away from a small Iowa town in futile search for the meaning of life, and *Marching Man* (1917), the story of a charismatic lawyer who tries unsuccessfully to reorganize the factory system in a small town. Both books reveal three of Anderson's preoccupations: the individual quest for self and social betterment, the small-town environment, and the distrust of modern industrial society. His third book *Winesburg, Ohio* consists of twenty-three thematically related sketches and stories. The narrative is united by the appearance of George Willard, a young reporter, who is in revolt against the narrowness of the small-town life and who acts as a counterpoint to the other people of the town. The book, which is written in simple language illuminated by a quiet lyricism, depicts how the lives of the characters have been profoundly distorted by the frustration and suppression of their desires. The individual tales of *Winesburg*, *Ohio*, and Anderson's other collections of short stories, *The Triumphs of the Egg* (1921), *Horses and Men* (1932), and *Death in the Woods* (1933), direct the American short story away from the neatly plotted tales of O. Henry and his imitators. His stories are characterized by a casual development, complexity of motivation, and an interest in psychological process.

In 1921 Anderson received the first *Dial* Award for his contribution to American literature. He travelled widely in Europe. After he returned to the United States, he settled down in New Orleans, where he shared an apartment with William Faulkner. He wrote, among others, the novel *Dark Laughter* (1925), which became a bestseller. However, he was never again as successful as he had been with the Winesburg stories either in depth of vision or in literary craft.

From New Orleans Anderson moved to New York, and from there finally to Marion, Virginia, where he built a country house, and worked as a farmer and journalist. He travelled again in Europe. To earn extra income he continued his series of lectures throughout the country. Anderson also wrote three personal narratives, which help us understand him as a man and a writer. Anderson died of peritonitis on a good-will tour to South America, at Christobal, Canal Zone, on March 8, 1941. After his death, Anderson's reputation soon declined, but since the 1970s, scholars and critics have found a new interest in his work.

For Anderson, life in an American small town is grotesque in some way. His characters are often lonely and isolated, dissatisfied with their

331

world and frustrated in their attempts to find something better. "He observed human grotesqueness and eccentricity from a Freudian psychological point of view and tried to reveal the abnormal states of mind in a more or less accurate way." [①] Stylistically, Anderson strives for the simplest possible prose, using brief or uncomplicated sentences and unsophisticated vocabulary appropriate to his typical characters. His style, which is deceptively simple, influences the styles of Ernest Hemingway and William Faulkner, whose early careers Anderson helped nurture.

Sophistication, Concerning Helen White

Introduction

"Sophistication, Concerning Helen White" is taken from *Winesburg, Ohio*, a book of the grotesque, which includes twenty-three stories. This cycle of stories has several unifying elements, including a single background, a prevailing tone, a central character and an underlying plot that is advanced or enriched by each of the stories. The underlying plot in *Winesburg, Ohio* is the growing up of George Willard, who is too young to understand the hope held for him by people in the small Midwestern town. Since people there cannot truly communicate with others, they have all become emotional cripples. Most of the grotesques are attracted one by one to George Willard with the belief that he might be able to speak what is in their hearts and thus re-establish their connection with mankind. Some critics have noted that the character of George is a not-well-disguised portrait of Anderson himself. In the story, George hopes to fulfill his dream of becoming a thoughtful writer. During a summer festival, George visits Helen White again. With her encouragement,

---

① Chang Yaoxin, *A Survey of American Literature* (Tianjin: Nankai University Press, 1990), 328.

he seeks to escape peer pressure from old and young citizens of the town by undertaking the rites of passage that every young person must endure.

Sophistication, Concerning Helen White

It was early evening of a day in, the late fall and the Winesburg County Fair had brought crowds of country people into town. The day had been clear and the night came on warm and pleasant. On the Trunion Pike, where the road after it left town stretched away between berry fields now covered with dry brown leaves, the dust from passing wagons arose in clouds. Children, curled into little balls, slept on the straw scattered on wagon beds. Their hair was full of dust and their fingers black and sticky. The dust rolled away over the fields and the departing sun set it ablaze with colors.

In the main street of Winesburg crowds filled the stores and the sidewalks. Night came on, horses whinnied, the clerks in the stores ran madly about, children became lost and cried lustily, an American town worked terribly at the task of amusing itself. [①]

Pushing his way through the crowds in Main Street, young George Willard concealed himself in the stairway leading to Doctor Reefy's office and looked at the people. With feverish eyes he watched the faces drifting past under the store lights. Thoughts kept coming into his head and he did not want to think. He stamped impatiently on the wooden steps and looked sharply about. "Well, is she going to stay with him all day? Have I done all this waiting for nothing?" he muttered.

George Willard, the Ohio village boy, was fast growing into manhood and new thoughts had been coming into his mind. All that day, amid the jam of people at the Fair, he had gone about feeling lonely. He was about to leave Winesburg to go away to some city where he hoped to get work on a city newspaper and he felt grown up. The mood that had taken possession of him was a thing known to men and unknown to boys. ② He felt old and a little tired. Memories awoke in him. To his mind his new sense of maturity set him apart, made of him a half-tragic figure. He wanted someone to understand the feeling that had taken possession of him after his mother's death.

There is a time in the life of every boy when he for the first time takes the backward view of life. Perhaps that is the moment when he crosses the line into manhood. The boy is walking through the street of his town. He is thinking of the future and of the figure he will cut in the world. ③ Ambitions and regrets awake within him. Suddenly something happens; he stops under a tree and waits as for a voice calling his name. Ghosts of old things creep into his consciousness; the voices outside of himself whisper a message concerning the limitations of life. From being quite sure of himself and his future he becomes not at all sure. If he be an imaginative boy a door is to open and for the first time he looks out upon the world, seeing, as though they marched in procession before him, the countless figures of men who before his time have come out of nothingness into the world, lived their lives and again disappeared into nothingness. The sadness of sophistication has come to the boy. With a little gasp he sees himself as merely a leaf blown by the wind through the streets of his village. He knows that in spite of all the stout talk of his fellows he must live and die in uncertainty, a thing blown by the winds, a thing destined like corn to wilt in the sun. He shivers and looks eagerly about. The eighteen years he has lived seem but a moment, a breathing space in the long march of humanity. Already he hears death calling. With all his heart he wants to come close to some other human, touch someone with his hands, be touched by the hand of another. If he prefers that the other be a woman, that is because he believes that a woman will be gentle, that she will understand. He wants, most of all, understanding.

When the moment of sophistication came to George Willard his mind turned to Helen White, the Winesburg banker's daughter. Always he had been conscious of the girl growing into womanhood as he grew into manhood. Once on a summer night when he was eighteen, he had walked with her on a country road and in her presence had given way to an impulse to boast, to make himself appear big and significant in her eyes. Now he wanted to see her for another purpose. He wanted to tell her of the new impulses that had come to him. He had tried to make her think of him as a man when he knew nothing of manhood and now he wanted to be with her and to try to make her feel the change he believed had taken place in his nature.

As for Helen White, she also had come to a period of change. What George felt, she in her young woman's way felt also. She was no longer a girl and hungered to reach into the grace and beauty of womanhood. She had come home from Cleveland, where she was attending college, to spend a day at the Fair. She also had begun to have memories. During the day she sat in the grand-stand with a young man, one of the instructors from the college, who was a guest of her mother's. The young man was of a pedantic turn of mind and she felt at once he would not do for her purpose. At the Fair she was glad to be seen in his company as he was well dressed and a stranger. She knew that the fact of his presence would create an impression. During the day she was happy, but when night came on she began to grow restless. She wanted to drive the instructor away, to get out of his presence. While they sat together in the grand-stand and while the eyes of former schoolmates were upon them, she paid so much attention to her escort that he grew interested. " A scholar needs money. I should marry a woman with money," he mused.

Helen White was thinking of George Willard even as he wandered gloomily through the crowds thinking of her. She remembered the summer evening when they had walked together and wanted to walk with him again. She thought that the months she had spent in the city, the going to theaters and the seeing of great crowds wandering in lighted thorough-fares, had changed her profoundly. She wanted him to feel and be conscious of the change in her nature.

The summer evening together that had left its mark on the memory of both the young man and woman had, when looked at quite sensibly, been rather stupidly spent. They had walked out of town along a country road. Then they had stopped by a fence near a field of young corn and George had taken off his coat and let it hang on his arm. "Well, I've stayed here in Winesburg—yes—I've not yet gone away but I'm growing up," he had said. "I've been reading books and I've been thinking. I'm going to try to amount to something in life.

"Well," he explained, "that isn't the point. Perhaps I'd better quit talking."

The confused boy put his hand on the girl's arm. His voice trembled. The two started to walk back along the road toward town. In his desperation George boasted, "I'm going to be a big man, the biggest that ever lived here in Winesburg," he declared. "I want you to do something, I don't know what. Perhaps it is none of my business. I want you to try to be different from other women. You see the point. It's none of my business I tell you. I want you to be a beautiful woman. You see what I want."

The boy's voice failed and in silence the two came back into town and went along the street to Helen White's house. At the gate he tried to say something impressive. Speeches he had thought out came into his head, but they seemed utterly pointless. "I thought—I used to think—I had it in my mind you would marry Seth Richmond. Now I know you won't," was all he could find to say as she went through the gate and toward the door of her house.

On the warm fall evening as he stood in the stairway and looked at the crowd drifting through Main Street, George thought of the talk beside the field of young corn and was ashamed of the figure he had made of himself. In the street the people surged up and down like cattle confined in a pen. Buggies and wagons almost filled the narrow thoroughfare. A band played and small boys raced along the sidewalk, diving between the legs of men. Young men with shining red faces walked awkwardly about with girls on their arms. In a room above one of the stores, where a dance was to be held, the fiddlers tuned their instruments. The broken sounds floated down through an open window and out across the murmur of voices and the loud blare of the horns of the band. The medley of sounds got on young Willard's nerves[④]. Everywhere, on all sides, the sense of crowding, moving life closed in about him. He wanted to run away by himself and think. "If she wants to stay with that fellow she may. Why should I care? What difference does it make to me?" he growled and went along Main Street and through Hern's Grocery into a side street.

George felt so utterly lonely and dejected that he wanted to weep but pride made him walk rapidly along, swinging his arms. He came to Wesley Moyer's livery barn and stopped in the shadows to listen to a group of men who talked of a race Wesley's stallion, Tony Tip, had won at the Fair during the afternoon. A crowd had gathered in front of the barn and before the crowd walked Wesley, prancing up and down boasting. He held a whip in his hand and kept tapping the ground. Little puffs of dust arose in the lamplight. "Hell, quit your talking," Wesley exclaimed. "I wasn't afraid, I knew I had 'em beat all the time. I wasn't afraid."

Ordinarily George Willard would have been intensely interested in the boasting of Moyer, the horseman. Now it made him angry. He turned and hurried away along the street. "Old Windbag," he sputtered. "Why does he want to be bragging? Why don't he shut up?"

George went into a vacant lot and, as he hurried along, fell over a pile of rubbish. A nail protruding from an empty barrel tore his trousers.

He sat down on the ground and swore. With a pin he mended the torn place and then arose and went on. "I'll go to Helen White's house, that's what I'll do. I'll walk right in. I'll say that I want to see her. I'll walk right in and sit down, that's what I'll do," he declared, climbing over a fence and beginning to run.

On the veranda of Banker White's house Helen was restless and distraught. The instructor sat between the mother and daughter. His talk wearied the girl. Although he had also been raised in an Ohio town, the instructor began to put on the airs of the city. He wanted to appear cosmopolitan. "I like the chance you have given me to study the background out of which most of our girls come," he declared. "It was good of you, Mrs. White, to have me down for the day." He turned to Helen and laughed. "Your life is still bound up with the life of this town?" he asked. "There are people here in whom you are interested?" To the girl his voice sounded pompous and heavy.

Helen arose and went into the house. At the door leading to a garden at the back she stopped and stood listening. Her mother began to talk. "There is no one here fit to associate with a girl of Helen's breeding," she said.

Helen ran down a flight of stairs at the back of the house and into the garden. In the darkness she stopped and stood trembling. It seemed to her that the world was full of meaningless people saying words. Afire with eagerness she ran through a garden gate and, turning a corner by the banker's barn, went into a little side street. "George! Where are you, George?" she cried, filled with nervous excitement. She stopped running, and leaned against a tree to laugh hysterically. Along the dark little street came George Willard, still saying words. "I'm going to walk right into her house. I'll go right in and sit down, " he declared as he came up to her. He stopped and stared stupidly. "Come on," he said and took hold of her hand. With hanging heads they walked away along the street under the trees. Dry leaves rustled under foot. Now that he had found her George wondered what he had better do and say.

At the upper end of the Fair Ground, in Winesburg, there is a half decayed old grand-stand. It has never been painted and the boards are all warped out of shape. The Fair Ground stands on top of a low hill rising out of the valley of Wine Creek and from the grand-stand one can see at night, over a cornfield, the lights of the town reflected against the sky.

George and Helen climbed the hill to the Fair Ground, coming by the path past Waterworks Pond. The feeling of loneliness and isolation that had come to the young man in the crowded streets of his town was both broken and intensified by the presence of Helen. What he felt was reflected in her.

In youth there are always two forces fighting in people. The warm unthinking little animal struggles against the thing that reflects and remembers, and the older, the more sophisticated thing had possession of George Willard. Sensing his mood, Helen walked beside him filled with respect. When they got to the grand-stand they climbed up under the roof and sat down on one of the long bench-like seats.

There is something memorable in the experience to be had by going into a fair ground that stands at the edge of a Middle Western town on a night after the annual fair has been held. The sensation is one never to be forgotten. On all sides are ghosts, not of the dead, but of living people. Here, during the day just passed, have come the people pouring in from the town and the country around. Farmers with their wives and children and all the people from the hundreds of little frame houses have gathered within these board walls. Young girls have laughed and men with beards have talked of the affairs of their lives. The place has been filled to overflowing with life. It has itched and squirmed with life and now it is night and the life has all gone away. The silence is almost terrifying. One conceals oneself standing silently beside the trunk of a tree and what there is of a reflective tendency in his nature is intensified. One shudders at the thought of the meaninglessness of life while at the same instant, and if the people of the town are his people, one loves life so intensely that tears come into the eyes.

In the darkness under the roof of the grand-stand, George Willard sat beside Helen White and felt very keenly his own insignificance in the scheme of existence. Now that he had come out of town where the presence of the people stirring about, busy with a multitude of affairs, had been so irritating, the irritation was all gone. The presence of Helen renewed and refreshed him. It was as though her woman's hand was assisting him to make some minute readjustment of the machinery of his life. He began to think of the people in the town where he had always lived with something like reverence. He had reverence for Helen. He wanted to love and to be loved by her, but he did not want at the moment to be confused by her womanhood. In the darkness he took hold of her hand and when she crept close put a hand on her shoulder. A wind began to blow and he shivered. With all his strength he tried to hold and to understand the mood that had come upon him. In that high place in the darkness the two oddly sensitive human atoms held each other tightly and waited. In the mind of each was the same thought. "I have come to this lonely place and here is this other," was the substance of the thing felt.

In Winesburg the crowded day had run itself out into the long night of the late fall. Farm horses jogged away along lonely country roads pulling their portion of weary people. Clerks began to bring samples of goods in off the sidewalks and lock the doors of stores. In the Opera House a crowd had gathered to see a show and further down Main Street the fiddlers, their instruments tuned, sweated and worked to keep the feet of youth flying over a dance floor.

In the darkness in the grand-stand Helen White and George Willard remained silent. Now and then the spell⑤ that held them was broken and they turned and tried in the dim light to see into each other's eyes. They kissed but that impulse did not last. At the upper end of the Fair Ground a half dozen men worked over horses that had raced during the afternoon. The men had built a fire and were heating kettles of water. Only their legs could be seen as they passed back and forth in the light. When the wind blew the little flames of the fire danced crazily about.

George and Helen arose and walked away into the darkness. They went along a path past a field of corn that had not yet been cut. The wind whispered among the dry corn blades. For a moment during the walk back into town the spell that held them was broken. When they had come to the crest of Waterworks Hill they stopped by a tree and George again put his hands on the girl's shoulders. She embraced him eagerly and then again they drew quickly back from that impulse. They stopped kissing and stood a little apart. Mutual respect grew big in them. They were both embarrassed and to relieve their embarrassment dropped into the animalism of youth. They laughed and began to pull and haul at each other. In some way chastened and purified by the mood they had been in, they became, not man and woman, not boy and girl, but excited little animals.

It was so they went down the hill. In the darkness they played like two splendid young things in a young world. Once, running swiftly forward, Helen tripped George and he fell. He squirmed and shouted. Shaking with laughter, he roiled down the hill. Helen ran after him. For just a moment she stopped in the darkness. There was no way of knowing what woman's thoughts went through her mind but, when the bottom of the hill was reached and she came up to the boy, she took his arm and walked beside him in dignified silence. For some reason they could not have explained they had both got from their silent evening together the thing needed. Man or boy, woman or girl, they had for a moment taken hold of the thing that makes the mature life of men and women in the modern world possible.

Notes

① **an American town worked terribly at the task of amusing itself**: an American town is now busy amusing itself.

② **The mood that had taken possession of him was a thing known to men and unknown to boys.** : Here, "the mood" refers to the mood of growing up, therefore, only men coming of age know it, boys can not.

③ **the figure he will cut in the world**: the image he will show to the world.

④ **got on young Willard's nerves**: make young Willard nervous.

⑤ **spell**: a piece of magic.

Questions for Reading Comprehension

1. What event is being celebrated in Winesburg? What does Winesburg work terribly at?

2. How does George Willard feel amid the jam of people at the Fair? Why?

3. For what purposes does George want to see Helen?

4. Who is Helen with during the day? Who is she thinking about at night? Why?

5. Why does George feel impatient with Moyer the horseman? Why is Helen not interested in the instructor?

6. How do George and Helen finally meet? Where do they go?

7. What do George and Helen have in common?

8. What do George and Helen want to share?

Discussion Questions for Appreciation

1. What kind of town is Winesburg as implied by Anderson?
2. What does Anderson suggest about adolescents in general?
3. What is the "sadness of sophistication" as suggested by Anderson?
4. What is "the thing that makes the mature life of men and women in the modern world possible" as suggested by Anderson at the end of the story?
5. Looking at the story as a whole, does the title "Sophistication" have a positive or negative connotation? Please justify yourself.

A Question for Writing

The twentieth century saw a tremendous shift in population as many young Americans left their rural communities for big cities. Does this story give you any insight into why they left? Do you think adolescents like George Willard were happy with the life they found in big cities? Why?

Ernest Hemingway（1899-1961）

Ernest Miller Hemingway was born in Oak Park, Illinois. In his childhood, his physician father frequently took him to camping, fishing and hunting, which were to become his life-long hobbies. He also attended concerts and operas and visited art museums with his mother, a music teacher, and a lover of high culture. Hemingway seemed to share his father's love of the outdoors more. In his teens, he became an amateur boxer and hurt one eye during boxing. In his high school years, he ran away from home twice, spending a few months on the road with tramps. Many of these experiences were used in his first volume of short stories, *In Our Time* (1925).

Hemingway started his career for the newspaper *Star* in Kansas City at the age of seventeen. There he learned to get to the heart of a story with direct, simple sentences. Eager to prove his manliness, Hemingway resigned after working for only six months at the *Star*, and attempted to enlist in the army, but was rejected because of poor vision. However, after the United States entered World War Ⅱ, he managed to join a volunteer ambulance unit in the Italian army, and was wounded near the Italian/Austrian front. Hospitalized, he fell in love with his nurse, yet the relationship ended in vain. However, his experience as a soldier and the love affair at the hospital provided him with materials for his novel *A Farewell to Arms* (1929).

After his return to the United States, Hemingway was celebrated as a war hero. However, living with his parents, who never quite appreciated what their son had been through, was difficult. His short story "Soldier's Home" reflects his feelings of frustration and shame upon returning home to a world that still has a romantic notion of war and fails to understand its psychological impact. Then, he became a reporter for Canadian and American newspapers and was soon sent back to Europe to cover such events as the Greek Revolution.

In 1920, Hemingway married Hadley Richardson and they moved to Paris in 1921. Then Hemingway worked his way to becoming a writer. Many of his political or military reports were "spot news" to be rushed by cable, and these cables shaped his most characteristic style—economy of expression. At the same time, Hemingway became a member of the group of expatriate Americans in Paris, where he made acquaintances with Ezra Pound, F. Scott Fitzgerald, and Gertrude Stein. Stein, in particular, influenced his spare style. And it was Stein who termed the loosely-knit group of artists and writers centered on the Left Bank of the Seine River the "Lost Generation". With the help of Fitzgerald and Anderson, Hemingway got his book of short stories *In Our Time* published in the United States in 1925. After the novel *The Sun Also Rises* (1926) brought Hemingway fame, he brought out his second collection of stories, *Men without Women* (1927). During this period, his first marriage broke up. In his life-time, he married four times. In 1928, Hemingway and his new bride, Pauline Pfeiffer, a fashion editor, moved to Florida, where he spent most of his days fishing.

In the 1930s and 1940s, Hemingway covered the Spanish Civil War, World War II, and the wars in China. He was fiercely anti-Nazi during World War II. His experiences as a reporter during the civil war in Spain were used as the background for his novel *For Whom the Bell Tolls* (1940).

Hemingway liked hunting, bullfighting and fishing. On a safari in Africa in 1953, he was badly injured in a plane crash; still, he continued to enjoy hunting and sport fishing, activities that inspired many of his works, such as *The Sun Also Rises*, "The Snows of Kilimanjaro" (1936), "The Short, Happy Life of Francis Macomber" (1936), and

345

The Old Man and the Sea (1952).

Hemingway shot himself to death in 1961. There are guesses about the reasons of his suicide—troubled family background, illness, or the belief that he was losing his gift for writing. His biggest theme of "grace under pressure," keeping one's dignity in the face of extreme situations, is one he strove to keep in his own life.

Hemingway's major works include: *The Sun Also Rises*, *A Farewell to Arms*, *For Whom the Bell Tolls* (1940), and *The Old Man and the Sea* (1952).

The Sun Also Rises paints the picture of the post-World War I generation, the Lost Generation. This novel features the Left Bank Paris in 1920s, and describes young English and American expatriates caught in the war and cut off from the old values. The protagonists, Jake Barnes, Robert Cohn, and Brett Ashley, wander aimlessly and restlessly, and they go fishing, swimming and bullfighting to avoid thinking seriously about a world that is meaningless and void. All their actions are futile in a world in which "all is vanity and vexation of spirit," yet Jake Barnes persists in living according to a self-conscious code of dignity, showing "grace under pressure".

A Farewell to Arms is the story of an American army officer, Frederick Henry, and a British nurse, Catherine Barkley, who meet in a hospital when Henry is wounded in the battlefield and hospitalized. They run away from war, trying to make "a separate peace", but their dream is shattered by the death of Catherine in childbirth. Thus, Henry is completely disillusioned. Instead of finding sacredness and glory in war, he finds the battle-field a slaughterhouse. This novel catches the mood of the post-war generation.

In 1937 Hemingway covered the Spanish Civil War between the

346

Fascist Franco Regime and the communist loyalists who supported the democratically elected government. Eventually the Franco-led rebels won the war in 1939. Hemingway wrote the novel *For Whom the Bell Tolls* based on his experiences in Spain. Robert Jordan, the protagonist, though keenly aware that he is fighting a losing battle, strives on. He loves a woman and joins her in the fighting. However, his love is shattered by the cruel reality. Yet, in the process of fighting and struggling, he finds himself no longer alone, but having a cause to work for and a group to fight with and, more importantly, someone to love and to die for.

The Old Man and the Sea is a short novel about an old fisherman's journey, his long and lonely struggle with a fish and the sea. The spirit Hemingway wants to praise is the fisherman's victory in defeat, or what Hemingway termed as "grace under pressure" in an interview. The short novel brought Hemingway the Pulitzer Prize of 1953, and was said to be central to his Nobel Prize of 1954.

Hemingway is famous for his style of economy of expression, or spare and tight journalistic type of prose. He likes to use the objective, detached point of view, and his vocabulary and sentence structure are deceptively simple. His "Iceberg Theory" best justifies his preference for understatement. He says "The dignity of movement of an iceberg is due to only one-eighth of it being above water."

Hemingway's subject matters are usually failure, moral bankruptcy, death, deception, and sterility in the post-WWI society. His heroes, fully aware of their tragic ending, still show inner moral discipline and guts in time of adversity.

A Clean, Well-lighted Place

Introduction

This story was published in 1933. Hemingway was living in Paris at this time and doing a lot of traveling in Europe. He saw and felt first-hand the effects of World War I and the severe economic and spiritual depression it caused. Europe was destroyed; a whole generation of young men died—nearly one third of all British young men, and nearly three fourths of all French and German young men. The suffering was horrible—and it became apparent that it was not for truth and justice, but for the prestige and profit of the leaders, who were quite willing to sacrifice the lives of their people for their own egotism.

One of the results of World War I was a loss of faith: People realized they could no longer trust their governments, and in the face of such pointless destruction, many could no longer trust their gods. People began to question every religious and social institution that had bound society together, and many came to the conclusion that no social or religious institution could be trusted.

One school of philosophy that incorporated this view was existentialism. There are different varieties of existentialism, but its basic belief is that there is no God, and therefore, life can have no inherent meaning. We are not put on earth for any purpose—our birth is an accident. There is no grand design to life—it is all chance. There is no order in the universe—it is all chaos. Our religions and our social structures are meant to help us avoid facing that terrifying truth. But this does not mean that life must be meaningless. It simply means that we, ourselves, must determine what the purpose of our lives is. We must set our own standards and live by them. If we fail to live up to our principles, then life is truly meaningless.

Hemingway subscribes, generally, to this theory. He believes that life is inherently meaningless, and that all we can do is to set high standards and adhere to them with dignity—all the while knowing that this dignity is all that keeps us from falling into despair.

A Clean, Well-lighted Place

It was very late and everyone had left the cafe except an old man who sat in the shadow the leaves of the tree made against the electric light. In the day time the street was dusty, but at night the dew settled the dust and the old man liked to sit late because he was deaf and now at night it was quiet and he felt the difference. The two waiters inside the cafe knew that the old man was a little drunk, and while he was a good client they knew that if he became too drunk he would leave without paying, so they kept watch on him.

"Last week he tried to commit suicide," one waiter said.

"Why?"

"He was in despair."

"What about?"

"Nothing."

"How do you know it was nothing?"

"He has plenty of money."

They sat together at a table that was close against the wall near the door of the cafe and looked at the terrace where the tables were all empty except where the old man sat in the shadow of the leaves of the tree that moved slightly in the wind. A girl and a soldier went by in the street. The street light shone on the brass number on his collar. The girl wore no head covering and hurried beside him.

"The guard will pick him up," [①] one waiter said.

"What does it matter if he gets what he's after?"

"He had better get off the street now. The guard will get him. They went by five minutes ago."

The old man sitting in the shadow rapped on his saucer with his glass. The younger waiter went over to him.

"What do you want?"

The old man looked at him. "Another brandy," he said.

"You'll be drunk," the waiter said. The old man looked at him. The waiter went away.

"He'll stay all night," he said to his colleague. "I'm sleepy now. I never get into bed before three o'clock. He should have killed himself last week."

The waiter took the brandy bottle and another saucer from the counter inside the cafe and marched out to the old man's table. He put down the saucer and poured the glass full of brandy.

"You should have killed yourself last week," he said to the deaf man. The old man motioned with his finger. "A little more," he said. The waiter poured on into the glass so that the brandy slopped over and ran down the stem into the top saucer of the pile. "Thank you," the old man said. The waiter took the bottle back inside the cafe. He sat down at the table with his colleague again.

"He's drunk now," he said.

"He's drunk every night."

"What did he want to kill himself for?"

"How should I know."

"How did he do it?"

"He hung himself with a rope."

"Who cut him down?"

"His niece."

"Why did they do it?"

"Fear for his soul."②

"How much money has he got?" "He's got plenty. "

"He must be eighty years old. "

"Anyway I should say he was eighty. "

"I wish he would go home. I never get to bed before three o'clock. What kind of hour is that to go to bed?"

"He stays up because he likes it. "

"He's lonely. I'm not lonely. I have a wife waiting in bed for me. "

"He had a wife once too. "

"A wife would be no good to him now. "

"You can't tell. He might be better with a wife. "

"His niece looks after him. You said she cut him down. "

"I know. " "I wouldn't want to be that old. An old man is a nasty thing. "

"Not always. This old man is clean. He drinks without spilling. Even now, drunk. Look at him. "

"I don't want to look at him. I wish he would go home. He has no regard for those who must work. "

The old man looked from his glass across the square, then over at the waiters.

"Another brandy," he said, pointing to his glass. The waiter who was in a hurry came over.

"Finished," he said, speaking with that omission of syntax stupid people employ when talking to drunken people or foreigners. "No more tonight. Close now. "

"Another," said the old man.

"No. Finished. " The waiter wiped the edge of the table with a towel and shook his head.

The old man stood up, slowly counted the saucers, took a leather coin purse from his pocket and paid for the drinks, leaving half a peseta[3] tip. The waiter watched him go down the street, a very old man walking unsteadily but with dignity.

"Why didn't you let him stay and drink?" the unhurried waiter asked. They were putting up the shutters. "It is not half-past two."

"I want to go home to bed."

"What is an hour?"

"More to me than to him."

"An hour is the same."

"You talk like an old man yourself. He can buy a bottle and drink at home."

"It's not the same."

"No, it is not," agreed the waiter with a wife. He did not wish to be unjust. He was only in a hurry.

"And you? You have no fear of going home before your usual hour?"

"Are you trying to insult me?"

"No, hombre, only to make a joke."

"No," the waiter who was in a hurry said, rising from pulling down the metal shutters. "I have confidence. I am all confidence."

"You have youth, confidence, and a job," the older waiter said. "You have everything."

"And what do you lack?"

"Everything but work."

"You have everything I have."

"No. I have never had confidence and I am not young."

"Come on. Stop talking nonsense and lock up."

"I am of those who like to stay late at the cafe," the older waiter said.

"With all those who do not want to go to bed. With all those who need a light for the night."

"I want to go home and into bed."

"We are of two different kinds," the older waiter said. He was now dressed to go home. "It is not only a question of youth and confidence although those things are very beautiful. Each night I am reluctant to close up because there may be some one who needs the cafe."

"Hombre, ④ there are bodegas open all night long."

"You do not understand. This is a clean and pleasant cafe. It is well lighted. The light is very good and also, now, there are shadows of the leaves."

"Good night," said the younger waiter.

"Good night," the other said. Turning off the electric light he continued the conversation with himself, it was the light of course but it is necessary that the place be clean and pleasant. You do not want music. Certainly you do not want music. Nor can you stand before a bar with dignity although that is all that is provided for these hours. What did he fear? It was not a fear or dread, It was a nothing that he knew too well. It was all a nothing and a man was a nothing too. It was only that and light was all it needed and a certain cleanness and order. Some lived in it and never felt it but he knew it all was nada y pues nada y nada y pues nada. ⑤ Our nada who art in nada, nada be thy name thy kingdom nada thy will be nada in nada as it is in nada. Give us this nada our daily nada and nada us our nada as we nada our nadas and nada us not into nada but deliver us from nada; pues nada. Hail nothing full of nothing, nothing is with thee. ⑥ He smiled and stood before a bar with a shining steam pressure coffee machine.

"What's yours?" asked the barman.

"Nada."

"Otro loco mas," said the barman and turned away.

"A little cup," said the waiter.

The barman poured it for him.

"The light is very bright and pleasant but the bar is unpolished," the waiter said.

The barman looked at him but did not answer. It was too late at night for conversation.

"You want another copita⑦?" the barman asked.

"No, thank you," said the waiter and went out. He disliked bars and bodegas. A clean, well-lighted cafe was a very different thing. Now, without thinking further, he would go home to his room. He would lie in the bed and finally, with daylight, he would go to sleep. After all, he said to himself, it's probably only insomnia. Many must have it.

Notes

① **The guard will pick him up**: The guard will arrest him for his neglect of duty.

② **Fear for his soul**: According to the Bible, suicide is a kind of crime as human births and deaths are decided by God.

③ **Peseta**: Spanish currency.

④ **hombre**: Spanish for "man". This is a friendly form of address.

⑤ **nada y pues nada**: "Nada", Spanish for "nothing". "Nada y pues nada" means "nothing and then nothing".

⑥ **Our nada who art in nada, nada be thy name thy kingdom nada thy will be nada in nada as it is in nada.... Hail nothing full of nothing, nothing is with thee.**: This is a paraphrase of the Lord's Prayer and the prayer to Virgin Mary. The Spanish word "nada" (nothing) takes the place of some of the English words. "Our Father, who art in heaven, Hallowed be thy name. Thy Kingdom come, Thy will be done, on earth as it is in heaven. Give us this day our daily bread. Forgive us our trespasses, as we forgive those who trespass against us. And lead us not into temptation, but deliver us from evil. Amen. Hail Mary, full of grace, the Lord is with thee".

⑦ **copita**: Spanish for "little cup".

Questions for Reading Comprehension

1. Why does the old man come to the café and get drunk every night?

2. What is the reason for the old man's attempted suicide?

3. Neither of the two waiters in the story is named, and their dialogue is not identified. However, the reader is still able to distinguish them, mainly through their different attitudes towards the old man drinking at the café. In what ways do the two waiters differ?

4. What different views do the two waiters hold towards life?

5. How does the old man carry himself when he leaves the café?

6. Why is the middle-aged waiter reluctant to close up for the night?

7. What does he do on the way home?

8. "Nothing" is the key word in the story. What deeper meaning does the author give it as the story unfolds?

Discussion Questions for Appreciation

1. Notice the contrast between "darkness" and "light" in the story. What symbolic meanings does the title of the story "A Clean, Well-lighted Place" bear?

2. What information can you gather about the social background and the setting of the story?

3. Lord's Prayer appears at the end of the story with some key words replaced by the Spanish word "nada", which means "nothing". Why?

4. What effect does Hemingway create by not naming any of his characters in the story? How do you understand the last sentence, "Many must have it"?

5. What are the principal features of Hemingway's style?

A Question for Writing

Hemingway's major theme is "grace under pressure," that is, keeping one's dignity in the face of extreme situations. How is this theme presented in the story?

William Faulkner (1897-1962)

William Faulkner was born on September 25, 1897, in New Albany, Mississippi. While he was still a child, the family settled in Oxford in north-central Mississippi. His great-grandfather was a colonel in the Civil War, lawyer, railroad builder, financier, politician, writer and public figure, a legend in Oxford. His own family history found its way into his novels, and the members of his family became valuable prototypes for his fictional characters.

At the age of thirteen, Faulkner began to write poetry. However, he dropped out of school and worked briefly in his grandfather's bank. During World War I, he enlisted in the Royal Canadian Air Force. However, the war was over before he was sent to the battlefield. His wartime service allowed him to study at the University of Mississippi, where he stayed only for a year. Then he moved to New York City, where he worked as a clerk in a bookstore. Then, he returned to Oxford and supported himself as a postmaster at the University of Mississippi.

The early works of Faulkner bear witness to his reading of Keats, Tennyson, and Swinburne. His first book, *The Marble Faun* (1924), was a collection of poems that appeared in 1924, but did not gain success. Then he drifted to New Orleans, where he met Sherwood Anderson, who encouraged him to write fiction rather than poetry, to develop his own style, and to use his region for materials. With Anderson's help, Faulkner published his first novel, *Soldier's Pay* (1926), which centers on the return of a soldier, who has been physically and psychologically disabled in the First World War. Written in the vein of the Lost Generation, it attracted favorable reviews.

Although Faulkner made brief trips to Europe and other parts of

America, he mostly remained in Oxford throughout his lifetime. In 1929 Faulkner wrote *Sartoris*, the first of fifteen novels set in Yoknapatawpha County, a fictional region of Mississippi—actually Yoknapatawpha was Lafayette County. Faulkner's Yoknapatawpha novels span the decades of economic decline from the American Civil War through the depression. Racism, class division, family as both life force and curse, are the recurring themes along with recurring characters and places. The narrative varies from the traditional storytelling in *Light in August* (1932) to series of snapshots in *As I Lay Dying* (1930) and interior monologue in *The Sound and the Fury* (1929) and *Absalom! Absalom!* (1932).

In 1929 Faulkner married Estelle Oldham, and settled in a large mansion in Rowan Oak, Oxford. To earn money to support Estelle and their children, Faulkner worked intermittently over the next twenty years in Hollywood on several screenplays, from *Today We Live* (1933) to *Land of the Pharaos* (1955).

When World War Ⅱ broke out, Faulkner's concern with social problems moved to the forefront. His writing became less experimental and more traditional. He began a series of books —the so-called Snopes Trilogy—about the rise of the poor white family named Snopes and the decline of the region's "aristocratic" families. Faulkner's second period of success started in 1946 with the publication of an anthology of his writings, *The Portable Faulkner* (1946), edited by the critic Malcolm Cowley. He became the center of critical attention. Then in 1948 he published *Intruder in the Dust*, which is perhaps the strongest expression of the antiracist theme he had examined throughout his works. This novel, together with the critical attention aroused by *The Portable Faulkner*, led him to the 1949 Nobel Prize for literature.

After receiving the Nobel Prize, numerous honors swarmed to him. However, hard drinking weakened Faulkner's physical and mental functioning. Besides these problems, his wife's drug addiction and declining health shadowed his life. In 1962, Faulkner died at the age of sixty-five of a heart attack.

Faulkner left behind numerous works that accomplished what he expressed in his Nobel speech as the writer's duty to write about the "human heart in conflict with itself which alone can make good writing because only that is worth writing about, worth the agony and the sweat."

Faulkner wrote altogether eighteen novels and three volumes of short stories. Most of his novels are set in his fictional world "Yoknapatawpha County". Of all his novels, *The Sound and the Fury*, *Absalom, Absalom!* and *Go Down, Moses* are judged as masterpieces. In these novels, histories of some southern aristocratic families such as the Compsons, the Sartorises, the Sutpens and the McCaslins are accounted. The fall of those families is doomed as they have displaced the Indians and enslaved the black race. What Faulkner is talking about concerns not merely the American South but the human situation in general.

The Sound and the Fury (1929), a sad story of the Compsons, has four sections, each told by a different narrator, supplying a different piece for the plot, except the last section, which uses a traditional omniscient point of view and provides a sequential narration, the other three jumped freely in time and space. The Civil War and Reconstruction devastated many of these once great Southern families economically, socially, and psychologically. Faulkner contends that in the process, the Compsons, and other similar Southern families, lost touch with the reality of the world around them and became lost in a haze of self-absorption. This self-absorption corrupted the core values these families once held dear and left the newer generations completely unequipped to deal with the realities of the modern world.

Faulkner's experiment with writing techniques makes his works sometimes difficult to read. He experiments in the use of stream-of-consciousness and the interior monologue. In some of his works, words often run together, with no capitalization and no proper punctuation. Sentences are not always clearly indicated; many long ones are pushed together in peculiar ways. Also, Faulkner experiments with narrative chronology, that is, the dislocation of narrative time, perhaps in order to create a sense of juxtaposition of the past and present, hence a way to respond to the modern confusion he feels.

Faulkner's fiction discusses issues of sex, class, race relations, obsessions, time, the past, his native South and the modern world. Today he is regarded as one of America's greatest novelist in the 20th century for his important interpretation of the universal theme of "the problems of the human heart in conflict with itself".

A Rose for Emily

Introduction

William Faulkner's "A Rose for Emily" was originally published in the April 30, 1930 issue of *Forum*. A slightly revised version was published in two collections of his short fiction, *These 13* (1931) and *Collected Stories* (1950). "A Rose for Emily" is the story of an eccentric spinster, Emily Grierson. Through unnamed narrator(s), we are able to see the strange circumstances of Emily's life and her odd relationships with her father, her lover, and the town of Jefferson, and the horrible secret she hides.

The setting of the story is Jefferson, the county seat of Yoknapatawpha, which is also a critical setting in much of Faulkner's fiction. As Frank A. Littler writes in *Notes on Mississippi Writers*, "A Rose for Emily" has been "read variously as a Gothic horror tale, a study in abnormal psychology, an allegory of the relations between North and South, a meditation on the nature of time, and a tragedy with Emily as a sort of tragic heroine."

A Rose for Emily

When Miss Emily Grierson died, our whole town went to her funeral: the men through a sort of respectful affection for a fallen monument, the women mostly out of curiosity to see the inside of her house, which no one save an old man-servant—a combined gardener and cook—had seen in at least ten years.

It was a big, squarish frame house that had once been white, decorated with cupolas and spires and scrolled balconies in the heavily lightsome style of the seventies, set on what had once been our most select street. But garages and cotton gins had encroached and obliterated even the august names of that neighborhood; only Miss Emily's house was left, lifting its stubborn and coquettish decay above the cotton wagons and the gasoline pumps—an eyesore among eyesores. And now Miss Emily had gone to join the representatives of those august names where they lay in the cedar-bemused cemetery among the ranked and anonymous graves of Union and Confederate soldiers who fell at the battle of Jefferson.

Alive, Miss Emily had been a tradition, a duty, and a care; a sort of hereditary obligation upon the town, dating from that day in 1894 when Colonel Sartoris[①], the mayor—he who fathered the edict that no Negro woman should appear on the streets without an apron-remitted her taxes, the dispensation dating from the death of her father on into perpetuity. Not that Miss Emily would have accepted charity. Colonel Sartoris invented an involved tale to the effect that Miss Emily's father had loaned money to the town, which the town, as a matter of business, preferred this way of repaying. Only a man of Colonel Sartoris' generation and thought could have invented it, and only a woman could have believed it.

When the next generation, with its more modern ideas, became mayors and aldermen, this arrangement created some little dissatisfaction. On the first of the year they mailed her a tax notice. February came, and there was no reply. They wrote her a formal letter, asking her to call at the sheriff's office at her convenience. A week later the mayor wrote her himself, offering to call or to send his car for her, and received in reply a note on paper of an archaic shape, in a thin, flowing calligraphy in faded ink, to the effect that she no longer went out at all. The tax notice was also enclosed, without comment.

They called a special meeting of the Board of Aldermen. A deputation waited upon her, knocked at the door through which no visitor had passed since she ceased giving china-painting lessons eight or ten years earlier. They were admitted by the old Negro into a dim hall from which a stairway mounted into still more shadow. It smelled of dust and disuse—a close, dank smell. The Negro led them into the parlor. It was furnished in heavy, leather-covered furniture. When the Negro opened the blinds of one window, they could see that the leather was cracked; and when they sat down, a faint dust rose sluggishly about their thighs, spinning with slow motes in the single sun-ray. On a tarnished gilt easel before the fireplace stood a crayon portrait of Miss Emily's father.

They rose when she entered—a small, fat woman in black, with a thin gold chain descending to her waist and vanishing into her belt, leaning on an ebony cane with a tarnished gold head. Her skeleton was small and spare; perhaps that was why what would have been merely plumpness in another was obesity in her. She looked bloated, like a body long submerged in motionless water, and of that pallid hue. Her eyes, lost in the fatty ridges of her face, looked like two small pieces of coal pressed into a lump of dough as they moved from one face to another while the visitors stated their errand.

She did not ask them to sit. She just stood in the door and listened quietly until the spokesman came to a stumbling halt. Then they could

361

hear the invisible watch ticking at the end of the gold chain.

Her voice was dry and cold. "I have no taxes in Jefferson. Colonel Sartoris explained it to me. Perhaps one of you can gain access to the city records and satisfy yourselves."

"But we have. We are the city authorities, Miss Emily. Didn't you get a notice from the sheriff, signed by him?"

"I received a paper, yes," Miss Emily said. "Perhaps he considers himself the sheriff. . . I have no taxes in Jefferson."

"But there is nothing on the books to show that, you see we must go by the—"

"See Colonel Sartoris. I have no taxes in Jefferson."

"But, Miss Emily—"

"See Colonel Sartoris." (Colonel Sartoris had been dead almost ten years.) "I have no taxes in Jefferson. Tobe!" The Negro appeared. "Show these gentlemen out."

II

So she vanquished them, horse and foot, just as she had vanquished their fathers thirty years before about the smell.

That was two years after her father's death and a short time after her sweetheart—the one we believed would marry her—had deserted her. After her father's death she went out very little; after her sweetheart went away, people hardly saw her at all. A few of the ladies had the temerity to call, but were not received, and the only sign of life about the place was the Negro man—a young man then—going in and out with a market basket.

"Just as if a man—any man—could keep a kitchen properly," the ladies said; so they were not surprised when the smell developed. It was another link between the gross, teeming world and the high and mighty Griersons.

A neighbor, a woman, complained to the mayor, Judge Stevens, eighty years old.

"But what will you have me do about it, madam?" he said.

"Why, send her word to stop it," the woman said. "Isn't there a law?"

"I'm sure that won't be necessary," Judge Stevens said. "It's probably just a snake or a rat that nigger of hers killed in the yard. I'll speak to him about it."

The next day he received two more complaints, one from a man who came in diffident deprecation. "We really must do something about it, Judge. I'd be the last one in the world to bother Miss Emily, but we've got to do something." That night the Board of Aldermen met—three graybeards and one younger man, a member of the rising generation.

"It's simple enough," he said. "Send her word to have her place cleaned up. Give her a certain time to do it in, and if she don't. . . "

"Dammit, sir," Judge Stevens said, "will you accuse a lady to her face of smelling bad?"

So the next night, after midnight, four men crossed Miss Emily's lawn and slunk about the house like burglars, sniffing along the base of the brickwork and at the cellar openings while one of them performed a regular sowing motion with his hand out of a sack slung from his shoulder. They broke open the cellar door and sprinkled lime there, and in all the outbuildings. As they recrossed the lawn, a window that had been dark was lighted and Miss Emily sat in it, the light behind her, and her upright torso motionless as that of an idol. They crept quietly across the lawn and into the shadow of the locusts that lined the street. After a week or two the smell went away.

That was when people had begun to feel really sorry for her. People in our town, remembering how old lady Wyatt, her great-aunt, had gone completely crazy at last, believed that the Griersons held themselves a

363

little too high for what they really were. None of the young men were quite good enough for Miss Emily and such. We had long thought of them as a tableau, Miss Emily a slender figure in white in the background, her father a spraddled silhouette in the foreground, his back to her and clutching a horsewhip[②], the two of them framed by the back-flung front door. So when she got to be thirty and was still single, we were not pleased exactly, but vindicated; even with insanity in the family she wouldn't have turned down all of her chances if they had really materialized.

When her father died, it got about that the house was all that was left to her; and in a way, people were glad. At last they could pity Miss Emily. Being left alone, and a pauper, she had become humanized. Now she too would know the old thrill and the old despair of a penny more or less.

The day after his death all the ladies prepared to call at the house and offer condolence and aid, as is our custom Miss Emily met them at the door, dressed as usual and with no trace of grief on her face. She told them that her father was not dead. She did that for three days, with the ministers calling on her, and the doctors, trying to persuade her to let them dispose of the body. Just as they were about to resort to law and force, she broke down, and they buried her father quickly.

We did not say she was crazy then. We believed she had to do that. We remembered all the young men her father had driven away, and we knew that with nothing left, she would have to cling to that which had robbed her, as people will.

III

She was sick for a long time. When we saw her again, her hair was cut short, making her look like a girl, with a vague resemblance to those angels in colored church windows—sort of tragic and serene.

The town had just let the contracts for paving the sidewalks, and in the summer after her father's death they began the work. The construction company came with riggers and mules and machinery, and a foreman named Homer Barron, a Yankee—a big, dark, ready man, with a big voice and eyes lighter than his face. The little boys would follow in groups to hear him cuss the riggers, and the riggers singing in time to the rise and fall of picks. Pretty soon he knew everybody in town. Whenever you heard a lot of laughing anywhere about the square, Homer Barron would be in the center of the group. Presently we began to see him and Miss Emily on Sunday afternoons driving in the yellow-wheeled buggy and the matched team of bays from the livery stable.

At first we were glad that Miss Emily would have an interest, because the ladies all said, "Of course a Grierson would not think seriously of a Northerner, a day laborer." But there were still others, older people, who said that even grief could not cause a real lady to forget *noblesse oblige*③—without calling it *noblesse oblige*. They just said, "Poor Emily. Her kinsfolk should come to her." She had some kin in Alabama; but years ago her father had fallen out with them over the estate of old lady Wyatt, the crazy woman, and there was no communication between the two families. They had not even been represented at the funeral.

And as soon as the old people said, "Poor Emily," the whispering began. "Do you suppose it's really so?" they said to one another. "Of course it is. What else could..." This behind their hands; rustling of craned silk and satin behind jalousies closed upon the sun of Sunday afternoon as the thin, swift clop-clop-clop of the matched team passed: "Poor Emily."

She carried her head high enough—even when we believed that she was fallen. It was as if she demanded more than ever the recognition of her dignity as the last Grierson; as if it had wanted that touch of earthiness to reaffirm her imperviousness. Like when she bought the rat poison, the arsenic. That was over a year after they had begun to say "Poor Emily," and while the two female cousins were visiting her.

"I want some poison," she said to the druggist. She was over thirty then, still a slight woman, though thinner than usual, with cold, haughty black eyes in a face the flesh of which was strained across the temples and about the eyesockets as you imagine a lighthouse-keeper's face ought to look. "I want some poison," she said.

"Yes, Miss Emily. What kind? For rats and such? I'd recom—"

"I want the best you have. I don't care what kind."

The druggist named several. "They'll kill anything up to an elephant. But what you want is—"

"Arsenic," Miss Emily said. "Is that a good one?"

"Is... arsenic? Yes, ma'am. But what you want—"

"I want arsenic."

The druggist looked down at her. She looked back at him, erect, her face like a strained flag. "Why, of course," the druggist said. "If that's what you want. But the law requires you to tell what you are going to use it for."

Miss Emily just stared at him, her head tilted back in order to look him eye for eye, until he looked away and went and got the arsenic and wrapped it up. The Negro delivery boy brought her the package; the druggist didn't come back. When she opened the package at home there was written on the box, under the skull and bones: "For rats."

IV

So the next day we all said, "She will kill herself"; and we said it would be the best thing. When she had first begun to be seen with Homer Barron, we had said, "She will marry him." Then we said, "She will persuade him yet," because Homer himself had remarked—he liked men, and it was known that he drank with the younger men in the Elks'

Club—that he was not a marrying man. Later we said, "Poor Emily" behind the jalousies as they passed on Sunday afternoon in the glittering buggy, Miss Emily with her head high and Homer Barron with his hat cocked and a cigar in his teeth, reins and whip in a yellow glove.

Then some of the ladies began to say that it was a disgrace to the town and a bad example to the young people. The men did not want to interfere, but at last the ladies forced the Baptist minister—Miss Emily's people were Episcopal—to call upon her. He would never divulge what happened during that interview, but he refused to go back again. The next Sunday they again drove about the streets, and the following day the minister's wife wrote to Miss Emily's relations in Alabama.

So she had blood-kin under her roof again and we sat back to watch developments. At first nothing happened. Then we were sure that they were to be married. We learned that Miss Emily had been to the jeweler's and ordered a man's toilet set in silver, with the letters H. B. on each piece. Two days later we learned that she had bought a complete outfit of men's clothing, including a nightshirt, and we said, "They are married." We were really glad. We were glad because the two female cousins were even more Grierson than Miss Emily had ever been.

So we were not surprised when Homer Barron—the streets had been finished some time since—was gone. We were a little disappointed that there was not a public blowing-off, but we believed that he had gone on to prepare for Miss Emily's coming, or to give her a chance to get rid of the cousins. (By that time it was a cabal, and we were all Miss Emily's allies to help circumvent the cousins.) Sure enough, after another week they departed. And, as we had expected all along, within three days Homer Barron was back in town. A neighbor saw the Negro man admit him at the kitchen door at dusk one evening.

And that was the last we saw of Homer Barron. And of Miss Emily for some time. The Negro man went in and out with the market basket, but the front door remained closed. Now and then we would see her at a window for a moment, as the men did that night when they sprinkled the lime, but for almost six months she did not appear on the streets. Then we knew that this was to be expected too; as if that quality of her father which had thwarted her woman's life so many times had been too virulent and too furious to die.

When we next saw Miss Emily, she had grown fat and her hair was turning gray. During the next few years it grew grayer and grayer until it attained an even pepper-and-salt iron-gray, when it ceased turning. Up to the day of her death at seventy-four it was still that vigorous iron-gray, like the hair of an active man.

From that time on her front door remained closed, save for a period of six or seven years, when she was about forty, during which she gave lessons in china-painting. She fitted up a studio in one of the downstairs rooms, where the daughters and granddaughters of Colonel Sartoris' contemporaries were sent to her with the same regularity and in the same spirit that they were sent to church on Sundays with a twenty-five-cent piece for the collection plate. Meanwhile her taxes had been remitted.

Then the newer generation became the backbone and the spirit of the town, and the painting pupils grew up and fell away and did not send their children to her with boxes of color and tedious brushes and pictures cut from the ladies' magazines. The front door closed upon the last one and remained closed for good. When the town got free postal delivery, Miss Emily alone refused to let them fasten the metal numbers above her door and attach a mailbox to it. She would not listen to them.

Daily, monthly, yearly we watched the Negro grow grayer and more stooped, going in and out with the market basket. Each December we sent her a tax notice, which would be returned by the post office a week later, unclaimed. Now and then we would see her in one of the down-stairs windows—she had evidently shut up the top floor of the house—

like the carven torso of an idol in a niche, looking or not looking at us, we could never tell which. Thus she passed from generation to generation—dear, inescapable, impervious, tranquil, and perverse.

And so she died. Fell ill in the house filled with dust and shadows, with only a doddering Negro man to wait on her. We did not even know she was sick; we had long since given up trying to get any information from the Negro

He talked to no one, probably not even to her, for his voice had grown harsh and rusty, as if from disuse.

She died in one of the downstairs rooms, in a heavy walnut bed with a curtain, her gray head propped on a pillow yellow and moldy with age and lack of sunlight.

V

The Negro met the first of the ladies at the front door and let them in, with their hushed, sibilant voices and their quick, curious glances, and then he disappeared. He walked right through the house and out the back and was not seen again.

The two female cousins came at once. They held the funeral on the second day, with the town coming to look at Miss Emily beneath a mass of bought flowers, with the crayon face of her father musing profoundly above the bier and the ladies sibilant and macabre; and the very old men—some in their brushed Confederate uniforms—on the porch and the lawn, talking of Miss Emily as if she had been a contemporary of theirs, believing that they had danced with her and courted her perhaps, confusing time with its mathematical progression, as the old do, to whom all the past is not a diminishing road but, instead, a huge meadow which no winter ever quite touches, divided from them now by the narrow bottleneck of the most recent decade of years.

Already we knew that there was one room in that region above stairs which no one had seen in forty years, and which would have to be

369

forced. They waited until Miss Emily was decently in the ground before they opened it.

The violence of breaking down the door seemed to fill this room with pervading dust. A thin, acrid pall as of the tomb seemed to lie everywhere upon this room decked and furnished as for a bridal: upon the valance curtains of faded rose color, upon the rose-shaded lights, upon the dressing table, upon the delicate array of crystal and the man's toilet things backed with tarnished silver, silver so tarnished that the monogram was obscured. Among them lay a collar and tie, as if they had just been removed, which, lifted, left upon the surface a pale crescent in the dust. Upon a chair hung the suit, carefully folded; beneath it the two mute shoes and the discarded socks.

The man himself lay in the bed.

For a long while we just stood there, looking down at the profound and fleshless grin. The body had apparently once lain in the attitude of an embrace, but now the long sleep that outlasts love, that conquers even the grimace of love, had cuckolded him. What was left of him, rotted beneath what was left of the nightshirt, had become inextricable from the bed in which he lay; and upon him and upon the pillow beside him lay that even coating of the patient and biding dust.

Then we noticed that in the second pillow was the indentation of a head. One of us lifted something from it, and leaning forward, that faint and invisible dust dry and acrid in the nostrils, we saw a long strand of iron-gray hair.

Notes

① **Colonel Sartoris**: a major figure among Faulkner's fictional inhabitants of Yoknapatawpha County.

② **horsewhip**: the legendary weapon used by American fathers to protect their daughters from unwelcome suitors.

③ **noblesse oblige**: the obligations of the upper class.

Questions for Reading Comprehension

1. Where is the story set?
2. Explain the basic plot in its chronological order. Is it in accordance with the narrative order?
3. Does Miss Emily love Homer Barron? And does he really love her?
4. What is Miss Emily's attitude towards her father? Why doesn't she cry when her father dies?
5. Why does Miss Emily kill Homer Barron? What motivates her to do that?
6. Why does Miss Emily keep Homer Barron's body in her room?
7. The character of Miss Emily is revealed in several episodes in the story. What kind of person is she? And what does she represent?
8. What is the attitude of the people of the town toward Miss Emily and her family?

Discussion Questions for Appreciation

1. What do Miss Emily's house and its surrounding suggest to you? What does the story say about the male-female relationships in American society of that time?
3. Except for the title, a rose is never mentioned in the story. Why do you think Faulkner chooses this title?
4. Who is the narrator of the story? What do you know about him? Can you list his "values"? Are his values shared by the town?
5. Is this narrator reliable? Does the sex identity of the narrator affect the narration in any way?

A Question for Writing

Many critics have interpreted Miss Emily as a symbol of the post-Civil-War American South. Do you agree with this interpretation?

Eugene O'Neill（1888-1953）

Eugene Gladstone O'Neill was born in a Broadway hotel room in New York City on October 16, 1888. His father, James O'Neill, was one of 19th century America's most popular actors. Young Eugene spent much of his early years on national tours with his father. However, as his mother was a morphine addict, and his brother an alcoholic, O'Neil's domestic life was full of tension and conflict.

In 1906 Eugene entered Princeton University but quit after a year. In 1909 he got married, had a son, and was divorced within three years. By 1912 O'Neill had taken various jobs. After a period of beach combing in Buenos Aires, he returned to New York, and spent most of his time in Greenwich Village—an area of lower Manhattan that was becoming home to artists and political radicals, frequenting the cheap saloons in that area. In 1912 he suffered a physical breakdown, and was sent to a sanatorium for six-month's rest. During his recovery, he was inspired to become a playwright after reading a wide range of dramatic literature such as Greek tragedies, Ibsen and Strindberg.

From 1913 to 1914, he wrote his fist play *The Web*, seven other one-act plays and two long plays. Then he joined the famous Professor Pierce Baker's Workshop at Harvard to learn to write better. In 1916 he joined a new experimental theatre group called the Provincetown Players in the Greenwich Village district of New York. The Provincetown Players staged O'Neill's first performed play, the one-act *Bound East for Cardiff*. During the period from 1913 to 1918, O'Neill wrote nineteen plays, and for some of his plays, the stage moved from the Greenwich Village to Broadway. With the New York production of *Beyond the Horizon* (1920), which he was awarded a Pulitzer Prize, O'Neill was acknowledged as the foremost creative American playwright of his time. For the next fourteen years, he stayed in Broadway and wrote *Emperor Jones* (1920), *Anna Christie* (1924), *The Hairy Ape* (1922), *Desire Under the Elms* (1924), *All God's Chillun Got Wings* (1924), *The Great God Brown* (1926), *Lazarus Laughed* (1926), *Strange Interlude* (1928), *Marco Millions* (1928), *Dynamo* (1929), *Mourning Becomes Electra* (1931), *Ah, Wilderness*! (1933), and *Days Without End* (1934). In 1936 O'Neill was awarded the Nobel Prize—the first and so far the only American playwright who won the honor.

In the 1930s O'Neill began to suffer from Parkinson's disease, and lived in relative seclusion for the last twenty years of his life. His production slowed down. And much of his work of the 1930s and 1940s remained in manuscript until after his death. The plays he wrote after the 1940s were reexamined and staged. These plays include *Long Day's Journey into Night* (1956), *A Moon for the Misbegotten* (1957), and *A Touch of the Poet* (1958). With *Long Day's Journey into Night*, O'Neill won another Pulitzer Prize four years after his death.

Long Days Journey into Night is considered to be O'Neill's autobiographical play, the production of which in 1956 revived worldwide interest in O'Neill's works. The story takes place in a single day in August 1912 at the summer home of the Tyrones. All the members of the family suffer frustrations and wish to escape from the harsh reality. They meet in the living room of the family's summer home and torment one another and themselves until midnight. The play explores the tragic nature of family relations, and questions the possibility of forgiveness and redemption.

As a premier playwright of America, O'Neill is credited with raising American dramatic theater from its narrow origins to an art form respected around the world. O'Neill's career as a playwright consists of three periods. His early plays, which are stark and naturalistic, utilize his own experiences, especially as a seaman. In these plays, the dialogues are crude, natural, and slangy. The settings of the plays are usually

373

ships' holds and sailors' bars instead of the elegant parlors of drawing room. In the 1920s, O'Neill became much interested in the theory of the psychologist Sigmund Freud. Influenced by Freud, O'Neill began to capture on the stage the forces behind human life. He began to experiment with techniques to convey inner emotions that usually were not openly expressed in dramatizable action. After the successive death of his parent and his brother in early 1920s, O'Neil began to dramatize the complicated pattern of his family's life. In his last period O'Neill returned to naturalistic writing. His later works, which most critics consider his best, turned to his life experiences for their story lines and themes.

Desire Under the Elms

Introduction

Desire Under the Elms was first produced in 1924 by the Provincetownv Playhouse in Greenwich Village, New York, and later moved to a Broadway theatre. The setting for the play is the Cabot Farm in Connecticut in 1850. The aging patriarch Ephraim Cabot returns to his farm with a new, young wife, Abbie Putnam. Eben, Ephraim's third son, believes that his father has killed his mother through overwork, and he has an affair with Abbie. The birth of the child parented by Eben and Abbie sets the family further at odds. In a desperate attempt to prove her love for Eben, Abbie murders the child.

The following excerpt is taken from Scene Three of Part II. In this scene, Abbie invites Eben to come to his mother's parlour so that she can carry out her plan of seduction. Under mixed feelings of physical attraction towards Abbie and revenge for his father, Eben finally succumbs to Abbie's seduction.

The control of the Oedipus complex over Eben is obvious in the play, so is the irresistible power of sexual attraction. Influenced by Freud's theory, O'Neil tries to convey the eternally tragic predicament of human beings, and to get at the root of human desires and frustrations. Some of the characters in the play are said to have their prototypes from Greek tragedies, such as *Medea*, *Oedipus* and *Hyppolytus*.

From *Desire Under the Elms*

. . .

A few minutes later. The interior of the parlor is shown. A grim, repressed room like a tomb in which the family has been interred alive. Abbie sits on the edge of the horsehair sofa. She has lighted all the candles and the room is revealed in all its preserved ugliness. A change has come over the woman. She looks awed and frightened now, ready to run away.

The door is opened and Eben appears. His face wears an expression of obsessed confusion. He stands staring at her, his arms hanging disjointedly from his shoulders, his feet bare, his hat in his hand.

ABBIE— (*after a pause—with a nervous, formal politeness*) Won't ye set?[①]

EBEN— (*dully*) Ay-eh. (*Mechanically he places his hat carefully on the floor near the door and sits stiffly beside her on the edge of the sofa. A pause. They both remain rigid, looking straight ahead with eyes full of fear.*)

ABBIE—When I fust come in—in the dark—they seemed somethin' here.

EBEN— (*simply*) Maw.

ABBIE—I kin still feel—somethin'.

EBEN—It's Maw[②].

ABBIE—At fust[③] I was feered o'it. I wanted t' yell an'run. Now—since yew come—seems like it's growin' soft an' kind t' me. (*addressing the air—queerly*) Thank yew.

EBEN—Maw allus[④] loved me.

ABBIE—Mebbe[⑤] it knows I love yew, too. Mebbe that makes it kind t'me.

EBEN— (*dully*) I dunno. [6] I should think she'd hate ye.

ABBIE— (*with certainty*) No. I kin[7] feel it don't—not no more.

EBEN—Hate ye fur stealin' her place—here in her hum—settin' in her parlor whar she was laid— (*He suddenly stops, staring stupidly before him.*)

ABBIE—What is it, Eben?

EBEN— (*in a whisper*) Seems like Maw didn't want me t' remind ye.

ABBIE— (*excitedly*) I knowed, Eben! It's kind t' me! It don't b'ar me no grudges fur what I never knowed an' couldn't help!

EBEN—Maw b'ars him a grudge.

ABBIE—Waal, so does all o'us.

EBEN—Ay-eh. (*with passion*) I does, by God!

ABBIE— (*taking one of his hands in hers and patting it*) Thar! Don't git riled thinkin' o' him. Think o'yer Maw who's kind t'us. Tell me about yer Maw, Eben.

EBEN—They hain't nothin' much. She was kind. She was good.

ABBIE— (*putting one arm over his shoulder. He does not seem to notice—passionatedly*) I'll be kind an'good t'ye!

EBEN—Sometimes she used t' sing fur me.

ABBIE—I'll sing fur ye!

EBEN—This was her hum. This was her farm.

ABBIE—This is my hum! This is my farm!

EBEN—He married her t'steal 'em. [8] She was soft an'easy. He couldn't 'preciate her.

ABBIE—He can't 'preciate[9] me!

EBEN—She died. (*a pause*) Sometimes she used to sing fur me. (*He bursts into a fit of sobbing.*)

ABBIE— (*both her arms around him—with wild passion*) I'll sing fur ye! I'll die fur ye! (*In spite of her overwhelming desire for him, there is a sincere maternal love in her manner and voice—a horribly frank mixture of lust and mother love.*) Don't cry, Eben! I'll take yer Maw's place! I'll be everyth's he was t' ye! Let me kiss ye, Eben! (*She pulls his head around. He makes a bewildered pretense of resistance. She is tender.*) Don't be afeered! I'll kiss ye pure, Eben—same ' s if I was a Maw t' ye—an'ye kin kiss me back ' s if yew was my son—my boy —sayin' good-night t'me! Kiss me, Eben. (*They kiss in restrained fashion. Then suddenly wild passion overcomes her. She kisses him lustfully again and again and he flings his arms about her and returns her kisses. Suddenly, as in the bedroom, he frees himself from her violently and springs to his feet. He is trembling all over, in a strange state of terror. Abbie strains her arms toward him with fierce pleading.*) Don't ye leave me, Eben! Can't ye see it hain't enuf—lovin' ye like a Maw— can't ye see it's got t'be that an'more—much more—a hundred times more—fur me t'be happy—fur yew t'be happy?

EBEN— (*to the presence he feels in the room*) Maw! Maw! What d'ye want? What air ye tellin' me?

ABBIE—She's tellin' ye t'love me. She knows I love ye an' I'll be good t'ye. Can't ye feel it? Don't ye know? She's tellin' ye t'love me, Eben!

EBEN—Ay-eh. I feel—mebbe she—but— I can't figger out— why — when ye've stole her place—here in her hum—in the parlor whar⑩ she was —

ABBIE— (*fiercely*) She knows I love ye!

EBEN— (*his face suddenly lighting up with a fierce, triumphant grin*) I see it! I sees why. It's her vengeance on him—so's she kin rest quiet in her grave!

ABBIE— (*wildly*) Vengeance O'God on the hull o'us! What d'we give a durn? I love ye, Eben! God knows I love ye! (*She stretches out her arms for him.*)

EBEN— (*throws himself on his knees beside the sofa and grabs her in his arms—releasing all his pent-up passion*) An' I love yew, Abbie! —now I kin say it! I been dyin'fur want o'ye—every hour since ye come! I love ye! (*Their lips meet in a fierce, bruising kiss.*)

Notes

① **Won't ye set**?: Won't you sit?

② **Maw**: Mum.

③ **fust**: first.

④ **allus**: always.

⑤ **Mebbe**: Maybe.

⑥ **dunno**: don't know.

⑦ **kin**: can.

⑧ **He married her t'steal 'em**: He married her to steal them.

⑨ **'preciate**: appreciate.

⑩ **whar**: where.

Questions for Reading Comprehension

1. Where exactly does this scene take place?

2. What is Abbie trying to do in this scene?

3. What means are employed by Abbie to carry out her scheme?

4. At first, Eben is quite hesitating, and even rejects Abbie's advance. What is the emotional conflict that he undergoes?

Discussion Questions for Appreciation

1. Abbie says that Eben's mother would be pleased that he does what she asks him to do. Does Eben believe in it or not? Why or why not?

2. It is in Eben's mother's parlor that Abbie finally succeeds seducing him. What is the significance of this arrangement?

3. In 1929, O'Neill says, "What has influenced my plays the most is my knowledge of drama of all time, —particularly Greek drama." Some critics also point out that Hippolytus, Phaedra and Medea serve as the prototypes of some of the characters in the play. With whom are Hippolytus and Phaedra identified in the play? And Medea?

Please justify your viewpoint.

4. One critic points out, "The meaning and unity of his [O'Neill's] work lies not in any controlling intellectual idea and certainly not in a 'message', but merely in the fact that each play is an experience of extraordinary intensity." Do you think that this play is an experience of extraordinary intensity?

A Question for Writing

O'Neill is said to be interested in the theory of the psychologist Sigmund Freud: the power of irrational drive, the existence of subconscious, the roles of repression, suppression, and inhibition in the formation of personality and in adult suffering; the importance of sex; and above all, the lifelong influence of parents. Can you justify at least two aspects of Freud's influence on O'Neill by quoting evidence from the excerpt?

Chapter Five   Post-war American Literature

(1945-   )

Historical Background

American society at the mid-20th-century was shaped by economic prosperity. A fierce desire for consumer goods and a steadily increasing standard of living—together with the tension of the cold war—imbued American culture. The postwar popularity of television reshaped leisure time and political life, creating a new kind of national community defined by the buying and selling of consumer goods.

1. The 1960s and the Counterculture Movement

The term "teenager" started entering standard usage only at the end of World War II. The fifteen years following the war saw unprecedented attention to America's adolescents. Deep fears were expressed about everything from teenage sexuality and juvenile delinquency to young people's driving habits, hairstyles, and choice of clothing. Teenagers often found themselves caught between their desire to carve out their own separate sphere and the pressure to become an adult as quickly as possible. Through the 1950s and into the 1960s teenagers had a major voice in determining America's cultural fads.

Some of the sharpest dissents from the cultural conformity of the day came from a group of writers known collectively as the Beats. Led by the novelist Jack Kerouac, who published *On the Road* in 1957, and the poet Allen Ginsberg, who published *Howl* in 1957, the Beats shared a distrust of the American virtues of progress, power, and material gain. They foreshadowed the mass youth rebellion and counterculture to come in the 1960s.

The 1960s witnessed the counterculture movement that gained momentum gradually: consensus was replaced by protest along a broad front, and energy multiplied as separated dissenters gathered in a fragile but potent coalition of resistance. The challenges were cultural as well as political: Blacks campaigned for civil rights, women demanded equality, and men and women of all races organized to stop the war in Vietnam. Virtually every established value was subjected to interrogation in an unprecedented search for alternatives.

In 1968 the bloodiest and most destructive fighting of the Vietnam War resulted in a stalemate that undermined the Americans' faith in their country. Disillusionment deepened in the spring of 1968 when Martin Luther King, Jr. and Robert Kennedy, two of the most revered political leaders, were struck down by assassins' bullets. The sharp divisions among the Americans in 1968, due to a large degree to President Johnson's policies in Vietnam, paved the way for the election of Richard M. Nixon.

2. The 1970s and the 1980s

In the 1970s the Americans faced an unfamiliar combination of skyrocketing prices, rising unemployment, and low economic growth. Economists termed this novel condition "stagflation." During the 1970s many Americans disengaged themselves from politics altogether. In 1976 nove-list Tom Wolfe coined the phrase "the Me Decade" to describe an era obsessed with personal well-being, happiness, and emotional security.

Elvis Presley gave place to Bruce Springsteen, who became the decade's most popular new rock artist with lyrics that often lamented the disappearance of the white working class.

The 1980s, though shrouded in a politically conservative climate, witnessed the rapid expansion of relatively new industries such as microelectronics, biotechnology, and computers. Service and information-based industries started to take center stage in the country's economy. In the mid-1980s the boom in cheap PCs capable of linking to the Internet began a population explosion in cyberspace.

3. Cultural Climate of the Late 20th Century

In 1993 the Oscar went to *Philadelphia*, a film that features gay men's lives. This reflects the great progress of the gay rights movement and the increasing tolerance of same-sex relations, although by 2002, most states had enacted laws defining marriage explicitly and exclusively as a heterosexual compact.

Some say that homosexuality is the last taboo in America. It is really hard to imagine teaching a course of American literature that eliminated all lesbian and male homosexual writers. How could one get through a course completely silent about Walt Whitman, Henry David Thoreau, Langston Hughes, Tennessee Williams, Allen Ginsberg, and Adrienne Rich! Most teachers assign these lesbian and gay writers without acknowledging them because their works that speak most clearly about their sexual orientation tend to be omitted.

Also in 1993, Toni Morrison won the Nobel Prize for Literature, which, among other things, is a signal that writings by minorities, both people of color and women, traditionally marginalized groups, had gained widespread respect. Morrison's best fiction includes *The Bluest Eye* (1970), her first novel, *Beloved* (1987), and *Jazz* (1992).

The Beats

The writers celebrated as the creators of a "beat generation" never thought of themselves as establishing an organized movement. The term properly applies only to a small circle of friends, particularly **Allen Ginsberg**, **Jack Kerouac**, **Lawrence Ferlinghetti**, **Gregory Corso.**

The "movement" became news after a public poetry reading in San Francisco on October 12, 1955 by poets including Gary Snyder and Allen Ginsberg, who crowned the evening by reading the just completed first part of his poem "Howl". Ginsberg cataloged, in the poem, the sins of the established political and sexual order, denouncing the bourgeois idols of marketplace and decorum with the zest of a prophet.

Jack Kerouac published *On the Road* in 1957, whose urgency and energy won itself status as a signature piece of the decade's discontent. Marred by its limits such as utter shapelessness and meager intellectual and moral furnishings, however, the novel manages to portray Sal Paradise, a cross-country rover, in an energetic manner, adding to a long line of opposition that reaches back through Jack London's Martin Eden to Mark Twain's Huck Finn and Thoreau's Civil Disobedience.

The recitings of Ginsberg's and Kerouac's writings attracted hordes of dissatisfied young people from all over the country to San Francisco's North Beach, where poetry readings flourished in coffeehouses. Well read in classic literature, Ginsberg and Kerouac produced writings that are contemplative, not action-provoking. Allen Ginsberg summarized the aim of the Beats' writings when he participated in a convocation that celebrated the 25th anniversary of the publication of *On the Road*: "The literary aspect or the spiritual aspect or the emotional aspect (of the Beat movement) was not so much protest at all but a declaration of unconditioned mind beyond protest, beyond resentment, beyond loser, beyond

383

winner. "

Kerouac coined the term "beat", which meant for him "a weariness with all the forms of the modern industrial state" [1] —pervasive conformity, militarism, and blind faith in technological progress. The Beat sensibility celebrates spontaneity, friendship, jazz, drug use, and the outcasts of American society. Beat writers received a largely antagonistic reception from the literary establishment. But Beat writers like Kerouac, Ginsberg, Gary Snyder, LeRoi Jones, and others continued to produce serious work that challenged America's official culture.

Postmodernism

The term came into prominence in the 1960s to distinguish the contemporary experimental writing of such authors as **Samuel Beckett**, **Jorge Luis Borges**, **John Barth**, **Thomas Pynchon** from such early-20th-century classics of modernism as James Joyce's *Ulysses* (1922) and T. S. Eliot's *The Wasteland* (1922). Although the classic modernists were thought to be revolutionary in their day, their works seem remote from today's society with its new interests in such things as feminism, gay and lesbian rights, and pop culture.

Postmodernist literature, both a continuation of modernist literature and a radical break with its dominant features is usually more politically concerned, more playful—it is given to parody and pastiche—and more closely related to the art forms of pop culture. In *Paracriticisms* (1975), Ahab Hassan provides suggestive lists of postmodernist footnotes on modernism. They include "anti-elitism, anti-authoritarianism; participa-

---

[1] John Mack Faragher, et al. *Out of Many: A History of the American People*, vol. II: Since 1865 (New Jersey: Prentice-Hall Inc., 2000), 832.

tion; and he says that art becomes communal, optional, anarchic. "①As opposed to modernism, Hassan adds that postmodernists produce "open, discontinuous, improvisational, indeterminate structures. "

It is hard to give a definition of postmodernism because no widespread agreement has been reached even on a definition of modernism. In the past two decades or so, critics intent on the debate over a definition of postmodernism have seemed to agree on one thing: the term resists comprehensive definition. In place of a strict logical definition, it is a good idea to list those characteristics that first made people notice a difference between modernism and postmodernism. Here is a noninclusive list that we suggest: (1) a propensity to contain and reuse all previous forms in a literature of exhaustion and replenishment; (2) a zone of the bizarre, where fantasy best expresses our sense of reality; (3) a turning away from penetration into the psychological depth of character as the primary goal of fiction; and (4) a propensity for metafiction, in which writing draws attention to the techniques and processes of its own creation.

385

The Culture War and the Opening Up of the American Literary Canon

The American literary canon refers to the body of those literary texts which are considered to be the most important in literary history. Does the American literary canon contain a constant set of texts from start to finish? The answer is a definite No.

Many Americans hold strong views on cultural value issues, which tend to divide public opinion sharply. This is partly because cultural is-

---

① Raman Selden et. al. *A Reader's Guide to Contemporary Literary Theory* (4th Edition, London: Prentice Hall, 1997), 202.

sues also form the test between the maintenance of the traditional western values that have informed America's history since its founding, and the accusation by others that those dominant values are racist, sexist, homophobic and oppressive. So significant has this conflict become that cultural matters appear to some commentators to be the key to whether the historically United States is now "disuniting" and, if so, whether, how and when that process can be halted.

The American literary canon, perhaps the most widely debated and politically charged issue in the culture war that has been raging since the 1980s, has undergone a tremendous transformation. The canon has always been highly varied despite the fact that certain authors, such as Poe, Twain, and James, and Whitman, have been permanent fixtures. But it chiefly contained the work of dead white males not because women or people from minority cultures did not write and publish, but because in the Euro-American world until fairly recently white males controlled the publishing industry and society. During the period from 1920 to 1970, literary critics as well as colleges and universities largely succeeded in drastically narrowing the canon of authors and works and in creating textbooks, curricula, departments, professional organizations, and interpretive studies based on that canon[1].

In the wake of the revolutionary 1960s, critics and readers have become increasingly aware of the voices of women, lesbians and gays, and members of minority cultures, including Native Americans, African Americans, Asian Americans, Latinos.

A generation ago decisions about what was worth teaching and what counted as 'culture' were still circumscribed by a relatively homogeneous class with a relatively common background. Today, new constituen-

---

[1] Paul Lauter, *Canons and Contexts* (New York: Oxford University Press, 1991), 22-97.

cies—women, blacks, gays, and immigrant groups from Asia and Latin America in particular—demand a say in how culture will be defined. [1]

As a consequence, works by these groups—giving voice to identities previously ignored by the larger society—are now included in the canon or taught in a range of literary courses.

Ethnic studies and women's studies are the two branches that benefit most from the Culture War. Asian American literature has thus been taught all across the United States.

Asian / Chinese American Literature

The Asian American Movement, which emerged in the 1960s, was energized by the national struggle for civil rights, and escalated by anti-Vietnam War activism. It gained momentum after the immigration reforms of 1965 effected major changes in the size of America's Asian population. The Asian American Movement privileged the term "Asian American" over the old choice, "Oriental," a word which to many second and third-generation Americans of Asian ancestry was negative in its connotations of marginality. What constitutes Asian American literature? King-Kok Cheung in the mid-1990s defined it as having been produced by writers of Asian descent who were either born in or who have migrated to North America—embracing both U. S. and Canadian citizens.

The development of Asian American literature can be roughly divided into two periods. It was marginalized and neglected in its first phase, although it has been published in the U. S. since the nineteenth century. The second period started in the mid-1970s, heralded by important anthologies of Asian American writing, particularly the now-

---

[1] Gerald Graff. *Beyond the Culture Wars: How Teaching the Conflicts Can Revitalizing American Education* (New York: Norton & Co. 1992), 8.

famous *Aiiieeeee* anthology (1974), and Chinese American writer Maxine Hong Kingston's two celebrated novels, *The Woman Warrior* (1976) and *China Men* (1980). The *Aiiieeeee* anthology, edited by Jeffrey Paul Chan, Frank Chin, Lawson Fusao Inada, and Shawn Wong, included only American-born writers of Chinese, Japanese, and Filipino ancestry. All these bushwhacked a space for Asian American writers in the thicket of American literature. From then on, the reading public and literary scholars in America began to pay attention to Asian/Chinese American writings. There is no doubt that Asian American literature, an indispensable strand in the canon of American literature, is prospering. The year 1991 alone saw the publication of the important works by five Chinese American fiction-writers: Amy Tan's *The Kitchen God's Wife*, Gish Jen's *Typical American*, David Wong Louie's *Pangs of Love*, Frank Chin's first novel, *Donald Duk*, and Gus Lee's *China Boy*.

Saul Bellow (1915-2005)

The acclaimed Jewish American writer, Saul Bellow was born in La-chine, Quebec, Canada, on June 10, 1905, shortly after his parents had emigrated from St. Petersburg, Russia. It was during his graduate work in anthropology at the University of Wisconsin that he discovered a more urgent calling—literature. Before Bellow started his career as a writer he wrote book reviews for ten dollars apiece, and spent years teaching. He was married five times. He died on April 5, 2005 in Brookline, Massachusetts.

By the time of his death, Bellow was regarded by many as the grea-test living novelist in English. His early books won him great reputation and numerous awards: *The Adventures of Augie March* (1953), *Herzog* (1964) and *Mr. Sammler's Planet* (1970) made him the first novelist to win the National Book Award three times; his 1975 novel *Humboldt's Gift* won the Pulitzer Prize and he won the Nobel Prize for literature in 1976. Between 1949 and 1954 Bellow also published his first short stories such as "Dora" and "Sermon by Dr. Pep" (1949), "The Trip to Galena" (1950), "Looking for Mr. Green" (1952), and "Leaving the Yellow House" (1954), among others. Through the last two decades of the 20th century, Bellow continued to publish steadily with *Him With His Foot in His Mouth* (1984), *More Die of Heartbreak* (1987), *A Theft* (1989), *The Bellarosa Connection* (1989), *It All Adds Up* (1994), and *The Actual* (1997).

Bellow's novels generally concern people alienated from but not de-feated by their urban environments. In spite of their endless failure, Bel-low said in his Nobel Prize speech that his anti-heroes "triumph nonethe-less, they are heroes nonetheless, since they never give up the realm of values in which man becomes human. " Bellow's heroes, usually thoughtful and humorously cynical, influenced a generation of American authors. His characters usually, in some way, refuse to accept the frantic society they have been placed in. Sometimes they merely battle inner demons and questions from within. In novels filled with exuberance, comic invention, and intellectual brilliance, Bellow dramatizes the lives of characters who seem misplaced, disoriented, trapped. Yet these characters come face to face with others who are tough, energetic, and streetwise. Bellow's achievement lies in his combination of cultural sophistication and the wisdom of the streets.

Bellow has commanded serious critical attention for more than fifty years. It is believed that after Hemingway, no writer did more to enliven and transform the American literary sentence, stirring mind and feelings, ideas and action, the premeditated and the unconscious, in a spicy mix of high and low speech. By now, he is undoubtedly one of the most studied American fiction writers of the contemporary period.

However, Bellow's critical reputation, along with that of most white male writers of his era, is currently under reconsideration. The majority of his novels are told as first-person male monologues which usually construct an androcentric world view. While such masculine dilemmas and sensibility are the principal source of comedy in the Bellow novel, this inevitably marginalises women. An increasing number of postcolonial critics, linguists, theorists, and cultural historians are investigating the racial ideologies embedded in Bellow's texts. Bellow's rather transparent propensity for meditating on issues of whiteness through racist and sexist perspectives is now a matter of scholarly inquiry.

Looking for Mr. Green

Introduction

Saul Bellow's story "Looking for Mr. Green", published in 1952, is a realistic depiction of George Grebe, a relief worker's dedicated attempt to search for an unemployed, crippled black man named Tulliver Green in the slums of Depression Chicago in order to deliver a welfare check. Grebe is a man who has been brought to an unaccustomed low in social position by the Great Depression, and whose job is, ironically, to deliver relief checks to those who have experienced even greater misfortune. The entire story takes place in the predominantly black section of Chicago where Grebe delivers government checks. The Depression has accelerated the already rapid decline of this neighborhood, an area which had been rebuilt only fifty years before, following the Great Fire. It appears that the entire story of "Looking for Mr. Green" is about a near-betrayal of Grebe's trust in the system he has been brought up in and his ultimate inability to comprehend that his cherished system does not actually work in an effective manner to better people's positions in society. Walking through the neighborhood, he starts to realize the futility of his search and the chaotic lack of organization in society, as he ponders the fact that he is trying to deliver a check "which no one visible asked for".

Grebe is Bellow's typical 20th-century character, having "an immense desire for certain durable human goods-truth, for instance, or freedom, or wisdom". Bellow's philosophical meditation on the human condition is played out in this story, as in his other fiction, against the landscape of Chicago, that "cultureless city pervaded nonetheless by Mind"[1]. The social indicators in the story are made prominent by vari-

---

[1] This is from Saul Bellow's acceptance speech for the Nobel Prize for literature in 1976.

ous stylistic devices, most notably including setting, imagery, tone, narrative, and use of peripheral characters.

Looking for Mr. Green

Whatsoever thy hand findeth to do, do it with thy might.... [1]

Hard work? No, it wasn't really so hard. He wasn't used to walking and stair-climbing, but the physical difficulty of his new job was not what George Grebe felt most. He was delivering Relief checks in the Negro district, and although he was a native Chicagoan this was not a part of the city he knew much about—it needed a depression to introduce him to it. No, it wasn't literally hard work, not as reckoned in foot-pounds, but yet he was beginning to feel the strain of it, to grow aware of its peculiar difficulty. He could find the streets and numbers, but the clients were not where they were supposed to be, and he felt like a hunter inexperienced in the camouflage of his game. It was an unfavorable day, too—fall, and cold, dark weather, windy. But, anyway, instead of shells in his deep trench coat pocket he had the cardboard of checks, punctured for the spindles of the file, the holes reminding him of the holes in player-piano paper. And he didn't look much like a hunter, either; he was a city figure entirely, belted up in this Irish conspirator's coat [2]. He was slender without being tall, stiff in the back, his legs looking shabby in a pair of old tweed pants gone through and fringy at the cuffs. With this stiffness, he kept his head forward, so that his face was red from the sharpness of the weather; and it was an indoors sort of face with gray eyes that persisted in some kind of thought and yet seemed to avoid definiteness of conclusion. He wore Sideburns that surprised you somewhat by the tough curl of the blond hair and the effect of assertion in their length. He was not so mild as he looked, nor so youthful; and nevertheless there was no effort on his part to seem what he was not. He was an educated man; he was a bachelor; he was in some ways simple; without lushing, he liked a drink; his luck had not been good. Nothing was deliberately hidden.

He felt that his luck was better than usual today. When he had reported for work that morning, he had expected to be shut up in the Relief office at a clerk's job, for he had been hired downtown as a clerk, and he was glad to have, instead, the freedom of the streets and welcomed, at least at first, the vigor of the cold and even the blowing of the hard wind. But on the other hand he was not getting on with the distribution of the checks. It was true that it was a city job; nobody expected you to push too hard at a city job. His supervisor, that young Mr. Raynor, had practically told him that. Still, he wanted to do well at it. For one thing, when he knew how quickly he could deliver a batch of checks, he would know also how much time he could expect to clip for himself. And then, too, the clients would be waiting for their money. That was not the most important consideration, though it certainly mattered to him. No, but he wanted to do well, simply for doing-well's sake, to acquit himself decently of a job because he so rarely had a job to do that required just this sort of energy. Of this peculiar energy he now had a superabundance; once it had started to flow, it flowed all too heavily. And, for the time being anyway, he was balked. He could not find Mr. Green.

So he stood in his big-skirted trench coat with a large envelope in his hand and papers showing from his pocket, wondering why people should be so hard to locate who were too feeble or sick to come to the station to collect their own checks. But Raynor had told him that tracking them down was not easy at first and had offered him some advice on how to proceed. "If you can see the postman, he's your first man to ask, and your best bet. If you can't connect with him, try the stores and tradespeople around. Then the janitor and the neighbors. But you'll find the closer you come to your man the less people will tell you. They don't want to tell you anything. "

"Because I'm a stranger. "

"Because you're white. We ought to have a Negro doing this, but we don't at the moment, and of course you've got to eat, too, and this is public employment. Jobs have to be made. Oh, that holds for me too. Mind you, I'm not letting myself out. I've got three years of seniority on you, that's all. And a law degree. Otherwise, you might be back of the desk and I might be going out into the field this cold day. The same dough pays us both and for the same, exact, identical reason. What's my law degree got to do with it? But you have to pass out these checks, Mr. Grebe, and if it'll help if you're stubborn, so I hope you are. "

"Yes, I'm fairly stubborn. "

Raynor sketched hard with an eraser in the old dirt of his desk, left-handed, and said, "Sure, what else can you answer to such a question. Anyhow, the trouble you're going to have is that they don't like to give information about anybody. They think you're a plain-clothes dick[3] or an installment collector, or summons-server[4] or something like that. Till you've been seen around the neighborhood for a few months and people know you're only from the Relief. "

It was dark, ground-freezing, pre-Thanksgiving weather, the wind played hob with the smoke, rushing it down, and Grebe missed his gloves, which he had left in Raynor's office. And no one would admit knowing Green. It was past three o'clock and the postman had made his last delivery. The nearest grocer, himself a Negro, had never heard the name Tulliver Green, or said he hadn't. Grebe was inclined to think that it was true, that he had in the end convinced the man that he wanted only to deliver a check. But he wasn't sure. He needed experience in interpreting looks and signs and, even more, the will not to be put off or denied and even the force to bully, if need be. If the grocer did know, he had got rid of him easily. But since most of his trade was with reliefers, why should he prevent the delivery of a check? Maybe Green, or Mrs. Green, if there was a Mrs. Green, patronized another grocer. And was there a Mrs. Green? It was one of Grebe's great handicaps that he hadn't looked at any of the case records. Raynor should have let him read files for a few hours. But he apparently saw no need for that, probably considering the job unimportant. Why prepare systematically to deliver a few checks?

But now it was time to look for the janitor. Grebe took in the building in the wind and gloom of the late November day—trampled, frost-hardened lots on one side; on the other, an automobile junk yard and then the infinite work of Elevated frames[5], weak-looking, gaping with rubbish fires; two sets of leaning brick porches three stories high and a flight of cement stairs to the cellar. Descending, he entered the underground passage, where he tried the doors until one opened and he found himself in the furnace room. There someone rose toward him and approached, scraping on the coal grit and bending under the canvas-jacketed pipes.

"Are you the janitor?"

"What do you want?"

"I'm looking for a man who's supposed to be living here. Green."

"What Green?"

"Oh, you maybe have more than one Green?" said Grebe with new, pleasant hope. This is Tulliver Green."

"I don't think I c'n help you, mister. I don't know any."

"A crippled man."

The janitor stood bent before him. Could it be that he was crippled?

Oh, God! what if he was. Grebe's gray eyes sought with excited difficulty to see. But no, he was only very short and stooped. A head awakened from meditation, a strong-haired beard, low, wide shoulders. A staleness of sweat and coal rose from his black shirt and the burlap sack he wore as an apron.

"Crippled how?"

Grebe thought and then answered with the light voice of unmixed candor, "I don't know. I've never seen him." This was damaging, but his only other choice was to make a lying guess, and he was not up to it. "I'm delivering checks for the Relief to shut-in cases[⑥]. If he weren't crippled he'd come to collect himself. That's why I said crippled. Bedridden, chair-ridden . . . is there anybody like that?"

This sort of frankness was one of Grebe's oldest talents, going back to childhood. But it gained him nothing here.

"No suh. I've got four buildin's same as this that I take care of. I don' know all the tenants, leave alone the tenants' tenants. The rooms turn over so fast, people movin' in and out every day. I can't tell you."

"Then where should I ask?"

The janitor opened his grimy lips but Grebe did not hear him in the piping of the valves and the consuming pull of air to flame in the body of the furnace. He knew, however, what he had said.

"Well, all the same, thanks. Sorry I bothered you. I'll prowl around upstairs again and see if I can turn up someone who knows him."

Once more in the cold air and early darkness, he made the short circle from the cellarway to the entrance crowded between the brickwork pillars and began to climb to the third floor. Pieces of plaster ground under his feet; strips of brass tape from which the carpeting had been torn away marked old boundaries at the sides. In the passage, the cold reached him worse than in the street; it touched him to the bone. The hall toilets ran like springs. He thought grimly as he heard the wind burning around the building with a sound like that of the furnace, that this was a great piece of constructed shelter. Then he struck a match in the gloom and searched for names and numbers among the writings and scribbles on the walls. He saw "WHOODY—DOODY GO TO JESUS," and zigzags, caricatures, sexual scrawls, and curses. So the sealed rooms of pyramids were also decorated, and the caves of human dawn.

The information on his card was, TULLIVER GREEN—APT 3D. There were no names, however, and no numbers. His shoulders drawn up, tears of cold in his eyes, breathing vapor, he went the length of the corridor and told himself that if he had been lucky enough to have the temperament for it he would bang on one of the doors and bawl out "Tulliver Green!" until he got results. But it wasn't in him to make an uproar and he continued to burn matches, passing the light over the walls. At the rear, in a corner off the hall, he discovered a door he had not seen before and he thought it best to investigate. It sounded empty when he knocked, but a young Negress answered, hardly more than a girl. She opened only a bit, to guard the warmth of the room.

"Yes suh?"

"I'm from the district Relief station on Prairie Avenue[7]. I'm looking for a man named Tulliver Green to give him his check. Do you know him?"

No, she didn't; but he thought she had not understood anything of what he had said. She had a dream-bound, dream-blind face, very soft and black, shut off. She wore a man's jacket and pulled the ends together at her throat. Her hair was parted in three directions, at the sides and transversely, standing up at the front in a dull puff.

"Is there somebody around here who might know?"

"I jus' taken this room las' week."

He observed that she shivered, but even her shiver was somnambulistic and there was no sharp consciousness of cold in the big smooth eyes other handsome face.

"All right, miss, thank you. Thanks," he said, and went to try another place.

Here he was admitted. He was grateful, for the room was warm. It was full of people, and they were silent as he entered—ten people, or a dozen, perhaps more, sitting on benches like a parliament. There was no light, properly speaking, but a tempered darkness that the window gave, and everyone seemed to him enormous, the men padded out in heavy work clothes and winter coats, and the women huge, too, in their sweaters, hats, and old furs. And, besides, bed and bedding, a black cooking range, a piano piled towering to the ceiling with papers, a dining-room table of the old style of prosperous Chicago. Among these people Grebe, with his cold-heightened fresh color and his smaller stature, entered like a schoolboy. Even though he was met with smiles and good will, he knew, before a single word was spoken, that all the currents ran against him and that he would make no headway. Nevertheless he began. "Does anybody here know how I can deliver a check to Mr. Tulliver Green?"

"Green?" It was the man that had let him in who answered. He was in short sleeves, in a checkered shirt, and had a queer, high head, profusely overgrown and long as a shako[8]; the veins entered it strongly from his forehead. "I never heard mention of him. Is this where he live?"

"This is the address they gave me at the station. He's a sick man, and he'll need his check. Can't anybody tell me where to find him?"

He stood his ground and waited for a reply, his crimson wool scarf wound about his neck and drooping outside his trench coat, pockets weighted with the block of checks and official forms. They must have realized that he was not a college boy employed afternoons by a bill collector, trying foxily to pass for a Relief clerk, recognized that he was an older man who knew himself what need was, who had had more than an average seasoning in hardship. It was evident enough if you looked at the marks under his eyes and at the sides of his mouth.

"Anybody know this sick man?"

"No suh. " On all sides he saw heads shaken and smiles of denial. No one knew. And maybe it was true, he considered, standing silent in the earthen, musky human gloom of the place as the rumble continued. But he could never really be sure.

"What's the matter with this man?" said shako-head.

"I've never seen him. All I can tell you is that he can't come in person for his money. It's my first day in this district. "

"Maybe they given you the wrong number?"

"I don't believe so. But where else can I ask about him?" He felt that this persistence amused them deeply, and in a way he shared their amusement that he should stand up so tenaciously to them. Though smaller, though slight, he was his own man, he retracted nothing about himself, and he looked back at them, gray-eyed, with amusement and also with a sort of courage. On the bench some man spoke in his throat, the words impossible to catch, and a woman answered with a wild, shrieking laugh, which was quickly cut off.

"Well, so nobody will tell me?"

"Ain't nobody who knows. "

"At least, if he lives here, he pays rent to someone. Who manages the building?"

"Greatham Company. That's on Thirty-ninth Street. "

Grebe wrote it in his pad. But, in the street again, a sheet of wind-driven paper clinging to his leg while he deliberated what direction to take next, it seemed a feeble lead to follow. Probably this Green didn't

399

rent a flat, but a room. Sometimes there were as many as twenty people in an apartment; the real-estate agent would know only the lessee. And not even the agent could tell you who the renters were. In some places the beds were even used in shifts, watchmen or jitney[9] drivers or short-order cooks in night joints turning out after a day's sleep and surrendering their beds to a sister, a nephew, or perhaps a stranger, just off the bus. There were large numbers of newcomers in this terrific, blight-bitten portion of the city between Cottage Grove and Ashland, wandering from house to house and room to room. When you saw them, how could you know them? They didn't carry bundles on their backs or look picturesque. You only saw a man, a Negro, walking in the street or riding in the car, like everyone else, with his thumb closed on a transfer. And therefore how were you supposed to tell? Grebe thought the Greatham agent would only laugh at his question.

But how much it would have simplified the job to be able to say that Green was old, or blind, or comsumptive. An hour in the files, taking a few notes, and he needn't have been at such a disadvantage. When Raynor gave him the block of checks he asked, "How much should I know about these people?" Then Raynor had looked as though he were preparing to accuse him of trying to make the job more important than it was. He smiled, because by then they were on fine terms, but nevertheless he had been getting ready to say something like that when the confusion began in the station over Staika and her children.

Grebe had waited a long time for this job. It came to him through the pull of an old schoolmate in the Corporation Counsel's office, never a close friend, but suddenly sympathetic and interested—pleased to show, moreover, how well he had done, how strongly he was coming on even in these miserable times. Well, he was coming through strongly, along with the Democratic administration[10] itself. Grebe had gone to see him in City Hall, and they had had a counter lunch or beers at least once a month for a year, and finally it had been possible to swing the job. He didn't mind being assigned the lowest clerical grade, nor even being a messenger, though Raynor thought he did.

This Raynor was an original sort of guy and Grebe had taken to him immediately. As was proper on the first day, Grebe had come early, but he waited long, for Raynor was late. At last he darted into his cubicle of an office as though he had just jumped from one of those hurtling huge red Indiana Avenue cars. His thin, rough face was wind-stung and he was grinning and saying something breathlessly to himself. In his hat, a small fedora[11] and his coat, the velvet collar a neat fit about his neck, and his silk muffler that set off the nervous twist of his chin, he swayed and turned himself in his swivel chair, feet leading the ground; so that he pranced a little as he sat. Meanwhile he took Grebe's measure out of his eyes, eyes of an unusual vertical length and slightly sardonic. So the two men sat for a while, saying nothing, while the supervisor raised his hat from his miscombed hair and put it in his lap. His cold-darkened hands were not clean. A steel beam passed through the little makeshift room, from which machine belts once had hung. The building was an old factory.

"I'm younger than you; I hope you won't find it hard taking orders from me," said Raynor. "But I don't make them up, either. You're how old, about?"

"Thirty-five."

"And you thought you'd be inside doing paper work. But it so happens I have to send you out."

"I don't mind."

"And it's mostly a Negro load we have in this district."

"So I thought it would be."

"Fine. You'll get along. *C'est un bon boulot.*[12] Do you know French?"

401

"Some."

"I thought you'd be a university man."

"Have you been in France?" said Grebe.

"No, that's the French of the Berlitz School. I've been at it for more than a year, just as I'm sure people have been, all over the world, office boys in China and braves[13] in Tanganyika[14]. In fact, I damn well know it. Such is the attractive power of civilization. It's overrated, but what do you want? *Que voulez-vous*[15]? I get *Le Rire*[16], and all the spicy papers, just like in Tanganyika. It must be mystifying, out there. But my reason is that I'm aiming at the diplomatic service. I have a cousin who's a courier, and the way he describes it is awfully attractive. He rides in the *wagon-lits*[17] and reads books. While we... What did you do before?"

"I sold."

"Where?"

"Canned meat at Stop and Shop. In the basement."

"And before that?"

"Window shades, at Goldblatt's."

"Steady work?"

"No, Thursdays and Saturdays. I also sold shoes."

"You've been a shoe-dog too. Well. And prior to that? Here it is in your folder." He opened the record. "Saint Olaf's College, instructor in classical languages. Fellow, University of Chicago 1926-1927. I've had Latin, too. Let's trade quotations— '*Dum spiro spero.*'"

"*Da dextram misero.*"

"*Alea jacta est.*"

"*Excelsior.*"[18]

Raynor shouted with laughter, and other workers came to look at him over the partition. Grebe also laughed, feeling pleased and easy. The luxury of fun on a nervous morning.

When they were done and no one was watching or listening, Raynor said rather seriously, "What made you study Latin in the first place? Was it for the priesthood?"

"No."

"Just for the hell of it? For the culture? Oh, the things people think they can pull!" He made his cry hilarious and tragic. I ran my pants off so I could study for the bar, and I've passed the bar, so I get twelve dollars a week more than you as a bonus for having seen life straight and whole. I'll tell you, as a man of culture, that even though nothing looks to be real, and everything stands for something else, and that thing for another thing, and that thing for a still further one—there ain't any comparison between twenty-five and thirty-seven dollars a week, regardless of the last reality. Don't you think that was clear to your Greeks? They were a thoughtful people, but they didn't part with their slaves."

This was a great deal more than Grebe had looked for in his first interview with his supervisor. He was too shy to show all the astonishment he felt. He laughed a little, aroused, and brushed at the sunbeam that covered his head with its dust. "Do you think my mistake was so terrible?"

"Damn right it was terrible, and you know it now that you've had the whip of hard times laid on your back. You should have been preparing yourself for trouble. Your people must have been well off to send you to the university. Stop me, if I'm stepping on your toes. Did your mother pamper you? Did your father give in to you? Were you brought up tenderly, with permission to go and find out what were the last things that everything else stands for while everybody else labored in the fallen world of appearances?"

"Well, no, it wasn't exactly like that." Grebe smiled. *The fallen world of appearances*! no less. But now it was his turn to deliver a surprise. "We weren't rich. My father was the last genuine English butler in Chicago. . . ."

"Are you kidding?"

"Why should I be?"

"In a livery?"

"In livery. Up on the Gold Coast. [19]"

"And he wanted you to be educated like a gentleman?"

"He did not. He sent me to the Armour Institute to study chemical engineering. But when he died I changed schools."

He stopped himself, and considered how quickly Raynor had reached him. In no time he had your valise on the table and all your stuff unpacked. And afterward, in the streets, he was still reviewing how far he might have gone, and how much he might have been led to tell if they had not been interrupted by Mrs. Staika's great noise.

But just then a young woman, one of Raynor's workers, ran into the cubicle exclaiming, "Haven't you heard all the fuss?"

"We haven't heard anything."

"It's Staika, giving out with all her might. The reporters are coming. She said she phoned the papers, and you know she did."

"But what is she up to?" said Raynor.

"She brought her wash and she's ironing it here, with our current, because the Relief won't pay her electric bill. She has her ironing board set up by the admitting desk, and her kids are with her, all six. They never are in school more than once a week. She's always dragging them around with her because of her reputation."

"I don't want to miss any of this," said Raynor, jumping up. Grebe, as he followed with the secretary, said, "Who is this Staika?"

"They call her the 'Blood Mother of Federal Street.' She's a professional donor at the hospitals. I think they pay ten dollars a pint. Of course it's no joke, but she makes a very big thing out of it and she and the kids are in the papers all the time."

A small crowd, staff and clients divided by a plywood barrier, stood in the narrow space of the entrance, and Staika was shouting in a gruff, mannish voice, plunging the iron on the board and slamming it on the metal rest.

"My father and mother came in a steerage, and I was born in our house, Robey by Huron. I'm no dirty immigrant. I'm a U. S. citizen. My husband is a gassed veteran from France with lungs weaker'n paper, that hardly can he go to the toilet by himself. These six children of mine, I have to buy the shoes for their feet with my own blood. Even a lousy little white Communion necktie, that's a couple of drops of blood; a little piece of mosquito veil for my Vadja so she won't be ashamed in church for the other girls, they take my blood for it by Goldblatt. That's how I keep goin'. A fine thing if I had to depend on the Relief. And there's plenty of people on the rolls—fakes! There's nothin' *they* can't get, that can go and wrap bacon at Swift and Armour any time. They're lookin' for them by the Yards. They never have to be out of work. Only they rather lay in their lousy beds and eat the public's money." She was not afraid, in a predominantly Negro station, to shout this way about Negroes.

Grebe and Raynor worked themselves forward to get a closer view of the woman. She was flaming with anger and with pleasure at herself, broad and huge, a golden-headed woman who wore a cotton cap laced with pink ribbon. She was barelegged and had on t black gym-shoes, her Hoover apron[20] was open and her great breasts, not much restrained by a man's undershirt, hampered her arms as she worked at the kid's dress on the ironing board. And the children, silent and white, with a kind of locked obstinacy, in sheepskins and lumberjackets, stood behind her. She had captured the station, and the pleasure this gave her was enormous. Yet her grievances were true grievances. She was telling the truth. But she behaved like a liar. The look other small eyes was hidden, and while she raged she also seemed to be spinning and planning.

"They send me out college case workers in silk pants to talk me out of what I got comin'. Are they better'n me? Who told them? Fire them. Let 'em go and get married, and then you won't have to cut electric from people's budget."

The chief supervisor, Mr. Ewing, couldn't silence her and he stood with folded arms at the head of his staff, bald, bald-headed, saying to his subordinates like the ex-school principal he was, "Pretty soon she'll be tired and go."

"No she won't," said Raynor to Grebe. "She'll get what she wants. She knows more about the Relief even then Ewing. She's been on the rolls for years, and she always gets what she wants because she puts on a noisy show. Ewing knows it. He'll give in soon. He's only saving face. If he gets bad publicity, the Commissioner'll have him on the carpet, downtown. She's got him submerged; she'll submerge everybody in time, and that includes nations and governments."

Grebe replied with his characteristic smile, disagreeing completely. Who would take Staika's orders, and what changes could her yelling ever bring about?

No, what Grebe saw in her, the power that made people listen, was that her cry expressed the war of flesh and blood, perhaps turned a little crazy and certainly ugly, on this place and this condition. And at first, when he went out, the spirit of Staika somehow presided over the whole district for him, and it took color from her; he saw her color, in the spotty curb fires, and the fires under the El, the straight alley of flamy gloom. Later, too, when he went into a tavern for a shot of rye, the sweat of beer, association with West Side Polish streets, made him think other again.

He wiped the comers of his mouth with his muffler, his handkerchief being inconvenient to reach for, and went out again to get on with the delivery of his checks. The air bit cold and hard and a few flakes of snow formed near him. A train struck by and left a quiver in the frames and a bristling icy hiss over the rails.

Crossing the street, he descended a flight of board steps into a basement grocery, setting off a little bell. It was a dark, long store and it caught you with its stinks of smoked meat, soap, dried peaches, and fish. There was a fire wrinkling and flapping in the little stove, and the proprietor was waiting, an Italian with a long, hollow face and stubborn bristles. He kept his hands warm under his apron.

No, he didn't know Green. You knew people but not names. The same man might not have the same name twice. The police didn't know, either, and mostly didn't care. When somebody was shot or knifed they took the body away and didn't look for the murderer. In the first place, nobody would tell them anything. So they made up a name for the coroner and called it quits. And in the second place, they didn't give a god-damn anyhow. But they couldn't get to the bottom of a thing even if they wanted to. Nobody would get to know even a tenth of what went on among these people. They stabbed and stole, they did every crime and abomination you ever heard of, men and men, women and women, parents and children, worse than the animals. They carried on their own way, and the horrors passed off like a smoke. There was never anything like it in the history of the whole world.

It was a long speech, deepening with every word in its fantasy and passion and becoming increasingly senseless and terrible: a swarm amassed by suggestion and invention, a huge, hugging, despairing knot, a human wheel of heads, legs, bellies, arms, rolling through his shop.

Grebe felt that he must interrupt him. He said sharply, "What are you talking about! All I asked was whether you knew this man."

"That isn't even the half of it. I been here six years. You probably don't want to believe this. But suppose it's true?"

"All the same," said Grebe, "there must be a way to find a person."

The Italian's close-spaced eyes had been queerly concentrated, as were his muscles, while he leaned across the counter trying to convince Grebe. Now he gave up the effort and sat down on his stool. "Oh... I suppose. Once in a while. But I been telling you, even the cops don't get anywhere."

"They're always after somebody. It's not the same thing."

"Well, keep trying if you want. I can't help you."

But he didn't keep trying. He had no more time to spend on Green. He slipped Green's check to the back of the block. The next name on the list was FIELD, WINSTON.

He found the back-yard bungalow without the least trouble; it shared a lot with another house, a few feet of yard between. Grebe knew these two-shack arrangements. They had been built in vast numbers in the days before the swamps were filled and the streets raised, and they were all the same—a boardwalk along the fence, well under street level, three or four ball-headed posts for clothes-lines, greening wood, dead shingles, and a long, long flight of stairs to the rear door.

A twelve-year-old boy let him into the kitchen, and there the old man was, sitting by the table in a wheel chair.

"Oh, it's a Government man," he said to the boy when Grebe drew out his checks. "Go bring me my box of papers." He cleared a space on the table.

"Oh, you don't have to go to all that trouble," said Grebe. But Field laid out his papers: Social Security card, Relief certification, letters from the state hospital in Manteno, and a naval discharge dated San Diego, 1920.

"That's plenty," Grebe said. "Just sign."

"You got to know who I am," the old man said. "You're from the Government. It's not your check, it's a Government check and you got no business to hand it over till everything is proved."

He loved the ceremony of it, and Grebe made no more objections. Field emptied his box and finished out the circle of cards and letters.

"There's everything I done and been. Just the death certificate and they can close book on me." He said this with a certain happy pride and magnificence. Still he did not sign; he merely held the little pen upright on the golden-green corduroy of his thigh. Grebe did not hurry him. He felt the old man's hunger for conversation.

"I got to get better coal," he said. "I send my little gran'son to the yard with my order and they fill his wagon with screening. The stove ain't made for it. It fall through the grate. The order says Franklin County egg-size coal."

"I'll report it and see what can be done."

"Nothing can be done, I expect. You know and I know. There ain't no little ways to make things better, and the only big thing is money. That's the only sunbeams, money. Nothing is black where it shines, and the only place you see black is where it ain't shining. What we colored have to have is our own rich. There ain't no other way."

Grebe sat, his reddened forehead bridged levelly by his close-cut hair and his cheeks lowered in the wings of his collar—the caked fire shone hard within the isinglass-and-iron frames but the room was not comfortable—sat and listened while the old man unfolded his scheme. This was to create one Negro millionaire a month by subscription. One clever, good-hearted young fellow elected every month would sign a contract to use the money to start a business employing Negroes. This would be advertised by chain letters and word of mouth, and every Negro wage earner would contribute a dollar a month. Within five years there would be sixty millionaires.

"That'll fetch respect," he said with a throat-stopped sound that came out like a foreign syllable. "You got to take and organize all the money that gets thrown away on the policy wheel and horse race. As long as they can take it away from you, they got no respect for you. Money, that's d' sun of human kind!" Field was a Negro of mixed blood, perhaps Cherokee[21], or Natchez[22]; his skin was reddish. And he sounded, speaking about a golden sun in this dark room, and looked, shaggy and slab-headed, with the mingled blood of his face and broad lips, the little pen still upright in his hand, like one of the underground kings of mythology, old judge Minos[23] himself.

And now he accepted the check and signed. Not to soil the slip, he held it down with his knuckles. The table budged and creaked, the center of the gloomy, heathen midden[24] of the kitchen covered with bread, meat, and cans, and the scramble of papers.

"Don't you think my scheme'd work?"

"It's worth thinking about. Something ought to be done, I agree."

"It'll work if people will do it. That's all. That's the only thing, any time. When they understand it in the same way, all of them."

"That's true," said Grebe, rising. His glance met the old man's.

"I know you got to go," he said. "Well, God bless you, boy, you ain't been sly with me. I can tell it in a minute."

He went back through the buried yard. Someone nursed a candle in a shed, where a man unloaded kindling wood from a sprawl-wheeled baby buggy and two voices carried on a high conversation. As he came up the sheltered passage he heard the hard boost of the wind in the branches and against the house fronts, and then, reaching the sidewalk, he saw the needle-eye red of cable towers in the open icy height hundreds of feet above the river and the factories those keen points. From here, his view was obstructed all the way to the South Branch and its timber

banks, and the cranes beside the water. Rebuilt after the Great Fire[25],
this part of the city was, not fifty years later, in ruins again, factories
boarded up, buildings deserted or fallen, gaps of prairie between. But it
wasn't desolation that this made you feel, but rather a faltering of organization that set free a huge energy, an escaped, unattached, unregulated
power from the giant raw place. Not only must people feel it but, it
seemed to Grebe, they were compelled to match it. In their very bodies.
He no less than others, he realized. Say that his parents had been servants in their time, whereas he was not supposed to be one. He thought
that they had never done any service like this, which no one visible
asked for, and probably flesh and blood could not even perform. Nor
could anyone show why it should be performed; or see where the per-
formance would lead. That did not mean that he wanted to be released
from it, he realized with a grimly pensive face. On the contrary. He had
something to do. To be compelled to feel this energy and yet have no
task to do—that was horrible; that was suffering; he knew what that
was. It was now quitting time. Six o'clock. He could go home if he
liked, to his room, that is, to wash in hot water, to pour a drink, lie
down on his quilt, read the paper, eat some liver paste on crackers before
going out to dinner. But to think of this actually made him feel a little sick,
as though he had swallowed hard air. He had six checks left, and he
was determined to deliver at least one of these: Mr. Green's check.

So he started again. He had four or five dark blocks to go, past
open lots, condemned houses, old foundations, closed schools, black
churches, mounds, and he reflected that there must be many people
alive who had once seen the neighborhood rebuilt and new. Now there
was a second layer of ruins; centuries of history accomplished through
human massing. Numbers had given the place forced growth; enormous
numbers had also broken it down. Objects once so new, so concrete that
it could have occurred to anyone they stood for other things, had crum-

411

bled. Therefore, reflected Grebe, the secret of them was out. It was that they stood for themselves by agreement, and were natural and not unnatural by agreement, and when the things themselves collapsed the agreement became visible. What was it, otherwise, that kept cities from looking peculiar? Rome, that was almost permanent, did not give rise to thoughts like these. And was it abidingly real? But in Chicago, where the cycles were so fast and the familiar died out, and again rose changed, and died again in thirty years, you saw the common agreement or covenant, and you were forced to think about appearances and realities. (He remembered Raynor and he smiled. Raynor was a clever boy.) Once you had grasped this, a great many things became intelligible. For instance, why Mr. Field should conceive such a scheme. Of course, if people were to agree to create a millionaire, a real millionaire would come into existence. And if you wanted to know how Mr. Field was inspired to think of this, why, he had within sight of his kitchen window the chart, the very bones of a successful scheme—the El with its blue and green confetti of signals. People consented to pay dimes and ride the crash-box cars, and so it was a success. Yet how absurd it looked; how little reality there was to start with. And yet Yerkes[26], the great financier who built it, had known that he could get people to agree to do it. Viewed as itself, what a scheme of a scheme it seemed, how close to an appearance. Then why wonder at Mr. Field's idea? He had grasped a principle. And then Grebe remembered, too, that Mr. Yerkes had established the Yerkes Observatory and endowed it with millions. Now how did the notion come to him in his New York museum of a palace or his Aegean-bound yacht to give money to astronomers? Was he awed by the success of his bizarre enterprise and therefore ready to spend money to find out where in the universe being and seeming were identical? Yes, he wanted to know what abides; and whether flesh is Bible grass[27]; and he offered money to be burned in the fire of suns. Okay, then. Grebe thought further, these things exist because people consent to exist with them—we have got so far—and also there is a reality which doesn't depend on consent but within which consent is a game. But what about need, the need that keeps so many vast thousands in position? You tell me that, you private little gentleman and *decent* soul—he used these words against himself scornfully. Why is the consent given to misery? And why so painfully ugly? Because there is *something* that is dismal and permanently ugly? Here he sighed and gave it up, and thought it was enough for the present moment that he had a real check in his pocket for a Mr. Green who must be real beyond question. If only his neighbors didn't think they had to conceal him.

This time he stopped at the second floor. He struck a match and found a door. Presently a man answered his knock and Grebe had the check ready and showed it even before he began. "Does Tulliver Green live here? I'm from the Relief."

The man narrowed the opening and spoke to someone at his back.

"Does he live here?"

"Uh-unh. No."

"Or anywhere in this building? He's a sick man and he can't come for his dough." He exhibited the check in the light, which was smoky—the air smelled of charred lard—and the man held off the brim of his cap to study it.

"Uh-unh. Never seen the name."

"There's nobody around here that uses crutches?"

He seemed to think, but it was Grebe's impression that he was simply waiting for a decent interval to pass.

"No, suh. Nobody I ever see."

"I've been looking for this man all afternoon" Grebe spoke out with sudden force, " and I'm going to have to carry this check back to the station. It seems strange not to be able to find a person to *give* him something when you're looking for him for a good reason. I suppose if I had bad news for him I'd find him quick enough. "

There was a responsive motion in the other man's face. "That's right, I reckon. "

"It almost doesn't do any good to have a name if you can't be found by it. It doesn't stand for anything. He might as well not have any," he went on, smiling. It was as much of a concession as he could make to his desire to laugh.

"Well, now, there's a little old knot-back man I see once in a while. He might be the one you lookin' for. Downstairs. "

"Where? Right side or left? Which door?"

"I don't know which. Thin-face little knot-back with a stick. "

But no one answered at any of the doors on the first floor. He went to the end of the corridor, searching by matchlight, and found only a stairless exit to the yard, a drop of about six feet. But there was a bungalow near the alley, an old house like Mr. Field's. To jump was unsafe. He ran from the front door, through the underground passage and into the yard. The place was occupied. There was a light through the curtains, upstairs. The name on the ticket under the broken, scoop-shaped mailbox was Green! He exultantly rang the bell and pressed against the locked door. Then the lock clicked faintly and a long staircase opened before him. Someone was slowly coming down—a woman. He had the impression in the weak light that she was shaping her hair as she came, making herself presentable, for he saw her arms raised. But it was for support that they were raised; she was feeling her way downward, down the wall, stumbling. Next he wondered about the pressure of her feet on the treads; she did not seem to be wearing shoes. And it was a freezing stairway. His ring had got her out of bed, perhaps, and she had forgotten to put them on. And then he saw that she was not only shoeless but naked; she was entirely naked, climbing down while she talked to herself, a heavy woman, naked and drunk. She blundered into him. The contact of her breasts, though they touched only his coat, made him go back against the door with a blind shock. See what he had tracked down, in his hunting game!

The woman was saying to herself, furious with insult, "So I cain't—, huh? I'll show that son-of-a-bitch kin' I, cain't I."

What should he do now? Grebe asked himself. Why, he should go. He should turn away and go. He couldn't talk to this woman. He couldn't keep her standing naked in the cold. But when he tried he found himself unable to turn away.

He said, "Is this where Mr. Green lives?"

But she was still talking to herself and did not hear him.

"Is this Mr. Green's house?"

At last she turned her furious drunken glance on him. "What do you want?"

Again her eyes wandered from him; there was a dot of blood in their enraged brilliance. He wondered why she didn't feel the cold.

"I'm from the Relief."

"Awright, what?"

"I've got a check for Tulliver Green."

This time she heard him and put out her hand.

"No, no, for *Mister* Green. He's got to sign," he said. How was he going to get Green's signature tonight!

"I'll take it. He cain't."

He desperately shook his head, thinking of Mr. Field's precautions about identification. "I can't let you have it. It's for him. Are you Mrs. Green?"

"Maybe I is, and maybe I ain't. Who want to know?"

"Is he upstairs?"

415

"Awright. Take it up yourself, you goddamn fool."

Sure, he was a goddamn fool. Of course he could not go up because Green would probably be drunk and naked, too. And perhaps he would appear on the landing soon. He looked eagerly upward. Under the light was a high narrow brown wall. Empty! It remained empty!

"Hell with you, then!" he heard her cry. To deliver a check for coal and clothes, he was keeping her in the cold. She did not feel it, but his face was burning with frost and self-ridicule. He backed away from her.

"I'll come tomorrow, tell him."

"Ah, hell with you. Don' never come. What you doin' here in the nighttime? Don' come back." She yelled so that he saw the breadth other tongue. She stood astride in the long cold box of the hall and held on to the banister and the wall. The bungalow itself was shaped something like a box, a clumsy, high box pointing into the freezing air with its sharp, wintry lights.

"If you are Mrs. Green, I'll give you the check," he said, changing his mind.

"Give here, then." She took it, took the pen offered with it in her left hand, and tried to sign the receipt on the wall. He looked around, almost as though to see whether his madness was being observed, and came near believing that someone was standing on a mountain of used tires in the auto-junking shop next door.

"But are you Mrs. Green?" he now thought to ask. But she was already climbing the stairs with the check, and it was too late, if he had made an error, if he was now in trouble, to undo the thing. But he wasn't going to worry about it. Though she might not be Mrs. Green, he was convinced that Mr. Green was upstairs. Whoever she was, the woman stood for Green, whom he was not to see this time. Well, you silly bastard, he said to himself, so you think you found him. So what?

Maybe you really did find him—what of it? But it was important that there was a real Mr. Green whom they could not keep him from reaching because he seemed to come as an emissary from hostile appearances. And though the self-ridicule was slow to diminish, and his face still blazed with it, he had, nevertheless, a feeling of elation, too. "For after all," he said, "he could be found!"

Notes

① ***Whatsoever thy hand findeth to do, do it with thy might...*** : From Ecclesiastes 9. 10; the verse continues, "for there is no work, no device, nor knowledge, no wisdom, in the grave, whither thou goest."

② **this Irish conspirator's coat**: a coat like those worn by members of the anti-British underground in Ireland.

③ **a plain-clothes dick**: a detective.

④ **Summons-server**: a person who sends a court order for attending a lawcourt.

⑤ **Elevated frames**: (abbr.) the "El", elevated urban railway.

⑥ **shut-in cases**: cases that need delivering to domicile.

⑦ **Prairie Avenue**: The Prairie Avenue District is an area steeped in Chicago's history. Following the Fire of 1871, it became the city's most fashionable neighborhood.

⑧ **shako**: stiff military headdress with a high crown and a plume, peaked military cap.

⑨ **jitney**: little bus.

⑩ **the Democratic administration**: The Corporation Counsel's Office provides professional legal services to the Village as a legal entity.

⑪ **fedora**: A low soft felt hat with a crown creased lengthways.

⑫ **C'est un bon boulot**: (French slang) It's a good job.

⑬ **braves**: American Indian warriors.

⑭ **Tanganyika**: an East African republic within the British Commonwealth, named after Lake Tanganyika.

⑮ **Que voulez-vous**: (French) What do you want?

⑯ **Le Rire**: a French humor journal.

⑰ **wagon-lits**: European railroad sleeping-cars.

⑱ **Excelsior**: The phrases are familiar Latin slogans, which are translated, in order, as follows: "Where there's life there's hope" (literally, "While I breathe I hope"); "Give the right hand to the wretched"; "The die is cast"; "Higher!"

⑲ **the Gold Coast**: one of Chicago's wealthiest sections.

⑳ **Hoover apron**: woman's overall, which was popular during World War Ⅰ.

㉑ **Cherokee**: an American Indian tribe formerly inhabiting much of the Southern US.

㉒ **Natchez**: a well-known tribe that formerly lived on and about St Catherine's Creek, east and south of the present city of Natchez, Mississipi.

㉓ **Minos**: legendary king of Crete, who commissioned Daedalus to build the Labyrinth.

㉔ **midden**: a refuse heap near a dwelling.

㉕ **the Great Fire**: the Chicago Fire of 1871.

㉖ **Yerkes**: Charles Tyson Yerkes (1837-1905), American financier who obtained a virtual monopoly of the surface and elevated railway service in Chicago.

㉗ **Bible grass**: See Isaiah 40:6. "All flesh is grass, and all the goodliness therefore is as the flower of the field."

Questions for Reading Comprehension

1. What is the purpose of Grebe's supervisor Raynor?

2. What is Bellow's attitude toward Raynor's cynical "wisdom"?

3. What is the purpose of the encounter with the Italian grocer who pre-

sents a hellish vision of the city with its chaotic masses of suffering humanity?

4. The old man Field offers this view of money— "Nothing is black where it shines and the only place you see black is where it ain't shining." What do you think of the scheme for creating black millionaires?

5. Why does Bellow include this scheme in the story?

6. What is the purpose of the Staika incident in the story?

7. Raynor sees Staika as embodiment of "the destructive force" that will "submerge everybody in time," including "nations and governments." In contrast, Grebe sees her as "the life force". Who is closer to truth?

8. The word "sun" and sun imagery are repeated throughout the story. Do they have any symbolic meaning?

Discussion Questions for Appreciation

1. David Demarest comments: "Grebe's stubborn idealism is nothing less than the basic human need to construct the world according to intelligent, moral principles." How do you understand this comment?

2. Bellow ends the story with Grebe's encounter with the drunken, naked black woman, who may be another embodiment of the spirit of Staika. Why does Bellow conclude the story this way? Has Grebe failed or succeeded? Is he deceiving himself?

A Question for Writing

One important theme of the story is the confrontation of appearance versus reality. How does Bellow present this theme?

Arthur Miller（1915-2005）

One of the major dramatists of the twentieth century, Arthur Asher Miller was born on 17 October 1915 in Manhattan, the second son of Isadore Miller, a prosperous Jewish coat-and-suit factory owner, who lost his wealth during the Great Depression and Augusta Barnett Miller, a schoolteacher. During Miller's years at the University of Michigan from 1934 on, most notable as the start of his playwriting career, he became aware of German expressionism, August Strindberg, and Henrik Ibsen, and he began to write plays. His second wife was the well-known Holywood actress Marilyn Monroe, whom he divorced in 1961. In 1962 he married Ingeborg Morath, a renowned photographer. Arthur Miller died in Connecticut on February 10, 2005.

Miller's early Broadway plays include *The Man Who Had All the Luck* (1944), which earned a Theater Guild award, *All My Sons* (1947), which claimed the New York Drama Critics Circle Award, and *Death of a Salesman* (1949), his masterpiece. Also in the same decade, Miller turned out *Focus* (1945), a novel about anti-Semitism. His major works of the following two decades include his adaptation of Henrik Ibsen's play *An Enemy of the People* (1950), *The Crucible* (1953), *A Memory of Two Mondays* (1955), *A View from the Bridge* (1955), *A View from the Bridge* (1956), *After the Fall* (1964) and *Incident at Vichy* (1964).

In the 1970s Miller produced three plays that reflect his continuing interest in morality, politics, and the Depression: *The Creation of the World and Other Business* (1972), *In the Country* (1977), and *The Archbishop's Ceiling* (1977). In the late 1970s he published *The Theater Essays of Arthur Miller* (1978), two screenplays for television—*Fame*

(1978) and *Playing for Time* (1980), and a book of reportage, *Chinese Encounters* (1979). His short pieces of the 1980s have been generally regarded as inferior to his early masterpieces, while his autobiography *Timebends: A Life* (1987), has been highly acclaimed. In the following decade his publications included *The Ride Down Mt. Morgan* (1992), *Homely Girl: A Life* (1992), *The Last Yankee* (1993), and *Broken Glass* (1994). Even in his 80s, Miller remained an active and important part of American theater, with the publication of *Echoes Down the Corridor* (2001).

Arthur Miller's work in all forms of writing—plays, scripts, novels, short stories, travel accounts, and essays—has made him one of America's most important literary figures. Throughout his career, he has continually addressed several distinct but related issues in both his dramatic and expository writings: the form of tragedy applicable to modern times and contemporary characters, the individual's relationship to society, and family relations, particularly interactions between fathers and sons. Insisting that "the individual is doomed to frustration when once he gains a consciousness of his own identity," Miller synthesizes elements from social and psychological realism to depict the individual's search for identity within a society that inhibits such endeavors. His plays have long been examined from the perspective of social criticism, realism, politics, and psychology, but later critics focus their attention on analyzing his work from feminist and cross-cultural perspectives and on exploring their theatrical innovation and figurative language.

Death of a Salesman

Introduction

After Arthur Miller's masterpiece, *Death of a Salesman*, opened on 10 February 1949 at the Morosco Theatre, it ran for 742 performances on

Broadway and toured the country, attracting enthusiastic audiences. Within a year of its premiere, the play was on stage in every major city in the United States, and within a few years it began its incredible run of international productions. It won important awards, including the New York Drama Critics' Circle Award and the Pulitzer Prize.

The play has been interpreted as a critique of the role of capitalism in American society. Written in realistic dialogue about ordinary people, the play is based in large part on the experiences of Miller's family during the Depression and his passionate belief in the honor of work and the difficulties of living the American dream. It illustrates Willy Loman's lifelong dream for economic success while he struggles to compete in the American economic system. Willy, a traveling salesman who has two sons, Biff and Happy, whom he has tried to raise to become men of influence and power, has been recently fired. He and his wife Linda are struggling to pay the bills, while the two sons are not helpful. As the play unfolds, it is revealed that Happy is a self-deluded, womanizing young man and Biff, home for a visit after a long absence, is a habitual thief who appears headed for a lifetime of failure. Willy, who has hoped for success for himself and his sons, feels that his best option is to commit suicide, thus giving his family some insurance money with which they will improve their lives. Throughout the play the Lomans in general cannot distinguish between reality and illusion, particularly Willy, who believes that he and his sons are great men who have what it takes to be successful and beat the business world. The problem of reality versus illusion, a major theme and a source of conflict in the play, eventually brings about Willy's downfall.

In theme and technique, the play accomplishes exactly what Miller wanted. As a modern tragedy, the play condemns human nature with pity and sorrow. Miller maintains through this play that modern literature does not require characters to be royalty or leaders and therefore fall from some great height to their demise, as in the tragedies of other eras, and that even a lowly man such as Willy could be considered a tragic hero when he is ready to lay down his life to secure his sense of personal dignity. The play is also a notable technical achievement, for in it Miller broke out of the realistic confinements of time, space and psychology, with the innovative interweaving of the "past" with the "present" and of events inside Willy's mind with those outside, which merges elements of both realism and expressionism.

The play is divided into three main parts, Act I, Act II, and the Requiem. Each section takes place on a different day. The selection includes the latter half of Act II and the short Requiem. Happy has arrived at Frank's Chop House where he and Biff and Willy are going to meet for dinner. Biff comes in, distraught, for he did not land the deal with Bill Oliver, his former boss, early that day, and now he has to somehow tell the bad news to Willy. Instead of obtaining any financial support from Oliver, Biff did not actually even see Oliver and even accidentally stole Oliver's fountain pen. Before joining his son for the dinner, Willy had a long discussion with his own boss Howard to ask for a job on the sales floor in New York instead of traveling around. But to his surprise, Howard, instead of being considerate toward the old man, fired him mercilessly. Though Happy keeps trying to turn Biff's story around so Willy will not be too upset, Biff tells the truth to Willy. Extremely depressed, Willy ends up leaving the table, and goes to the restroom where he lapses into a flashback, his habitual behavior. Late that evening, Biff and Happy return home, while Willy is outside planting the garden and talking to Uncle Ben in his illusion. The climax of the play occurs during the following huge argument between Biff and Willy. As the house settles down, Willy gets in his car and drives to his death.

From *Death of a Salesman*
Act II

CHARLEY[①]: Jesus!

[CHARLEY *stares after him a moment and follows. All light blades out. Suddenly raucous music is heard, and a red glow rises behind the screen at right. STANLEY, a young waiter, appears, carrying a tabled, allowed by* HAPPY, *who is carrying two chairs.*]

STANLEY [*putting the table down*]: That's all right, Mr Loman, I can handle it myself. [*He turn and takes the chairs from* HAPPY *and places them at the table.*]

HAPPY [*glancing around*]: Oh, this is better.

STANLEY: Sure, in the front there you're in the middle of all kinds a noise. Whenever you got a party, Mr Loman, you just tell me and I'll put you back here. Y'know, there's a lotta people they don't like it private, because when they go out they like to see a lotta action around them because they're sick and tired to stay in the house by theirself. But I know you, you ain't from Hackensack[②]. You know what I mean?

HAPPY [*sitting down*]: So how's it coming, Stanley?

STANLEY: An, it's a dog's life. I only wish during the war they'd a took me in the Army. I coulda been dead by now.

HAPPY: My brother's back, Stanley.

STANLEY: Oh, he come back, heh? From the Far West.

HAPPY: Yeah, big cattle man, my brother, so treat him right. And my father's coming too.

STANLEY: Oh, your father too!

HAPPY: You got a couple of nice lobsters?

STANLEY: Hundred per cent, big.

HAPPY: I want them with the claws.

STANLEY: Don't worry, I don't give you no mice. [HAPPY *laughs.*]
How about some wine? It'll put a head on the meal.

HAPPY: No, You remember, Stanley, that recipe I brought you from
overseas? With the champagne in it?

STANLEY: Oh, yeah, sure. I still got it tacked up yet in the kitchen.
But that'll have to cost a buck apiece anyways.

HAPPY: That's all right.

STANLEY: What'd you, hit a number or somethin'?

HAPPY: No, it's a little celebration. My brother is—I think he pulled
off a big deal today. I think we're going into business together.

STANLEY: Great! That's the best for you. Because a family business,
you know what I mean? —that's the best.

HAPPY: That's what I think.

STANLEY: 'Cause what's the difference? Somebody steals? It's in the
family. Know what I mean? [*Sotto voce*]③ Like this bartender here.
The boss is goin' crazy what kinda leak he's got in the cash register.
You put it in but it don't come out.

HAPPY [*raising his head*]: Sh!

STANLEY: What?

HAPPY: You notice I wasn't lookin' right or left, was I?

STANLEY: No.

HAPPY: And my eyes are closed.

STANLEY: So what's the—?

HAPPY: Strudel's comin'.

STANLEY [*catching on, looks around*]: Ah, no, there's no—
[*He breaks off as a furred, lavishly dressed girl enters and sits at the
next table. Both, allow her with their eyes.*]

STANLEY: Geez④, how'd ya know?

HAPPY: I got radar or something. [*Staring directly at her profile*]
Ooooooooo . . . Stanley.

STANLEY: I think that's for you, Mr Loman.

HAPPY: Look at that mouth. Oh, God. And the binoculars.

STANLEY: Geez, you got a life, Mr Loman.

HAPPY: Wait on her.

STANLEY [*going to the girl's table*]: Would you like a menu, ma'am?

GIRL: I'm expecting someone, but I'd like a—

HAPPY: Why don't you bring her—excuse me, miss, do you mind? I sell champagne, and I'd like you to try my brand. Bring her a champagne, Stanley.

GIRL: That's awfully nice of you.

HAPPY: Don't mention it. It's all company money. [*He laughs.*]

GIRL: That's a charming product to be selling, isn't it?

HAPPY: Oh, gets to be like everything else. Selling is selling, y' know.

GIRL: I suppose.

HAPPY: You don't happen to sell, do you?

GIRL: No, I don't sell.

HAPPY: Would you object to a compliment from a stranger? You ought to be on a magazine cover.

GIRL [*looking at him a little archly*]: I have been.

[STANLEY *comes in with a glass of champagne.*]

HAPPY: What'd I say before, Stanley? You see? She's a cover girl.

STANLEY: Oh, I could see, I could see.

HAPPY [*to the* GERL]: What magazine?

GIRL: Oh, a lot of them. [*She takes the drink.*] Thank you

HAPPY: You know what they say in France, don't you? 'Champagne is the drink of the complexion'⑤—Hya, Biff! [BIFF *has entered and sits with* HAPPY.]

BIFF: Hello, kid. Sorry I'm late.

HAPPY: I just got here. Uh, Miss—?

GIRL：Forsythe.

HAPPY：Miss Forsythe, this is my brother.

BIFF：Is Dad here?

HAPPY：His name is Biff. You might've heard of him Great football player.

GIRL：Really? What team?

HAPPY：Are you familiar with football?

GIRL：No, I'm afraid I'm not.

HAPPY：Biff is quarterback with the New York Giants[6].

GIRL：Well, that is nice, isn't it? [*She drinks.*]

HAPPY：Good health.

GIRL：I'm happy to meet you.

HAPPY：That's my name. Hap. It's really Harold, but at West Point they called me Happy.

GIRL [*now really impressed*]：Oh, I see. How do you do? [*She turns her profile.* [7]]

BIFF：Isn't Dad coming?

HAPPY：You want her?

BIFF：Oh, I could never make that.

HAPPY：I remember the time that idea would never come into your head. Where's the old confidence, Biff?

BIFF：I just saw Oliver—[8]

HAPPY：Wait a minute. I've got to see that old confidence again. Do you want her? She's on call.

BIFF：Oh, no. [*He turns to look at the* GIRL.]

HAPPY：I'm telling you. Watch this. [*Turning to the* GIRL] Honey? [*She turns to him.*] Are you busy?

GIRL：Well, I am. . . but I could make a phone call.

HAPPY：Do that, will you, honey? And see if you can get a friend. We'll be here for while. Biff is one of the greatest football players in the country.

GIRL [*standing up*]: Well, I'm certainly happy to meet you.

HAPPY: Come back soon.

GIRL: I'll try.

HAPPY: Don't try, honey, try hard.

[*The* GIRL *exits.* STANLEY *follows, shaking his head in bewildered admiration.*]

HAPPY: Isn't that a shame now? A beautiful girl like that? That's why I can't get married. There's not a good woman in a thousand. New York is loaded with them, kid!

BIFF: Hap, look—

HAPPY: I told you she was on call!

BIFF [*strangely unnerved*]: Cut it out, will ya? I want to say something to you.

HAPPY: Did you see Oliver?

BIFF: I saw him all right. Now look, I want to tell Dad a couple of things and I want you to help me.

HAPPY: What? Is he going to back you?

BIFF: Are you crazy? You're out of your goddam head, you know that?

HAPPY: Why? What happened?

BIFF [*breathlessly*]: I did a terrible thing today, Hap. It's been the strangest day I ever went through. I'm all numb, I swear.

HAPPY: You mean he wouldn't see you?

BIFF: Well, I waited six hours for him, see? All day. Kept, sending my name in. Even tried to date his secretary so she'd get me to him, but no soap[⑨].

HAPPY: Because you're not showin' the old confidence. Biff. He remembered you, didn't he?

BIFF [*stopping* HAPPY *with a gesture*]: Finally, about five o'clock, he comes out. Didn't remember who I was or anything. I felt like such an idiot, Hap.

HAPPY: Did you tell him my Florida idea[10]?

BIFF: He walked away. I saw him for one minute. I got so mad I could've torn the walls down! How the hell did I ever get the idea I was a salesman there? I even believed myself that I'd been a salesman for him! And then he gave me one look and—I realized what a ridiculous lie my whole life has been. We've been talking in a dream for fifteen years. I was a shipping clerk.

HAPPY: What'd you do?

BIFF [*with great tension and wonder*]: Well, he left, see. And the secretary went out. I was all alone in the waiting-room. I don't know what came over me. Hap, The next thing I know I'm in his office—panelled walls, everything. I can't explain it. I—Hap, I took his fountain pen.

HAPPY: Geez, did he catch you?

BIFF: I ran out. I ran down all eleven flights. I ran and ran and ran.

HAPPY: That was an awful dumb—what'd you do that for?

BIFF [agonized]: I don't know, I just—wanted to take something, I don't know. You gotta help me, Hap, I'm gonna tell Pop.

HAPPY: You crazy? What for?

BIFF: Hap, he's got to understand that I'm not the man somebody lends that kind of money to. He thinks I've been spiting him all these years and it's eating him up.

HAPPY: That's just it. You tell him something nice.

BIFF: I can't.

HAPPY: Say you got a lunch date with Oliver tomorrow.

BIFF: So what do I do tomorrow?

HAPPY: You leave the house tomorrow and come back at night and say Oliver is thinking it over. And he thinks it over for a couple of weeks, and gradually it fades away and nobody's the worse.

BIFF: But it'll go on for ever!

HAPPY: Dad is never so happy as when he's looking forward to something!

[WILLY *enters.*]

HAPPY: Hello, scout!

WILLY: Gee, I haven't been here in years!

[STANLEY *has followed* WILLY *in and sets a chair for him.* STANLEY *starts off but* HAPPY *stops* him]

HAPPY: Stanley!

[STANLEY *stands by, waiting for an order.*]

BIFF [*going to* WILLY *with guilt, as to an invalid*]: Sit down, Pop. You want a drink?

WILLY: Sure, I don't mind.

BIFF: Let's get a load on.

WILLY: You look worried.

BIFF: N—no. [*To* STANLEY] Scotch all around. Make it doubles.

STANLEY: Doubles, right. [*He goes.*]

WILLY: You had a couple already, didn't you?

BIFF: Just a couple, yeah.

WILLY: Well, what happened, boy? [*Nodding affirmatively, with a smile*] Everything go all right?

BIFF [*takes a breath, then reaches out and grasps* WILLY'S *hand*]: Pal ... [*He is smiling bravely, and* WILLY *is smiling too.*] I had an experience today.

HAPPY: Terrific, Pop.

WILLY: That so? What happened?

BIFF [*high, slightly alcoholic above the earth*]: I'm going to tell you everything from first to last. It's been a strange day. [*Silence. He looks, around composes himself as best he can, but his breath keeps breaking the rhythm of his voice.*] I had to wait quite a while for him, and—

WILLY: Oliver?

BIFF: Yeah, Oliver. All day, as a matter of cold fact. And a lot of—instances—facts, Pop, facts about my life came back to me. Who was it, Pop? Who ever said I was a salesman with Oliver?

WILLY: Well, you were.

BIFF: No, Dad, I was a shipping clerk.

WILLY: But you were practically—

BIFF [with determination]: Dad, I don't know who said it first, but I was never a salesman for Bill Oliver.

WILLY: What're you talking about?

BIFF: Let's hold on to the facts. Tonight, Pop. We're not going to get anywhere bullin' around. I was a shipping clerk.

WILLY [angrily]: All right, now listen to me—

BIFF: Why don't you, let me finish?

WILLY: I'm not interested in stone about the past or any crap of that kind because the woods are burning boys, you understand? There's a big blaze going on all around. I was fired today.

BIFF [shocked]: How could you be?

WILLY: I was fired, and I'm looking for a little good news to tell your mother, because, the woman has waited and the woman has suffered. The gist of it is, that I haven't got a story left in my head, Biff. So, don't give me a lecture about facts and aspects. I am not interested. Now what've you got to say to me?

[STANLBY enters with three drinks. They wait until he leaves.]

WILLY: Did you see Oliver?

BIFF: Jesus, Dad!

WILLY: You mean you didn't go up there?

HAPPY: Sure he went up there.

BIFF: I did. I—saw him. How could they fire you?

WILLY [*on the edge of his chair*]: What kind of a welcome did he give you?

BIFF: He won't even let you work on commission?

WILLY: I'm out! [*Driving*] So tell me, he gave you a warm welcome?

HAPPY: Sure, Pop, sure!

BIFF [*driven*]: Well, it was kind of—

WILLY: I was wondering if he'd remember you. [*To* HAPPY] Imagine, man doesn't see him for ten, twelve years and gives him that kind of a welcome!

HAPPY: Damn right!

BIFF [*trying to return to the offensive*]: Pop, look—

WILLY: You know why he remembered you, don't you? Because you impressed him in those days.

BIFF: Let's talk quietly and get this down to the facts, huh?

WILLY [*as though* BIFF *had been interrupting*]: Well, what happened? It's great news. Biff. Did he take you into his office or'd you talk in the waiting-room?

BIFF: Well, he came in, see, and—

WILLY [*with a big smile*]: What'd he say? Betcha he threw his arm around you.

BIFF: Well, he kinda—

WILLY: He's a fine man. [*To* HAPPY] Very hard man to see, y'know.

HAPPY [*agreeing*]: Oh, I know.

WILLY [*to* BIFF]: Is that where you had the drinks?

BIFF: Yeah, he gave me a couple of—no, no!

HAPPY [*cutting in*]: He told him my Florida idea.

WILLY: Don't interrupt. [*To* BIFF] How'd he react to the Florida idea?

BIFF: Dad, will you give me a minute to explain?

WILLY: I've been waiting for you to explain since I sat down here! What happened? He took you into his office and what?

BIFF: Well—I talked. And—and he listened, see.

WILLY: Famous for the way he listens, y'know. What was his answer?

BIFF: His answer was— [*He breaks off, suddenly angry.*] Dad, you're not letting me tell you what I want to tell you!

WILLY [*accusing, angered*]: You didn't see him, did you?

BIFF: I did see him!

WILLY: What'd you insult him or something? You insulted him, didn't you?

BIFF: Listen, will you let me out of it, will you just let me out of it!

HAPPY: What the hell!

WILLY: Tell me what happened!

BIFF [*to* HAPPY]: I can't talk to him!

[*A single trumpet note jars the ear. The light of green leaves stains the house, which holds the air of night and a dream. YOUNG BER-NARD*⑪ *enters and knocks on the door of the house.*]

YOUNG BERNARD [*frantically*]: Mrs Loman, Mrs Loman!

HAPPY: Tell him what happened!

BIFF [*to* HAPPY]: Shut up and leave me alone!

WILLY: No, no! You had to go and flunk math!

BIFF: What math? What're you talking about?

YOUNG BERNARD: Mrs Loman, Mrs Loman!

[LINDA *appears in the house, as of old.* ⑫]

WILLY [*wildly*]: Math, math, math!

BIFF: Take it easy. Pop!

YOUNG BERNARD: Mrs Loman!

WILLY [*furiously*]: If you hadn't flunked you'd've been set by now!

BIFF: Now, look, I m gonna tell you what happened, and you're going to listen to me.

YOUNG BERNARD: Mrs Loman!

BIFF: I waited six hours—

HAPPY: What the hell are you saying?

BIFF: I kept sending in my name but he wouldn't see me. So finally he ... [*He continues unheard as light fades low on the restaurant.*]

YOUNG BERNARD: Biff flunked math!

LINDA: No!

YOUNG BERNARD: Birnbaum⑬ flunked him! They won't graduate him!

LINDA: But they have to. He's gotta go to the university, Where is he? Biff! Biff!

YONG BERNARD: No, he left. He went to Grand Central⑭.

LINDA: Grand—You mean he went to Boston!

YOUNG BERNARD: Is Uncle Willy in Boston?

LINDA: Oh, maybe Willy can talk to the teacher. Oh, the poor, poor boy!

[*Light on house area snaps out.*]

BIFF [*at the table, now audible, holding up a gold fountain pen*]: ... so I'm washed up with Oliver, you understand? Are you listening to me?

WILLY [*at a loss*]: Yeah, sure. If you hadn't flunked—

BIFF: Flunked what? What're you talking about?

WILLY: Don't blame everything on me! I didn't flunk math—you did! What pen?

HAPPY: That was awful dumb, Biff a pen like that is worth—

WILLY [*seeing the pen for the first time*]: You took Oliver's pen?

BIFF [*weakening*]: Dad, I just explained it to you.

WILLY: You stole Bill Oliver's fountain pen!

BIFF: I didn't exactly steal it! That's just what I've been explaining to you!

HAPPY: He had it in his hand and just then Oliver walked in, so he got nervous and stuck it in his pocket!

WILLY: My God, Biff!

BIFF: I never intended to do it. Dad!

OPERATOR'S VOICE: Standish Arms⑮, good evening!

WILLY [shouting]: I'm not in my room!

BIFF [frightened]: Dad, what's the matter? [He and HAPPY stand up.]

OPERATOR: Ringing Mr Loman for you!

WILLY: I'm not there, stop it!

BIFF [horrified, gets down on one knee before WILLY]: Dad, I'll make good, I'll make good. [WILLY tries to get to his feet. biff holds him down.] Sit down now.

WILLY: No, you're no good, you're no good for anything.

BIFF: I am. Dad, I'll find something else, you understand? Now don't worry about—anything. [He holds up WILLY'S face.] Talk to me. Dad.

OPERATOR: Mr Loman does not answer. Shall I page him?

WILLY [attempting to stand, as though to rush and silence the OPERATOR]: No, no, no!

HAPPY: He'll strike something. Pop.

WILLY: No, no...

BIFF [desperately, standing over WILLY]: Pop, listen! Listen to me! I'm telling you something good. Oliver talked to his partner about the Florida idea. You listening? He—he talked to his partner, and he came to me ... I'm going to be all right, you hear? Dad, listen to me, he said it was just a question of the amount!

WILLY: Then you... got it?

HAPPY: He's gonna be terrific. Pop!

WILLY [trying to stand]: Then you got it, haven't you? You got it! You got it!

BIFF [agonized, holds WILLY down]: No, no. Look, Pop. I'm sup-

435

posed to have lunch with them tomorrow. I'm just telling you this so you'll know that I can still make an impression. Pop. And I'll make good somewhere, but I can't go tomorrow, see?

WILLY: Why not? You simply—

BIFF: But the pen. Pop!

WILLY: You give it to him and tell him it was an oversight!

HAPPY: Sure, have lunch tomorrow!

BIFF: I can't say that—

WILLY: You were doing a crossword puzzle and accidentally used his pen!

BIFF: Listen, kid, I took those balls years ago, now I walk in with his fountain pen? That clinches it, don't you see? I can't face him like that! I'll try elsewhere.

PAGE'S VOICE: Paging Mr Loman!

WILLY: Don't you want to be anything?

BIFF: Pop, how can I go back?

WILLY: You don't want to be anything, is that what's behind it?

BIFF [*now angry at* WILLY *for not crediting his sympathy*]: Don't take it that way! You think it was easy walking into that office after what I'd done to him? A team of horses couldn't have dragged me back to Bill Oliver!

WILLY: Then why'd you go?

BIFF: Why did I go? Why did I go? Look at you! Look at what's become of you!

[*Off left, the* WOMAN[16] *laughs.*]

WILLY: Biff, you're going to go to that lunch tomorrow, or—

BIFF: I can't go. I've got no appointment!

HAPPY: Biff, for. . . !

WILLY: Are you spiting me?

BIFF: Don't take it that way! Goddammit!

WILLY [*strikes* BIFF *and falters away from the table*]: You rotten little louse! Are you spiting me?

THE WOMAN: Someone's at the door, Willy!

BIFF: I'm no good, can't you see what I am?

HAPPY [*separating them*]: Hey, you're in a restaurant! Now cut it out, both of you! [*The girls enter.*] Hello, girls, sit down.

[*The* WOMAN *laughs, off left.*]

MISS FORSYTHE: I guess we might as well. This is Letta[17].

THE WOMAN: Willy, are you going to wake up?

BIFF [*ignoring* WILLY]: How're ya, miss, sit down. What do you drink?

MISS FORSYTHE: Letta might not be able to stay long.

LETTA: I gotta get up very early tomorrow. I got jury duty. I'm so excited! Were you fellows ever on a jury?

BIFF: No, but I been in front of them! [*The girls laugh.*] This is my father.

LETTA: Isn't he cute? Sit down with us, Pop.

HAPPY: Sit him down, Biff!

BIFF [*going to him*]: Come on, slugger, drink us under the table. To hell with it! Come on, sit down, pal.

[*On* BIFF'S *last insistence,* WILLY *is about to sit.*]

THE WOMAN [*now urgently*]: Willy, are you going to answer the door!

[*The* WOMAN'S *call pulls* WILLY *back. He starts right, befuddled.*]

BIFF: Hey, where are you going?

WILLY: Open the door.

BIFF: The door?

WILLY: The washroom. . . the door. . . where's the door?

BIFF [*leading* WILLY *to the left*]: Just go straight down.

[WILLY *moves left.*]

THE WOMAN: Willy, Willy, are you going to get up, get up, get up, get up?

[WILLY *exits left.*]

LETTA: I think it's sweet you bring your daddy along.

MISS FORSYTHE: Oh, he isn't really your father!

BIFF [*at left, turning to her resentfully*]: Miss Forsythe, you've just seen a prince walk by. A fine troubled prince. A hard-working, unappreciated prince. A pal, you understand? A good companion. Always for his boys.

LETTA: That's so sweet.

HAPPY: Well, girls, what's the programme? We're wasting time. Come on, Biff Gather round. Where would you like to go?

BIFF: Why don't you do something for him?

HAPPY: Me!

BIFF: Don't you give a damn for him Hap?

HAPPY: What're you talking about? I'm the one who—

BIFF: I sense it, you don't give a good goddam about him. [*He takes the rolled-up hose from his pocket and puts it on the table in front of HAPPY.*] Look what I found in the cellar, for Christ's sake. How can you bear to let it go on?

HAPPY: Me? Who goes away? Who runs off and—

BIFF: Yeah, but he doesn't mean anything to you. You could help him—I can't. Don't you understand what I'm talking about? He's going to kill himself, don't you know that?

HAPPY: Don't I know it! Me!

BIFF: Hap, help him! Jesus... help him... Help me, help me, I can't bear to look at his face! [*Ready to weep, he hurries out, up right.*]

HAPPY [*starting after him*]: Where are you going?

MISS FORSYTHE: What's he so mad about?

HAPPY: Come on, girls, we'll catch up with him.

MISS FORSYTHE [*as* HAPPY *pushes her out*]: Say, I don't like that temper of his!

HAPPY: He's just a little overstrung, he'll be all right!

WILLY [*off left, as the* WOAMN *laughs*]: Don't answer! Don't answer!

LETTA: Don't you want to tell your father—

HAPPY: No, that's not my father. He's just a guy. Come on, we'll catch Biff, and, honey, we're going to paint this town[⑱]! Stanley where's the check! Hey, Stanley!

[*They exit.* STANLEY *looks toward left.*]

STANLEY [*calling to* HAPPY *indignantly*]: Mr Loman! Mr Loman!

[STANLEY *picks up a chair and follows them off. Knocking is heard off left. The* WOMAN *enters, laughing.* WILLY *follows her. She is in a black slip; he is buttoning his shirt. Raw, sensuous music accompanies their speech.*]

WILLY: Will you stop laughing? Will you stop?

THE WOMAN: Aren't you going to answer the door? He'll wake the whole hotel.

WILLY: I'm not expecting anybody.

THE WOMAN: Whyn't you have another drink, honey, and stop being so damn self-centred?

WILLY: I'm so lonely.

THE WOMAN: You know you ruined me, Willy? From now on, whenever you come to the office, I'll see that you go right through to the buyers. No waiting at my desk any more, Willy. You ruined me.

WILLY: That's nice of you to say that.

THE WOMAN: Gee, you are self-centred! Why so sad? You are the saddest, self-centredest soul I ever did see-saw. [*She laughs. He kisses her.*] Come on inside, drummer boy[⑲]. It's silly to be dressing in the middle of the night. [*As knocking is heard*] Aren't you going to answer the door?

WILLY: They're knocking on the wrong door.

THE WOMAN: But I felt the knocking. And he heard us talking in here. Maybe the hotel's on fire!

WILLY [*his terror rising*]: It's a mistake.

THE WOMAN: Then tell him to go away!

WILLY: There's nobody there.

THE WOMAN: It's getting on my nerves, Willy. There's somebody standing out there and it's getting on my nerves!

WILLY [*pushing her away from him*]: All right, stay in the bathroom here, and don't come out. I n think there's a law in Massachusetts about it, so don't come out. It may be that new room clerk. He looked very mean. So don't come out. It's a mistake, there's no fire.

[*The knocking is heard again. He takes a few steps away from her, and she vanishes into the wing. The light follows him, and now he is facing* YOUNG BIFF, *who carries a suitcase.* BIFF *steps toward him. The music is gone.*]

BIFF: Why didn't you answer?

WILLY: Biff! What are you doing in Boston?

BIFF: Why didn't you answer! I've been knocking for five minutes. I called you on the phone—

WILLY: I just heard you. I was in the bathroom and had the door shut. Did anything happen home?

BIFF: Dad—I let you down.

WILLY: What do you mean?

BIFF: Dad . . .

WILLY: Biffo[20], what's this about? [*Putting his arm around* BIFF] Come on, let's go downstairs and get you a malted.

BIFF: Dad, I flunked math.

WILLY: Not for the term?

BIFF: The term. I haven't got enough credits to graduate.

WILLY: You mean to say Bernard wouldn't give you the answers?

BIFF: He did, he tried, but I only got a sixty-one.

WILLY: And they wouldn't give you four points?㉑

BIFF: Birnbaum refused absolutely. I begged him. Pop, but he won't give me those points. You gotta talk to him before they close the school. Because if he saw the kind of man you are, and you just talked to him in your way, I'm sure he'd come through for me. The class came right before practice, see, and I didn't go enough. Would you talk to him? He'd like you, Pop. You know the way you could talk.

WILLY: You're on. We'll drive right back.

BIFF: Oh, Dad, good work! Fm sure he'll change it for you!

WILLY: Go downstairs and tell the clerk I'm checkin' out. Go right down.

BIFF: Yes, sir! See, the reason he hates me. Pop—one day he was late for class so I got up at the blackboard and imitated him. I crossed my eyes and talked with a lithp㉒.

WILLY [*laughing*]: You did? The kids like it?

BIFF: They nearly died laughing!

WILLY: Yeah? What'd you do?

BIFF: The thquare root of thixthy twee is㉓... [WILLY *bursts out laughing*; BIFF *joins him.*] And in the middle of it he walked in!

[WILLY *laughs and the* WOMAN *joins in offstage.*]

WILLY [*without hesitation*]: Hurry downstairs and—

BIFF: Somebody in there?

WILLY: No, that was next door.

[The WOMAN *laugh offstage.*]

BIFF: Somebody got in your bathroom!

WILLY: No, it's the next room, there's a party—

THE WOMAN [*enters, laughing. She lisps this*]: Can I come in? There's something in the bathtub, Willy, and it's moving!

[WILLY *looks at* BIFF, *who is staring open-mouthed and horrified at the* WOMAN]

WILLY: Ah—you better go back to your room. They must be finished painting by now. They're painting her room so I let her take a shower here. Go back, go back... [*He pushes her.*]

THE WOMAN [*resisting*]: But I've got to get dressed, Willy, I can't—

WILLY: Get out of here! Go back, go back... [*Suddenly striving for the ordinary*] This is Miss Francis, Biff, she's a buyer. They're painting her room. Go back. Miss Francis, go back ...

THE WOMAN: But my clothes, I can't go out naked in the hall!

WILLY [*pushing her offstage*]: Get outa here ! Go back, go back!

[BIFF *slowly sits down on his suitcase as the argument continues offstage.*]

THE WOMAN: Where's my stockings? You promised me stockings, Willy!

WILLY: I have no stockings here!

THE WOMAN: You had two boxes of size nine sheers for me, and I want them!

WILLY: Here, for God's sake, will you get outa here!

THE WOMAN [*enters, holding a box of stockings*]: I just hope there's nobody in the hall. That's all I hope. [*To* BIFF] Are you football or baseball?

BIFF: Football.

THE WOMAN [*angry, humiliated*]: That's me too. G'night. [*She snatches her clothes from* WILLY, *and walks out.*]

WILLY [*after a pause*]: Well, better get going. I want to get to the school first thing in the morning. Get my suits out of the closet. I'll get my valise. [BIFF *doesn't move.*] What's the matter? [BIFF re-

mains motionless, tears falling.] She's buyer. Buys for J. H. Simmons[24]. She lives down the hall—they're painting. You don't imagine— [*He breaks off. After a pause*] Now listen, pal, she's just a buyer. She sees merchandise in her room and they have to keep it looking just so... [*Pause. Assuming command*] All right, get my suits. [BIFF *doesn't move.*] Now stop crying and do as I say. I gave you an order. Biff, I gave you an order! Is that what you do when I give you an order? How dare you cry? [*Putting his arms around* BIFF] Now look, Biff when you grow up you'll understand about these things. You mustn't—you mustn't over-emphasize a thing like this. I'll see Birnbaum first thing in the morning.

BIFF: Never mind.

WILLY [*getting down beside* BIFF]: Never mind! He's going to give you those points, I'll see to it.

BIFF: He wouldn't listen to you.

WILLY: He certainly will listen to me. You need those points for the U. S. of Virginia.

BIFF: I'm not going there,

WILLY: Heh? If I can't get him to change that mark you'll make it up in summer school. You've got all summer to—

BIFF [*his weeping breaking from him*]: Dad...

WILLY [*infected by it*]: Oh, my boy...

BIFF: Dad...

WILLY: She's nothing to me. Biff. I was lonely, I was terribly lonely.

BIFF: You—you gave her Mama's stockings! [*His tears break through and he rises to go.*]

WILLY [*grabbing for* BIFF]: I gave you an order!

BIFF: Don't touch me, you liar!

WILLY: Apologize for that!

BIFF: You fake! You phony little fake! You fake! [*Overcome, he turns quickly and weeping fully goes out with his suitcase.* WILLY *is left on the floor on his knees.*]

WILLY: I gave you an order! Biff, come back here or I'll beat you I Come back here I'll whip you!

[STANLEY *comes quickly in from the right and stands in front of* WILLY.]

WILLY [*shouts at* STANLEY]: I gave you an order...

STANLEY: Hey, let's pick it up, pick it up, Mr Loman. [*He helps* WILLY *to his feet.*] Your boys left with the chippies. They said they'll see you home.

[*A second waiter watches some distance away.*]

WILLY: But we were supposed to have dinner together.

[*Music is heard,* WILLY' S *theme.*]

STANLEY: Can you make it?

WILLY: I'll—sure, I can make it. [*Suddenly concerned about his clothes.*] Do I—I look all right?

STANLEY: Sure, you look all right. [*He flicks a speck off* WILLY'S *lapel.*]

WILLY: Here—here's a dollar.

STANLEY: Oh, your son paid me. It's all right.

WILLY [*putting it in* STANLEY'S *hand*]: No, take it. You're a good boy.

STANLEY: Oh, no, you don't have to...

WILLY: Here—here's some more. I don't need it any more. [*After a slight pause*] Tell me—is there a seed store in the neighbourhood?

STANLEY: Seeds? You mean like to plant?

[*As* WILLY *turns,* STANLEY *slips the money back into his jacket pocket.*]

WILLY: Yes. Carrots, peas...

STANLEY: Well, there's hardware stores on Sixth Avenue, but it may be too late now.

WILLY [*anxiously*]: Oh, I'd better hurry. I've got to get some seeds. [*He starts off to the right.*] I've got to get some seeds, right away. Nothing's planted. I don't have a thing in the ground.

[*WILLY hurries out as the light goes down. STANLEY moves over to the right after him watches him off. The other waiter has been staring at WILLY.*]

STANLEY [*to the waiter*]: Well, whatta you looking at?

[*The waiter picks up the chairs and moves off right. STANLEY takes the table and/allows him. The light fades on this area. There is a long pause, the sound of the flute coming over. The light gradually rises on the kitchen, which is empty. HAPPY appears at the door of the house, followed by BIFF. HAPPY is carrying a large bunch of long-stemmed roses. He enters the kitchen, looks around for LINDA. Not seeing her, he turns to BIFF, who is just outside the house door, and makes a gesture with his hands, indicating 'Not here, I guess'. He looks into the living-room and freezes. Inside, LINDA, unseen, is seated, WILLY'S coat on her lap. She rises ominously and quietly and moves toward HAPPY, who backs up into the kitchen, afraid.*]

HAPPY: Hey, what're you doing up? [*LINDA says nothing but moves toward him implacably.*] Where's Pop? [*He keeps backing to the right, and now LINDA is in full view in the doorway to the living-room.*] Is he sleeping?

LINDA: Where were you?

HAPPY [*trying to laugh it off*]: We met two girls, Mom, very fine types. Here, we brought you some flowers. [*Offering them to her*] Put them in your room, Ma.

[*She knocks them to the floor at BIFF'S feet. He has now come inside and closed the door behind him. She stares at BIFF, silent.*]

HAPPY: Now what'd you do that for? Mom, I want you to have some flowers—

LINDA [*cutting* HAPPY *off, violently to* BIFF]: Don't you care whether he lives or dies?

HAPPY [*going to the stairs*]: Come upstairs, Biff.

BIFF [*with a flare of disgust, to* HAPPY]: Go away from me!

[*To* LINDA] What do you mean, lives or dies? Nobody's dying around here, pal.

LINDA: Get out of my sight! Get out of here!

BIFF: I wanna see the boss㉕.

LINDA: You're not going near him!

BIFF: Where is he? [*He moves into the living-room and* LINDA *follows.*]

LINDA: [*shouting after* BIFF]: You invite him to dinner. He looks forward to it all day— [BIFF *appears in his parents' bedroom, looks around, and exits.*] —and then you desert him there. There's no stranger you'd do that to!

HAPPY: Why? He had a swell time with us. Listen, when I— [LINDA *comes back into the kitchen*] —desert him I hope I don't outlive the day!

LINDA: Get out of here!

HAPPY: Now look, Mom. . .

LINDA: Did you have to go to women tonight? You and your lousy rotten whores!

[BIFF *re-enters the kitchen.*]

HAPPY: Mom, all we did was follow BIFF around trying to cheer him up! [*To* BIFF] Boy what a night you gave me!

LINDA: Get out of here, both of you, and don't come back! I don't want you tormenting him any more. Go on now, get your things together! [*To* BIFF] you can sleep in his apartment. [*She starts to pickup the flowers and stops herself.*] Pick up this stuff, I'm not your maid any more. Pick it up, you bum, you!

[HAPPY *turns his back to her in refusal.* BIFF *slowly moves over and gets down on his knees, picking up the flowers.*]

LINDA: You're a pair of animals! Not one, not another living soul would have had the cruelty to walk out on that man in a restaurant!

BIFF [*not looking at her*]: Is that what he said?

LINDA: He didn't have to say anything. He was so humiliated he nearly limped when he came in.

HAPPY: But, Mom, he had a great time with us—

BIFF [*cutting him off violently*]: Shut up!

[*Without another word,* HAPPY *goes upstairs.*]

LINDA: You! You didn't even go in to see if he was all right!

BIFF [*still on the floor in front of* LINDA, *the flowers in his hand; with self-loathing*]: No. Didn't. Didn't do a damned thing. How do you like that, heh? Left him babbling in a toilet.

LINDA: You louse. You...

BIFF: Now you hit it on the nose! [26] [*He gets up, throws the flowers in the wastebasket.*] The scum of the earth, and you're looking at him!

LINDA: Get out of here!

BIFF: I gotta talk to the boss, Mom. Where is he?

LINDA: You're not going near him. Get out of this house!

BIFF [*with absolute assurance, determination*]: No. We're gonna have an abrupt conversation, him and me.

LINDA: You're not talking to him!

[*Hammering is heard from outside the house, off tight.* biff *turns toward the noise.*]

LINDA [*suddenly pleading*]: Will you please leave him alone?

BIFF: What's he doing out there?

LINDA: He's planting the garden!

BIFF [*quietly*]: Now? Oh, my God!

447

[BIFF *moves outside*, LINDA *following. The light dies down on them and comes up on the centre of the apron as* WILLY *walks into it. He is carrying a flashlight, a hoe, and a handful of seed packets. He raps the top of the hoe sharply to for it firmly, and then moves to the left, measuring off the distance with his foot. He holds the flashlight to look at the seed packets, reading off the instructions. He is in the blue of night.*]

WILLY: Carrots ... quarter-inch apart. Rows ... one-foot rows. [*He measures it off.*] One foot. [*He puts down a, package and measures off.*] Beets. [*He puts down another package and measures again.*] Lettuce. [*He reads the package, puts it down.*] One foot— [*He breaks off as and appears at the right and moves slowly down to him.*] What a proposition, ts, ts. Terrific, terrific. 'Cause she's suffered, Ben[27], the woman has suffered. You understand me? A man can't go out the way he came in, Ben, a man has got to add up to something. You can't, you can't— [BEN *moves toward him as though to interrupt.*] You gotta consider, now. Don't answer so quick. Remember, it's a guaranteed twenty-thousand-dollar proposition[28]. Now look, Ben, I want you to go through the ins and outs of this thing with me. I've got nobody to talk to, Ben, and the woman has suffered, you hear me?

BEN [*standing still, considering*]: What's the proposition?

WILLY: It's twenty thousand dollars on the barrelhead. Guaranteed, gilt-edged, you understand?

BEN: You don't want to make a fool of yourself. They might not honour the policy.

WILLY: How can they dare refuse? Didn't I work like a coolie to meet every premium on the nose? And now they don't pay off! Impossible!

BEN: It's called a cowardly thing, William.

WILLY: Why? Does it take more guts to stand here the rest of my life ringing up a zero?

BEN [*yielding*]: That's a point, William. [*He moves, thinking, turns.*] And twenty thousand—that is something one can fell with the hand, it is there.

WILLY [*now assured, with rising power*]: Oh, Ben, that's the whole beauty of it! I see it like a diamond, shining in the dark, hard and rough, that I can pick up and touch in my hand. Not like—like an appointment! This would not be another damned-fool appointment, Ben, and it changes all the aspects. Because he thinks I'm nothing, see, and so he spites me. But the funeral— [*Straightening up*] Ben, that funeral will be massive! The come from Maine, Massachusetts, Vermont, New Hampshire! All the old-timers with the strange licence plates—that boy will be thunder-struck, Ben, because he never realized—I am known! Rhode Island, New York, New Jersey—I am known, Ben, and he'll see it with his eyes once and for all. He'll see what I am, Ben! He's in for a shock, that boy!

BEN [*coming down to the edge of the garden*]: Hell call you a coward,

WILLY [*suddenly fearful*]: No, that would be terrible.

BEN: Yes. And a damned fool.

WILLY: No, no, he mustn't, I won't have that! [*He is broken and desperate.*]

BEN: He'll hate you, William.

[*The gay music of the boys is heard.*]

WILLY: Oh, Ben, how do we get back to all the great times? Used to he so full of light, and comradeship, the sleigh-riding in winter, and the ruddiness on his checks. And always some kind of good news coming up, always something nice coming up ahead. And never even let me carry the valises in the house, and simonizing, simonizing that little red car! Why, why can't I give him something and not have him hate me?

BEN: Let me think about it. [*He glances at his watch.*] I still have a little time. Remarkable proposition, but you've got to be sure you're not making a fool of yourself. [BEN *drifts off upstage and goes out of sight.* BIFF *comes down from the left.*]

WILLY [*suddenly conscious of* BIFF, *turns and looks up at him, then begins picking up the packages of seeds in confusion*]: Where the hell is that seed? [*Indignantly*] You can't see nothing out here! They boxed in the whole goddam neighbourhood[29]!

BIFF: There are people all around here. Don't you realize that?

WILLY: I'm busy. Don't bother me.

BIFF [*taking the hoe from* WILLY]: I'm saying good-bye to you, Pop. [WILLY *looks at him, silent, unable to move.*] I'm not coming back any more.

WILLY: You're not going to see Oliver tomorrow?

BIFF: I've got no appointment, Dad.

WILLY: He put his arm around you, and you've got no appointment?

BIFF: Pop, get this now, will you? Every time I've left it's been a fight that sent me out of here. Today I realized something about myself and I tried to explain it to you and I—I think I'm just not smart enough to make any sense out of it for you. To hell with whose fault it is or anything like that. [*He takes* WILLY'S *arm.*] Let's just wrap it up, heh? Come on in, we'll tell Mom. [*He gently tries to pull* WILLY *to left.*]

WILLY [*frozen, immobile, with guilt in his voice*]: No, I don't want to see her.

BIFF: Come on! [*He pulls again, and* WILLY *tries to pull away.*]

WILLY [*highly nervous*]: No, no, I don't want to see her.

BIFF [*tries to look into* WILLY'S *face, as if to find the answer there*]: Why don't you want to see her?

WILLY [*more harshly now*]: Don't bother me, will you?

BIFF: What do you mean, you don't want to see her? You don't want them calling you yellow, do you? This isn't your fault; it's me, I'm a bum. Now come inside! [WILLY *strains to get away.*] Did you hear what I said to you?

[WILLY *pulls away and quickly goes by himself into the house.* BIFF *follows.*]

LINDA [*to* WILLY]: Did you plant, dear?

BIFF [*at the door, to* LINDA]: All right, we had it out. I'm going and I'm not writing any more. LINDA [going to WILLY in the kitchen]: I think that's the best way, dear. 'Cause there's no use drawing it out, you'll just never get along.

[WILLY *doesn't respond.*]

BIFF: People ask where I am and what I'm doing, you don't know, and you don't care. That way it'll be off your mind and you can start brightening up again. All right? That clears it, doesn't it? [WILLY *is silent, and* BIFF *goes to him.*] You gonna wish me luck, scout! [*He extends his hand.*] What do you say?

LINDA: Shake his hand, Willy.

WILLY [*turning to her, seething with hurt*]: There's no necessity to mention the pen at all, y'know.

BIFF [*gently*]: I've got no appointment. Dad.

WILLY [*erupting fiercely*]: He put his arm around. . . ?

BIFF: Dad, you're never going to see what I am, so what's the use of arguing? If I strike oil I'll send you a cheque. Meantime forget I'm alive.

WILLY [*to* LINDA]: Spite, see?

BIFF: Shake hands, Dad.

WILLY: Not my hand.

BIFF: I was hoping not to go this way.

WILLY: Well, this is the way you're going. Good-bye.

[BIFF *looks at him a moment, then turns sharply and goes to the* stairs.]

WILLY [*stops him with*]: May you rot in hell if you leave this house!

BIFF [*turning*]: Exactly what is it that you want from me?

WILLY: I want you to know, on the train, in the mountains, in the valleys, wherever you go, that you cut down your life for spite!

BIFF: No, no.

WILLY: Spite, spite, is the word of your undoing! And when you're down and out, remember what did it. When you re rotting somewhere beside die railroad tracks, remember, and don't you dare blame it on me!

BIFF: I'm not blaming it on you!

WILLY: I won't take the rap for this, you hear?

[HAPPY *comes down the stairs and stands on the bottom step, watching.*]

BIFF: That's just what I'm telling you!

WILLY [*sinking into a chair at the table with full accusation*]: You're trying to put a knife in me—don't think I don't know what you're doing!

BIFF: All right, phony! Then let's lay it on the line. [*He whips the rubber tube out of his pocket and puts it on the table.*]

HAPPY: You crazy—

LINDA: Biff! [*She moves to grab the hose, but* BIFF *holds it down with his hand.*]

BIFF: Leave it there! Don't move it!

WILLY [*not looking at it*]: What is that?

BIFF: You know goddam well what that is.

WILLY [*caged, wanting to escape*]: I never saw that.

BIFF: You saw it. The mice didn't bring it into the cellar! What is this supposed to do, make a hero out of you? This supposed to make me sorry for you?

WILLY: Never heard of it.

BIFF: There'll be no pity for you, you hear it? No pity!

WILLY [*to* LINDA]: You hear the spite!

BIFF: No, you're going to hear the truth—what you are and what I am!

LINDA: Stop it!

WILLY: Spite!

HAPPY [*coming down toward* BIFF]: You cut it now!

BIFF [*to* HAPPY]: The man don't know who we are I The man is gonna know! [*To* WILLY] We never told the truth for ten minutes in this house!

HAPPY: We always told the truth!

BIFF [*turning on him*]: You big blow③, are you die assistant buyer? You're one of the two assistants to the assistant, aren't you?

HAPPY: Well, I'm practically—

BIFF: You're practically full of it! We all are! And I'm through with it. [*To* WILLY] Now hear this, Willy, this is me.

WILLY: I know you!

BIFF: You know why I had no address for three months? I stole a suit in Kansas City and I was in jail. [*To* LINDA, *who is sobbing*] Stop crying, I'm through with it.

[LINDA *turns away from them, her hands covering her face.*]

WILLY: I suppose that's my fault!

BIFF: I stole myself out of every good job since high school!

WILLY: And whose fault is that?

BIFF: And I never got anywhere because you blew me so full of hot air I could never stand taking orders from anybody! That's whose fault it is!

WILLY: I hear that!

LINDA: Don't, Biff!

BIFF: It's goddam time you heard that! I had to be boss big shot③ in two weeks, and I'm through with it!

WILLY: Then hang yourself! For spite, hang yourself!

BIFF: No! Nobody's hanging himself, Willy! I ran down eleven flights[②] with a pen in my hand today. And suddenly I stopped, you hear me? And in the middle of that office building, do you hear this? I stopped in the middle of that building and I saw—the sky. I saw the things that I love in this world. The work and the food and time to sit and smoke. And I looked at the pen and said to myself, what the hell am I grabbing this for? Why am I trying to become what I don't want to be? What am I doing m an office, making a contemptuous, begging fool of myself, when all I want is out there, waiting for me the minute I say I know who I am! Why can't I say that, Willy? [*He tries to make* WILLY *face him, but* WILLY *pulls away and moves to the left.*]

WILLY [*with hatred threateningly*]: The door of your life is wide open!

BIFF: Pop! I'm a dime a dozen[③], and so are you!

WILLY [*turning on him now in an uncontrolled outburst*] I am not a dime a dozen! I am Willy Loman, and you are Biff Loman!

[BIFF *starts for* WILLY, *but is blocked by* HAPPY. *In his fury* BIFF *seems on the verge of attacking his father.*]

BIFF: I am not a leader of men, Willy, and neither are you. You were never anything but a hard-working drummer who landed m the ash-can like all the rest of them! I'm one dollar ax hour, Willy! I tried seven states and couldn't raise it. A buck an hour! Do you gather my meaning? I'm not bringing home any prizes any more, and you're going to stop waiting for me to bring them home!

WILLY [*directly to* BIFF]: You vengeful, spiteful mut!

[BIFF *breaks from* HAPPY. WILLY, *in fright, starts up the stairs.* BIFF *grabs him.*]

BIFF [*at the peak of his fury*]: Pop, I'm nothing! I'm nothing, Pop. Can't you understand that? There's no spite m it any more. I'm just what I am, that's all.

［BIFF'S *fury has spent itself, and he breaks down, sobbing, holding on to* WILLY, *who dumbly fumbles for* BIFF'S *face.*］

WILLY［*astonished*］: What're you doing? What're you doing?［*To* LINDA］Why is he crying?

BIFF［*crying, broken*］: Will you let me go, for Christ's sake? Will you take that phony dream and burn it before something happens?［*Struggling to contain himself, he pulls away and moves to the stairs.*］I'll go in the morning. Put him—put him to bed.［*Exhausted,* BIFF *moves up the stairs to his room.*］

WILLY［*after a long pause, astonished, elevated*］: Isn't that—isn't that remarkable? Biff—he likes me!

LINDA: He loves you, Willy!

HAPPY［*deeply moved*］: Always did. Pop.

WILLY: Oh, Biff!［*Staring wildly*］He cried! Cried to me.［*He is choking with his love, and now cries out his promise*］That boy—that boy is going to be magnificent!

［BEN *appears in the light just outside the kitchen.*］

BEN: Yes, outstanding, with twenty thousand behind him.

LINDA［*sensing the racing of his mind*㉞, *fearfully carefully*］: Now come to bed, Willy. It's all settled now.

WILLY［*finding it difficult not to rush out of the house*］: Yes, we'll sleep. Come on. Go to sleep, Hap.

BEN: And it does take a great kind of a man to crack the jungle.

［*In accents of dread,* BEN'S *idyllic music starts up.*］

HAPPY［*his arm around* LINDA］: I'm getting married. Pop, don't forget it. I'm changing everything. I'm gonna run that department before the year is up. You'll see. Mom.［*He kisses her.*］

BEN: The jungle is dark but full of diamonds, Willy.

［WILLY *turns, moves, listening to* BEN.］

LINDA. Be good. You're both good boys, just act that way, that's all.

HAPPY: 'Night, Pop. [*He goes upstairs.*]

LINDA [*to* WILLY]: Come, dear.

BEN [*with greater force*]: One must go in to fetch a diamond out.

WILLY [*to* LINDA, *as he moves slowly along the edge of the kitchen, toward the door*]: I just want to get settled down, Linda. Let me sit alone for a little.

LINDA [*almost uttering her fear*]: I want you upstairs.

WILLY [*taking her in his arms*]: In a few minutes, Linda. I couldn't sleep right now. Go on, you look awful tired. [*He kisses her.*]

BEN: Not like an appointment at all. A diamond is rough and hard to the touch.

WILLY: Go on now. I'll be right up.

LINDA: I think this is the only way, Willy.

WILLY: Sure, it's the best thing.

BEN: Best thing!

WILLY: The only way. Everything is gonna be—go on, kid, get to bed. You look so tired.

LINDA: Come right up.

WILLY: Two minutes.

[LINDA *goes into the living-room, then reappears in her bedroom.* WILLY *moves just outside the kitchen door.*]

WILLY: Loves me. [*Wonderingly*] Always loved me. Isn't that a remarkable thing? Ben, he'll worship me for it!

BEN [*with promise*]: It's dark there, but full of diamonds.

WILLY: Can you imagine that magnificence with twenty thousand dollars in his pocket?

LINDA [*calling from her room*] Willy! Come up!

WILLY [*calling into the kitchen*]: Yes! Yes. Coming! It's very smart, you realize that, don't you, sweetheart? Even Ben sees it. I gotta go, baby. 'Bye! 'Bye! [*Going over to* BEN, *almost dancing*] Imagine?

When the mail comes he'll be ahead of Bernard again!

BEN: A perfect proposition all around.

WILLY: Did you see how he cried to me? Oh, if I could kiss him, Ben!

BEN: Time, William, time!

WILLY: Oh, Ben, I always knew one way or another we were gonna make it, Biff and I!

BEN [*looking at his watch*]: The boat. We'll be late. [*He moves slowly off into the darkness.*]

WILLY [*elegiacally, turning to the house*]: Now when you kick off, boy I want a seventy-yard boot, and get right down the field under the ball, and when you hit, hit low and hit hard, because it's important, boy. [*He swings around and faces the audience.*] There s all lands of important people in the stands, and the first dung you know... [*Suddenly realizing he is alone*] Ben! Ben, where do I...? [*He makes a sudden movement of search.*] Ben, how do I...?

LINDA [*calling*]: Willy, you coming up?

WILLY [*uttering a gasp of fear, whirling about as if to quiet her*]: Sh! [*He turns around as if to find his way; sounds, faces, voices, seem to be swarming in upon him and he flicks at them, crying, 'Sh! Sh! ' Suddenly music, faint and high, stops him. It rises in intensity, almost to an unbearable scream. He goes up and down on his toes, and rushes off around the house.*] Shhh!

LINDA: Willy?

[*There is no answer. LINDA waits. BIFF gets up off his bed. He is still in his clothes. HAPPY sits up. BIFF stands listening.*]

LINDA [*with real fear*]: Willy, answer me! Willy!

[*There is the sound of a car starting and moving away at full speed.*]

LINDA: No!

BIFF [*rushing down the stairs*]: Pop!

[*As the car speeds off, the music crashes down in a frenzy of sound, which becomes the soft pulsation of a single cello string BIFF slowly returns to his bedroom. He and HAPPY gravely don their jackets. LINDA slowly walks out of her room. The music has developed into a dead march. The leaves of day are appearing over everything. CHARLEY and BERNARD, sombrely dressed, appear and knock on the kitchen door. BIFF and HAPPY slowly descend the stairs to the kitchen as CHARLEY and BERNARD enter. All stop a moment when LINDA, in clothes of mourning, bearing a little bunch of rose, comes through the draped doorway into the kitchen. She goes to CHARLEY and takes his arm. Now all move toward the audience, through the wall-line of the kitchen. At the limit of the apron, LINDA lays down the flowers, kneels, and sits back on her heels. All stare down at the grave.*]

Requiem

CHARLEY: It's getting dark, Linda.

[LINDA *doesn't react. She stares at the grave.*]

BIFF: How about it Mom? Better get some rest, heh? They'll be closing the gate soon.

[LINDA *makes no move. Pause.*]

HAPPY [*deeply angered*]: He had no right to do that. There was no necessity for it. We would've helped him.

CHARLEY [*grunting*]: Hmmm.

BIFF: Come along, Mom.

LINDA: Why didn't anybody come?

CHARLEY: It was a very nice funeral.

LINDA: But where are all the people he knew? Maybe they blame him.

CHARLEY: Naa. It's a rough world, Linda. They wouldn't blame him.

LINDA: I can't understand it. At this time especially. First time in thirty-five years we were just about free and clear[35]. He only needed a little salary. He was even finished with the dentists.

CHARLEY: No man only needs a little salary.

LINDA: I can't understand it.

BIFF: There were a lot of nice days. When he'd come home from a trip-or on Sundays, making the stoop; finishing the cellar; putting on the new porch; when he built the extra bathroom; and put up the garage. You know something, Charley, there's more of him in that front stoop than in all the sales he ever made.

CHARLEY: Yeah. He was a happy man with a batch of cement.

LINDA: He was so wonderful with his hands.

BIFF: He had the wrong dreams. All, all, wrong.

HAPPY [*almost ready to fight* BIFF]: Don't say that!

BIFF: He never knew who he was.

CHARLEY [*stopping* HAPPY'S *movement and reply. To* BIFF]: Nobody dast blame this man. You don't understand; Willy was a salesman. And for a salesman, there is no rock bottom to the life. He don't put a bolt to a nut, he don't tell you the law or give you medicine. He's a man way out there in the blue, riding on a smile and a shoeshine. And when they start not smiling back—that's an earthquake. And then you get yourself a couple of spots on your hat, and you're finished. Nobody dast blame this man. A salesman is got to dream, boy. It comes with the territory.

BIFF: Charley, the man didn't know who he was.

HAPPY [*infuriated*]: Don't say that!

BIFF: Why don't you come with me, Happy?

HAPPY: I'm not licked that easily. I'm staying right in this city, and I'm gonna beat this racket![36] [*He looks at* BIFF, *his chin set.*] The Loman Brothers!

BIFF: I know who I am, kid.

HAPPY: All right, boy. I'm gonna show you and everybody else that

459

Willy Loman did not die in vain. He had a good dream. It's the only dream you can have—to come out number—one man. He fought it out here, and this is where I'm gonna win it for him.

BIFF [*with a hopeless glance at* HAPPY, *bends toward his mother*]: Let's go, Mom.

LINDA: I'll be with you in a minute. Go on, Charley. [*He hesitates.*] I want to, just for a minute. I never had a chance to say good-bye.

[CHARLEY *moves away*; *followed by* HAPPY. BIFF *remains a slight distance up and left of* LINDA. *She sits there, summoning herself. The flute begins, not far away, playing behind her speech.*]

LINDA: Forgive me, dear. I can't cry. I don't know what it is, but I can't cry. I don't understand it. Why did you ever do that? Help me, Willy, I can't cry. It seems to me that you're just on another trip. I keep expecting you. Willy, dear, I can't cry. Why did you do it? I search and search and I search, and I can't understand it, Willy. I made the last payment on the house today. Today, dear. And there'll be nobody home. [*A sob rises in her throat.*] We're free and dear. [*Sobbing more fully, released*] We're free. [BIFF *comes slowly toward her.*] We're free... We're free...

[BIFF *lifts her to her feet and moves out up right with her in his arms.* LINDA *sobs quietly.* BERNARD *and* CHARLEY *come together and follow them, followed by* HAPPY. *Only the music of the flute is left on the darkening stage as over the house the hard towers of the apartment buildings rise into sharp focus.*]

Notes

① **Charley**: Bernard's father, the Lomans' next door neighbor who owns his own sales firm. He and Willy do not get along very well, but they are friends nonetheless. Charliey is always the voice of reality in the play, trying to set Willy straight on the facts of Willy's situation, but he refuses to listen.

② **Hackensack**：a big city in the State of New Jersey.

③ **Sotto voce**：at a very low volume—used as a direction in music and drama.

④ **Geez**：(exclamation) gee whiz, an expression of surprise, enthusiasm, annoyance.

⑤ **Champagne is the drink of the complexion**：This is a popular French saying about the advantage of drinking champagne, making charming complexion.

⑥ **New York Giants**：a football team in New York.

⑦ **She turns her profile**：She turns her side towards the audience.

⑧ **Oliver**：Bill Oliver, Biff's former boss.

⑨ **no soap**：(Amer. slang) no way.

⑩ **Florida idea**：Biff and Happy think of a job that would enable Biff to settle down in New York. They plan to ask Bill Oliver for a loan of ten thousand dollars to begin a business of their own.

⑪ **Young Bernard**：a childhood friend of Biff, who always studied and eventually became a successful lawyer, something that Willy has trouble dealing with.

⑫ **as of old**：just as she was before.

⑬ **Birnbaum**：Biff's maths teacher.

⑭ **Grand Central**：the city's railway station.

⑮ **Standish Arms**：Myles Stanley (1584—1656) was a famous military officer in the Plymouth Colony. Here Stanley Arms is the name of the hotel where Biff found his father having an affair with a strange woman.

⑯ **Woman**：Willy's mistress.

⑰ **Letta**：Miss Forsythe and Letta are the two girls that Happy picks up at the restaurant.

⑱ **paint this town**：go out and enjoy a lively, boisterous time in bars, night-clubs, etc.

⑲ **drummer boy**: traveling salesman.

⑳ **Biffo**: Dear little Biff.

㉑ **four points**: The passing grade in US schools is 65 instead of 60. That's why Biff needs four more points to pass the exam.

㉒ **lithp**: lisp, a thick-tongued speech.

㉓ **The thquare root of thixthy twee is**: The square root of sixty-three is . . .

㉔ **J. H. Simmons**: name of a company.

㉕ **the boss**: my father, Willy.

㉖ **Now you hit it on the nose**: Now you are exactly right.

㉗ **Ben**: Willy's dead brother who appears to Willy during his flashbacks and times of trouble. Ben was a rich man who made it big in the diamond mines of Africa. Willy once was given the chance to become partners with Ben, but he refused and instead he chose the life that he currently lives.

㉘ **a guaranteed twenty-thousand-dollar proposition**: It refers to the twenty-thousand-dollar claim of compensation from a life-insurance company.

㉙ **They boxed in the whole goddam neighbourhood**: The neighborhood was enclosed by the increasing population.

㉚ **You big blow**: You big liar.

㉛ **boss big shot**: very fast.

㉜ **flights**: stories.

㉝ **a dime a dozen**: It means "I'm nothing."

㉞ **the racing of his mind**: a mental disorder.

㉟ **free and clear**: with no debts.

㊱ **beat this racket**: to be a successful salesman.

Questions for Reading Comprehension

1. What is the significance of Willy's suicide attempts? What does he expect will result from his death? Will that happen?

2. What is the meaning of the flute music heard at various points throughout the play? What/Who is this music associated with? Why is it significant that Willy's father was supposedly a flute maker and salesman?

3. What is the significance and role of the farm and farming imagery? How does it relate to business and urban life?

4. What does Willy miss about the old days? What has changed?

5. In what context does the expression "death of a salesman" occur in the play?

6. What is the meaning of Happy's comments at Willy's funeral? How about Linda's final words, "We're free . . . We're free . . . "

7. Why is the flute music the last sound to be heard?

8. Charley repeatedly tells Willy to "grow up". Is he right to think that Willy never did "grow up"?

463

Discussion Questions for Appreciation

1. How is Willy's last name expressive of his lacks and needs? What is the origin of his needs and desires?

2. Is Linda a loving wife or a self-deceiving "enabler" of family pathologies? Is she aware of Willy's infidelity?

3. What forces entrap Willy and drive him to self-destruction? What commentary on modern commerce do you think that Arthur Miller means to make?

4. What is Charley's explanation of his own success? How is Charley's son, Bernard's story significant or revealing in reference to the concerns of the play?

5. Why does Miller conceive of Happy as an even more desperate cha-

racter than Biff? Is his name Happy ironic?

A Question for Writing

The noted drama critic Eric Bentley argued that the elements of social drama in *Death of a Salesman* keep the "tragedy" from having genuinely tragic stature. Describing Willy as a "little man," Bentley insisted that such a person is "too little and too passive to play the tragic hero". Bentley and others said that, according to Miller's own definition, Willy's death is merely "pathetic" rather than tragic. Is Willy Loman a tragic figure? Or is he pathetic?

Jerome David Salinger （1919-　）

No other writer since the 1920s has achieved the heights of popularity of J. D. Salinger. But unlike Fitzgerald and Hemingway, Salinger has refused to live in public the role of American Author, and the known facts of his life are sparse and undramatic. On 1 January 1919 in New York City, Salinger was born of a prosperous Jewish father and an Irish Catholic mother. In the 1930s, he was enrolled in several institutes and had his first short story "The Young Folks" published in the March-April issue of *Story* in 1940. After that Salinger began to place his pieces in various magazines. In 1942 Salinger was drafted into the army and served until the end of World War II, during which he continued to produce commercially viable short fiction for popular magazines. Repulsed by his literary celebrity and clamoring admirers since the publication of *The Catcher in the Rye* (1951), Salinger began to withdraw into guarded seclusion during the mid-1950s. He married Claire Douglas in 1955 and they had two children. The marriage ended in 1967.

He published thirty-five short stories in various publications, including those in magazines such as *Esquire*, *Collier's*, *The Saturday Evening Post*, *Mademoiselle*, *Good Housekeeping*, and *Cosmopolitan* between 1940 and 1946, and almost exclusively the *New Yorker* from 1946 until 1951. Thirteen of these stories were collected for his three books, *Nine Stories* (1953), *Franny and Zooey* (1961), and *Raise High the Roof Beam*, *Carpenters and Seymour: An Introduction* (1963). The remaining twenty-two stories were never officially published by Salinger outside their original magazine appearances. He has published nothing since his final published work in 1965, "Hapworth 16, 1924" in *The New Yorker*. Salinger's life and literary activity since the mid-1960s are shrouded in obscurity and speculation.

His cold relationship with his father and his traumatic experiences in World War II were negative aspects of Salinger's life, which shaped his personality and his fiction. His small body of mature fiction is unified by a preoccupation with several core themes: the deprivation of childhood innocence and integrity by insensitive, superficial adults; the longing for kinship and unconditional love amid the alienation and absurdity of modern life; and the quest for spiritual enlightenment in a materialistic world. All Salinger's work is remarkable for his command of the brisk, nervous, defensive speech of young, upper-middle-class Manhattanites. His work is a unique phenomenon, important as the voice of a "silent generation" in revolt against a "phony world" and in search of mystical escapes from a deteriorating society. Events are not very important to Salinger; little happens in his stories. Although he has a sharp eye for detail, the background, setting, or locale seems to matter less than it does for almost any other American writer. Even character, as it is usually understood, seems not finally a major interest. What does interest Salinger is the human voice.

Yet despite his limited body of work, Salinger remained for at least a dozen years, from 1951 to 1963, the most popular American fiction writer with serious high-school and college students, as well as many adults alienated by the stultifying conformity of the Eisenhower years. No legitimate history of post-World War II American fiction can be written without awarding him a place in the first rank. While Salinger's fictional characters have been endlessly analyzed and discussed, the author himself has remained a mystery.

The Catcher in the Rye

Introduction

The Catcher in the Rye was the culminating project of the first three decades of J. D. Salinger's life. Within two weeks after its publication in 1951, it was listed number one on *The New York Times* best-seller list, and it stayed there for thirty weeks. It remained immensely popular for many years, especially among teenagers and young adults, largely because of its fresh, brash style and anti-establishment attitudes—typical attributes of many people emerging from the physical and psychological turmoil of adolescence. Despite its widespread popularity, some critics argue that it is too vulgar, immoral, and immature to be considered serious literature. Moreover, a few teachers and parents have censored the novel because they feel that it will corrupt children who read it.

The Catcher in the Rye portrays the emotional and physical deterioration of Holden Caulfield, a self-conscious sixteen-year-old boy whose idealistic resistance to the hypocrisy and immorality of his peers and the adult world results in his mounting estrangement. The entire novel is a flashback of the events that led up to his emotional destruction. The flashback begins with Holden leaving Pencey, the boarding school he has been attending, because of poor grades. The first-person narrative, recounted from an unspecified mental institute where Holden is convalescing after a nervous breakdown, describes his flight from Pencey and his subsequent experiences in New York City shortly before Christmas.

467

One Saturday night, after an unpleasant experience with his history teacher "Old Spencer," his roommate Stradlater and the boy next door, Robert Ackley, Holden decides to leave Pencey four days early for Christmas break. To avoid confronting his disapproving parents, Holden wanders about New York in search of meaning and companionship. His episodic rite of passage involves unsatisfying encounters with various acquaintances and strangers, including a prostitute whom he solicits though refuses to employ, resulting in a beating by her pimp; a date with his childhood friend Sally Hayes, who abandons Holden after angrily rejecting his wild suggestion that they run off together; and a brief respite with an admired teacher, Mr. Antolini, whose ambiguous late-night affection Holden reviles as a homosexual advance. Finally, he meets his sister, Phoebe, who tells him that she wants to run away with him and that she will never go back to school. Holden sees himself in her, finally changes his mind and decides to go back to his parents. He then is sent to a mental hospital for treatment.

The special point of view of the novel results in its richness of texture. By making such an unorthodox and unreliable character as Holden the narrator, Salinger subtly suggests the reader must always read between the lines like a detective looking for hints and clues that might help explain which of Holden's insights are valid and which are as phony as the phoniness he condemns. The success of the novel also lies in its elaborate structure that on the surface seems rambling and inconclusive. Instead of focusing primarily on plot development like most traditional novels, *The Catcher in the Rye* focuses more on character development. For all its seriousness, It is one of the funniest novels in American literature, and much has been said relating its humor to Mark Twain's *Huckleberry Finn*. Perhaps of equal importance with its connections to the past is the role of *Catcher* in the development of the post-World War II "black" humor, the humor that has occasional elements of cruelty, despair, and insanity.

Chapter 22 centers on the conversation between Holden and his younger sister, Phoebe, who of all of the characters in the novel, ranks as one of the most mature and perceptive. She realizes that Holden's major problem is his overwhelmingly negative attitude toward everything and everyone around him and confronts him on this fault. To the question, raised by Phoebe, of what he actually likes, Holden has difficulty finding an answer. His appreciation of the suicide of James Castle indicates his own emotional state and gives greater credence to earlier foreshadowing that Holden also will attempt to kill himself. His idealization of his younger brother, Allie, and his dream of becoming a "catcher in the rye" show Holden's affection for childhood innocence.

From *The Catcher in the Rye*
Chapter 22

When I came back, she had the pillow off her head all right—I knew she would—but she still wouldn't look at me, even though she was laying on her back and all. When I came around the side of the bed and sat down again, she turned her crazy face the other way. She was ostracizing the hell out of me. Just like the fencing team at Pencey when I left all the goddam foils on the subway.

'How's old Hazel Weatherfield?' I said. 'You write any new stories about her? I got that one you sent me right in my suitcase. It's down at the station. It's very good.'

'Daddy'll *kill* you.'

Boy, she really gets something on her mind when she gets something on her mind.

'No, he won't. The worst he'll do, he'll give me hell again, and then he'll send me to that goddam military school. That's all he'll do to me. And m the *first* place, I won't even be around. I'll be away. I'll be—I'll probably be in Colorado on this ranch.'

'Don't make me laugh. You can't even ride a horse.'

'Who can't? Sure I can. Certainly I can. They can teach you in about two minutes,' I said. 'Stop picking at that.' She was picking at that adhesive tape on her arm. 'Who gave you that haircut?' I asked her. I just noticed what a stupid haircut somebody gave her. It was way too short.

'None of your business,' she said. She can be very snotty sometimes. She can be quite snotty. 'I suppose you failed in every single subject again,' she said—very snotty. It was sort of funny, too, in a way. She sounds like a goddam school teacher sometimes, and she's only a little child.

'No, I didn't ' I said. 'I passed English. ' Then, just for the hell of it, I gave her a pinch on the behind. It was sticking way out in the breeze, the way she was laying on her side. She has hardly any behind. I didn't do it hard, but she tried to hit my hand anyway, but she missed.

Then all of a sudden, she said, 'Oh, why did you *do* it?' She meant why did I get the axe[①] again. It made me sort of sad, the way she said it.

'Oh, God, Phoebe[②], don't ask me. I'm sick of everybody asking me that,' I said. 'A million reasons why. It was one of the worst schools I ever went to. It was full of phonies. And mean guys. You never saw so many mean guys in your life. For instance, if you were having a bull session in somebody's room, and somebody wanted to come in, nobody'd let them in if they were some dopey, pimply guy. Everybody was always locking their door when somebody wanted to come in. And they had this goddam secret fraternity that I was too yellow not to join. There was this one pimply, boring guy, Robert Ackley[③], that wanted to get in. He kept trying to join, and they wouldn't let him. Just because he was boring and pimply. I don't even fell like talking about it. It was a stinking school. Take my word. '

Old Phoebe didn't say anything, but she was listening. I could tell by the back of her neck that she was listening. She always listens when you tell her something. And the funny part is she knows, half the time, what the hell you're talking about. She really does.

I kept talking about old Pencey. I sort of felt like it.

'Even the couple of *nice* teachers on the faculty, they were phonies, too,' I said. 'There was this one old guy, Mr Spencer[④]. His wife was always giving you hot chocolate and all that stuff, and they were

470

really pretty nice. But you should've seen him when the headmaster, old Thurmer, came in the History class and sat down in the back of the room. He was always coming in and sitting down in the back of the room for about a half an hour. He was supposed to be incognito or something. After a while, he'd be sitting back there and then he'd start interrupting what old Spencer was saying to crack a lot of corny jokes. Old Spencer'd practically kill himself chuckling and smiling and all, like as if Thurmer was a goddam *prince* or something'.

'Don't swear so much.'

'It would've made you puke, I swear it would,' I said. "Then, on Veterans' Day. They have this day, Veterans' Day, that all the jerks that graduated from Pencey around 1776 come back and walk all over the place, with their wives and children and everybody. You should've seen this one old guy that was about fifty. What he did was, he came in our room and knocked on the door and asked us if we'd mind if he used the bathroom. The bathroom was at the end of the corridor—I don't know why the hell he asked *us*. You know what he said? He said he wanted to see if his initials were still in one of the can doors. What he did, he carved his goddam stupid sad old initials in one of the can doors about ninety years ago, and he wanted to see if they were still there. So my room-mate and I walked him down to the bathroom and all, and we had to stand there while he looked for his initials in all the can doors. He kept talking to us the whole time, telling us how when he was at Pencey they were the happiest days of his life, and giving us a lot of advice for the future and all. Boy, did he depress me! I don't mean he was a bad guy—he wasn't. But you don't have to be a bad guy to depress somebody— you can be *good* guy and do it. All you have to do to depress somebody is to give them a lot of phoney advice while you're looking for your initials in some can door—that's all you have to do. I don't know. Maybe it wouldn't have been so bad if he hadn't been all out of breath. He was all out of breath from just climbing up the stairs, and the whole time he was looking for his initials, he kept breathing hard, with his nostrils all funny and sad, while he kept telling Stradlater⑤ and I to get all we could out of Pencey. God, Phoebe! I can't explain. I just didn't like anything that was happening at Pencey. I can't explain.'

Old Phoebe said something then, but I couldn't hear her. She had the side of her mouth right smack on the pillow, and I couldn't hear her.

'What?' I said. 'Take your mouth away. I can't hear you with your mouth that way.'

'You don't like *anything* that's happening.'

It made me even more depressed when she said that.

'Yes, I do. Yes, I do. Sure I do. Don't say that. Why the hell do you say that?'

'Because you don't. You don't like any schools. You don't like a million things. You *don't*.'

'I do! That's where you're wrong—that's exactly where you're wrong! Why the hell do you have to say that?' I said. Boy, was she depressing me.

'Because you don't she,' said. 'Name one thing.'

'One thing? One thing I like?' I said. 'Okay.'

The trouble was, I couldn't concentrate too hot. Sometimes it's hard to concentrate.

'One thing I like a lot, you mean?' I asked her.

She didn't answer me, though. She was in a cockeyed position way the hell over on the other side of the bed. She was about a thousand miles away. 'C'mon, answer me,' I said. 'One thing I like a lot, or one thing I just like?'

'You like a lot.'

'All right,' I said. But the trouble was, I couldn't concentrate. About all I could think of were those two nuns⑥ that went around collecting dough in those beat-up old straw baskets. Especially the one with die glasses with those iron rims. And this boy I knew at Elkton Hills. There was this one boy at Elkton Hills, named James Castle, that wouldn't take back something he said about this very conceited boy, Phil Stabile. James Castle called him a very conceited guy, and one of Stabile's lousy friends went and squealed on him to Stabile. So Stabile, with about six other dirty bastards, went down to James Castle's room and went in and locked the goddam door and tried to make him take back what he said, but he wouldn't do it. So they started in on him. I won't even tell you what they did to him—it's too repulsive—but he *still* wouldn't take it back, old James Castle. And you should've seen him. He was a skinny little weak-looking guy, with wrists about as big as pencils. Finally, what he did, instead of taking back what he said, he jumped out the window. I was in the shower and all, and even I could hear him land outside. But I just thought something fell out the window, a radio or a desk or something, not a *boy* or anything. Then I heard everybody running through the corridor and down the stairs, so I put on my bathrobe and I ran downstairs, too, and there was old James Castle laying right on the stone steps and all. He was dead, and his teeth, and blood, were all over the place, and nobody would even go near him. He had on this turtleneck sweater I'd lent him. All they did with the guys that were in the room with him was expel them. They didn't even go to gaol.

That was about all I could think of, though. Those two nuns I saw at breakfast and this boy James Castle I knew at Elkton Hills. The funny part is, I hardly even know James Castle, if you want to know the truth. He was one of these very quiet guys. He was in my Maths class, but he was way over on the other side of the room, and he hardly ever got up to recite or go to the blackboard or anything. Some guys in school hardly ever get up to recite or go to the blackboard. I think the only time I ever

473

even had a conversation with him was that time he asked me if he could borrow this turtleneck sweater I had. I damn near dropped dead when he asked me, I was so surprised and all. I remember I was brushing my teeth, in the can, when he asked me. He said his cousin was coming up to take him for a drive and all. I didn't even know he knew I *had* a turtleneck sweater. All I knew about him was that his name was always right ahead of me at roll call. Cabel, R., Cabel, W., Castle, Caulfield—I can still remember it. If you want to know the truth, I almost didn't lend him my sweater. Just because I didn't know him too well.

'What?' I said to old Phoebe. She said something to me, but I didn't hear her.

'You can't even think of one thing. '

'Yes, I can. Yes, I can. '

'Well, do it, then. '

'I like Allie[7], ' I said. 'And I like doing what I'm doing right now. Sitting here with you, and talking, and thinking about stuff, and—'

'Allie's *dead*. You always say that! If somebody's dead and everything, and in *Heaven*, then it isn't really—'

'I know he's dead! Don't you think I know that? I can still like him though, can't I? Just because somebody's dead, you don't just stop liking them, for God's sake—especially if they were about a thousand times nicer than the people you know that're *alive* and all. '

Old Phoebe didn't say anything. When she can't think of anything to say, she doesn't say a goddam word.

'Anyway, I like it now, ' I said. 'I mean right now. Sitting here with you and just chewing the fat and horsing[8]—'

'That isn't anything *really*! '

'It is so something *really*! Certainly it is! Why the hell isn't it?

People never think anything is anything *really*. I'm getting goddam sick of it. '

'Stop swearing. All right, name something else. Name something you'd like to *be*. Like a scientist. Or a lawyer or something. '

'I couldn't be a scientist. I'm no good in Science'.

'Well, a lawyer—like Daddy and all'

'Lawyers are all right, I guess—but it doesn't appeal to me,' I said. 'I mean they're all right if they go around saving innocent guys' lives all the time, and like that, but you don't *do* that kind of stuff if you're a lawyer. All you do is make a lot of dough and play golf and play bridge and buy cars and drink martinis and look like a hot-shot. And besides. Even if you did go around saving guys' lives and all, how would you know if you did it because you really *wanted* to save guys' lives, or you did it because what you *really* wanted to do was be a terrific lawyer, with everybody slapping you on the back and congratulating you in court when the goddam trial was over, the reporters and everybody, the way it is in the dirty movies? How would you know you weren't being a phoney? The trouble is, you *wouldn't*. '

I'm not too sure old Phoebe knew what the hell I was talking about. I mean she's only a little child and all. But she was listening, at least. If somebody at least listens, it's not too bad.

'Daddy's going to kill you. He's going to *kill* you, ' she said.

I wasn't listening, though. I was thinking about something else—something crazy. 'You know what I'd like to be?' I said. 'You know what I'd like to be? I mean if I had my goddam choice?'

'What? Stop swearing. '

'You know that song "If a body catch a body comin' through the rye"? I 'd like—'

'It's "If a body *meet* a body coining through the rye"! ' old Phoede said. 'It's a poem. By Robert *Bums*. '

475

'I *know* it's a poem by Robert Burns. '

She was right, though. It *is* "If a body meet a body coming through the rye'. I didn't know it then, though.

'I thought it was "If a body catch a body", ' I said. 'Anyway, I keep picturing all these little kids playing some game in this big field of rye and all. Thousands of little kids, and nobody's around—nobody big, I mean—except me. And I'm standing on the edge of some crazy cliff. What I have to do, I have to catch everybody if they start to go over the cliff—I mean if they're running and they don't look where they're going I have to come out from somewhere and *catch* them. That's all I'd do all day. I'd just be the catcher in the rye and all. I know it's crazy, but that's the only thing I'd really like to be. I know it's crazy. '

Old Phoebe didn't say anything for a long time. Then, when she said something, all she said was, 'Daddy's going to kill you. '

'I don't give a damn if he does, ' I said. I got up from the bed then, because what I wanted to do, I wanted to phone up this guy that was my English teacher at Elkton Hills, Mr Antolini⑨. He lived in New York now. He quit Elkton Hills. He took this job teaching English at N. Y. U. 'I have to make a phone call, ' I told Phoebe. 'I'll be right back. Don't go to sleep. ' I didn't want her to go to sleep while I was in the living-room. I knew she wouldn't, but I said it anyway, just to make sure.

While I was walking towards the door, old Phoebe said, 'Holden! ' and I turned round.

She was sitting way up in bed. She looked so pretty. 'I'm taking belching lessons from this girl, Phyllis Margulies, ' she said. 'Listen. '

I listened, and I heard something, but it wasn't much. 'Good, ' I said. Then I went out in the living-room and called up this teacher I had, Mr Antolini.

Notes

① **get the axe**: be removed or dismissed from his school.

② **Phoebe**: Holden's younger sister, a smart kid. She and Holden mutually adore and respect each other. Holden thinks about Phoebe many times during his time in New York City, and finally risks getting caught by his parents to sneak into their apartment and visit her.

③ **Robert Ackley**: Holden's unpleasant next door neighbor in his dorm at Pencey Prep, whose personal habits are dirty and whose room stinks. Holden finds Ackley disgusting but appears to feel sorry for him at the same time.

④ **Mr Spencer**: Holden's history teacher at Pencey Prep. He is at home in a bathrobe, suffering from a cold when Holden visits him for the last time before leaving Pencey. Holden wants to say goodbye to Mr. Spencer, but then regrets his choice when Mr. Spencer grills him about his future.

⑤ **Stradlater**: Holden's roommate at Pencey Prep, whom Holden calls a 'secret slob,' because, although he is handsome and well kept, his razor is rusted and cruddy. Stradlater often walks around without a shirt on and is popular with the girls.

⑥ **those two nuns**: Holden meets the two nuns, who are actually school teachers, in Grand Central Station, with whom Holden has a nice conversation at a coffee shop.

⑦ **Allie**: Allie Caulfield, Holden's younger brother, who died of leukemia, which distressed Holden to the point that he punched out all the windows in the garage. Allie had bright red hair and wrote poems all over his baseball mitt so he would have something to read on the field. Holden remembers him as extremely kind and intelligent.

⑧ **chewing the fat and horsing**: talking about something in a grumbling and playful way.

⑨ **Mr Antolini**: a favorite ex-English teacher of Holden's, whom Hold-

477

en calls later in the evening. Mr. Antolini seems kind and concerned, and gives Holden some advice about keeping his head up. Holden flees Antolini's apartment in the middle of the night, however, after he wakes up to find the teacher patting his head, fearing it is some 'perverty' move.

Questions for Reading Comprehension

1. To what does Holden compare Phoebe's behavior when she finds out that he was expelled from Pencey?

2. Where does Holden say that his father will send him when he learns that Holden has been expelled?

3. Even though Holden likes Mr. Spencer, he considers him a phony, why?

4. What was the Pencey alumnus looking for when he came to Holden and Stradlater's dorm?

5. When Holden thinks about the nuns, what does he picture them doing?

6. One of Holden's classmates, James Castle, commits suicide by jumping from a dormitory window while wearing Holden's sweater. What do you make of this?

7. What does Holden think of his dead younger brother, Allie?

8. Discuss Holden's relationship with Phoebe citing specifics from their conversations.

Discussion Questions for Appreciation

1. In *The Catcher in the Rye*, Holden seems to be talking to another person. Who do you think that person is?

2. Why do you think this novel is frequently subject to censorship efforts in public schools and libraries? How might you defend the book against efforts to remove it from school libraries?

3. Though Holden never describes his psychological breakdown directly, it becomes clear as the novel progresses that he is growing increasingly unstable. How does Salinger indicate this instability to the reader while protecting his narrator's reticence?

4. Humor plays an important role in this story. Can you find some examples in this chapter? What does this imply about Salinger's view of the human condition?

5. Holden often behaves like a prophet or a saint, pointing out the phoniness and wickedness in the world around him. Are there instances where Holden is phony, too? What do these moments reveal about his character and his psychological problems?

6. What do you think Holden's future will be?

A Question for Writing

Examine carefully the description of the "catcher in the rye." Analyze the symbols in this description. What are the kids falling into? What does "the rye" symbolize? Why does Holden want to be the catcher in the rye? What are the positive and negative aspects of his fantasy?

479

Flannery O'Connor（1925-1964）

Flannery O'Connor died, at the age of thirty-nine, a victim of the lupus that had crippled her and kept her tied to her home in Milledgeville, Georgia, home for fifteen years. Today, she is considered one of the most important American writers of short fiction. O'Connor published two novels, *Wise Blood* (1952) and *The Violent Bear It Away* (1960), but her greatest achievements lie in her dozen short stories: *The Complete Stories*, published posthumously in 1971, won the National Book Award for Fiction. Her best known major stories include "A Good Man Is Hard to Find," "The Life You Save May Be Your Own," "Good Country People," and "Everything That Rises Must Converge."

Many critical works have emphasized the bizarre effects of reading O'Connor's fiction, which, at its best, powerfully blends the elements of Southwestern humor, the Southern grotesque, Catholic and Christian theology and philosophy, realism and romance. It is probably the comic irony of her stories that proves fundamentally attractive—from the religious to the atheistic humanists who she loves to ridicule in some of her best fiction, a fiction that questions the modern disbelief in the mysteries of Christianity. Her stories teem with images of the grotesque, and her characters include a gallery of men and women who are mentally or physically twisted. In one story after another, O'Connor explores the frustration or the sheer boredom that leads to violence, to murder, suicide, or cold despair. A Catholic, she believes in evil and grace, that is, salvation through Christ.

Although O'Connor's purpose is largely instructional, her short stories are far from being didactic abstractions. Her grotesque characters are firmly rooted in the world she saw around her. The incongruity re-

sults from the conflict between the ideal held by the grotesque character
and his actual deformed condition; that is, the effect of the grotesque relies heavily on the delicate balance between the terrible and the comic.
Hugh Holman sees comedy or humor in O'Connor not as merely a comic
relief from the tragic elements with which it coexists, but as central to
her vision of mankind:

Her vision of man is not of a cloud-scraping demigod, a wielder of
vast powers, but of a frail, weak creature, imperfect and incomplete in
all his parts. To embody such a vision calls for either comedy or pathos,
and pathos was alien to Flannery O'Connor's nature and beliefs. ①

A typical O'Connor's story deals with hubris—that is, overweening
pride and arrogance—and the characters' arrogance often takes on a spiritual dimension. A proud protagonist—usually a woman—considers herself impeccable as regards her own abilities, her Christian goodness, and
her property. But the central character has hidden fears that are brought
to the surface, always comically, through an outsider figure—often an
ironic agent of God, who serves to transform the protagonist's perception.

O'Connor's South is a place of primitive emotion, ugliness, and bad
luck, relieved only at long intervals by humor, synonymous with beauty
or hope. The grotesque in fiction flourishes during times of cultural crisis. O'Connor's fiction reflects the tenor of the South in her lifetime; it
has been forced into a cultural crisis more intense than that of other regions because it is faced with keeping pace with the rest of the country,
while striving to maintain its identity. "The Southern grotesque is kept
alive in the 1980s by Bobbie Ann Mason. Mason's grotesque is grandchild

481

----

① 135, "The Freak Endures: The Southern Grotesque," form *Since Flannery
O'Connor*, *Essays on the contemporary American Short Story*, Loren Logsdon and
Charles W. Mayer (eds.), 1987, Western Illinois University.

of the grotesque as described and practiced by Flannery O'Connor. "①
Less apparent in its moral intent than that of O'Connor's fiction, Mason's
Shiloh and Other Stories (1982) also dramatizes the incongruities resulting from the clash between traditional Southern lifestyles and encroa-
ching modern life. O'Connor's influence, of course, goes beyond the
South. In his essay "On Writing," Raymond Carver confesses that not
until he read Flannery O'Connor's essay did he meet anyone who shared
what he had thought was his "uncomfortable secret" of not knowing often
where a story was going, and he acknowledges being greatly heartened
by O'Connor's belief that the writing process is itself an "act of
discovery". Such remarks, however, underestimate the extent of
Carver's respect for the intensity of O'Connor's vision and the sophistication of her narrative artistry. In fact, they are like soul-mates in that
they both use humor when faced with disaster in their fiction.

482

The Life You Save May Be Your Own

Introduction

"The Life You Save May Be Your Own" is one of the ten short stories collected in Flannery O'Conner's first published collection *A Good
Man Is Hard to Find and Other Stories* (1955), which even more than
her first novel, quickly established her as a masterful storyteller, endowed with vision, an unfailing sense for language and a supreme feeling
for the use of irony. The collection is an excellent place to start exploring
her work. The characters in this collection, mostly Southerners, are mis-
fits, wanderers, and souls searching for faith and absolution. The end-

---

① 137, "The Freak Endures; The Southern Grotesque," from *since Flannery
O'Connor, Essays on the Contemporary American Short Story*. Loren Logsolon and
Charles W. Mayer (eds.), 1987, Western Illinois University.

ings of O'Connor's stories are as far from your standard happy ending as you can imagine.

The short story "The Life You Save May Be Your Own" is counted among O'Connor's six winners of the O. Henry Award for Short Fiction. "The Life You Save May Be Your Own", a cautionary road sign commonly seen in the 1950s, becomes the title and motto of the story about a wanderer's encounter with a mother and her handicapped daughter who take him in, only to use that purported charity to their own advantage. A one-armed tramp, appropriately named "Mr. Shiftlet", walks up to a run-down farm where an old woman, Mrs. Crater, and her mute, retarded daughter, Lucynell live. Mr. Shiftlet persuades the old woman to hire him for work around the farm and for repairing a car. Over a period of a few weeks he repairs the car, which is what he really wants, and accepts the mother's offering to marry Lucynell if her mother will give him some money. Mr. Shiftlet convinces Mrs. Crater that he must take Lucynell on a real honeymoon in Mrs. Crater's car he has fixed up. After the wedding Mr. Shiftlet takes Lucynell on a honeymoon, but abandons her in a country diner the first day, claiming she's a hitchhiker. This story finds two unsavory characters using each other. Mr. Shiftlet wants the car; Lucynell's mother wants to get rid of Lucynell in some "clean" way. In the end, they both get what they want, while Lucynell is left dozing in some diner, unable to communicate, miles from home. The ironic tone all through this work is both humorous and painful. The title is, of course, ironic. Not only are no lives saved, several are damaged.

Through imagery, dialogue, and moments of revelation, O'Connor explores the themes of morality and religion, both frequent concerns in her work. Within the sparse, apparently simple plot of the story, O'Connor constructs a world torn between renewal and emptiness, natural beauty and crass materialism, compassion and cruelty.

483

The Life You Save May Be Your Own

The old woman and her daughter were sitting on their porch when Mr. Shiftlet came up their road for the first time. The old woman slid to the edge of her chair and leaned forward, shading her eyes from the piercing sunset with her hand. The daughter could not see far in front of her and continued to play with her fingers. Although the old woman lived in this desolate spot with only her daughter and she had never seen Mr. Shiftlet before, she could tell, even from a distance, that he was a tramp and no one to be afraid of. His left coat sleeve was folded up to show there was only half an arm in it and his gaunt figure listed slightly to the side as if the breeze were pushing him. He had on a black town suit and a brown felt hat that was turned up in the front and down in the back and he carried a tin tool box by a handle. He came on, at an amble, up her road, his face turned toward the sun which appeared to be balancing itself on the peak of a small mountain.

The old woman didn't change her position until he was almost into her yard; then she rose with one hand fisted on her hip. The daughter, a large girl in a short blue organdy dress, saw him all at once and jumped up and began to stamp and point and make excited speechless sounds.

Mr. Shiftlet stopped just inside the yard and set his box on the ground and tipped his hat at her as if she were not in the least afflicted; then he turned toward the old woman and swung the hat all the way off. He had long black slick hair that hung flat from a part in the middle to beyond the tips of his ears on either side. His face descended in forehead for more than half its length and ended suddenly with his features just balanced over a jutting steel-trap jaw. He seemed to be a young man but he had a look of composed dissatisfaction as if he understood life thoroughly.

"Good evening," the old woman said. She was about the size of a cedar fence post and she had a man's gray hat pulled down low over her head.

The tramp stood looking at her and didn't answer. He turned his back and faced the sunset. He swung both his whole and his short arm up slowly so that they indicated an expanse of sky and his figure formed a crooked cross. The old woman watched him with her arms folded across her chest as if she were the owner of the sun, and the daughter watched, her head thrust forward and her fat helpless hands hanging at the wrists. She had long pink-gold hair and eyes as blue as a peacock's neck.

He held the pose for almost fifty seconds and then he picked up his box and came on to the porch and dropped down on the bottom step. "Lady," he said in a firm nasal voice, "I'd give a fortune to live where I could see me a sun do that every evening."

"Does it every evening," the old woman said and sat back down. The daughter sat down too and watched him with a cautious sly look as if he were a bird that had come up very close. He leaned to one side, rooting in his pants pocket, and in a second he brought out a package of chewing gum and offered her a piece. She took it and unpeeled it and began to chew without taking her eyes off him. He offered the old woman a piece but she only raised her upper lip to indicate she had no teeth.

Mr. Shiftlet's pale sharp glance had already passed over everything in the yard—the pump near the corner of the house and the big fig tree that three or four chickens were preparing to roost in—and had moved to a shed where he saw the square rusted back of an automobile. "You ladies drive?" he asked.

"That car ain't run in fifteen year," the old woman said. "The day my husband died, it quit running."

"Nothing is like it used to be, lady," he said. "The world is almost rotten."

485

"That's right," the old woman said. "You from around here?"

"Name Tom T. Shiftlet," he murmured, looking at the tires.

"I'm pleased to meet you," the old woman said. "Name Lucynell Crater and daughter Lucynell Crater. What you doing around here, Mr. Shiftlet?"

He judged the car to be about a 1928 or '29 Ford. "Lady," he said, and turned and gave her his full attention, "lemme tell you something. There's one of these doctors in Atlanta that's taken a knife and cut the human heart-the human heart," he repeated, leaning forward, "out of a man's chest and held it in his hand," and he held his hand out, palm up, as if it were slightly weighted with the human heart, "and studied it like it was a day-old chicken, and lady," he said, allowing a long significant pause in which his head slid forward and his clay-colored eyes brightened, "he don't know no more about it than you or me."

"That's right," the old woman said.

"Why, if he was to take that knife and cut into every corner of it, he still wouldn't know no more than you or me. What you want to bet?"

"Nothing," the old woman said wisely. "Where you come from, Mr. Shiftlet?"

He didn't answer. He reached into his pocket and brought out a sack of tobacco and a package of cigarette papers and rolled himself a cigarette, expertly with one hand, and attached it in a hanging position to his upper lip. Then he took a box of wooden matches from his pocket and struck one on his shoe. He held the burning match as if he were studying the mystery of flame while it traveled dangerously toward his skin. The daughter began to make loud noises and to point to his hand and shake her finger at him, but when the flame was just before touching him, he leaned down with his hand cupped over it as if he were going to set fire to his nose and lit the cigarette.

He flipped away the dead match and blew a stream of gray into the evening. A sly look came over his face. "Lady," he said, "nowadays, people'll do anything anyways. I can tell you my name is Tom T. Shiftlet and I come from Tarwater, Tennessee, but you never have seen me before: how you know I ain't lying? How you know my name ain't Aaron Sparks, lady, and I come from Singleberry, Georgia, or how you know it's not George Speeds and I come from Lucy, Alabama, or how you know I ain't Thompson Bright from Toolafalls, Mississippi?"

"I don't know nothing about you," the old woman muttered, irked.

"Lady," he said, "people don't care how they lie. Maybe the best I can tell you is, I'm a man; but listen lady," he said and paused and made his tone more ominous still, "what is a man?"

The old woman began to gum a seed. "What you carry in that tin box, Mr. Shiftlet?" she asked.

"Tools," he said, put back. "I'm a carpenter."

"Well, if you come out here to work, I'll be able to feed you and give you a place to sleep but I can't pay. I'll tell you that before you begin," she said.

There was no answer at once and no particular expression on his face. He leaned back against the two-by-four that helped support the porch roof. "Lady," he said slowly, "there's some men that some things mean more to them than money." The old woman rocked without comment and the daughter watched the trigger that moved up and down in his neck. He told the old woman then that all most people were interested in was money, but he asked what a man was made for. He asked her if a. man was made for money, or what. He asked her what she thought she was made for but she didn't answer, she only sat rocking and wondered if a one-armed man could put a new roof on her garden house. He asked a lot of questions that she didn't answer. He told her that he was twenty-eight years old and had lived a varied life. He had been a gospel singer, a foreman on the railroad, an assistant in an undertaking parlor, and he had come over the radio for three months with Uncle Roy and his Red Creek Wranglers. He said he had fought and bled in the Arm Service of his country and visited every foreign land and that everywhere he had seen people that didn't care if they did a thing one way or another. He said he hadn't been raised thataway.

A fat yellow moon appeared in the branches of the fig tree as if it were going to roost there with the chickens. He said that a man had to escape to the country to see the world whole and that he wished he lived in a desolate place like this where he could see the sun go down every evening like God made it to do.

"Are you married or are you single?" the old woman asked.

There was a long silence. "Lady," he asked finally, "where would you find you an innocent woman today'? I wouldn't have any of this trash I could just pick up."

The daughter was leaning very far down, hanging her head almost between her knees, watching him through a triangular door she had made in her overturned hair; and she suddenly fell in a heap on the floor and began to whimper. Mr. Shiftlet straightened her out and helped her get back in the chair.

"Is she your baby girl?" he asked.

"My only," the old woman said, "and she's the sweetest girl in the world. I wouldn't give her up for nothing on earth. She's smart too. She can sweep the floor, cook, wash, feed the chickens, and hoe. I wouldn't give her up for a casket of jewels."

"No," he said kindly, "don't ever let any man take her away from you."

"Any man come after her," the old woman said, " 'll have to stay around the place."

Mr. Shiftlet's eye in the darkness was focused on a part of the automobile bumper that glittered in the distance. "Lady," he said, jerking his short arm up as if he could point with it to her house and yard and pump, "there ain't a broken thing on this plantation that I couldn't fix for you, one-arm jackleg or not. I'm a man," he said with a sullen dignity, "even if I ain't a whole one. I got," he said, tapping his knuckles on the floor to emphasize the immensity of what he was going to say, "a moral intelligence!" and his face pierced out of the darkness into a shaft of doorlight and he stared at her as if he were astonished himself at this impossible truth.

The old woman was not impressed with the phrase. "I told you you could hang around and work for food," she said, "if you don't mind sleeping in that car yonder."

"Why listen, Lady," he said with a grin of delight, "the monks of old slept in their coffins!"

"They wasn't as advanced as we are," the old woman said.

The next morning he began on the roof of the garden house while Lucynell, the daughter, sat on a rock and watched him work. He had not been around a week before the change he had made in the place was apparent. He had patched the front and back steps, built a new hog pen, restored a fence, and taught Lucynell, who was completely deaf and had never said a word in her life, to say the word "bird."

The big rosy-faced girl followed him everywhere, saying "Burrttddt ddbirrrttdt," and clapping her hands. The old woman watched from a distance, secretly pleased. She was ravenous for a son-in-law.

Mr. Shiftlet slept on the hard narrow back seat of the car with his feet out the side window. He had his razor and a can of water on a crate that served him as a bedside table and he put up a piece of mirror against the back glass and kept his coat neatly on a hanger that he hung over one of the windows.

In the evenings he sat on the steps and talked while the old woman

489

and Lucynell rocked violently in their chairs on either side of him. The old woman's three mountains were black against the dark blue sky and were visited off and on by various planets and by the moon after it had left the chickens. Mr. Shiftlet pointed out that the reason he had improved this plantation was because he had taken a personal interest in it. He said he was even going to make the automobile run.

He had raised the hood and studied the mechanism and he said he could tell that the car had been built in the days when cars were really built. "You take now," he said, "one man puts in one bolt and another man puts in another bolt and another man puts in another bolt so that it's a man for a bolt. That's why you have to pay so much for a car: you're paying all those men. Now if you didn't have to pay but one man, you could get you a cheaper car and one that had had a personal interest taken in it, and it would be a better car." The old woman agreed with him that this was so.

Mr. Shiftlet said that the trouble with the world was that nobody cared, or stopped and took any trouble. He said he never would have been able to teach Lucynell to say a word if he hadn't cared and stopped long enough.

"Teach her to say something else," the old woman said.

"What you want her to say next?" Mr. Shiftlet asked.

The old woman's smile was broad and toothless and suggestive. "Teach her to say 'sugarpie,'" she said.

Mr. Shiftlet already knew what was on her mind.

The next day he began to tinker with the automobile and that evening he told her that if she would buy a fan belt, he would be able to make the car run.

The old woman said she would give him the money. "You see that girl yonder?" she asked, pointing to Lucynell who was sitting on the floor a foot away, watching him, her eyes blue even in the dark. "If it was ever a man wanted to take her away, I would say, 'No man on earth is going to take that sweet girl of mine away from me!' but if he was to say, 'Lady, I don't want to take her away, I want her right here,' I would say, 'Mister, I don't blame you none. I wouldn't pass up a chance to live in a permanent place and get the sweetest girl in the world myself. You ain't no fool,' I would say."

"How old is she?" Mr. Shiftlet asked casually.

"Fifteen, sixteen," the old woman said. The girl was nearly thirty but because of her innocence it was impossible to guess.

"It would be a good idea to paint it too," Mr. Shiftlet remarked. "You don't want it to rust out."

"We'll see about that later," the old woman said.

The next day he walked into town and returned with the parts he needed and a can of gasoline. Late in the afternoon, terrible noises issued from the shed and the old woman rushed out of the house, thinking Lucynell was somewhere having a fit. Lucynell was sitting on a chicken crate, stamping her feet and screaming, "Burrddttt! bddurrddtttt!" but her fuss was drowned out by the car. With a volley of blasts it emerged from the shed, moving in a fierce and stately way. Mr. Shiftlet was in the driver's seat, sitting very erect. He had an expression of serious modesty on his face as if he had just raised the dead.

That night, rocking on the porch, the old woman began her business at once. "You want you an innocent woman, don't you?" she asked sympathetically. "You don't want none of this trash."

"No'm, I don't," Mr. Shiftlet said.

"One that can't talk," she continued, "can't sass you back or use foul language. That's the kind for you to have. Right there," and she pointed to Lucynell sitting cross-legged in her chair, holding both feet in her hands.

"That's right," he admitted. "She wouldn't give me any trouble."

491

"Saturday," the old woman said, "you and her and me can drive into town and get married."

Mr. Shiftlet eased his position on the steps.

"I can't get married right now," he said. "Everything you want to do takes money and I ain't got any."

"What you need with money?" she asked.

"It takes money," he said. "Some people'll do anything anyhow these days, but the way I think, I wouldn't marry no woman that I couldn't take on a trip like she was somebody. I mean take her to a hotel and treat her. I wouldn't marry the Duchesser Windson[①]," he said firmly, "unless I could take her to a hotel and give her something good to eat."

"I was raised thataway and there ain't a thing I can do about it. My old mother taught me how to do."

"Lucynell don't even know what a hotel is," the old woman muttered. "Listen here, Mr. Shiftlet," she said, sliding forward in her chair, "you'd be getting a permanent house and a deep well and the most innocent girl in the world. You don't need no money. Lemme tell you something: there ain't any place in the world for a poor disabled friendless drifting man."

The ugly words settled in Mr. Shiftlet's head like a group of buzzards in the top of a tree. He didn't answer at once. He rolled himself a cigarette and lit it and then he said in an even voice, "Lady, a man is divided into two parts, body and spirit."

The old woman clamped her gums together.

"A body and a spirit," he repeated. "The body, lady, is like a house: it don't go anywhere; but the spirit, lady, is like a automobile: always on the move, always . . ."

"Listen, Mr. Shiftlet," she said, "my well never goes dry and my house is always warm in the winter and there's no mortgage on a thing about this place. You can go to the courthouse and see for yourself. And yonder under that shed is a fine automobile." She laid the bait carefully. "You can have it painted by Saturday. I'll pay for the paint."

In the darkness, Mr. Shiftlet's smile stretched like a weary snake waking up by a fire. After a second he recalled himself and said, "I'm only saying a man's spirit means more to him than anything else. I would have to take my wife off for the week end without no regards at all for cost. I got to follow where my spirit says to go."

"I'll give you fifteen dollars for a week-end trip," the old woman said in a crabbed voice. "That's the best I can do."

"That wouldn't hardly pay for more than the gas and the hotel," he said. "It wouldn't feed her."

"Seventeen-fifty," the old woman said. "That's all I got so it isn't any use you trying to milk me. You can take a lunch."

Mr. Shiftlet was deeply hurt by the word "milk." He didn't doubt that she had more money sewed up in her mattress but he had already told her he was not interested in her money. "I'll make that do," he said and rose and walked off without treating② with her further.

On Saturday the three of them drove into town in the car that the paint had barely dried on and Mr. Shiftlet and Lucynell were married in the Ordinary's③ office while the old woman witnessed. As they came out of the courthouse, Mr. Shiftlet began twisting his neck in his collar. He looked morose and bitter as if he had been insulted while someone held him. "That didn't satisfy me none," he said. "That was just something a woman in an office did, nothing but paper work and blood tests. What do they know about my blood? If they was to take my heart and cut it out," he said, "they wouldn't know a thing about me. It didn't satisfy me at all."

"It satisfied the law," the old woman said sharply.

"The law," Mr. Shiftlet said and spit. "It's the law that don't satisfy me. "

He had painted the car dark green with a yellow band around it just under the windows. The three of them climbed in the front seat and the old woman said, "Don't Lucynell look pretty? Looks like a baby doll." Lucynell was dressed up in a white dress that her mother had uprooted from a trunk and there was a Panama hat on her head with a bunch of red wooden cherries on the brim. Every now and then her placid expression was changed by a sly isolated little thought like a shoot of green in the desert. "You got a prize!" the old woman said.

Mr. Shiftlet didn't even look at her.

They drove back to the house to let the old woman off and pick up the lunch. When they were ready to leave, she stood staring in the window of the car, with her fingers clenched around the glass. Tears began to seep sideways out of her eyes and run along the dirty creases in her face. "I ain't ever been parted with her for two days before," she said.

Mr. Shiftlet started the motor.

"And I wouldn't let no man have her but you because I seen you would do right. Good-bye, Sugarbaby," she said, clutching at the sleeve of the white dress. Lucynell looked straight at her and didn't seem to see her there at all. Mr. Shiftlet eased the car forward so that she had to move her hands.

The early afternoon was clear and open and surrounded by pale blue sky. Although the car would go only thirty miles an hour, Mr. Shiftlet imagined a terrific climb and dip and swerve that went entirely to his head so that he forgot his morning bitterness. He had always wanted an automobile but he had never been able to afford one before. He drove very fast because he wanted to make Mobile[④] by nightfall.

Occasionally he stopped his thoughts long enough to look at Lucynell in the seat beside him. She had eaten the lunch as soon as they were out of the yard and now she was pulling the cherries off the hat one by one and throwing them out the window. He became depressed in spite of the car. He had driven about a hundred miles when he decided that she must be hungry again and at the next small town they came to, he stopped in front of an aluminum-painted eating place called The Hot Spot and took her in and ordered her a plate of ham and grits. The ride had made her sleepy and as soon as she got up on the stool, she rested her head on the counter and shut her eyes. There was no one in The Hot Spot but Mr. Shiftlet and the boy behind the counter, a pale youth with a greasy rag hung over his shoulder. Before he could dish up the food, she was snoring gently.

"Give it to her when she wakes up," Mr. Shiftlet said. "I'll pay for it now."

The boy bent over her and stared at the long pink-gold hair and the half-shut sleeping eyes. Then he looked up and stared at Mr. Shiftlet. "She looks like an angel of Gawd," he murmured.

"Hitch-hiker," Mr. Shiftlet explained. "I can't wait. I got to make Tuscaloosa⑤."

The boy bent over again and very carefully touched his finger to a strand of the golden hair and Mr. Shiftlet left.

He was more depressed than ever as he drove on by himself. The late afternoon had grown hot and sultry and the country had flattened out. Deep in the sky a storm was preparing very slowly and without thunder as if it meant to drain every drop of air from the earth before it broke. There were times when Mr. Shiftlet preferred not to be alone. He felt too that a man with a car had a responsibility to others and he kept his eye out for a hitch-hiker. Occasionally he saw a sign that warned: "Drive carefully. The life you save may be your own."

The narrow road dropped off on either side into dry fields and here and there a shack or a filling station stood in a clearing. The sun began to set directly in front of the automobile. It was a reddening ball that through his windshield was slightly flat on the bottom and top. He saw a boy in overalls and a gray hat standing on the edge of the road and he slowed the car down and stopped in front of him. The boy didn't have his hand raised to thumb the ride, he was only standing there, but he had a small cardboard suitcase and his hat was set on his head in a way to indicate that he had left somewhere for good. "Son," Mr. Shiftlet said, "I see you want a ride."

The boy didn't say he did or he didn't but he opened the door of the car and got in, and Mr. Shiftlet started driving again. The child held the suitcase on his lap and folded his arms on top of it. He turned his head and looked out the window away from Mr. Shiftlet. Mr. Shiftlet felt oppressed. "Son," he said after a minute, "I got the best old mother in the world so I reckon you only got the second best."

The boy gave him a quick dark glance and then turned his face back out the window.

"It's nothing so sweet," Mr. Shiftlet continued, "as a boy's mother. She taught him his first prayers at her knee, she give him love when no other would, she told him what was right and what wasn't, and she seen that he done the right thing. Son," he said, "I never rued a day in my life like the one I rued when I left that old mother of mine."

The boy shifted in his seat but he didn't look at Mr. Shiftlet. He unfolded his arms and put one hand on the door handle.

"My mother was a angel of Gawd," Mr. Shiftlet said in a very strained voice. "He took her from heaven and giver to me and I left her." His eyes were instantly clouded over with a mist of tears. The car was barely moving.

The boy turned angrily in the seat. "You go to the devil!" he cried. "My old woman is a flea bag and yours is a stinking pole cat!" and with that he flung the door open and jumped out with his suitcase into the ditch.

Mr. Shiftlet was so shocked that for about a hundred feet he drove along slowly with the door stiff open. A cloud, the exact color of the boy's hat and shaped like a turnip, had descended over the sun, and another, worse looking, crouched behind the car. Mr. Shiftlet felt that the rottenness of the world was about to engulf him. He raised his arm and let it fall again to his breast. "Oh Lord!" he prayed. "Break forth and wash the slime from this earth!"

The turnip continued slowly to descend. After a few minutes there was a guffawing peal of thunder from behind and fantastic raindrops, like tin-can tops, crashed over the rear of Mr. Shiftlet's car. Very quickly he stepped on the gas and with his stump sticking out the window he raced the galloping shower into Mobile.

Notes

① **Duchesser Windsor**: Shiftlet is referring to the American woman for whom Britain's King Edward VIII gave up the throne in 1936. The new King gave them the titles Duke and Duchess of Windsor.

② **treating**: negotiating or discussing terms.

③ **Ordinary**: A local judge who, in many states, is called the "justice of the peace."

④ **Mobile**: a port city in southwestern Alabama.

⑤ **Tuscaloosa**: a city nearly 200 miles north of Mobile, in west central Alabama.

Questions for Reading Comprehension

1. Does the title of the story sound like a noble or a mean slogan? Does it carry any thematic implication?

2. How do you measure the significance of the setting of the story, the wasteland, a "desolate spot"?

3. Both the mother and the daughter are named Lucynell Crater in the

story. How would you understand the relationship between the mother and the daughter?

4. Does the description of the characters' physical appearances have anything to do with their spiritual personalities?

5. What symbolic significance would you associate with the word "bird" in regard to Lucynell? The boy in the restaurant refers to Lucynell as "an angel of Gawd". Which other person is referred to by the same phrase?

6. What prayer does Mr. Shiftlet say to God? And how is he answered?

Discussion Questions for Appreciation

1. According to O'Connor, a grotesque character is one who is "forced to meet the extremes of his own nature". How do the characters in this story fit into this characterization?

2. In many of O'Connor's stories there is a conflict between the world of the spirit and the world of the body. In this story, Mr. Shiftlet claims to be more concerned with things of the spirit than with objects as he says, "Lady, a man is divided into two parts, body and spirit. . . The body, lady, is like a house: it don't go anywhere; but the spirit, lady, is like a automobile, always on the move. . . . " How do the characters in this story deal with their own conflicts between the spirit and the body?

3. Flannery O'Connor once said she had some trouble with the end of that story, "I got it up to his taking the girl away and leaving her. I knew I wanted to do that much, and I did it. But the story wasn't complete. I needed that little boy on the side of the road, and that little boy is what makes the story work. " What does the boy appearing near the end of the story represent?

A Question for Writing

O'Connor once said, "All of my stories are about the action of grace on a character who is not very willing to support it." Evaluate the characters in this story in terms of this quotation.

Allen Ginsberg（1926-1997）

Allen Ginsberg is one of the most celebrated poets in contemporary America and a prominent figure in the counterculture and antiwar movements of the 1960s, as well as a leading member of the Beat Generation. His private life has informed much of the critical discussion of his works. Born in Newark, New Jersey in 1926, Ginsberg suffered an emotionally troubled childhood that is reflected in many of his poems. Witnessing his mother's mental illness had a traumatic effect on Ginsberg, who wrote poetry about her unstable condition for the rest of his life. Contributing to Ginsberg's confusion and isolation during these years was his increasing awareness of his homosexuality, which he concealed from both his peers and his parents until he was in his twenties. He later fell in love with a young artist's model, Peter Orlovsky, who was to remain his companion for the next forty years. To experiment with various psychedelic stimulants to create visionary poetry, Ginsberg traveled with Orlovsky to South America, Europe, Morocco, and India. In his remaining years, publishing steadily and traveling tirelessly despite increasing health problems with diabetes and the aftereffects of a stroke, Ginsberg gave readings in Russia, China, Europe, and the South Pacific. He died of liver cancer at his home in New York City on April 5, 1997.

As the most provocative poetic voice of the second half of the twentieth century, Ginsberg's public reading and publication of "Howl" in 1955 set standards for poetry readings throughout the United States and established him as a leading voice of the Beat movement. In 1957 *Howl and Other Poems* became the subject of a landmark obscenity trial, during the furor of the which, he assembled the manuscript later published

as his novel *Naked Lunch* (1959). Ginsberg's works of the 1960s and
early 1970s include his second volume, *Kaddish and Other Poems:
1958-1960* (1961), *Reality Sandwiches* (1963), *Planet News* (1968),
The Gates of Wrath: Rhymed Poems, 1948-1952 (1973), *The Fall of
America: Poems of These States 1965-1971* (1973), and *Mind Breaths:
Poems 1972-1977* (1978). His later publications include *Plutonian Ode*
(1982), *Collected Poems: 1947-1980* (1984), *White Shroud: Poems
1980-1985* (1986), *Cosmopolitan Greetings: Poems, 1986-1992*
(1994), *Selected Poems, 1947-1995* (1996), and *Death* and *Fame:
Last Poems, 1993-1997* (1999).

A modern transcendentalist, Ginsberg attacked the formalism of the
postwar conventions to create works which gave voice to the disenfranchised, the ostracized, and the oppressed. Most of his poems use varieties of the long line, with cadences and cuts suited to the poet's inspiration. Ginsberg often worked in a "stream of consciousness" manner and
experimented with substances such as marijuana and Benzedrine in order
to expand his mind and achieve a higher spiritual plateau. He felt that
the poet's duty was to bring a visionary consciousness of reality to his
readers.

501

Ginsberg was the recipient of numerous honors and awards during
his lifetime, including the Woodbury Poetry Prize, a Guggenheim fellowship, the National Book Award for Poetry, NEA grants and a Lifetime
Achievement Award from the Before Columbus Foundation. Commentators have been sharply divided in their opinions of Ginsberg's work.
Many prominent writers have acknowledged Ginsberg's contribution in introducing and legitimizing experimental poetry to a wider audience, while
his openness concerning his homosexuality and his use of graphic sexual
language have been strongly objected to by some critics.

A Supermarket in California

Introduction

Allen Ginsberg's *Howl and Other Poems* (1956) was the best known and most widely circulated book of poems of its time, and the pocket Bible of the Beat generation. "A Supermarket in California", written in 1955 and later included in the collection, with its movement from exclamations to sad questioning, is Ginsberg's melancholy reminder of what had become Walt Whitman's vision of American plenty pronounced in his "Song of Myself" a century earlier. By 1955, when Ginsberg wrote the poem in Berkeley, California, the phenomenon of a chain of large self-service stores had signaled progress and abundance for many Americans. But for Ginsberg, such a place prompted a sense of loneliness, as well as nostalgia. The poem is a tribute to Whitman's legacy of writing about the world in which he lived and is an expression of Ginsberg's sense of isolation from the mainstream values of America in the 1950s. As an artist who was at the forefront of a counterculture movement during the Eisenhower years, Ginsberg was an outsider on a suburban street. Readers are meant to compare Whitman's vision of plenty in America with the much more contained and less natural world that Ginsberg later observed.

In the first stanza, Ginsberg summons Whitman into his thought during a moonlit stroll to relieve the pain of self-reflection. The poet then confronts his reader with a smattering of images, the entire scene of which takes on a fantastic quality. Ginsberg's affinity with Whitman is evident in the next stanza in which the old poet suddenly appears as an incongruous, yet welcome, element. In his imagination, Ginsberg follows Whitman and the two are trailed by "the store detective", as if they are suspect and illicit variables marring the respectable veneer of mainstream America. Constantly alluding to various aspects of Whitman's poetry and life in the poem, Ginsberg ironically and humorously measures himself against Whitman's grandiose poetic self-depiction and compares Whitman's view of America with what it has actually become. The third stanza begins with Ginsberg's question "Where are we going Walt Whitman?", which signals the ending of their indulgence in sensual, edible pleasures and the return of Ginsberg's uncertainty about the world. By asking Whitman which way the country is headed for, Ginsberg demonstrates his own confusion in reading present reality. That Whitman himself offers no resolution to Ginsberg's questions suggests that the country is beyond logic and repair, and has entered the very dream-world to which Ginsberg has escaped. The final stanza begins with another question, which again underscores Ginsberg's sense of isolation from mainstream America. The poem then ends with Ginsberg's unsettling question to his great predecessor: What America was left to you when the last spark of your consciousness was extinguished by death?

503

If we look at "A Supermarket in California" in relation to the other poems in *Howl*, we can see that Ginsberg's stance toward America is unequivocally bleak. By setting the poem in a supermarket, no longer can Ginsberg innocently "loiter" and "loaf" in the claustrophobic space of the supermarket. He zeroes in on what is almost an embarrassment of riches and choice in the industrialized Western world. The America that Ginsberg bemoans lacks the spiritual fellowship once envisioned by Whitman. In its place is a world in which one achieves personal identity through consumerism and conformity.

A Supermarket in California

What thoughts I have of you tonight, Walt Whitman, for I walked down the sidestreets under the trees with a headache self-conscious looking at the full moon.

In my hungry fatigue, and shopping for images, I went into the neon fruit supermarket, dreaming of your enumerations!

What peaches and what penumbras[①]! Whole families shopping at night! Aisles full of husbands! Wives in the avocados, babies in the tomatoes! —and you, Garcia Lorca[②], what were you doing down by the watermelons?

I saw you, Walt Whitman, childless, lonely old grubber, poking among the meats in the refrigerator and eyeing the grocery boys.

I heard you asking questions of each: Who killed the pork chops? What price bananas? Are you my Angel?

I wandered in and out of the brilliant stacks of cans following you, and followed in my imagination by the store detective.

We strode down in the open corridors together in our solitary fancy tasting artichokes, possessing every frozen delicacy, and never passing the cashier.

Where are we going, Walt Whitman? The doors close in an hour. Which way does your beard point tonight?

(I touch your book and dream of our odyssey in the supermarket and feel absurd.)

Will we walk all night through solitary streets? The trees add shade to shade, lights out in the houses, we'll both be lonely.

Will we stroll dreaming to the lost America of love past blue automobiles in driveways, home to our silent cottage?

Ah, dear father, graybeard, lonely old courage-teacher, what America did you have when Charon[③] quit poling his ferry and you got out on a smoking bank and stood watching the boat disappear on the black waters of Lethe[④]?

Notes

① **penumbras**: partial shadows.

② **Garcia Lorca**: Federico Garcia Lorca (1899-1936), a Spanish poet and dramatist, who like Whitman and Ginsberg, is a homosexual.

③ **Charon**: (Greek mythology,) the boatman who ferried the dead across the Lethe, the river of forgetfulness in Hades, the Underworld.

④ **Lethe**: the river of forgetfulness in Hades.

Questions for Reading Comprehension

1. In the first stanza, Ginsberg introduces Whitman's "enumerations", which refer to the lists or catalogs of people and images from the world he observed in his poems, and the Spanish poet and dramatist Garcia Lorca, who was famous for portraying the interconnectedness of dreams and reality in his characters' lives. How do these elements contribute to the quality of the entire scene in the supermarket?

2. What does the poet share with Whitman in the second stanza?

3. In the third stanza, Ginsberg professes, "I touch your book and dream of our Odyssey in the supermarket and feel absurd." It is believed that Ginsberg is like Odysseus in Homer's *Odyssey* who is trying to get home. How do you understand this allusion?

4. In Greek mythology, Charon was the aged boatman charged with the responsibility of ferrying the souls of the deceased to the realm of Hades, the god of death. The poem ends with the boat disappearing on the Lethe, the underworld's river of forgetfulness. What is the implication of the Greek myth in this poem?

5. What is Ginsberg's relation to Walt Whitman in "A Supermarket in California"? Why does Ginsberg envision the older poet in such a setting? Is the setting relevant to Ginsberg's understanding of his own poetry?

Discussion Questions for Appreciation

1. What feelings about American society does Ginsberg express in "A Supermarket in California?"

2. Allen Ginsberg was the leader of the Hippy or "Beat" movement and the major spokesman for its "philosophy". How is the world of the Hippies represented in his poetry?

3. In what way are Ginsberg's vision and his poetic techniques similar to Whitman's? In what ways does he differ from Whitman?

A Question for Writing

Allen Ginsberg's use of long lines is a deliberate experiment. How does this device contribute to the effect of the poem?

Raymond Carver (1938-1988)

Carver's premature death at the age of 50 cut short the career of one of the most influential short story writers in contemporary America. By the time of his death, Carver had published four collections of short fiction: *Will You Please Be Quiet, Please* (1976), *Furious Seasons* (1977), *What We Talk About When We Talk About Love* (1981), and *Cathedral* (1983). Most of the stories in these collections were gathered for the posthumously published *Where I'm Calling From* (1988), which contains virtually all his major fiction. Carver also wrote five collections of poetry, although his reputation as a poet has lagged behind the view of him as the major short story writer of his generation.

Carver got married at nineteen and fathered two children by the time he was twenty. To support them, Carver had to toil in a series of dead-end jobs. Determined to be a writer, Carver moved his family from Washington to California in 1958, and enrolled as a part-time student at Chico State College. There he took creative writing and published his first story. He then transferred to Humboldt State College in California and enrolled for a seminar called "What Is Existentialism?" The class introduced the young writer to writers whose influence proved lasting: Dostoevsky, Nietzsche, Kafka, Sartre, and Camus. It is no wonder that the abiding motifs in Carver's fiction are displacement, betrayal, miscommunication, violence, guilt, insecurity, and impotence.

To render such bleakness feasible in his stories, an unusual variation on traditional black humor appears, where menace not only co-exists inherently with humor but is meanwhile promoted by it. Carver's creativity lies in the fact that the menace in his stories tends to be unidentifiable or psychological at best. Therefore, his protagonists have to suffer des-

507

perately, but quietly, too. In the eyes of black humorists, "Life is like a joke." Jokes abound in a number of Carver's stories, among them "The Bridle" and "Careful." Some stories are jokes themselves, such as "One More Thing" and "They're Not Your Husband."

The characterization of Mel, the male protagonist of "What We Talk About When We Talk About Love," is in fact full of comic incongruity, an essential feature of black humor. Mel does not practice what he preaches. He believes that love is an absolute and claims that nothing he has experienced as love can match what he finds in the elderly couple bandaged head to foot in casts because of an auto accident. He then negates this standard and judgment by laughing at his wife's former boyfriend, Ed, another man who defines love in an absolute manner and deems life not worth living without her. The story ends in what Carver once described as "a sense of menace". Some sort of fear looms large in the story. Nothing in it ultimately relieves the sense of insecurity plaguing both Mel and Terri.

Carver's first marriage was tumultuous and he divorced in 1977. 1977 was a watershed year for Carver in that he gave up drinking after being hospitalized a number of times and told by a doctor that he would die if he continued alcoholism. Alcohol is a central figure in such stories as "What We Talk About When We Talk About Love," "Careful," "Vitamins," and "Where I'm Calling From." Carver's protagonist, including those of "The Bath" and "Neighbors," often bear a rage against the deadening roles and rituals of family life. The writer himself recalled the bone-deep alienation he felt in the early 1960s, when his existence seemed defined by his roles as husband, father, and son. "There were good times back there, of course, he allowed, "But I'd take poison before I'd go through that time again". Consequently, critics and readers alike have sought biographical connections between the struggles of his characters and specific struggles Carver faced in his personal life. Such connections, though understandable, tend to distract readers from fully appreciating the stories themselves.

An admirer of Sherwood Anderson and an follower of Hemingway, Carver pared his fiction down to its leanest, attracting the criticism of himself as a minimalist writer, a misleading label that fails to do his fiction justice. Carver's influence on the American short fiction in the late 20th century, however, has been nearly as large as Ernest Hemingway's influence on an earlier generation. His work portrays, with economy and grace, how working-class people live, especially how men and women relate to each other, in the fragmented world of late 20th century America.

What We Talk About When We Talk About Love

Introduction

The dominant obsessions of the seventeen stories in Raymond Carver's third collection *What We Talk About When We Talk About Love* (1981) were the same as those of his previous work, but the stories were much darker, reflecting the hell of marital discord and alcoholism, the feelings of dislocation and lost identity and an awareness of random, uncontrollable changes in life. The collection is also Carver's most violence-riddled one where murder, suicide, sudden death, domestic mayhem, and mute but volatile fury are the rule rather than the exception. Carver's colloquial dialogue, replete with mundane observations that are suggestive of unsatisfied emotions and desires, often controls the stories while other narrative elements, such as description, setting, and characterization, are minimal. The stories, which reach the extreme of stark understatement, have been denoted minimalist masterpieces by some critics, and laconic, empty failures by others.

The title story "What We Talk About When We Talk About Love"

509

is the longest and undoubtedly the best of the collection, and it is a fitting climax to the volume. Although its plot is rather thin, several of the obsessions that have run through the collection—the difficulty of sustaining relationships, the effect of alcoholism as a contributing factor to that difficulty, the problem of communication—are given their most extensive treatment. Compared to the blue-collar inhabitants of Carver's fiction, the four characters—the narrator, Nick; his wife, Laura; their friend Mel McGinnis, a cardiologist; and his wife, Terri—are relatively well-educated, but they share a sense of bafflement over matters of the heart. After their divorce Terri's abusive first husband threatens to kill her before committing suicide himself. Mel, her second husband, says that if given the chance he would murder his former wife, Marjorie, who is bleeding him dry financially. The other married couple, Nick and Laura, believes they are too much in love to be torn apart by external circumstances. But who knows what impels and sustains the feeling of love or how it might end? Sitting around the table drinking gin, the more these characters talk about love, the less they feel they know, so that rather than moving towards understanding, they are eased by the growing darkness.

510

What We Talk About When We Talk About Love

My friend Mel McGinrds was talking. Mel McGinnis is a cardiologist, and sometimes that gives him the right.

The four of us were sitting around his kitchen table drinking gin. Sunlight filled the kitchen from the big window behind the sink. There were Mel and me and his second wife, Teresa—Terri, we called her—and my wife, Laura. We lived in Albuquerque① then. But we were all from somewhere else.

There was an ice bucket on the table. The gin and the tonic water kept going around, and we somehow got on the subject of love. Mel thought real love was nothing less than spiritual love. He said he'd spent five years in a seminary② before quitting to go to medical school. He said he still looked back on those years in the seminary as the most important years in his life.

Terri said the man she lived with before she lived with Mel loved her so much, he tried to kill her. Then Terri said, "He beat me up one night. He dragged me around the living room by my ankles. He kept saying, 'I love you, I love you, you bitch. ' He went on dragging me around the living room. My head kept knocking on things. " Terri looked around the table. "What do you do with love like that?"

She was a bone-thin woman with a pretty face, dark eyes, and brown hair that hung down her back. She liked necklaces made of turquoise③ , and long pendant earrings.

"My God, don't be silly. That's not love, and you know it," Mel said. "I don't know what you'd call it, but I sure know you wouldn't call it love".

"Say what you want to, but I know it was," Terri said. "It may sound crazy to you, but it's true just the same. People are different, Mel. Sure, sometimes the may have acted crazy. Okay. But lie loved me. In his own way maybe, but he loved me. There was love there, Mel. Don't say there wasn't. "

Mel let out his breath. He held his glass and turned to Laura and me. "The man threatened to kill me," Mel said. He finished his drink and reached for the gin bottle. "Terri's a romantic. Terri's of the kick-me-so-I'll-know-you-love-me school. Terri, hon, don't look that way. " Mel reached across the table and touched Terri's cheek with his fingers. He grinned at her.

"Now he wants to make up," Terri said.

"Make up what?" Mel said. "What is there to make up? I know what I know. That's all. "

"How'd we get started on this subject, anyway?" Terri said. She

raised her glass and drank from it. "Mel always has love on his mind."
she said. "Don't you, honey?" She smiled, and I thought that was the
last of it.

"I just wouldn't call Ed's behavior love. That's all I'm saying, honey," Mel said. "What about you guys?" Mel said to Laura and me.
"Does that sound like love to you?"

"I'm the wrong person to ask," I said. "I didn't even know the
man. I've only heard his name mentioned in passing. I wouldn't know.
You'd have to know the particulars. But I think what you're saying is that
love is an absolute."

Mel said, "The kind of love I'm talking about is. The kind of love
I'm talking about, you don't try to kill people."

Laura said, "I don't know anything about Ed, or anything about the
situation. But who can judge anyone else's situation?"

I touched the back of Laura's hand. She gave me a quick smile. I
picked up Laura's hand. It was warm, the nails polished, perfectly manicured. I encircled the broad wrist with my fingers, and I held her.

"When I left, he drank rat poison," Terri said. She clasped her
arms with her hands. "They took him to the hospital in Sante Fe. That's
where we lived then, about ten miles out. They saved his life. But his
gums went crazy from it. I mean they pulled away from his teeth. After
that, his teeth stood out like fangs. My God," Terri said. She waited a
minute, then let go of her arms and picked up her glass.

"What people won't do!" Laura said.

"He's out of the action now," Mel said. "He's dead."

Mel handed me the saucer of limes. I took a section, squeezed it
over.

"It gets worse," Terri said. "He shot himself in the mouth. But he
bungled[④] that too. Poor Ed," she said. Terri shook her head.

"Poor Ed nothing" Mel said. "He was dangerous."

Mel was forty-five years old. He was tall and rangy with curly soft hair. His face and arms were brown from the tennis he played. When he was sober, his gestures, all his movements, were precise, very careful.

"He did love me though. Mel. Grant me that," Terri said. "That's all I'm asking. He didn't love me the way you love me. I'm not saying that. But he loved me. You can grant me that, can't you?"

"What do you mean, he bungled it?" I said.

Laura leaned forward with her glass. She put her elbows on the table and held her glass in both hands. She glanced from Mel to Terri and waited with a look of bewilderment on her open face, as if amazed that such things happened to people you were friendly with.

"How'd he bungle it when he killed himself?" I said.

"I'll tell you what happened," Mel said. "He took this twenty-two pistol he'd bought to threaten Terri and me with. Oh, I'm serious, the man was always threatening. You should have seen the way we lived in those days. Like fugitives⑤. I even bought a gun myself. Can you believe it? A guy like me? But I did. I bought one for self-defense and carried it in the glove compartment. Sometimes I'd have to leave the apartment in the middle of the night. To go to the hospital, you know? Terri and I weren't married then, and my first wife had the house and kids, the dog, everything, and Terri and I were living in this apartment here. Sometimes, as I say, I'd get a call in the middle of the night and have to go in to the hospital at two or three in the morning. It'd be dark out there in the parking lot, and I'd break into a sweat before I could even get to my car. I never knew if he was going to come up out of the shrubbery or from behind a car and start shooting. I mean, the man was crazy. He was capable of wiring a bomb, anything. He used to call my service at all hours and say he needed to talk to the doctor, and when I'd return the call, he'd say, 'Son of a bitch, your days are numbered.' Little things like that. It was scary, I'm telling you."

"I still feel sorry for him," Terri said.

"It sounds like a nightmare," Laura said. "But what exactly happened after he shot himself?"

Laura is a legal secretary. We'd met in a professional capacity. Before we knew it, it was a courtship, She's thirty-five, three years younger than I am. In addition to being in love, we like each other and enjoy one another's company. She's easy to be with.

"What happened?" Laura said.

Mel said, "He shot himself in the mouth in his room. Someone heard the shot and told the manager. They came in with a passkey, saw what had happened, and called an ambulance. I happened to be there when they brought him in, alive but past recall. The man lived for three days. His head swelled up to twice the size of a normal head. I'd never seen anything like it, and I hope I never do again. Terri wanted to go in and sit with him when she found oat about it . We had a fight over it. I didn't think she should see him like that. 1 didn't think she should see him, and I still don't. "

"Who won the fight?" Laura said.

"I was in the room with him when he died," Terri said. "He never came up out of it. But I sat with him. He didn't have anyone else. "

"He was dangerous," Mel said. "If you call that love, you can have it. "

"It was love," Terri said. "Sure, it's abnormal in most people's eyes. But he was willing to die for it. He did die for it. "

"I sure as hell wouldn't call it love," Mel said. "I mean, no one knows what he did it for. I've seen a lot of suicides, and I couldn't say anyone ever knew what they did it for. "

Mel put his hands behind his neck and tilted his chair back. "I'm not interested in that kind of love," he said. "If that's love, you can have it. "

Terri said, "We were afraid. Mel even made a will out and wrote to his brother in California who used to be a Green Beret[6]. Mel told him who to look for if something happened to him."

Terri drank from her glass. She said, "But Mel's right—we lived like fugitives. We were afraid. Mel was, weren't you, honey? I even called the police at one point, but they were no help. They said they couldn't do anything until Ed actually did something. Isn't that a laugh?" Terry said.

She poured the last of the gin into her glass and waggled the bottle. Mel got up from the table and went to the cupboard. He took down another bottle.

"Well, Nick and I know what love is," Laura said. "For us, I mean," Laura said. She bumped my knee with her knee. "You're supposed to say something now," Laura said, and turned her smile on me.

For an answer, I took Laura's hand and raised it to my lips. I made a big production out of kissing her hand. Everyone was amused.

"We're lucky," I said.

"You guys," Terri said. "Stop that now. You're making me sick. You're still on the honeymoon, for God's sake. You're still gaga[7], for crying out loud. Just wait. How long have you been together now? How long has it been? A year? Longer than a year?"

"Going on a year and a half," Laura said, flushed and smiling.

"Oh, now," Terri said. "Wait awhile."

She held her drink and gazed at Laura.

"I'm only kidding," Terri said.

Mel opened the gin and went around the table with the bottle.

"Here, you guys," he said. "Let's have a toast. I want to propose a toast. A toast to love. To true love," Mel said.

We touched glasses.

"To love," we said.

Outside in the backyard, one of the dogs began to bark. The leaves of the aspen[8] that leaned past the window ticked against the glass. The afternoon sun was like a presence in this room, the spacious light of ease and generosity. We could have been anywhere, somewhere enchanted. We raised our glasses again and grinned at each other like children who had agreed on something forbidden.

"I'll tell you what real love is," Mel said. "I mean, I'll give you a good example. And then you can draw your own conclusions." He poured more gin into his glass. He added an ice cube and a sliver of lime. We waited and sipped our drinks. Laura and I touched knees again. I put a hand on her warm thigh and left it there.

"What do any of us really know about love?" Mel said. "It seems to me we're just beginners at love. We say we love each other and we do, I don't doubt it. I love Terri and Terri loves me, and you guys love each other too. You know the kind of love I'm talking about now. Physical love, that impulse that drives you to someone special, as well as love of the other person's being, his or her essence, as it were. Carnal love and, well, call it sentimental love, the day-to-day caring about the other person. But sometimes I have a hard time accounting for the fact that I must have loved my first wife too. But I did, I know I did. So I suppose I am like Terri in that regard. Terri and Ed." He thought about it and then he went on. "There was a time when I thought I loved my first wife more than life itself. But now I hate her guts. I do. How do you explain that? What happened to that love? What happened to it, is what I'd like to know. I wish someone could tell me. Then there's Ed. Okay, we're back to Ed. He loves Terri so much he tries to kill her and he winds up killing himself." Mel stopped talking and swallowed from his glass. "You guys have been together eighteen months and you love each other.

It shows all over you. You glow with it. But you both loved other people before you met each other. You've both been married before, just like us. And you probably loved other people before that too, even. Terri and I have been together five years, been married for four. And the terrible thing, the terrible thing is, but the good thing too, the saving grace, you might say, is that if something happened to one of us—excuse me for saying this—but if something happened to one of us tomorrow I think the other one, the other person, would grieve for a while, you know, but then the surviving party would go out and love again, have someone else soon enough. All this, all of this love we're talking about, it would just be a memory. Maybe not even a memory. Am I wrong? Am I way off base? Because I want you to set me straight if you think I'm wrong. I want to know. I mean, I don't know anything, and I'm the first one to admit it. "

"Mel, for God's sake," Terri said. She reached out and took hold of his wrist. "Are you getting drunk? Honey? Are you drunk?"

"Honey, I'm just talking," Mel said. "All right? I don't have to be drunk to say what I think. I mean, we're all just talking, right?" Mel said. He fixed his eyes on her.

"Sweetie, I'm not criticizing," Terri said.

She picked up her glass.

"I'm not on call today," Mel said. "Let me remind you of that. I am not on call," he said.

"Mel, we love you," Laura said.

Mel looked at Laura. He looked at her as if he could not place her, as if she was not the woman she was.

"Love you too, Laura," Mel said. "And you, Nick, love you too. You know something?" Mel said. "You guys are our pals," Mel said.

He picked up his glass.

Mel said, "I was going to tell you about something. I mean, I was going to prove a point. You see, this happened a few months ago, but it's still going on right now and it ought to make us feel ashamed when we talk like we know what we're talking about when we talk above love."

"Come on now," Terri said. "Don't talk like you're drunk if you're not drunk."

"Just shut up for once in your life," Mel said very quietly. "Will you do me a favor and do that for a minute? So as I was saying there's this old couple who had this car wreck out on the interstate. A kid hit them and they were all torn to shit and nobody was giving them much chance to pull through."

Terri looked at us and then back at Mel. She seemed anxious, or maybe that's too strong a word.

Mel was handing the bottle around the table.

"I was on call that night," Mel said. "It was May or maybe it was June. Terri and I had just sat down to dinner when the hospital called. There'd been this thing out on the interstate. Drunk kid, teenager, plowed his dad's pickup into this camper with this old couple in it. They were up in their mid-seventies, that couple. The kid—eighteen, nineteen, something—he was DOA[9]. Taken the steering wheel through his sternum. The old couple, they were alive, you understand. I mean, just barely. But they had everything. Multiple fractures, internal injuries, hemorrhaging, contusions, lacerations, the works, and they each of them had themselves concussions. They were in a bad way, believe me. And, of course, their age was two strikes against them. I'd say she was worse off than he was. Ruptured spleen along with everything else. Both kneecaps broken. But they'd been wearing their seatbelts and, God knows, that's what saved them for the time being."

"Folks, this is an advertisement for the National Safety Council,"

Terri said. "This is your spokesman, Dr. Melvin R. McGinnis, talking." Terri laughed. "Mel," she said, "sometimes you're just too much. But I love you, hon," she said.

"Honey, I love you," Mel said.

He leaned across the table. Terri met him halfway. They kissed.

"Tern's right," Mel said as he settled himself again. "Get those seatbelts on. But seriously, they were in some shape, those oldsters. By the time I got down there, the kid was dead, as I said. He was off in a corner, laid out on a gurney. I took one look at the old couple and told the ER[⑩] nurse to get me a neurologist and an orthopedic man and a couple of surgeons down there right away."

He drank from his glass. "I'll try to keep this short," he said. "So we took the two of them up to OR[⑪] and worked like fuck on them most of the night. They had these incredible reserves, those two. You see that once in a while. So we did everything that could be done, and toward morning we're giving them a fifty-fifty chance, maybe less than that for her. Sphere they are, still alive the next morning. So, okay, we move them into the ICU[⑫], which is where they both kept plugging away at it for two weeks, hitting it better and better on all the scopes. So we transfer them out to their own room."

Mel stopped talking. "Here," he said, "let's drink this cheapo gin the hell up. Then we're going to dinner, right? Terri and I know a new place. That's where we'll go, to this new place we know about. But we're not going until we finish up this cut-rate, lousy gin[⑬]."

Terri said, "We haven't actually eaten there yet. But it looks good. From the outside, you know."

"I like food," Mel said. "If I had it to do all over again, I'd be a chef, you know? Right, Terri?" Mel said.

He laughed. He fingered the ice in his glass.

"Terri knows," he said. "Terri can tell you. But let me say this.

If I could come back again in a different life, a different tune and all, you know what? I'd like to come back as a knight. You were pretty safe wearing all that armor. It was all right being a knight until gunpowder and muskets and pistols came along. "

"Mel would like to ride a horse and carry a lance. " Terri said.

"Carry a woman's scarf with you everywhere. " Laura said.

"Or just a woman" Mel said.

"Shame on you," Laura said.

Terri said, "Suppose you came back as a serf. The serfs didn't have it so good in those days," Terri said.

"The serfs never had it good," Mel said. "But I guess even the knights were vessels to someone. Isn't that the way it worked? But then everyone is always a vessel⑭ to someone. Isn't that right? Terri? But what I liked about knights, besides their ladies, was that they had that suit of armor, you know, and they couldn't get hurt very easy. No cars in those days, you know? No drunk teenagers to tear into your ass. "

"Vassals⑮, " Terri said.

"What?" Mel said.

"Vassals," Terri said. "They were called vassals, not vessels. "

"Vassals, vessels," Met said, "what the fuck's the difference? You knew what I meant anyway. All right," Mel said. "So I'm not educated. I learned my stuff. I'm a heart surgeon, sure, but I'm just a mechanic. I go in and I fuck around and I fix things. Shit," Mel said.

"Modesty doesn't become you. " Terri said.

"He's just a humble sawbones⑯," I said. "But sometimes they suffocated in all that armor, Mel. They'd even have heart attacks if it got too hot and they were too tired and worn out. I read somewhere that they'd fall off their horses and not be able to get up because they were too tired to stand with all that armor on them. They got trampled by their own horses sometimes. "

"That's terrible," Mel said. "That's a terrible thing, Nicky. I guess they'd just lay there and wait until somebody came along and made a shish kebab[17] out of them. "

"Some other vessel," Terri said.

"That's right," Mel said. "Some vassal would come along and spear the bastard in the name of love. Or whatever the fuck it was they fought over in those days. "

"Same things we fight over these days," Terri said.

Laura said, "Nothing's changed. "

The color was still high in Laura's cheeks. Her eyes were bright. She brought her glass to her lips.

Mel poured himself another drink. He looked at the label closely as if studying a long row of numbers. Then he slowly put the bottle down on the table and slowly reached for the tonic water[18].

"What about the old couple?" Laura said. "You didn't finish that story you started. "

Laura was having a hard time lighting her cigarette. Her matches kept going out.

The sunshine inside the room was different now, changing, getting thinner. But the leaves outside the window were still shimmering, and I stared at the pattern they made on the panes and on the Formica[19] counter. They weren't the same patterns, of course.

"What about the old couple?" I said.

"Older but wiser," Terri said.

Mel stared at her.

Terri said, "Go on with your story, hon. I was only kidding. Then what happened?"

"Terri, sometimes," Mel said.

"Please, Mel," Terri said. "Don't always be so serious, sweetie. Can't you take a joke?"

"Where's the joke?" Mel said.

He held his glass and gazed steadily at his wife.

"What happened?" Laura said.

Mel fastened his eyes on Laura. He said, "Laura, if I didn't have Terri and if I didn't love her so much, and if Nick wasn't my best friend, I'd fall in love with you, I'd carry you off, honey," he said.

"Tell your story," Terri said. "Then we'll go to that new place, okay?"

"Okay," Mel said. "Where was I?" he said. He stared at the table and then he began again.

"I dropped in to see each of them every day, sometimes twice a day if I was up doing other calls anyway. Casts and bandages, head to foot, the both of them. You know, you've seen it in the movies. That's just the way they looked, just like in the movies. Little eye-holes and nose-holes and mouth-holes. And she had to have her legs slung up on top of it. Well, the husband was very depressed for the longest while. Even after he found out that his wife was going to pull through, he was still very depressed. Not about the accident, though. I mean, the accident was one thing, but it wasn't everything. I'd get up to his mouth-hole, you know, and he'd say no, it wasn't the accident exactly but it was because he couldn't see her through his eye-holes. He said that was what was making him feel so bad. Can you imagine? I'm telling you, the man's heart was breaking because he couldn't turn his goddamn head and see his goddamn wife."

Mel looked around the table and shook his head at what he was filing to say.

"I mean, it was killing the old fart just because he couldn't look at the fucking woman."

We all looked at Mel.

"Do you see what I'm saying?" he said.

Maybe we were a little drunk by then. I know it was hard keeping things in focus. The light was draining out of the room, going back through the window where it had come from. Yet nobody made a move to get up from the table to turn on the overhead light.

"Listen," Mel said. "Let's finish this fucking gin. There's about enough left here for one shooter all around. Then let's go eat. Let's go to the new place."

"He's depressed," Terri said. "Mel, why don't you take a pill?"

Mel shook his head. "I've taken everything there is."

"We all need a pill now and then," I said.

"Some people are born needing them," Terri said.

She was using her finger to rub at something on the table. Then she stopped rubbing.

"I think I want to call my kids," Mel said. "Is that all right with everybody? I'll call my kids," he said.

Terri said, "What if Marjorie[20] answers the phone? You guys, you've heard us on the subject of Marjorie? Honey, you know you don't want to talk to Marjorie. It'll make you feel even worse."

"I don't want to talk to Marjorie," Mel said. "But I want to talk to my kids."

"There isn't a day goes by that Mel doesn't say he wishes she'd get married again. Or else die," Terri said. "For one thing," Terri said, "she's bankrupting us. Mel says it's just to spite him that she won't get married again. She has a boyfriend who lives with her and the kids, so Mel is supporting the boyfriend too."

"She's allergic to bees," Mel said. "If I'm not praying she'll get married again, I'm praying she'll get herself stung to death by a swarm of fucking bees. "

"Shame on you," Laura said.

"Bzzzzzzz," Mel said, turning his fingers into bees and buzzing them at Tern's throat. Then he let his hands drop all the way to his sides.

"She's vicious," Mel said. "Sometimes I think I'll go up there dressed like a beekeeper. You know, that hat that's like a helmet with the plate that comes down over your face, the big gloves, and the padded coat? I'll knock on the door and let loose a hive of bees in the house. But first I'd make sure the kids were out, of course. "

He crossed one leg over the other. It seemed to take him a lot of time to do it. Then he put both feet on the floor and leaned forward, elbows on the table, his chin cupped in his hands.

"Maybe I won't call the kids, after all. Maybe it isn't such a hot idea. Maybe we'll just go eat. How does that sound?"

Notes

① **Albuquerque**: a city in New Mexico.

② **seminary**: a college for training priests or rabbis.

③ **turquoise**: a valuable greenish-blue stone or a jewel that is made from this.

④ **bungle**: spoil a task through tack of skill.

⑤ **fugitive**: a person who is running away or escaping.

⑥ **Green Beret**: (*colloq.*) a British or American commando.

⑦ **gaga**: fatuous, slightly crazy.

⑧ **aspen**: a poplar tree, with especially tremulous leaves.

⑨ **DOA**: (*abbr.*) dead on arrival (at hospital etc.).

⑩ **ER**: Emergency Room.

⑪ **OR**: Operation Room.

⑫ **ICU**: Intensive Care Unit.

⑬ **lousy gin**: disgusting gin sold at a reduced price.

⑭ **vessel**: tube-like structures in the body of an animal or a plant.

⑮ **Vassals**: (in the Middle Ages) men promising to fight for and be loyal to a king or lord in return for the right to hold land.

⑯ **sawbones**: (*slang*) a doctor or surgeon.

⑰ **shish kebab**: a dish of pieces of marinated meat and vegetables cooked and served on skewers.

⑱ **tonic water**: a carbonated mineral water containing quinine.

⑲ **Formica**: a hard durable plastic laminate used for working surfaces, cupboard doors, etc.

⑳ **Marjorie**: Mel's first wife.

Questions for Reading Comprehension

1. The image of the human "heart" takes on figurative connotation in the story, as it is referred to in both the mechanical sense, of the functioning of the human heart, and the symbolic sense, as the organ of love. Find examples from the story to further illustrate the double meaning "heart" takes on.

2. A central element of figurative speech in this story revolves around Mel's fascination with the protective armor of knights as he explains: "What I like about knights, besides their ladies, was that they had that suit of armor, you know, and they couldn't get hurt very easy." How do you understand Mel's need and desire for the knight's armor?

3. Mel misuses the term "vessel" when he means "vassals", as he points out, "But then everyone is always a vessel to someone." Though at this point Terri corrects him, supplying the proper term vassal for vessel, this play on words is intentionally designed. What's the intention?

4. The imagery of "taking a pill" combines several figurative themes in

the story. Find examples from the story to illustrate it.

5. Do Mel and Terri propose similar or different definitions of "real love"?

6. Can the participants of the talk agree on what is "real love" at the end of the story? What are the variations of love that are discussed in the story?

Discussion Questions for Appreciation

1. Carver was his own most discerning critic. He once said to a friend, "I knew I had gone as far as I could or wanted to go, cutting everything down to the marrow, not just the bone. Any further in that direction and I'd be at a dead end—writing stuff and publishing stuff I wouldn't want to read myself. " How do you understand Carver's comment on his own work?

2. "Carver's is not a particularly lyrical prose," says Bruce Weber in his *New York Times Magazine* article: "A typical sentence is blunt and uncomplicated, eschewing the ornaments of descriptive adverbs and parenthetical phrases. His rhythms are often repetitive or brusque, as if to suggest the strain of people learning to express newly felt things, fresh emotions. . . . Dialogue is usually clipped, and it is studded with commonplace observations of the concrete objects on the table or on the wall rather than the elusive, important issues in the air. " Do you agree with Weber on his opinion of the story?

3. Do the characters know what they are talking about when they talk about love? Do the readers know?

4. What is the comic incongruity in Mel's character?

5. Nick and Laura come close to embodying a simple yet profound enjoyment of each other's company. But when Nick kisses Laura's hand, Mel and Terri find it more amusing than tender. What does Terri's gentle warning— "Wait a while" —suggest?

6. Is love "absolute" or unpredictable? Can you sum up the nature of love as discussed in the story?

A Question for Writing

Shortly before *What We Talk About When We Talk About Love* was published, Carver expressed his literary stance in his essay "A Storyteller's Shoptalk" (later published as "On Writing") : "Get in, get out. Don't linger. Go on." and celebrated the tension-producing value of "the things that are left out, that are implied, the landscape just under the smooth (but sometimes broken and unsettled) surface of things." How do you think Carver implements this literary technique in this short story?

Alice Walker（1944-　）

Born into a family of sharecroppers in Georgia, Alice Walker was a high school teacher and lecturer before she became a writer. Her father defied death threats to cast the first black vote in Georgia, and this tradition of resistance has continued both in Walker's life and in her writing. She has been active in voter registration campaigns in the South. One of black American feminism's most powerful literary voices, she has written poems, plays, short stories, essays and novels. Almost all her work concerns the plight, but also celebrates the strength, of women oppressed not only by sexism but also by racism. Walker's attention to black women's voices *In Love and Trouble* (1973, her first short-story volume), where "Everyday Use" is a central story, is significant in that perhaps for the first time in contemporary U. S. literary history, a writer has featured a variety of Southern black women's perspectives. The traditional literary stereotypes of Southern black women have been either "the mammy" or "the wench."

Walker listed, among the "random influences" on her work, *Their Eyes Were Watching God* (1937) by Zora Neale Hurston, a novel that emphasizes a Southern black woman's search for her own voice. In Walker's eyes, Hurston "was incapable of being embarrassed by anything black people did, and so was able to write about everything with freedom and fluency." Understanding the importance of Hurston's legacy to American literature, Alice Walker is a major force in the rediscovery of her maternal ancestor's works, to the extent that today, in significant measure because of her efforts, Hurston is now considered a great American writer.

The Color Purple (1983), written as a series of letters, is about women, love, individuality and understanding. Walker packs in this cluster of themes by using the effective technique of the two letter writers, Celie and her long-lost sister Nettie. The letters record the experience of Celie's oppression and liberation: her early letters describe how her brutish father, finding his wife unable to meet his sexual needs, turns to Celie and rapes her. Eventually she will find the comradeship she needs in women, in her letters to Nettie and in her love for Shug Avery, her husband's mistress. The novel won the Pulitzer Prize and was made into a popular but not highly satisfactory film (1985). But Walker has been condemned, especially by black men, for her "demonizing" black males in the novel.

The "womanist" essays that Walker collected in the volume *In Search of Our Mothers' Gardens* (1983) celebrate the generations of female creativity and endurance, the cooking, gardening, and quilting, whose beauty is tied to human use. Actually, in the title essay of the volume, "In Search of Our Mothers' Gardens" (1974), Walker celebrates the creative legacy, symbolized by the quilt that women like her mother had bestowed on her and other contemporary black women writers. In the 1980s, partially inspired by Walker's work, many studies, including those by cultural and feminist critics, explored the relationship between the quilt as metaphor and American culture. In her book Sister's Choice, named after Walker's name for Celie's quilt in *The Color Purple*, Elaine Showalter investigates the history of the quilt in relation to American culture, ranging from 19th century women's literature to the AIDS Quilt so important in American society. African American women's writing today has also responded to Walker's metaphor of the quilt as an articulation of women's culture. Critics have noticed the importance of the quilt in *Song of Solomon* (1977) and *Beloved* (1987), both Toni Morrison's novels.

In an interview in 1973, Walker described the three circles of black women that she was about to explore in her fiction. The first type is those whose spirits and bodies are both mutilated, sometimes driven to madness. The second type is those who are psychically conflicted in their attempt to become part of mainstream American life. In Walker's third circle are those black women who come to a new consciousness about their right to be themselves and to shape the world.

Everyday Use

Introduction

"Everyday Use", published early in Alice Walker's writing career, appeared in her collection *In Love and Trouble*: *Stories of Black Women* (1973). Most of the protagonists in this volume are Southern black women who, often against their own conscious wills in the face of pain, abuse, and even death, challenge the conventions of sex, race, and age that attempt to restrict them. The stories reflect Alice Walker's precision in rendering the psychological states of the women characters who she describes as "mad, raging, loving, resentful, hateful, strong, ugly, weak, pitiful, and magnificent," women trying to live with the loyalty to black men that characterize their lives. She portrays these troubled personalities as products of a dehumanizing culture, and as victims of sexual and racial oppression.

"Everyday Use" was enthusiastically reviewed upon publication and has since been considered by some critics the best of Walker's short stories. It is narrated by the unrefined voice of a rural black woman, in the author's attempt to give a voice to a traditionally disenfranchised segment of the population. It tells the story of a mother and her two daughters who have conflicting ideas about their identities and ancestry. The mother narrates a story of the day when one daughter, Dee, a smart but rather ruthless college girl, returns home on a visit and clashes with the other daughter, Maggie, a sweet but ineffectual homebody, over the possession of some heirloom quilts. The contrast between Dee's beliefs and those of her mother and sister is emphasized by the different values the characters place on the old quilts and other objects in the home. The story confronts us with two characters with very different values, addressing the question of how we should honor our heritage. The motif of quilting has since become central to Walker's concerns, because it suggests the strength to be found in connecting with one's roots and one's past.

Everyday Use

For Your Grandmama

I will wait for her in the yard that Maggie and I made so clean and wavy yesterday afternoon. A yard like this is more comfortable than most people know. It is not just a yard. It is like an extended living room. When the hard clay is swept clean as a floor and the fine sand around the edges lined with tiny, irregular grooves, anyone can come and sit and look up into the elm tree and wait for the breezes that never come inside the house.

Maggie will be nervous until after her sister goes: she will stand hopelessly in corners, homely and ashamed of the burn scars down her arms and legs, eyeing her sister with a mixture of envy and awe. She thinks her sister has held life always in the palm of one hand, that "no" is a word the world never learned to say to her.

You've no doubt seen those TV shows where the child who has "made it" is confronted, as a surprise, by her own mother and father, tottering in weakly from backstage. (A pleasant surprise, of course: What would they do if parent and child came on the show only to curse out and insult each other?) On TV mother and child embrace and smile into each other's faces. Sometimes the mother and father weep, the child wraps them in her arms and leans across the table to tell how she would not have made it without their help. I have seen these programs.

Sometimes I dream a dream in which Dee and I are suddenly brought together on a TV program of this sort. Out of a dark and soft-seated limousine I am ushered into a bright room filled with many people. There I meet a smiling, gray, sporty man like Johnny Carson who shakes my hand and tells me what a fine girl I have. Then we are on the stage and Dee is embracing me with tears in her eyes. She pins on my dress a large orchid, even though she has told me once that she thinks orchids are tacky flowers.

In real life I am a large, big-boned woman with rough, man-working hands. In the winter I wear flannel nightgowns to bed and overalls during the day. I can kill and clean a hog as mercilessly as a man. My fat keeps me hot in zero weather. I can work outside all day, breaking ice to get water for washing; I can eat pork liver cooked over the open fire minutes after it comes steaming from the hog. One winter I knocked a bull calf straight in the brain between the eyes with a sledge hammer and had the meat hung up to chill before nightfall. But of course all this does not show on television. I am the way my daughter would want me to be: a hundred pounds lighter, my skin like an uncooked barley pancake. My hair glistens in the hot bright lights. Johnny Carson has much to do to keep up with my quick and witty tongue.

But that is a mistake. I know even before I wake up. Who ever knew a Johnson with a quick tongue? Who can even imagine me looking a strange white man in the eye? It seems to me I have talked to them always with one foot raised in flight, with my head turned in whichever way is farthest from them. Dee, though. She would always look anyone in the eye. Hesitation was no part of her nature.

"How do I look, Mama?" Maggie says, showing just enough of her thin body enveloped in pink skirt and red blouse for me to know she's there, almost hidden by the door.

"Come out into the yard," I say.

Have you ever seen a lame animal, perhaps a dog run over by some careless person rich enough to own a car, sidle up to someone who is ignorant enough to be kind to them? That is the way my Maggie walks. She has been like this, chin on chest, eyes on ground, feet in shuffle, ever since the fire that burned the other house to the ground.

Dee is lighter than Maggie, with nicer hair and a fuller figure. She's a woman now, though sometimes I forget. How long ago was it that the other house burned? Ten, twelve years? Sometimes I can still hear the flames and feel Maggie's arms sticking to me, her hair smoking and her dress falling off her in little black papery flakes. Her eyes seemed stretched open, blazed open by the flames reflected in them. And Dee. I see her standing off under the sweet gum tree she used to dig gum out of; a look of concentration on her face as she watched the last dingy gray board of the house fall in toward the red-hot brick chimney. Why don't you do a dance around the ashes? I'd wanted to ask her. She had hated the house that much.

I used to think she hated Maggie, too. But that was before we raised the money, the church and me, to send her to Augusta to school. She used to read to us without pity; forcing words, lies, other folks' habits, whole lives upon us two, sitting trapped and ignorant underneath her voice. She washed us in a river of make-believe, burned us with a lot of knowledge we didn't necessarily need to know. Pressed us to her with the serious way she read, to shove us away at just the moment, like dimwits, we seemed about to understand.

Dee wanted nice things. A yellow organdy dress to wear to her graduation from high school; black pumps to match a green suit she'd made from an old suit somebody gave me. She was determined to stare down any disaster in her efforts. Her eyelids would not flicker for minutes at a time. Often I fought off the temptation to shake her. At sixteen she had a style of her own: and knew what style was.

I never had an education myself. After second grade the school was closed down. Don't ask me why: in 1927 colored asked fewer questions than they do now. Sometimes Maggie reads to me. She stumbles along good-naturedly but can't see well. She knows she is not bright. Like good looks and money, quickness passed her by. She will marry John Thomas (who has mossy teeth in an earnest face) and then I'll be free to sit here and I guess just sing church songs to myself. Although I never was a good singer. Never could carry a tune. I was always better at a man's job. I used to love to milk till I was hooked in the side in '49. Cows are soothing and slow and don't bother you, unless you try to milk them the wrong way.

I have deliberately turned my back on the house. It is three rooms, just like the on that burned, except the roof is tin; they don't make shingle roofs any more. There are no real windows, just some holes cut in the sides, like the portholes in a ship, but not round and not square, with rawhide holding the shutters up on the outside. This house is in a pasture, too, like the other one. No doubt when Dee sees it she will want to tear it down. She wrote me once that no matter where we "choose" to live, she will manage to come see us. But she will never bring her friends. Maggie and I thought about this and Maggie asked me, "Mama, when did Dee ever *have* any friends?"

She had a few. Furtive boys in pink shirts hanging about on washday after school. Nervous girls who never laughed. Impressed with her they worshiped the well-turned phrase, the cute shape, the scalding humor that erupted like bubbles in lye. She read to them.

When she was courting Jimmy T, she didn't have much time to pay to us, but turned all her faultfinding power on him. He *flew* to marry a cheap city girl from a family of ignorant flashy people. She hardly had time to recompose herself.

When she comes I will meet—but there they are!

Maggie attempts to make a dash for the house, in her shuffling way, but I stay her with my hand. "Come back here," I say. And she stops and tries to dig a well in the sand with her toe.

It is hard to see them clearly through the strong sun. But even the first glimpse of leg out of the car tells me it is Dee. Her feet were always neat-looking, as if God himself had shaped them with a certain style. From the other side of the car comes a short, stocky man. Hair is all over his head a foot long and hanging from his chin like a kinky mule tail. I hear Maggie suck in her breath. "Uhnnnh" is what it sounds like. Like when you see the wriggling end of a snake just in front of your foot on the road. "Uhnnnh."

Dee next. A dress down to the ground, in this hot weather. A dress so loud it hurts my eyes. There are yellows and oranges enough to throw back the light of the sun. I feel my whole face warming from the heat waves it throws out. Earrings gold, too, and hanging down to her shoulders. Bracelets dangling and making noises when she moves her arm up to shake the folds of the dress out of her armpits. The dress is loose and flows, and as she walks closer, I like it. I hear Maggie go "Uhnnnh" again. It is her sister's hair. It stands straight up like the wool on a sheep. It is black as night and around the edges are two long pigtails that rope about like small lizards disappearing behind her ears.

"Wa-su-zo-Tean-o!"[①] she says, coming on in that gliding way the dress makes her move. The short stocky fellow with the hair to his navel is all grinning and he follows up with "Asalamalakim[②], my mother and sister!" He moves to hug Maggie but she falls back, right up against the back of my chair. I feel her trembling there and when I look up I see the perspiration falling off her chin.

"Don't get up," says Dee. Since I am stout it takes something of a push. You can see me trying to move a second or two before I make it.

535

She turns, showing white heels through her sandals, and goes back to the car. Out she peeks next with a Polaroid. She stoops down quickly and lines up picture after picture of me sitting there in front of the house with Maggie cowering behind me. She never takes a shot without making sure the house is included. When a cow comes nibbling around the edge of the yard she snaps it and me and Maggie *and* the house. Then she puts the Polaroid in the back seat of the car, and comes up and kisses me on the forehead.

Meanwhile Asalamalakim is going through motions with Maggie's hand. Maggie's hand is as limp as a fish, and probably as cold, despite the sweat, and she keeps trying to pull it back. It looks like Asalamalakim wants to shake hands but wants to do it fancy. Or maybe he don't know how people shake hands. Anyhow, he soon gives up on Maggie.

"Well," I say. "Dee."

"No, Mama," she says. "Not 'Dee,' Wangero Leewanika Kemanjo!③"

"What happened to 'Dee'?" I wanted to know.

"She's dead," Wangero said. "I couldn't bear it any longer, being named after the people who oppress me."

"You know as well as me you was named after your aunt Dicie," I said. Dicie is my sister. She named Dee. We called her "Big Dee" after Dee was born.

"But who was *she* named after?" asked Wangero.

"I guess after Grandma Dee" I said.

"And who was she named after?" asked Wangero.

"Her mother," I said, and saw Wangero was getting tired. "That's about as far back as I can trace it," I said. Though, in fact, I probably could have carried it back beyond the Civil War through the branches.

"Well," said Asalamalakim, "there you are."

"Uhnnnh," I heard Maggie say.

"There I was not," I said, "before 'Dicie' cropped up in our family, so why should I try to trace it that far back?"

He just stood there grinning, looking down on me like somebody inspecting a Model A car. Every once in a while he and Wangero sent eye signals over my head.

"How do you pronounce this name?" I asked.

"You don't have to call me by it if you don't want to," said Wangero.

"Why shouldn't I?" I asked. "If that's what you want us to call you, we'll call you."

"I know it might sound awkward at first," said Wangero.

"I'll get used to it," I said. "Ream it out again."

Well, soon we got the name out of the way. Asalamalakim had a name twice as long and three times as hard. After I tripped over it two or three times he told me to just call him Hakim[4]—abarber. I wanted to ask him was he a barber, but I didn't really think he was, so I didn't ask.

"You must belong to those beef-cattle peoples down the road," I said. They said "Asalamalakim" when they met you, too, but they didn't shake hands. Always too busy: feeding the cattle, fixing the fences, putting up saltlick shelters, throwing down hay. When the white folks poisoned some of the herd the men stayed up all night with rifles in their hands. I walked a mile and a half just to see the sight.

Hakim-a-barber said, "I accept some of their doctrines, but farming and raising cattle is not my style." (They didn't tell me, and I didn't ask, whether Wangero (Dee) had really gone and married him.)

We sat down to eat and right away he said he didn't eat collards and pork was unclean. Wangero, though, went on through the chitlins and corn bread, the greens and everything else. She talked a blue streak over the sweet potatoes. Everything delighted her. Even the fact that we

537

still used the benches her daddy made for the table when we couldn't afford to buy chairs.

"Oh, Mama!" she cried. Then turned to Hakim-a-barber. "I never knew how lovely these benches are. You can feel the rump prints," she said, running her hands underneath her and along the bench. Then she gave a sigh and her hand closed over Grandma Dee's butter dish. "That's it!" she said. "I knew there was something I wanted to ask you if I could have." She jumped up from the table and went over in the corner where the churn stood, the milk in it clabber by now. She looked at the churn and looked at it.

"This churn top is what I need," she said. "Didn't Uncle Buddy whittle it out of a tree you all used to have?"

"Yes," I said.

"Uh huh" she said happily. "And I want the dasher, too."

"Uncle Buddy whittle that, too?" asked the barber.

Dee (Wangero) looked up at me.

"Aunt Dee's first husband whittled the dash," said Maggie so low you almost couldn't hear her. "His name was Henry, but they called him Stash."

"Maggie's brain is like an elephant's," Wangero said, laughing. "I can use the churn top as a centerpiece for the alcove table," she said, sliding a plate over the churn, "and I think of something artistic to do with the dasher."

When she finished wrapping the dasher the handle stuck out. I took it for a moment in my hands. You didn't even have to look close to see where hands pushing the dasher up and down to make butter had left a kind of sink in the wood. In fact, there were a lot of small sinks; you could see where thumbs and fingers had sunk into the wood. It was beautiful light yellow wood, from a tree that grew in the yard where Big Dee and Stash had lived.

After dinner Dee (Wangero) went to the trunk at the foot of my bed and started rifling through it. Maggie hung back in the kitchen over the dishpan. Out came Wangero with two quilts. They had been pieced by Grandma Dee and then Big Dee and me had hung them on the quilt frames on the front porch and quilted them. One was in the Lone Star pattern. The other was Walk Around the Mountain. In both of them were scraps of dresses Grandma Dee had worn fifty and more years ago. Bits and pieces of Grandpa Jarrell's Paisley shirts. And one teeny faded blue piece, about the size of a penny matchbox, that was from Great Grandpa Ezra's uniform that he wore in the Civil War.

"Mama," Wangero said sweet as a bird. "Can I have these old quilts?"

I heard something fall in the kitchen, and a minute later the kitchen door slammed.

"Why don't you take one or two of the others?" I asked. "These old things was just done by me and Big Dee from some tops your grandma pieced before she died."

"No," said Wangero. "I don't want those. They are stitched around the borders by machine."

"That'll make them last better," I said.

"That's not the point," said Wangero. "These are all pieces of dresses Grandma used to wear. She did all this stitching by hand. Imagine!" She held the quilts securely in her arms, stroking them.

"Some of the pieces, like those lavender ones, come from old clothes her mother handed down to her," I said, moving up to touch the quilts. Dee (Wangero) moved back just enough so that I couldn't reach the quilts. They already belonged to her.

"Imagine!" she breathed again, clutching them closely to her bosom.

"The truth is," I said, "I promised to give them quilts to Maggie, for when she marries John Thomas. "

She gasped like a bee had stung her.

"Maggie cant appreciate these quilts!" she said. "She'd probably be backward enough to put them to everyday use. "

"I reckon she would," I said. "God knows I been saving 'em for long enough with nobody using 'em. I hope she will!" I didn't want to bring up how I had offered Dee (Wangero) a quilt when she went away to college. Then she had told me they were old-fashioned, out of style.

"But they're *priceless*!" she was saying now, furiously; for she has a temper. "Maggie would put them on the bed and in five years they'd be in rags. Less than that!"

"She can always make some more," I said. "Maggie knows how to quilt. "

Dee (Wangero) looked at me with hatred. "You just will not understand. The point is these quilts, *these* quilts!"

"Well," I said, stumped. "What would *you* do with them?"

"Hang them," she said. As if that was the only thing you *could* do with quilts.

Maggie by now was standing in the door. I could almost hear the sound her feet made as they scraped over each other.

"She can have them, Mama," she said, like somebody used to never winning anything, or having anything reserved for her. "I can member Grandma Dee without the quilts. "

I looked at her hard. She had filled her bottom lip with checkerberry snuff and it gave her a face a kind of dopey, hangdog look. It was Grandma Dee and Big Dee who taught her how to quilt herself. She stood there with he scarred hands hidden in the folds of her skirt. She looked at her sister with something like fear but she wasn't mad at her. This was Maggie's portion. This was the way she knew God to work.

When I looked at her like that something hit me in the top of my head and ran down to the soles of my feet. Just like when I'm in church and the spirit of God touches me and I get happy and shout. I did something I never had done before: hugged Maggie to me, then dragged her on into the room, snatched the quilts out of Miss Wangero's hands and dumped them into Maggie's lap. Maggie just sat there on my bed with her mouth open.

"Take one or two of the others," I said to Dee.

But she turned without a word and went out to Hakim-a-barber.

"You just don't understand," she said, as Maggie and I came out to the car.

"What don't I understand?" I wanted to know.

"Your heritage," she said. And then she turned to Maggie, kissed her, and said, "You ought to try to make something of yourself, too, Maggie. It's really a new day, for us. But from the way you and Mama still live you'd never know it."

She put on some sunglasses that hid everything above the tip of her nose and her chin.

Maggie smiled; maybe at the sunglasses. But a real smile, not scared. After we watched the car dust settle I asked Maggie to bring me a dip of snuff. And then the two of us sat there just enjoying, until it was time to go in the house and go to bed.

541

Notes

① **Wa-su-zo-Tean-o**: a phrase showing how the people of Uganda say "Good morning", translated as "I hope you have slept well".

② **Asalamalakim**: the well known Arab greeting "as-salam alaykum", which means "peace be with you".

③ **Wangero Leewanika Kemanjo**: Dee's self-given name which sounds authentically African but has no relationship to either a person she knew, or to the personal history that sustained her.

④ **Hakim**: an Arabic word meaning ruler or leader.

Questions for Reading Comprehension

1. When offered the quilts before she left for college, Dee refused them, ashamed to own such "old fashioned" items. Upon her return, Dee covets the folk-art objects that comprise everyday reality for her mother and sister. What accounts for Dee's change of heart?

2. Has she learned to appreciate her mother and her heritage?

3. By what process do the quilts get made? What is remarkable about the social occasions which bring them into being?

4. Which of the various facts about the quilts do Maggie and Dee "single out" as what is "essential" about the quilts for them?

5. What are the differences in character between Dee and Maggie, and how do these show up in the differences between what the quilts mean to them?

6. In "Everyday Use," Walker presents two very different perceptions of heritage and values as narrated through the viewpoint of a mother observing her two daughters. How does she describe each child? What use does the mother anticipate that Dee and Maggie would put the quilts to?

7. What does the mother think of Dee's new name and the gentleman who accompanies Dee?

8. The narrator indicates that she has not had much of an education, and that she is a strong, mannish, earthy woman. Is the narrator really as ignorant as she claims?

Discussion Questions for Appreciation

1. How do the two daughters act as foils to each other? What values does each represent, and how does Walker lead us to prefer one daughter to another?

2. Walker's story poses an important question: "How can we best both honor and preserve our heritage?" Is it through the careful safeguarding of artifacts, such as the quilts in the story, or the passing of memories of these artifacts? Most readers agree that Maggie is the more deserving of the daughters. However, would the quilts be safer for posterity with Dee?

3. How might this story be different if it were written from the point of view of one of the daughters?

4. Dee and Maggie seem as different as night and day. Does either of them have any character traits in common with their mother? If so, what are they? What traits don't they share with their mother?

5. Walker has often been considered a black feminist writer. Does this story carry with it a feminist message?

6. What is your own heritage, and how do you preserve it? Are you proud of your family and where you came from? Do you empathize with Dee, who wishes to preserve the things of her heritage, but who is ashamed of her family?

A Question for Writing

How does the story invite us to evaluate these opposing sets of values? With whom does Walker invite us to side, to identify? Which sort of values do you think the author thinks people ought to hold dear?

Gish Jen（1956-　）

　　Gish Jen was born Lillian C. Jen to immigrant Chinese-American parents in New York City. After earning a B. A. at Harvard, Jen attended the Iowa Writers' Workshop and received her M. F. A. in 1983.

　　Generally speaking, before the commercial success of Amy Tan's *Joy Luck Club* (1989), it was not easy for Asian American writers to have their works accepted by major publishers. Jen was no exception. Yet against all odds, she continued to write and won national acclaim with the publication of her first novel *Typical American* (1991) and her second novel *Mona in the Promised Land* (1996), both finalists for the National Book Critics' Circle. *Typical American*, named "the Notable Book of the Year" by *The New York Times*, chronicles a Chinese American family's pursuit of the American dream, while *Mona in the Promised Land* continues the saga of the family but focuses on the younger daughter Mona's attempt to convert to Judaism. Gish Jen's third novel, *The Love Wife*, published in 2004, continues in a humorous vein the interest in cultural clashes.

　　Although Jen's first short story collection *Who's Irish?: Stories* (1999) appeared after the novels, she had been writing short stories since the beginning of her writing career, and it was her skill with short fiction that first caught the interest of keen readers. What's more important, Jen's stories do not exclusively deal with the Asian American experience or Asian American subjects. In the 1980s, she published short stories in many literary magazines, such as *The New Yorker*, *Atlantic Monthly*, *Southern Review*, and *Fiction International*. Meanwhile she won a number of awards for her short fiction, including a National Endowment for the Arts Award (1988) and Massachusetts Artists Foundation Fellowship (1988), as well as prizes from the Katherine Ann Porter Contest (1987).

Like her novels, the majority of Jen's short stories explore the themes of assimilation, identity, displacement, generational conflict, interracial relationships, and the American dream. *Who's Irish?* is composed of eight funny stories in which Jen looks at Chinese Americans making their way in American society. In these stories, cultures collide. The title story "Who's Irish?," for example, focuses on the conflicts between the narrator and her Americanized daughter and Irish American son-in-law. A family takes its first and comically disastrous step towards joining a country club in "In the American Society." The longest piece of the collection, "House, House, Home," portrays a character that defies the expectations of her immigrant parents. Of course, by no means limited to Chinese American experiences, *Who's Irish?* covers a variety of characters and subjects. As always, "Gish Jen charts her characters' lives with both tenderness and wit, while cutting to the core of what is absurd and comic—and sometimes tragic—in our existence."①

In "Asian American Short Fiction: An Introduction and Critical Survey," Rachel Lee notes that Jen's short stories "deliberately resist the narrow ways 'real' Asian American literature has been defined,"② uncovering the effect of isolation and racism inside families, subverting the myth of Asian Americans as the model minority. All the above attests that Jen is not recognized merely as an ethnic writer or a woman writer but as an important contemporary American author.

---

① Gish Jen, *Who's Irish?* (London: Granta Books, 1999), back cover.

② Guiyou Huang (ed.), *Asian American Short Story Writers: an A-to-Z guide* (Westport, CT: Greenwood Press, 2003), 106.

In the American Society

Introduction

"In the American Society" is the oldest story in *Who's Irish*, a collection of eight short stories published in 1999. Most of the stories in this book had been published previously to high acclaim. Although the specific plots and topics of the stories in *Who's Irish?* are diverse, the major themes of the collection seem to be ethnic interaction, immigration, and the complexities of a multicultural world. They also use Asian Americans and other Americans to address other subjects, such as art and religion.

"In the American Society" is a portrait of Ralph Chang, a father, who owns a successful pancake restaurant in a suburb of New York. On the surface, he might appear to be living the American Dream, but it turns out that the American Dream involves a conflict between selves. The story narrates an episode in the life of the Chang family from the point of view of the eldest daughter, Callie Chang. The two-part structure of the story offers us a view of the father's feudal lord behavior in two different settings. In the first, one of Ralph's workers at the pancake house, Fernando, is fired, and he eventually denounces Ralph, who treats his employees like servants. In the second, the same arrogant impulse stands him in good stead when confronting racism. The debate about whether one's own society is preferable to "American society" is raised in the last part of the story, when the Changs are invited to a party at a country club. In her eagerness to fit in, Helen, the mother, accepts the invitation. The humor in the situation arises from the incongruity between the expensive outfits the Changs wear to the party and the Bermuda shorts or "wrap skirts" worn by most of the other guests. The episode depicts the Changs' grim realization of their marginal status when Ralph is harassed and insulted by Jeremy, a guest who has had too much to drink and who repeatedly bosses Ralph around, finally asking: "Who are you?" The structure gives us a clear picture of Ralph Chang's background, personality and his misadventures in assimilation, thus enabling us to consider the appropriateness of social behavior based on class and cultural differences.

In the American Society

His Own Society

When my father took over the pancake house, it was to send my little sister, Mona, and me to college. We were only in junior high at the time, but my father believed in getting a jump on things. "Those Americans always saying it," he told us. "Smart guys thinking in advance." My mother elaborated, explaining that businesses took bringing up, like children. They could take years to get going, she said, years.

In this case, though, we got rich right away. At two months, we were breaking even, and at four, those same hotcakes that could barely withstand the weight of butter and syrup were supporting our family with ease. My mother bought a station wagon with air conditioning, my father an oversized red vinyl recliner for the back room; and as time went on and the business continued to thrive, my father started to talk about his grandfather, and the village he had reigned over in China—things my father had never talked about when he worked for other people. He told us about the bags of rice his family would give out to the poor at New Year's, and about the people who came to beg, on their hands and knees, for his grandfather to intercede for the more wayward of their relatives. "Like that Godfather in the movie," he would tell us as, feet up, he distributed paychecks. Sometimes an employee would get two green envelopes instead of one, which meant that Jimmy needed a tooth pulled, say, or that Tiffany's husband was in the clinker[①] again. "It's nothing, nothing," he would insist, sinking back into his chair. "Who else is going to taking care of you people?"

My mother would mostly just sigh about it. "Your father thinks this is China," she would say, and then she would go back to her mending. Once in a while, though, when my father had given away a particularly large sum, she would exclaim, outraged, "But this here is the *U—S— of—A*!" —this apparently having been what she used to tell immigrant stock boys when they came in late.

She didn't work at the supermarket anymore; but she had made it to the rank of manager before she left, and this had given her not only new words and phrases but new ideas about herself, and about America, and about what was what in general. She had opinions about how downtown should be zoned; she could pump her own gas and check her own oil; and for all that she used to chide Mona and me for being copycats, she herself was now interested in espadrilles, and wallpaper, and, most recently, the town country club.

"So join already," said Mona, flicking a fly off her knee.

My mother enumerated the problems as she sliced up a quarter round of watermelon. There was the cost. There was the waiting list. There was the fact that no one in our family played either tennis or golf.

"So what?" said Mona.

"It would be waste," said my mother.

"Me and Callie can swim in the pool."

"Anyway, you need that recommendation letter from a member."

"Come on" said Mona. "Annie's mom'd write you a letter in a sec[②]."

My mother's knife glinted in the early-summer sun. I spread some more newspaper on the picnic table.

"Plus, you have to eat there twice a month. You know what that means." My mother cut another, enormous slice of fruit.

"No, I don't know what that means," said Mona.

"It means Dad would have to wear a Jacket, dummy[3]," I said.

"Oh! Oh! Oh!" said Mona, clasping her hand to her breast. "Oh! Oh! Oh! Oh! Oh!"

We all laughed: My father had no use for nice clothes, and would wear only ten-year-old shirts, with grease-spotted pants, to show how little he cared what anyone thought.

"Your father doesn't believe in joining the American society," said my mother. "He wants to have his own society."

"So go to dinner without him." Mona shot her seeds out in long arcs over the lawn. "Who cares what he thinks?"

But of course, we all did care, and knew my mother could not simply up and do as she pleased. For to embrace what my father embraced was to love him; and to embrace something else was to betray him.

549

He demanded a similar sort of loyalty of his workers, whom he treated more like servants than employees. Not in the beginning, of course. In the beginning, all he wanted was for them to keep on doing what they used to do, to which end he concentrated mostly on leaving them alone. As the months passed, though, he expected more and more of them, with the result that, for all his largesse, he began to have trouble keeping help. The cooks and busboys complained that he asked them to fix radiators and trim hedges, not only at the restaurant but at our house; the waitresses, that he sent them on errands, and made them chauffeur him around. Our headwaitress, Gertrude, claimed that he once even asked her to scratch his back.

"Its not just the blacks don't believe in slavery," she said when she quit.

My father never quite registered her complaints, though, nor those of the others who left. Even after Eleanor quit, then Tiffany, and Gerald, and Jimmy, and even his best cook. Eureka Andy, for whom he had bought new glasses, he remained mostly convinced that the fault lay with them.

"All they understand is that assemble line," he lamented. "Robots, they are. They want to be robots."

There were occasions when the clear running truth seemed to eddy, when he would pinch the vinyl of his chair up into little peaks and wonder if he was doing things right. But with time he would always smooth the peaks back down; and when business started to slide in the spring, he kept on like a horse in his ways.

By the summer, our dish boy was overwhelmed with scraping. It was no longer Just the hash browns that people were leaving for trash, and the service was as bad as the food. The waitresses served up French pancakes instead of German, apple Juice instead of orange. They spilled things on laps, on coats. On the Fourth of July, some greenhorn[4] sent an entire side of fries slaloming[5] down a lady's *Massif Central*[6]. Meanwhile, in the back room, my father labored through articles on the economy.

"What is housing starts?" he puzzled. "What is GNP?"

Mona and I did what we could, filling in as busgirls and dishwashers, and, one afternoon, stuffing the comments box by the cashier's desk. That was Mona's idea. We rustled up a variety of pens and pencils, checked boxes for an hour, smeared the cards with coffee and grease, and waited. It took a few days for my father to notice that the box was full, and he didn't say anything about it for a few days more. Finally, though, he started to complain of fatigue; and then he began to complain that the staff was not what it could be. We encouraged him in this—pointing out, for instance, how many dishes got chipped. But in the end all that happened was that, for the first time since we took over the restaurant, my father got it into his head to fire someone. Skip, a skinny busboy who was saving up for a sports car, said nothing as my father mumbled on about the price of dishes. My father's hands shook as he wrote out the severance check; and once it was over, he spent the rest of the day napping in his chair.

Since it was going on midsummer, Skip wasn't easy to replace. We hung a sign in the window and advertised in the paper, but no one called the first week, and the person who called the second didn't show up for his interview. The third week, my father phoned Skip to see if he would come back, but a friend of his had already sold him a Corvette for cheap.

Finally, a Chinese guy named Booker turned up. He couldn't have been more than thirty, and was wearing a lighthearted seersucker suit, but he looked as though life had him pinned. His eyes were bloodshot and his chest sunken, and the muscles of his neck seemed to strain with the effort of holding his head up. In a single dry breath he told us that he had never bused tables but was willing to learn, and that he was on the lam from the deportation authorities.

"I do not want to lie to you, he kept saying. " He had come to the United States on a student visa but had run out of money and was now in a bind. He was loath to go back to Taiwan, as it happened—he looked up at this point, to be sure my father wasn't pro-KMT—but all he had was a phony Social Security card, and a willingness to absorb all blame, should anything untoward come to pass.

"I do not think, anyway, that it is against law to hire me, only to be me," he said, smiling faintly.

Anyone else would have examined him on this, but my father conceived of laws as speed bumps⑦ rather than curbs⑧. He wiped the counter with his sleeve, and told Booker to report the next morning.

"I will be good worker," said Booker.

"Good," said my father.

"Anything you want me to do, I will do."

My father nodded.

Booker seemed to sink into himself for a moment. "Thank you," he said finally. "I am appreciate your help. I am very, very appreciate for everything."

My father looked at him. "Did you eat today?" he asked in Mandarin.

Booker pulled at the hem of his jacket.

"Sit down," said my father. "Please, have a seat."

My father didn't tell my mother about Booker, and my mother didn't tell my father about the country club. She would never have applied, except that Mona, while over at Annie's, had let it drop that our mother wanted to join. Mrs. Lardner came by the very next day.

"Why, I'd be honored and delighted to write you people a letter," she said. Her skirt billowed around her.

"Thank you so much," said my mother. "But it's too much trouble for you, and also my husband is. . . "

"Oh, it's no trouble at all, no trouble at all. I tell you." She leaned forward, so that her chest freckles showed. "I know just how it is. It's a secret of course, but, you know, my natural father was Jewish. Can you see it? Just look at my skin."

"My husband," said my mother.

"I'd be honored and delighted," said Mrs. Lardner, with a little wave other hands. "Just honored and delighted."

552

Mona was triumphant. "See, Mom," she said, waltzing around the kitchen when Mrs. Lardner left. "What did I tell you? 'I'm honored and delighted, just honored and delighted.' " She waved her hands in the air.

"You know, the Chinese have a saying," said my mother. "To do nothing is better than to overdo. You mean well, but you tell me now what will happen."

"I'll talk Dad into it," said Mona, still waltzing. "Or I bet Callie can. He'll do anything Callie says."

"I can try, anyway," I said.

"Did you hear what I said?" said my mother. Mona bumped into the broom closet door. "You're not going to talk anything. You've already made enough trouble." She started on the dishes with a clatter.

Mona poked diffidently at a mop.

I sponged off the counter. "Anyway," I ventured. "I bet our name'll never even come up."

"That's if we're lucky," said my mother.

"There's all these people waiting," I said.

"Good." She started on a pot.

I looked over at Mona, who was still cowering in the broom closet. "In fact, there's some black family's been waiting so long, they're going to sue," I said.

My mother turned off the water. "Where'd you hear that?"

"Patty told me."

She turned the water back on, started to wash a dish, then put it down and shut the faucet.

"I'm sorry," said Mona.

"Forget it," said my mother. "Just forget it."

Booker turned out to be a model worker, whose boundless gratitude translated into a willingness to do anything. As he also learned quickly, he soon knew not only how to bus but how to cook, and how to wait tables, and how to keep the books. He fixed the walk-in door so that it stayed shut, reupholstered the torn seats in the dining room, and devised a system for tracking inventory. The only stone in the rice was that he tended to be sickly; but, reliable even in illness, he would always send a friend to take his place. In this way, we got to know Ronald, Lynn, Dirk, and Cedric, all of whom, like Booker, had problems with their legal status, and were anxious to please. They weren't all as capable as Booker, though, with the exception of Cedric, whom my father often hired even when Booker was well. A round wag of a man who called Mona and me *shou hou*—skinny monkeys—he was a professed nonsmoker who was nevertheless always begging drags off other people's cigarettes. This last habit drove our head cook, Fernando, crazy, especially since, when refused a hit, Cedric would occasionally snitch one. Winking impishly at Mona and me, he would steal up to an ashtray, take a quick puff, and then break out laughing, so that the smoke came rolling out of his mouth in a great incriminatory cloud. Fernando accused him of stealing fresh cigarettes, too, even whole packs.

"Why else do you think he's weaseling around in the back of the store all the time?" he said. His face was blotchy with anger. "The man is a frigging thief."

Other members of the staff supported him in this contention, and joined in on an "Operation Identification,"⑨ which involved numbering and initialing their cigarettes—even though what they seemed to fear for wasn't so much their cigarettes as their jobs. Then one of the cooks quit; and, rather than promote someone, my father hired Cedric for the position. Rumor had it that Cedric was taking only half the normal salary; that Alex had been pressured to resign; and that my father was looking for a position with which to placate Booker, who had been bypassed because of his health.

The result was that Fernando categorically refused to work with Cedric.

"The only way I'll cook with that piece of slime," he said, shaking his huge, tattooed fist, "is if it's his ass frying on the grill."

My father cajoled and cajoled, but in the end was simply forced to put them on different schedules.

The next week, Fernando got caught stealing a carton of minute steaks. My father would not tell even Mona and me how he knew to be standing by the back door when Fernando was on his way out, but everyone suspected Booker. Everyone but Fernando, that is, who was sure Cedric had been the tip-off. My father held a staff meeting, in which he tried to reassure everyone that Alex had left on his own, and that he had no intention of firing anyone. But though he was careful not to mention Fernando, everyone was so amazed that he was being allowed to stay that Fernando was incensed nonetheless.

"Don't you all be putting your bug eyes on me," he said. "He's the frigging crook." He grabbed Cedric by the collar.

Cedric raised an eyebrow. "Cook, you mean," he said.

At this, Fernando punched Cedric in the mouth; and, the words he had just uttered notwithstanding, my father fired Fernando on the spot.

With everything that was happening, Mona and I were ready to be finishing up at the restaurant. It was almost time: The days were still stuffy with summer, but our window shade had started flapping in the evening as if gearing up to go out. That year, the breezes were full of salt, as they sometimes were when they came in from the east, and they blew anchors and docks through my mind like so many tumbleweeds, filling my dreams with wherries and lobsters and grainy-faced men who squinted, day in and day out, at the sky.

It was time for a change—you could feel it—and yet the pancake house was the same as ever. The day before school started, my father came home with bad news.

"Fernando called police," he said, wiping his hand on his pant leg.

My mother naturally wanted to know what police; and so, with much coughing and hawing, the long story began, the latest installment of which had the police calling Immigration, and Immigration sending an investigator. My mother sat stiff as whalebone as my father described how the man had summarily refused lunch on the house, and how my father had admitted, under pressure, that he knew there were "things" about his workers.

"So now what happens?"

My father didn't know. "Booker and Cedric went with him to the jail," he said. "But me, here I am." He laughed uncomfortably.

The next day, my father posted bail for "his boys," and waited apprehensively for something to happen. The day after that, he waited again, and the day after that, he called our neighbor's law student son, who suggested my father call the Immigration Department under an alias. My father took his advice; and it was thus that he discovered that Booker was right. It was illegal for aliens to work, but it wasn't to hire them.

In the happy interval that ensued, my father apologized to my mother, who in turn confessed about the country club, for which my father had no choice but to forgive her. Then he turned his attention back to "his boys."

My mother didn't see that there was anything to do.

"I like to talking to the judge," said my father.

"This is not China," said my mother.

"I'm only talking to him. I'm not give him money unless he wants it."

"You're going to land up in jail."

"So what else I should do?" My father threw up his hands. "Those are my boys."

"Your boys!" exploded my mother. "What about your family? What about your wife?"

My father took a long sip of tea. "You know," he said finally, "in the war my father sent our cook to the soldiers to use. He always said it—the province comes before the town, the town comes before the family."

"A restaurant is not a town," said my mother.

My father sipped at his tea again. "You know, when I first come to the United States, I also had to hide-and-seek with those deportation guys. If people did not helping me, I am not here today."

My mother scrutinized her hem.

After a minute, I volunteered that before seeing a judge, he might try a lawyer.

He turned. "Since when did you become so afraid like your mother?"

I started to say that it wasn't a matter of fear, but he cut me off.

"What I need today," he said, "is a son."

My father and I spent the better part of the next day standing on lines at the Immigration office. He did not get to speak to a judge, but with much persistence he managed to speak to a special clerk, who tried to persuade him that it was not her place to extend him advice. My father, though, shamelessly plied her with compliments and offers of free pancakes, until she finally conceded that she personally doubted anything would happen to either Cedric or Booker.

"Especially if they're 'needed workers,'" she said, rubbing at the red marks her glasses left on her nose. She yawned. "Have you thought about sponsoring them to become permanent residents?"

Could he do that? My father was overjoyed. And what if he saw to it right away? Would she perhaps put in a good word with the judge?

She yawned again, her nostrils flaring. "Don't worry," she said. "They'll get a fair hearing."

My father returned jubilant. Booker and Cedric hailed him as their savior. He was like a father to them, they said; and, laughing and clapping, they made him tell the story over and over, sorting through the details like jewels. And how old was the assistant judge? And what did she say?

That evening, my father tipped the paperboy a dollar and bought a pot of mums for my mother, who suffered them to be placed on the dining room table. The next night, he took us all out to dinner. Then on Saturday, Mona found a letter and some money in an envelope on my father's chair at the restaurant.

Dear Mr. Chang,

You are the grat boss. But, we do not like to trial, so will runing away now. Plese to excus us. People saying the law in America is fears like dragon. Here is only $140. We hope some day we can pay back the rest bale. You will getting intrest, as you diserving, so grat a boss you are. Thank you for every flung. In next life you will be burn in rich family, with no more *pancaks.*

Yours truley,

Booker + Cedric

In the weeks that followed, my father went to the pancake house for crises, but otherwise hung around our house, fiddling idly with the sump pump and boiler in an effort, he said, to get ready for winter. It was as though he had gone into retirement, except that instead of moving south, he had moved to the basement. He even took to showering my mother with little attentions, and to calling her "old girl," and when we finally heard that the club had entertained all the applications it could for the year, he was so sympathetic that he seemed more disappointed than my mother.

In the American Society

Mrs. Lardner tempered the bad news with an invitation to a bon voyage bash she was throwing for her friend Jeremy Brothers, who was going to Greece for six months.

"Do come" she urged. "You'll meet everyone, and then, you know, if things open up in the spring. . . " She waved her hands.

My mother wondered if it would be appropriate to show up at a party for someone they didn't know, but "the honest truth" was that this was an annual affair. "If it's not Greece, its Italy," sighed Mrs. Lardner. "We really just do it because his wife left him and his daughter doesn't speak to him, and poor Jeremy just feels so unloved!"

She also invited Mona and me to the goings-on, to keep Annie out of the champagne. I wasn't too keen on the idea, but before I could say anything, she had already thanked us for so generously agreeing to honor her with our presence.

"A pair of little princesses, you are!" she told us. "A pair of princesses!"

The party was that Sunday. On Saturday, my mother took my father out shopping for a suit. Since it was the end of September, she insisted that he buy a worsted rather than a seersucker, even though it was only 10, rather than 50, percent off. My father protested that the weather was as hot as ever, which was true—a thick Indian summer had cozied murderously up to us—but to no avail. Summer clothes, said my mother, were not properly worn after Labor Day[10].

The suit was unfortunately as extravagant in length as it was in price, which posed an additional quandary, since the tailor wouldn't be in until Monday. The salesgirl, though, found a way of tacking it up temporarily.

"Maybe this suit not fit me," fretted my father. "Just don't take your jacket off," said the salesgirl. He gave her a tip before they left, but when he got home, he refused to remove the price tag.

"I like to asking the tailor about the size," he insisted.

"You mean you're going to *wear* it and then *return* it?" Mona rolled her eyes.

"I didn't say I'm return it," said my father stiffly. "I like to asking the tailor, that's all."

The party started off swimmingly, except that most people were wearing Bermudas or wrap skirts. Still, my parents carried on, sharing with great feeling the complaints about the heat. Of course, my father tried to eat a cracker full of shallots, and burned himself in an attempt to help Mr. Lardner turn the coals of the barbecue; but on the whole, he seemed to be doing all right. Not nearly so well as my mother, though, who had accepted an entire cupful of Mrs. Lardner's magic punch and indeed seemed to be under some spell. As Mona and Annie skirmished over whether some boy in their class inhaled when he smoked, I watched my mother take off her shoes, laughing and laughing as a man with a beard regaled her with navy stories by the pool. Apparently he had been stationed in the Orient and remembered a few words of Chinese, which made my mother laugh still more. My father excused himself to go to the bathroom, then drifted back and weighed anchor at the hors d' oeuvres[①] table, while my mother sailed on to a group of women, who tinkled at length over the clarity of her complexion. I dug out a book I had brought.

Just when I'd cracked the spine, though, Mrs. Lardner came by to bewail her shortage of servers. Her caterers were criminals, I agreed; and the next thing I knew, I was handing out bits of marine life as amiably as I could.

"Here you go, Dad," I said, when I got to the hors d'oeuvres table.

"Everything is fine," he said.

I hesitated to leave him alone; but then the man with the beard zeroed in on him, and though he talked of nothing but my mother, I thought it would be okay to get back to work. Just at that moment, though, Jeremy Brothers lurched our way, an empty, albeit corked, wine bottle in hand. He was a slim, well-proportioned man, with a Roman nose and small eyes and a nice manly jaw that he allowed to hang agape.

"Hello," he said drunkenly. "Pleased to meet you."

"Pleased to meeting you," said my father.

"Right," said Jeremy. "Right. Listen. I have this bottle here, this most recalcitrant[②] bottle. You see that it refuses to do my bidding. I bid it open sesame, please, and it does nothing. " He pulled the cork out with his teeth, then turned the bottle upside down.

My father nodded.

"Would you have a word with it, please?" said Jeremy. The man with the beard excused himself. "Would you please have a goddamned word with it?"

My father laughed uncomfortably.

"Ah!" Jeremy bowed a little. "Excuse me, excuse me, excuse me. You are not my man, not my man at all. " He bowed again and started to leave, but then circled back. "Viticulture is not your forte. Yes, I can see that, see that plainly. But may I trouble you on another matter? Forget the damned bottle. " He threw it into the pool, winking at the people he splashed. "I have another matter. Do you speak Chinese?"

My father said he did not, but Jeremy pulled out a handkerchief with some characters on it anyway, saying that his daughter had sent it from Hong Kong and that he thought the characters might be some secret message.

"Long life," said my father.

"But you haven't looked at it yet. "

"I know what it says without looking. " My father winked at me.

"You do?"

"Yes, I do. "

"You're making fun of me, aren't you?"

"No, no, no," said my father, winking again.

"*Who are you anyway?*" said Jeremy.

His smile fading, my father shrugged.

"Who are you?"

My rather shrugged again.

Jeremy began to roar. "This is my party, my party, and I've never seen you before in my life." My father backed up as Jeremy came toward him. "*Who are you? WHO ARE YOU?*"

Just as my father was going to step into the pool, Mrs. Lardner came running up. Jeremy informed her that there was a man crashing his party.

"Nonsense," said Mrs. Lardner. "This is Ralph Chang, whom I invited extra specially so he could meet you." She straightened the collar of Jeremy's peach-colored polo shirt for him.

"Yes, well we've had a chance to chat," said Jeremy.

She whispered in his ear; he mumbled something; she whispered something more.

"I do apologize," he said finally.

My father didn't say anything.

"I do." Jeremy seemed genuinely contrive. "Doubtless you've seen drunks before, haven't you? You must have them in China."

"Okay," said my father.

As Mrs. Lardner glided off, Jeremy clapped his arm over my father's shoulders. "You know, I really am quite sorry, quite sorry."

My father nodded.

"What can I do? How can I make it up to you?"

"No, thank you."

"No, tell me, tell me," wheedled Jeremy. "Tickets to casino night?" My father shook his head. "You don't gamble. Dinner at Bartholomew's?" My father shook his head again. "You don't eat." Jeremy scratched his chin. "You know, my wife was like you. Old Annabelle could never let me make things up—never, never, never, never, never".

My father wriggled out from under his arm.

"How about sport clothes? You are rather overdressed, you know. Excuse me for saying so. But here." He took off his polo shirt and folded it up. "You can have this with my most profound apologies." He ruffled his chest hairs with his free hand.

"No, thank you," said my father.

"No, take it, take it. Accept my apologies." He thrust the shirt into my father's arms. "I'm so very sorry, so very sorry. Please, try it on."

Helplessly holding the shirt, my father searched the crowd for my mother.

"Here, I'll help you with your coat."

My father froze.

Jeremy reached over and took the jacket off. "Milton's, one hundred twenty-five dollars reduced to one hundred twelve-fifty," he read. "What a bargain, what a bargain!"

"Please give it back," pleaded my father. "Please."

"Now for your shirt," ordered Jeremy.

Heads began to turn.

"Take off your shirt."

"I do not taking orders like a servant," announced my father stiffly.

"Take off your shirt, or I'm going to throw this jacket right into the pool, just right into this little pool here." Jeremy held it over the water.

"Go ahead."

"One hundred twelve-fifty," taunted Jeremy. "One hundred twelve..."

My father flung the polo shirt into the water with such force that part of it bounced back up into the air like a fluorescent fountain. Then it settled into a soft heap on top of the water. My mother hurried up.

"You're a sport!" said Jeremy, suddenly breaking into a smile, and slapping my father on the back. "You're a sport⑬! I like that. A man with spirit, that's what you are. A man with panache⑭. Allow me to return to you your jacket." He handed it back to my father. "Good value you got on that. good value."

My father hurled the coat into the pool, too. "We're leaving," he said grimly. "Leaving!"

"Now, Ralphie," said Mrs. Lardner, bustling up; but my father was already stomping off.

"Get your sister," he told me. To my mother: "Get your shoes."

"That was *great*, Dad," said Mona as we walked to the car. "You were *stupendous*."

"Way to show 'em," I said.

"What?" said my father offhandedly.

Although it was only just dusk, we were in a gulch⑮, which made it hard to see anything except the gleam of his white shirt moving up the hill ahead of us.

"It was all my fault," began my mother.

"Forget it," said my father grandly. Then he said, "The only trouble is, I left those keys in my jacket pocket."

"Oh no," said Mona.

"Oh no is right," said my mother.

"So we'll walk home" I said.

"But how're we going to get into the *house*?" said Mona.

The noise of the party churned through the silence.

"Someone has to going back," said my father.

"Let's go to the pancake house first," suggested my mother. "We can wait there until the party is finished, and then call Mrs. Lardner."

Having all agreed that was a good plan, we started walking again.

"God, just think," said Mona. "We're going to have to *dive* for them."

My father stopped a moment. We waited.

"You girls are good swimmers," he said finally. "Not like me."

Then his shirt started moving again, and we trooped up the hill after it, into the dark.

Notes

① **clinker**: (*slang*) a mistake or a blunder.

② **sec**: in a second.

③ **dummy**: (*slang*) a stupid person.

④ **greenhorn**: an inexperienced or foolish person; a new recruit.

⑤ **slaloming**: moving like a ski-race down a zigzag course defined by artificial obstacles.

⑥ **Massif Central**: the keystone of France, holding the country together by the sheer force of its grandeur. Here it refers to part of a lady's body.

⑦ **speed bump**: a transverse ridge on the road to control the speed of vehicles.

⑧ **curb**: restraint, control.

⑨ **Operation Identification**: a program designed to discourage theft of valuables from your home and other locations and provide a way to easily identify stolen property.

⑩ **Labor Day**: the first Monday in September in US and Canada.

⑪ **hors d' oeuvres**: a French appetizer or starter; outside of the main dishes.

⑫ **recalcitrant**: obstinately disobedient.

⑬ **sport**: (*slang*) a person behaving in a special way, esp. regarding games, rules, etc.

⑭ **panache**: assertiveness or flamboyant confidence of style or manner.

⑮ **gulch**: a ravine, esp. one in which a torrent flows.

Questions for Reading Comprehension

1. What are the dynamics of this nuclear family? What is the relationship between each family member with the others?

2. This story is narrated by Callie Chang. Does she narrate the story as an adult remembering in hindsight, or as a teenager in junior high?

3. What allows Ralph Chang to open up and discuss his grandfather? Why do you think he is reluctant to tell his daughters about his grandfather?

4. What does the Booker-and-Cedric incident reveal about the immigrant experience and American society?

5. Is Ralph Chang's act of throwing his jacket into the pool an act of foolishness or autonomy? What motivates his action?

6. What are the implications of Ralph Chang's action for the Chang family?

567

Discussion Questions for Appreciation

1. This story is divided into two parts, one focusing on the private world of the Chang family and the other on the public face they assume for "American society". Is there an ironic contrast between the two sections?

2. In what ways does the Changs' private society intrude on their ability to thrive in mainstream American society?

3. Does the dialogue seem realistic? How does the writer use dialogue to convey the characters' attitudes towards race, sex and class?

4. Identify the source of humor in this story. How does humor contri-

bute to the tone, mood, and overall message of the story?

A Question for Writing

Many of Jen's stories explore concepts of ethnicity and Americaness. How do the Changs fit into "American society"? What do they do to try to embrace the culture of the "U. S. *of A*"?

References

Abrams, M. H. *A Glossary of Literary Terms*. New York: Harcourt Brace College Publishers. 1999.

Baym, Nina ed. *The Norton Anthology of American Literature*. Vol. 2. 5th Edition. New York: W. W. Norton & Company, 1998.

Baym, Nina et al. , eds. *The Norton Anthology of American Literature*. Third Shorter Edition. New York: W. W. Norton and Company, 1989.

Booz, Elisabeth B. *A Brief Introduction to Modern American Literature*. Shanghai: Shanghai Foreign Language Education Press. 1982.

Chang Yaoxin. *A Survey of American Literature*. Tianjin: Nankai University Press. 1990, 2003.

Charters, Ann ed. *The Story and Its Writer: an Introduction to Short Fiction*. New York: St. Martin's Press, Inc. 1995.

Coffman, Stanley. *Imagism, A Chapter for the History of Modern Poetry*. New York: Farrar, Strauss, and Groux. 1972.

Conn, Peter. *Literature in America: An Illustrated History*. Cambridge: Cambridge University Press. 1989.

Faragher, John Mack et al. *Out of Many, a History of the American People*. Volume II: Since 1865. New Jersey: Prentice-Hall, Inc. . 2000.

Graff, Gerald. *Beyond the Culture Wars: How Teaching the Conflicts Can Revitalizing American Education*. New York: Norton & Co. 1992.

Hart, James D. *The Oxford Companion to American Literature*. New York: Oxford University Press. 1965.

Holman, C. Hugh. *A Handbook to Literature*. Indianapolis and New York: The Odyssey Press. 1972.

Horton, R. W. *Backgrounds of American Literary Thought*. Englewood Cliffs, N. J.: Prentice-Hall, Inc. 1974.

Hu Yintong, Liu Shusen eds. *A Course in American Literature*. Tianjin: Nankai University Press. 1995.

Huang Guiyou. ed. *Asian American Short Story Writers: an A-to-Z guide*. Westport, CT: Greenwood Press. 2003.

Jen, Gish. *Who's Irish?* London: Granta Books. 1999.

Kermode, Frank ed. *Selected Prose of T. S. Eliot*. London: Faber & Faber. 1987.

Lauter, Paul. *Canons and Contexts*. New York: Oxford University Press. 1991.

Logsdon, Loren, and Charles W. Mayer eds. *Since Flannery O'Connor, Essays on the Contemporary American Short Story*. Macomb: Western Illinois University Press. 1987.

May, Charles. *The Short Story: the Reality of Artifice*. New York and London: Routledge. 2002.

McMichael, George et. , ed. *Anthology of American Literature Vol. 1 & Vol. 2*. New York: Macmillan Publishing Co. , Inc. , and London: Collier Macmillan Publishers. 1980.

Poe, Edgar Allan. "The Philosophy of Composition", from *Graham's Magazine*, April 1846.

Poupard, Dennis ed. *Twentieth-Century Literary Criticism*. 11 Vols. Detroit: Gale Research Company. 1983.

Pratt, William. *The Imagist Poem*. New York: E. P. Dutton & Co. Inc. 1963.

Rubinstein, Annette T. *American Literature: Root and Flower*. Beijing: Foreign Language Teaching and Research Press. 1988.

Selden, Raman et al. *A Reader's Guide to Contemporary Literary Theory*. 4th Edition. London: Prentice Hall. 1997.

Tao Jie. *Selected Readings of American Literature*. Beijing: High Education Press. 2000.

Toming. *A History of American Literature*. Nanjing: Yilin Press. 2002.

Walker, Alice. *In Search of Our Mother's Gardens: Womanist Prose*. San Diego: Harcourt Brace Jovanovich. 1983.

Wang Leng. ed. *Selected Readings in American Literature*. Shanghai: Shanghai Jiaotong University. 2003.

Wu Dinbai. *An Outline of American Literature*. Shanghai: Shanghai Foreign Language Press. 1998.

Wu Weiren. *History and Anthology of American Literature*. Beijing: Foreign Language Teaching and Research Press. 1990.